THE OUTNUMBERED

To My Father

THE
OUTNUMBERED

A Novel by
CATHERINE HUTTER

THE REPRINT SOCIETY
LONDON

FIRST PUBLISHED 1944

＊

THIS EDITION PUBLISHED BY THE REPRINT SOCIETY LTD.
BY ARRANGEMENT WITH CHATTO AND WINDUS
1946

Printed in Great Britain by T. and A. Constable Ltd.
at the University Press, Edinburgh

CONTENTS

*

CONTENTS

Chapter One

IN the month of March, in the year 1924, when Adolf Hitler was dictating *Mein Kampf* to Rudolf Hess in Landsberg, the fortress in which both were confined, the Jewish pedlar Moishe dropped dead in the village of Pritnitz, just where a dirt road leads off into the hills to the Sanatorium Strubl.

Moishe died of a heart attack. This was evident by the blueness of his lips, which were still soft and warm and slightly puffed as he lay with his face upturned to the sky. At first they looked as if they were about to whistle, then they flattened out and blackened and bared his teeth like fangs, giving him a savage expression which he had never had in life. His skin, always sallow, was ashen, and he lay quite still, only his curls, the *pajes*, one over each ear, stirring as the wind moved them.

He looked little and cramped as he lay there, although he had the whole road to lie on, a road wide enough to let two carts pass at the same time. The snows on the mountains were melting and a cold stream of water flowed down the road day and night, forming a rivulet independent of the brook on the other side, which never dried up, not even in the hot month of August. This seasonal brook of melted snow and ice formed a rut which the farmers cursed and which Dr. Sapponyi, the owner of the Sanatorium, had filled up every year in May when the ground hardened. This he did, not because he was kindly disposed toward the farmers, but because his patients might injure their sick lungs by the bumping and shaking on their trips to and from the railway station in Pritnitz.

Moishe lay upslope, and a tiny tributary of icy water trickled up his trouser leg, which caused him no discomfort because he was dead. His wife, Dworje, however, knelt down beside him and moved his leg to avoid the cold stream. She stared at him with horrified eyes, her mouth open, and grunted softly with every breath that left her parted lips, "*Uchhh . . . uchhh . . . uchhh . . .*"

At Moishe's feet stood his daughter, a child about six years old, judging by her size. Her matted black hair was dull with the dust of the road, her face sun- and wind-burned, her eyes brown in their oval frames of thick black lashes, her nose straight and thin and rounded at the tip, with sensitive, flaring nostrils. Her mouth was small, its full lips red and slightly pouting in repose, giving her an expression both serious and womanly. She had a high, prettily rounded forehead. She resembled neither her father nor her mother.

She was chubby, not with the robust chubbiness of a healthy child, but with the flabby plumpness which results from eating only poor, starchy foods. Her stomach protruded a little.

She was dressed all in black. Her clothes showed grey dust in the creases as though they had not been changed for a long time. Her stockings were woollen, home-knit, her boots high and buttoned at the side. They were badly scuffed but whole, and the dust lay in a thick scum on them because they had been greased to make them waterproof. The heels and soles and an inch up the side were caked with mud.

She, too, stared at her recumbent father but did not kneel. She let her hands dangle at her sides with astonishment for a moment, then she began to suck her thumb.

Dworje covered her lined yellow face with one bony hand, and the big tears trickled from between her fingers, down her arm, on to her black dress, on to the earth. She had stopped groaning. Her crying made no sound.

It was the time of the year when the snow roses, those big white mountain anemones, were already high on their thick green stems. They were always worth picking, right to the end. You could find them first by digging under the icy covering of the melting spring snow for their buds, down-turned, white and crisp, like mammoth snowdrops. Later you could pick them easily, above the black earth, free of the snow, open wide like lotus flowers, their white blossoms slowly turning brown, then copper-red and, finally, pale green, but never withering. They only grew more and more transparent. All the year round the ground in the woods was carpeted with their big, rhododendronlike leaves.

CHAPTER ONE

Dworje rocked back and forth, and tears trickled in a steady stream between her fingers. The sun shone overhead in a cloudless sky of porcelain blue.

Diagonally opposite from where Moishe lay stood an inn, its shabby white façade touched by the sunlight. The German Gothic letters, "To the White Hart," were faded. The sign of the White Hart had long since been beaten down by storm and never been replaced. At lilac time this inn enjoyed a few weeks of glory because the bushes in the front yard were old and grown big and, when their time came, thick with purple blossoms. Then the White Hart was hidden behind them like a sleeping beauty. But at this time of the year the leaves were barely sprouting, and the Hart looked what it was—a poor man's tavern.

Two young men were drinking beer at a wooden table by the window. Through the sparse trees they could see what was happening on the road. They nudged one another and watched the scene a while in stolid silence. Then one said, in the dialect of that region, "Let's go," threw a coin on the table, and walked out in advance of his friend.

There was something weather-beaten but aristocratic in his appearance which the other, who was all peasant, lacked. The peasant boy's face was bland, his companion's cruel, with a seeking expression born of a dissatisfaction that came, not from physical want, but from some psychic frustration. He looked full of suppressed aggressiveness. He scuffed as he walked, kicked the gate open, and spat out of the corner of his mouth as he moved toward the group in the road.

Both boys came to a standstill beside the dead pedlar and looked down at him. Dworje did not change her attitude, but the child stared up at them, then backed away a step.

"The Jew is your father?" the aggressive one asked idly, just for something to say.

The child kept her thumb in her mouth, and her large eyes on him, but she did not answer.

"That's good," the young man went on. "One swine-Jew less." Then they, too, stared silently.

Two peasant girls came cycling down the road. When they saw the group, they dismounted and advanced slowly, wheeling their bicycles. "Look," said one, "a dead Jew."

The young man repeated, "That's good. One swine-Jew less."

The girl answered him gaily in the same dialect, "Ay, Conrad, you're heartless! Didn't you learn in church that before God we're all alike?"

Conrad threw back his head impatiently. "The church? Nonsense! You still fall for such silly stuff!" He pointed contemptuously at the dead man. "Can the priest make you believe that you're like this one?" Then he pointed to the child. "Have you ever seen such a dirt heap in your life before? *Pfui!*" And he spat.

The girls laughed.

The child looked from one to the other. Her world was still in the process of taking shape. Clear in her mind were several fundamental things—bad smells in the room she lived in, good smells in the out-of-doors, poor food that often made her sick because her mother stuffed her, the sensual comfort of her mother's breast which she had not been weaned from, the relief of her father's arms which carried her when she was tired, the indifference of the people with whom they stayed as they wandered from place to place. Finally, and most vividly, she was aware of the unkindness of all people in the world except those who were like them and gave them shelter in the winter months. Her awakening soul had already learned to cringe when a human being opened his mouth to speak. Sometimes it turned out that there was nothing for her to fear—she was not going to be yelled at, pushed, or kicked; but more often than not she was right to back away and run as fast as her little legs and a shortness of breath would let her.

She was therefore not surprised at the contempt and derision facing her now. Although she had never seen anyone strike her mother, she had a fleeting idea that the boy who had said, "One swine-Jew less," might do that, and she wanted to pluck at her mother's sleeve and tell her to look out and not remain in such a defenceless position. But fear kept her motionless at her father's feet, sucking her thumb, her soft eyes watching, aware.

Moishe's pack lay beside him. He had been carrying it in his arms when he dropped dead. He had taken it off his back because he had felt a sudden pain there and had just said to his wife that he thought, after all, they had better rest a few days in Gutenberg, two villages farther away, where there was a Jew who would take them in, before starting on the long trek across the mountains. Then he had stopped speaking in the middle of a sentence, made a grimace, and dropped dead.

Conrad picked up the pack. It was surprisingly heavy. He opened it and began to examine its contents. Moishe's long black kaftan flapped protestingly in the wind.

The girls propped their bicycles against a tree and crossed over to Moishe's side. One, Ströcker's Lisl, wore her black hair in braids round her head. She was the daughter of the tree-tapper Ströcker.

The trees here were tapped for their poor sap or resin. Most of the men in the district were tree-tappers. Higher and higher from year to year grew the bare red patches where the bark was cut away. The sap dripped slowly into tin pails, spilling hardened and white like wax on a gutted candle down the wounded trunk of the tree. When the pails were full, the men carried them down to the refinery in Pritnitz.

They didn't make enough to keep body and soul together, for the trees here were as poor as everything that grew on thickly populated European soil. For too many years the peasant had taken from the tired earth for it to give him rich returns now.

The other girl, a farmer's daughter, wore her light hair in more up-to-date fashion in a knot at the nape of her neck, with the short hairs curling loose about her face.

In the long valley between Strubl and Pritnitz lived only three farmers. They were well off in comparison with the tree-tappers. They worked their own land, owned two, perhaps three cows, one or two horses, pigs, goats.

This farmer's daughter walking across the road to look at Moishe was "Brandstetter's Poldi." She had nothing to do but work her father's land until she got married, and she would marry well. She was what was called a good match, because with her went an

Old-World dowry of cash, a trousseau of fine linen, and a part of the farm.

The tree-tapper's children had nothing like this to look forward to. They would go into domestic service at Strubl, which absorbed so many of them, generation after generation—the men in the capacity of groom, coachman, chauffeur, doorman, cook's help, shoe-cleaner; the women to wash, wait at table, do kitchen work, or look after the children of patients. Some of them would find work in less exotic surroundings, at one of the inns in or around Pritnitz. And some would go to work in the glue factory in Waldeck.

But Ströcker's Lisl and Brandstetter's Poldi were both too young for either factory or marriage. They were fourteen, and in their last year at school. Now they stood side by side, looking down at Moishe, moved by nothing but curiosity and a faint, pleasant sensation of disgust.

They wore dirndl dresses faded from many washings, and their feet were bare—they had given up wearing shoes a few days ago for the warm weather months ahead. Only the girls who worked in the factory wore shoes and stockings all the year round.

Both girls wore earrings of thin gold, hand-carved by peasant jewellers. Lisl's set had a ruby inserted in a scroll, Poldi's a tiny pearl dangling from a golden shell. They had worn these little ornaments since their small pricked lobes could hold them. A little gold cross hung from a chain around Poldi's neck. She had received it at first communion; Lisl had one, too, but hers was of silver and hidden in her blouse.

As they looked down at Moishe, Poldi began to giggle, then Lisl began to laugh, and finally the boys joined in.

From the opposite direction came a small boy, also barefoot. He wore a pair of threadbare Tirolean trousers upheld by the customary embroidered leather braces from which sunshine and age had erased every semblance of colour and pattern. His brown young face and neck rose up out of a clean white shirt.

"Look!" Poldi cried. "A dead Jew!"

The boy joined them. He was tree-tapper Reicher's Walter,

and he couldn't have been much over ten years old. The sight of the Jew gave him a shudder. He was scared of Jews. He was scared of dead people. He was scared of most things. But he knew well enough, already at his tender age, that in the world he lived in it would be fatal to give himself away on that score.

"Nice and dirty," he said, as he came edging closer. He spoke in a low voice and said these disparaging words to hide his fear. Then he looked away sheepishly in the direction he was heading for.

Poldi nudged Conrad and said, "Look at the child."

She was still watching them, her eyes profound, showing none of the fear she felt. "*Unheimlich*," said Poldi, by which she meant queer, strange, and a little terrifying.

She moved closer to Conrad, who began to perspire as he felt desire running through him. He looked at the little gold cross that was slipping into the groove of the girl's full breasts where the tightly buttoned bodice pressed them close together. He wanted to run up to the Sanatorium then and there and lie with the third-floor maid, Hilda, who let him come night after night. His head grew dizzy when he thought of her and what she let him do to her, and he closed his eyes for a moment. "Isn't it so?" said Poldi, moving closer.

"Dirty Jew-child," said Conrad, shaking himself out of it, but his voice had lost its aggressiveness and was suddenly soft. The child cast down her eyes, and her lips puckered as though she would cry.

"Look," said Lisl, "*die Julie*." In her language the name was pronounced "You-ly."

Julie came from the inn. She was the innkeeper's daughter and a half-wit. Her face was sallow, plain and curiously flat, her eyes a limpid blue and watery, with sore, reddened rims; her teeth were irregular; her nose ran unheeded. She dragged one leg slightly as she walked and she had a habit of lifting her arms with a jerky motion when she wanted to say something. Then she would let them fall beside her again apathetically in a gesture of despair. This she could do so poignantly that even those who knew she could not talk would pause for a second as though to see if she were really going to say anything. Then they would shrug their shoulders and look away as she let her arms drop in the familiar gesture of despair, muttering, "Stupid wretch!" or, "Poor thing!"

Julie came shambling across to the group. "Here you have a dead 'un!" shouted Conrad. "Now you can pray."

Julie knelt down beside the dead man, opposite Dworje. She crossed herself, pressed her hands together, the tips of her fingers touching, and began to pray. Her lips moved to form the words she could not say aloud, not because she was mute, but because chronic fear of the world in which she lived kept her dumb. Dworje moved her hand for a moment to look at the newcomer, then she covered her face again and wept harder than ever.

Suddenly Julie stopped praying. She stared at the child for a moment, and, leaning forward, stretched out her long bony hand toward her. The child backed away. Julie motioned to the child that she, too, should kneel. The child shook her head. Then Julie turned up her face to heaven again, and as she prayed in an agony of devotion, her body, like Dworje's, began to sway.

The sun fell on Julie's hair. In it lay all the beauty which God had denied her everywhere else in her poor body. It was thick and fine and the colour of spun gold. She wore it loose, brushed until it glowed by a tight-lipped, unhappy mother who had given birth to only one child, and that an idiot.

The Jewish child moved closer, stretched out a hand, and touched the golden river. Julie opened her eyes and smiled.

The child took her thumb out of her mouth and smiled at Julie. She showed a row of pearly white teeth and dimples on either side of her mouth.

"Why, she's pretty!" cried Lisl, and none of the others could deny it.

Except for the *gluck-glucking* of the water it was very quiet. Suddenly Walter said, "Shouldn't we call Schreiner?" Schreiner was the district doctor.

"*He* won't come to the Jew," said Conrad.

"Why not?" said Lisl. "He goes up to Strubl to see Sapponyi's patients, and Sapponyi's a Jew."

"He only goes up to sign death-certificates," said Poldi, and laughed as Conrad reddened with anger. "Sapponyi doesn't need him for anything else!"

That made them laugh, Conrad excepted, for they all knew of the district doctor's hatred of Sapponyi, how Schreiner, whose patients were hard to get at and thankless to cure, envied the famous Jew Sapponyi with his cosmopolitan clientèle.

Conrad found his voice. "Shut your trap!" he said to Poldi, and glowered at the others. "Anybody else want to say anything against Schreiner?"

Nobody did. They did not wear Poldi's armour of desirableness. They stopped laughing, all except Poldi, who knew very well what she had made Conrad feel a moment ago, and that what she had to offer was far more potent than his loud mouth.

She was an easy-going girl who hated a quarrel, and she could see as plain as day the difference between Medizinalrat Sapponyi at Strubl and this queer creature lying dead in the road.

"But this one here's a *Polnischer*," she said, meaning a Polish Jew. "Schreiner'll never come to the *Polnischer*." And Conrad was mollified.

The others saw the difference too, and nodded their heads.

"Let's go to the Lamb," said Poldi, "and call up Sapponyi. He'll come down and fix the Jew."

Everybody stared at her silently, then suddenly their faces lit up. Telephone! If the Jew's death gave them the chance to use the one public telephone in Pritnitz, then he had not died in vain!

Conrad laughed contemptuously. The morons! He had telephoned. Often. Once, even, long distance to Munich. He let the pack swing from one hand. The others forgot the telephone for a moment and Poldi asked, "What's in it?"

"What do you suppose is in it?" said Conrad, moving the pack more behind his back. "Junk. What else would the Jew be peddling?"

But he opened it for them all to see. Shoe-laces, safety-pins, sewing tackle, and—"Oh!" gasped Poldi as something glistened. Gold. Cheap imitation jewellery from Gablonz in Czechoslovakia

—brooches, rings, earrings, each stuck on a stiff white card. They looked into the pack, then at one another, then down at the ground and away. Walter shifted from one foot to the other.

"I'd better be going," he said, thinking he'd hung around long enough to prove he wasn't squeamish, and off he went with a lump in his throat.

"Conrad can go up to Schreiner's and phone," said Poldi.

"No!" cried Lisl and Conrad's companion simultaneously, because if Conrad telephoned from Schreiner's office they would miss their big chance.

"I wouldn't bother him with this . . . here," said Conrad softly, touching the foot of the corpse with his boot in a display of indifference, not really kicking it . . . after all, a dead man . . . Conrad was still very young. His eyes caught the child's steady gaze, and he quickly lifted his to the mountain-tops.

None of them had ever used the telephone of Pritnitz's largest inn, the Golden Lamb, kept by Heinrich Grabautschnik. The Lamb, unlike the White Hart, had a large, intricate sign of wrought iron which no storm could tear down. The building was white-washed every year, in a garden at the back were tables and chairs. Its rooms were clean, and there were toilets with weakly-flushing water on every floor and a tap from which you could fetch as much water as you liked at the end of every passage, and a can of hot water was brought to you for washing if you wanted it in the morning. That was the sort of place the Lamb was, with its public telephone hanging on the wall in the passage as you went in.

"All right, we'll go to the Lamb," said Conrad. "But who's going to spend ten *Groschen* on the Jew?"

The idea of telephoning was sensational, but it did involve the spending of ten *Groschen*.

At first nobody had a solution. Then Lisl said, "Sapponyi'll give it back."

That wasn't the point. Which one of them had ten *Groschen* on him?

Poldi dug in the pocket of her dirndl and stretched out a round arm to Conrad. "Here," the farmer's daughter said graciously. "You don't have to return it, either."

Conrad took the coin, angry because the two beers had taken all his money. Then they all ran off, leaving only Julie behind. When they came back again, they had their teacher with them.

Melita Bahr had come to the valley a month ago to teach at the school in the village that nestled around Strubl. This village was even smaller than Pritnitz. Its name was Fichtenbach, but it might as well have had no name at all since it had no railway, no bus stop, no church, and no post office. Nobody ever said, "I'm going to Fichtenbach"; but, "I'm going up Strubl way." Still, in the civic registry it was inscribed as "Community of Fichtenbach. Number of inhabitants—54."

Since the establishment of the Republic, which had at once tried to alleviate overcrowding in schools, Fichtenbach had its own school. Here Melita taught twenty-four children of all ages in one room at the same time. At fourteen they were through with learning and ready for a lifetime of hard labour, interspersed by sickness.

Fichtenbach's first teacher had been a Bohemian whom everybody hated. "*Der Böhme!*" they had called him contemptuously, and ostracized him. This poor fellow had been a member of the Social Democratic Party of Austria and had one day appeared in Vienna with the plea to be placed somewhere else. "The narrow-mindedness of the peasants in the backwater where you have chosen to place me is indescribable," he wrote in his official appeal, "and I have come to believe that the ostracism of the Austrian peasant is the most baneful humanly possible. I don't know why they hate me except for the fact that I am a Bohemian. I think you would do well to send them one of their own kind."

Adolf Hitler, who at that very time was preparing to create the legend of *Ein Volk, ein Reich, ein Führer*, including just this type of Bohemian in his idea of "one people," could not hear the harassed schoolmaster's words. But the board did and gave the post to Melita Bahr.

Melita was a Social Democrat too, but she was a blonde Viennese.

17

She looked like the girl the peasants saw on the old-fashioned picture postcards which they bought for birthdays, confirmations, and weddings. Melita had just that kind of Old-World face and figure. That she had a very up-to-date mind they could not comprehend, and she tackled her job with so much serious tact that they never noticed they were being made over into civilians of a twentieth-century world. Not until they lost her did they realize that life, under her regime, had been good. Then it was too late.

Melita was still suffering from homesickness for Vienna, which was only a little over fifty miles away but, seen from the perspective of Fichtenbach, might have been on another planet.

Moritz Behrendt, one of their party leaders, the man with whom she thought she was in love, had known what he was talking about when he had urged her to take the post, saying, "You know, Melly, we have so much yet to gain in the provinces. If we don't win them over, they will one day strangle us. It is your duty to go."

Duty! The word was enough to send Melita flying to the four corners of the earth, even if it had not been Behrendt who had spoken them.

Behrendt had been right. There was plenty to be done here—everything, in fact. It was like starting from scratch with very small children. Melita was glad she had come, but she still suffered from nostalgia for—for what? Not for anything personal or private, nothing as small as that; not for her brother Anton, whom she saw at week-ends . . . after all, she was not a child . . . not for Behrendt . . . she was not a love-sick adolescent. . . . No. What Melita missed was the common stride of which they were all a part, the community life, the community of the workers of Vienna. She could close her eyes and see them, a vast sea of ardent people —her people, of whom she was a part. Now, fifty miles away from Vienna, she was lonely, lonely like an exile. But she was knuckling down to her job manfully.

Melita had met the children at the Lamb. She had too much understanding to interfere with their red-letter mission. Not until Lisl and the peasant boy had tried to make the connection and failed, and Poldi had succeeded, like the little woman of the world she was cut out to be, had Melita taken the receiver and explained the situation as she understood it from the children's laconic telling. It was not lost on her that the urge to telephone had far outweighed any desire to help the afflicted family on the road.

Now, as she came up to the group, Conrad at her side, the others behind her, she said, "Oh, but that looks sad!"

She went up to the dead man and bent over him. Julie she took no notice of; she was already used to the girl's strange ways. She undid the Jew's kaftan across his chest and laid her hand on his silent heart. Yes, he was dead.

Then she looked at the child, who was staring at her, intending to look away again, but finding her gaze lingering to stare back. The child was so exotic, so picturesque . . . like those Arab children, thought Melita, in that educational picture she had seen with Anton the night before she had left Vienna. As she looked at the child she could hear again the tinkling sound of tambourines.

Melita looked away at last and now tried to attract Dworje's attention. She shook her gently by the shoulder. Nothing happened. She tried to take Dworje's hand away from her face, but it seemed frozen to it. The desperate woman shook her off, silently, and went on weeping and rocking back and forth.

"I hope the Herr Medizinalrat comes soon," said Melita, and she looked anxiously down the road that led to Strubl. If only he would come soon!

She had not spoken to him personally, but to Sister Andrea, who had said she would call the Herr Medizinalrat at once. But with women like Andrea you never could tell. A single encounter with Strubl's head nurse had given Melita the impression that Andrea belonged to the type of woman who takes a matter into her own hands whether it is her affair or not.

Melita went over to a tree stump, sat down and lit a cigarette. Andrea would tell Sapponyi when she saw fit. Meanwhile the children were once again busying themselves with Moishe's pack.

"You must hand it over to the *gendarme*," Melita told them. Two of the country police, called *gendarmes*, had their quarters at the Lamb.

Conrad said to the others, "D'ye hear what she says? Put it all back. Come on, now!"

He saw to it that nobody kept any of the shoe-laces, barrettes, pins, needles, thread, and other knick-knacks in the pack. But a little gold thimble he handed to Poldi. "Here," he said, "I give that to you."

Poldi dimpled and smiled and said, "Thanks." The child's eyes flickered as she watched the transaction.

Melita could feel herself break into a sweat of embarrassment and shame. Dworje's grief and the child's apathy were easier to bear than the heartlessness of the girls and boys. That was a sight she wanted to put away from her because it made her ashamed of the humanity she was so anxious to save and must therefore be able to love. If only the Herr Medizinalrat would come soon!

She looked up into the blue opaqueness of the sky, then down at the sharp shadows which the sun cast on the road as it filtered through the sparse birch trees. The shadows of the bicycles standing propped against them made wheels on the ground. Nature had no respect for tragedy either. We don't count so much, thought Melita, and felt uncomfortable. Her life was built to such a great extent on the idea that people were important.

Others passed by and stopped to stare at the dead Jew. By the time Sapponyi's car drew up, there were fifteen spectators, five of them adults.

Melita rose from her tree stump and went to meet the doctor as he got out of the car. "Grüss Gott, Herr Medizinalrat," she said, giving him his title, Mr. Medicinal-Adviser. "This is as good as a fair. Look."

Sapponyi was wearing the dress of the Austrian country squire, the grey *loden* suit with the forest-green collar, revers, and cuffs and deer-horn buttons, and on his head a Tirolean hat with brush.

As he got out of his ten-year-old Steyrer touring car, those standing around the dead Jew moved aside to make room for him, and they hung on what he would do, their mouths agape, looking idiotic. It was as though an old king had arrived on the scene of a medieval fairy-tale; and in a way that was what Sapponyi was to the peasants of that vicinity.

They never saw the Count, who owned the land which was not Sapponyi's, which spread out around them as far as they could see, to whom they paid their rentals. Some did not even know his name. He lived in a castle in Carinthia, far away, where he owned as much land again. Sapponyi, in his car, in his dress of the Austrian aristocracy, was the visible ruler of the valley, Jew or no Jew. Schreiner could talk his head off. He couldn't break that spell. They made way for the Herr Medizinalrat beside the dead man.

Sapponyi was a small man of delicate build. His eyes were colourless behind thick glasses, his face was pale, and a slight moustache hid the contours of his lips, which gave the impression of being thin. His face was not unkind, but nervous—apprehensive, Melita thought—and that was what Sapponyi was, an apprehensive man.

He was the youngest son of a Hungarian baronet and landowner who had been a Jew only incidentally. Sapponyi's father had been knighted by a benevolent monarch. Anti-semitism was something Sapponyi's father, living splendidly under the Austro-Hungarian Monarchy, which understood how to handle its minorities so that they were not all too conscious of oppression, had not been made to feel. In Sapponyi's day, however, it had become inescapable; it had kept the son of the baronet from a professorship; there was no getting away from it however busy one might be.

Sapponyi had never felt like an Israelite. How could he? Judaism was as strange a thing to him as to his anti-semitic colleagues. But he felt equally ill at ease in his acquired Catholicism. What the peasants did not know, because Sapponyi's material support of their Church was too obvious, was that Sapponyi was not religious. But, unlike Melita, he had no faith in the justice or stability of any political creed either. His mind being more keen than Melita's, he could find contradictions and dangerous gaps in practically every material belief, which produced in him an irritability toward humanity in general. Sapponyi had no faith and no belief, and his private life was without complications. Thus his mind was free to occupy

21

itself with his profession. This had made him an unusually good doctor. He treated his patients like machines that had come to be mended, which did not help to make him popular, but his medical reputation was impeccable and doctors from all parts of the Continent sent their patients to him.

But sometimes even his work failed to give Sapponyi assurance. Because he had vision, he had to fear for the future, not his future— he was near sixty—nor that of his wife, Thérèse. Thérèse was safe within herself from any danger. But he feared for Strubl and for his fortune, which was to go to his daughter and her aristocratic husband who had brought with him a fine old name but no hope of even self-support and he feared for his three grandchildren, for whom he felt responsible.

He could see nothing good ahead for these children, tainted as they were with Jewish blood. He was perhaps the only man in Austria who in 1924 took the new German menace seriously.

The sight of Melita, so blatantly Gentile, galled him. He shouldn't have married, he shouldn't have had a child, the entire Jewish race should be wiped out.

In this mood he shook hands with her. Not only her impeccable Gentileness irritated him, her beliefs did, too. Being a Social Democrat was as bad, as hopeless, as being a Jew. Why couldn't she be satisfied with her enviable position racially instead of spoiling her life by picking out a belief that could only be a handicap?

Sapponyi examined the dead man more thoroughly than Melita had done, but he came to the same conclusion. Then he leaned forward and with a swift, sure gesture wrenched Dworje's hand away from her face. Blank eyes stared at him, at Moishe, then the woman flung herself on the body and began to wail.

Sapponyi, with a gentleness customarily used toward such creatures as Julie who, in small communities, held almost the position of mascots, tapped the idiot girl lightly on the shoulder. She opened her eyes and, when she saw the doctor, rose, curtsied, and stood in gawky silence until she was gradually pushed into the background by the staring onlookers. Finally, she walked away, her lame leg dragging, deep in her jumbled thoughts.

Sapponyi said, "Go to the inn, Conrad, and tell Reischenbacher to send the cart. Tell Keppler we'll need a coffin. Anything he has on hand will do. Hurry."

Conrad may have despised Sapponyi, but Sapponyi was the big boss of the valley, so he hurried to obey.

"Who's going to pay?" he stopped to turn and shout back. "Keppler'll want to know."

"Tell Keppler I will pay," said Sapponyi, whose voice carried without his having to raise it.

Conrad ran off.

Pritnitz had an undertaker because Strubl gave up its frequent dead. For this reason the cemetery was disproportionately large for so small a community, and exotic names such as Vassilopilu, Efenkeshi, Uruu, Semjinyatil, mingled with the Ströckers and Brandstetters and other old peasant families who had lived in Pritnitz and its environments for centuries. But Keppler turned out even more coffins than there were foreign graves to show, for the wealthiest patients took their dead home for burial in his elaborately embossed caskets. Keppler had moved to Pritnitz from a Viennese suburb because business was so good in this valley of the Vienna woods.

The number of dead cast no reflection on Sapponyi. It was simply that too many came when it was too late, died, and were then embalmed and encased by Keppler, to lie behind the Pritnitz cemetery's wrought-iron railings, a gift from Sapponyi, under an Austrian sky—Greeks, Turks, Bulgars, Roumanians, Hungarians, Slovenes, Serbs, Letts, Lithuanians, Esthonians, Russians—all lying peacefully side by side. "My league of nations," Sapponyi had once fondly termed them.

Now he looked down at the man he was about to give a more elegant and solidly built bed than he had ever lain on in his lifetime. Why was he doing it? Why had the sight of this wizened old face with its traditional beard and *pajes*—why had it moved him? He had felt the same way when he had shown Thérèse the ghetto in Krakau . . . the Kazimierz. They had gone into a store, just to show her what it was like inside, and the woman had had cherries for sale, ripe, pink cherries. Sapponyi had suddenly wanted to buy some, but Thérèse had laid a restraining hand on his arm and said, in French, so that the woman should not understand—oh, her consideration was flawless!—"Don't, Manfred, they'll make you ill. Everything here is very picturesque, but so dirty!" And she had wrinkled her fine little nose, and he could see that she was trying to breathe as little as possible.

It had rankled. "Blood is thicker than water." The silly words often came to him. They came to him now. There lay the Jewish pedlar, reminding him of his origin, its strangeness, its unshakable individualism in the face of an eternally overwhelming and inimical majority, race, race, race . . . like a reproach from God! Where was there a community where he, Sapponyi, might feel at home?

The cart was soon there. When the procession reached Schreiner's house, he was at the front door and motioned them to the back. Here, in a small anteroom, Moishe was laid on a bench. Schreiner soon terminated the brief examination. Keppler had provided a very fine coffin, originally ordered for a patient at Strubl and then discarded for another. Dworje's horror-filled eyes watched them lay Moishe in it and nail down the top. Reischenbacher helped Keppler do it. The child stood by and sucked her thumb.

Melita said to Sapponyi, "It's a good thing she's too little to feel anything."

Sapponyi answered, "I'm sure it will make some sort of impression on her, and not a good one."

Schreiner watched the proceedings, arms akimbo, head on one side, his whole attitude one of patient indifference. Schreiner was a National Socialist, an inscribed party member, a link in the firmly moulded chain of the National Socialist German Workers' Party known as the N.S.D.A.P., or Nazi Party.

Schreiner had first heard of the movement in Munich, Germany, in the year 1921, when he had been visiting his married sister. In those days he had been a little country doctor in Innsbruck, that model of an Alpine town, huddled at the foot of a steep mountain whose summit gleams white even in early autumn. From Innsbruck to the south the way lay open to Vienna; all one had to do was turn one's back on the mountain and go straight ahead; and from Innsbruck to the north one of the best constructed mountain highways in Europe led to Munich, which was the seat of the *Bewegung*, or Movement.

Here Schreiner heard one Adolf Hitler speak for the first time. His sister, who personally knew the speaker, had taken Schreiner to the party rally in the Circus Krone, and introduced him to the man with the forelock who was still sweating from the agitation of his speech, his flesh loose on his face, his eye wild and unable, or unwilling, to focus. Schreiner had mumbled a few admiring words and, as his adulation had penetrated to the ecstatic figure, the eyes had seemed to gather their concentrative strength and had given Schreiner a piercing glance. Schreiner looked into the coldest, clearest, most penetrating blue eyes he had ever seen.

At that moment he fell under the sway of the leader. Although it was not his good fortune to have speech with the great man again —a cult was already being established around him—he was able to converse with some of the other leaders. He told them of his position in Innsbruck, that he was about to break up his house and office there and move to Pritnitz in Lower Austria, near Vienna, where his mother's brother, also a doctor, had died and left a better business and a house and a bit of land for him to take over. In Pritnitz he would be the district doctor, and he would not have to put up with unfair Jewish encroachment as he had to in Innsbruck. He did not mention the other Gentile doctors there whose business was better than his. With them Schreiner could not plead the excuse of "cunning Jew"; they were just better doctors. But, Schreiner finished his story, he would gladly sell the property in Pritnitz if these men thought he could do more for the Movement in Innsbruck.

On the contrary, thought these men, the contribution from Innsbruck was already the largest from the Ostmark. They would be glad to have a faithful party member in Lower Austria, where the Social Democrats, "the Reds," as they called them, were so strong. And so Kurt Schreiner was instructed in the preliminaries of what he was to do to propagate the Movement in Lower Austria.

There was one reason why Kurt Schreiner would have been glad if they had told him to stay in Innsbruck. He did not relish the idea of living at such close quarters to his illegitimate child, Conrad, and of seeing again the child's mother, Toni.

Toni had been the first woman in his life. He had been twenty years old and visiting his uncle, the one who had just died, when he had seen her first, watering her father's cows, her legs bare, her skirt tucked up all round above her knees, her sweaty blouse sticking to her breasts, showing their firmness. They were breasts you could cup with one big hand. He hadn't looked at her face until much later and never had paid much attention to it even then, which was unfair because Toni was beautiful in a primitive way. Hers was a serene face with rather dull, big eyes, regular features, good teeth, and long, thick black hair in a knot of braids at the nape of her neck. She had let it down later on when, at her suggestion, they had sat in the hay-field to watch the sun set. She had wiggled her bare toes to get them free of hay, and he had tickled her feet.

She had taken him in the most motherly way; it had been a very comforting experience. She had guided his inexperienced body and he had not, for one moment, felt clumsy. He had never been quite as happy again. But of course, a man like himself, an academic man, could never marry a peasant girl like Toni. Neither had Toni expected marriage, not even when, several weeks later, she had realized that she was pregnant. When she had written to him, then back in Innsbruck, he had sent her money at once and had continued to send a little over the required amount as regular as a clock in the years that followed. But he had never come to Pritnitz again.

Toni had married three years later, the second richest farmer in the valley, and told Schreiner that he need send no more money for Conrad; she could now look after the boy herself. Schreiner had discontinued the payments, feeling neither relief nor regret.

Toni had continued to produce children. Conrad grew up with three brothers and two sisters, but he was different from them all. His mother seemed to prefer the other children; his father—Conrad had known nothing of Schreiner—certainly did.

Conrad hated the lot of them, his mother most of all. Of her he was afraid. The man who he thought was his father beat him; of him he was not afraid. But of his mother's contemptuous, quiet gaze—the time they'd caught him stealing and brought him home, for instance, and at other times, after minor meannesses—the way she didn't say anything, but turned away as though he were beyond repair, as though she wanted to turn her back on him and could—that was it, and could! That galled, that rankled.

On the evening of his arrival in Pritnitz Schreiner had walked up the road toward Strubl and turned into the valley's first crevice, eager to get this visit to Toni out of the way. He felt no embarrassment at the thought of meeting Toni's husband. There was nothing unusual about his position. Nearly all the women here had had one child or more before their marriage, and rarely was the father the man they finally married.

But he saw nobody except Toni. Her husband had gone to market and would not be back until the next day.

Toni knew that Schreiner had come to Pritnitz to live. The gossip of the village had told her that. She had listened with an expressionless face, nodding her head and thinking of something else. She met him now with very little emotion. He was dreadfully unattractive, she thought. She could hardly recall what he had been like twelve years ago when she had let him love her in the hay.

"*Grüss Gott*, Toni," said Schreiner, in a rather pompous voice.

She was standing in front of the house facing him, as though waiting for him. But she hadn't been waiting for him. From here you could see the sun set unhindered over the Schneeberg, and sunsets still appealed to her.

"*Grüss Gott*, Schreiner," she said. It would never have occurred to her to call him by his first name.

Schreiner felt how right he had been not to want to see her again. There was no respect in her greeting—she had never respected him —but then, twelve years ago, she had at least made him feel good. Now there was nothing.

After a brief pause she said, "Do you want to come in? Sit down for a while?" But she made no hospitable move to show him the way.

"Let's stay out here," said Schreiner, pointing to the wooden bench against the wall of the house. "Then you can see the sun set. You always did like that."

She thanked him with an abstracted smile, and they both sat down.

"I've come to stay," he said.

"I know," she answered him.

"Are you glad?" He could have bitten his tongue for saying that, for giving her the chance to say, as she did, "What difference does it make? What have we two got to do with each other now?"

Schreiner swallowed. "There's the child," he said. "I'd like to see the boy."

Her features hardened. "If you want to see the boy," she said, "you'll have to go to Wiener-Neustadt. He's in a reform school there. He was caught stealing for the third time. So they took him away."

Schreiner was too taken aback to speak. "He's got bad blood," Toni went on, "that boy has. He's no good."

Schreiner rose angrily and drew himself up to his full height. "Bad blood!" he snorted. "Bad blood? If he's a bad boy it's because he's had a bad upbringing. What could I expect of a lot of slovenly Austrian peasants?"

She didn't get angry. It didn't seem to make any difference to her what he thought of her or of them all. She said quietly, "The others aren't like that."

Schreiner ignored the thrust and said, "I will go to Wiener-Neustadt and fetch the boy and keep him with me. I suppose you have no objection?"

She looked straight at him then and said quietly, "That would be quite all right with me."

She gave him the address in Wiener-Neustadt and they parted. He found the boy, an overgrown eleven-year-old, looking like fourteen, physically as fit as Siegfried, mentally completely awry. For the last three years now Conrad had been living with him, and both men felt that they had gained dignity in each other's company. Schreiner saw possibilities in Conrad which Toni could not have

28

seen. He realized the boy's smartness, which could be trained into useful channels. The boy felt that he was being appreciated and grew less belligerent. He did not steal again. Schreiner did not expect to make a gentleman of him, not even an academic man. The future he had in mind for Conrad was one with which the boy could be completely satisfied. He was to be trained for the Movement.

Schreiner and Conrad had returned from a visit to the Reich just a few days before Moishe had dropped dead on the road. They had gone to witness the trial of Adolf Hitler for the attempted *Putsch* in Munich four months ago, and had heared the verdict—five years' confinement in the fortress of Landsberg on the Lech, with the possibility of parole after six months' good behaviour. Six months . . . they would pass, Schreiner had explained to the boy. They were less than a day, less than a second in the great future that was in store for them all. A weak Republic had let them off easily. Schreiner's lips curled contemptuously at the thought of such a ridiculous institution, and his contempt included the Social Democrats of the Ostmark, who, because they had not been able to get their own way when the Austrian Republic had been founded in 1918, had retired from the Government and thought they had a future in democratic opposition. Numskulls! He despised them more than he despised the Jews. They weren't even enemies. They were merely weaklings.

His contempt included Melita. How he had been deceived, at first, by her Nordic appearance! He looked at her now, earnestly conversing with Sapponyi, and felt fury that this girl should flaunt her liberalism in his domain. But not for long! The future belonged to his kind, the new, upsurging, ruthless kind.

Sapponyi tapped him lightly on the shoulder. "Wouldn't you like to get on with this?" he said, his hand raised in a gesture that indicated Dworje and the child.

Schreiner started. "Yes. Of course," he said curtly. "I need her credentials."

Dworje had no credentials. The borders they crossed were marked by no customs and passport office. They were the "green borders." . . . You walked across them on foot, not knowing when you had passed from Austrian fields into Hungarian ones. Nature drew no national demarcation lines.

Schreiner said, "Your name, Jewess?"

Dworje's eyes were on the sealed coffin. "He needs it for the record," urged Sapponyi in a kindlier voice.

Dworje's lips parted. They were dry and stuck a little. Her voice was parched as she said, "Dworje."

"Your last name, Dworje," said Sapponyi, and pointed to the coffin. "His name."

She shook her head.

"What is your last name, Dworje?"

Again she shook her head.

"What was his name?"

The same effort to speak, the same harsh voice coming from dry lips, "Moishe."

"Haven't you any last name, Dworje?"

She shook her head.

Sapponyi said to Schreiner, "Oh, they're that kind." And when he saw the district doctor and Keppler, and even Melita Bahr, staring at him uncomprehendingly, he said, "They have no second name."

"That a person should have no second name!" mumbled Keppler, more to himself.

"These are poor Jews," Sapponyi explained, although he knew that Schreiner wasn't at all interested. "Where they come from, some God-forsaken little village in Poland or Roumania, probably, the Jew has no surname. I suppose they've never settled down long enough anywhere to need a name. Or they'd have got an ugly one, like Stinky-water or Asshole—that is, unless they had enough money to bribe the official to give them a fine name like Cohn, which comes from the Hebrew *kochan* and means High Priest—or Levi, or Simeon, or Reuben, the names of their oldest tribes. But what do I have to tell you all that for? You know similar cases. The Jew in Gutenberg . . . *Süssleib*—Sweetbody. Not such a good name for a hunchback!"

Schreiner pretended that he wasn't listening. He was getting the papers ready which had to be filled up because the Jew had died in his district. Sapponyi went on, addressing himself to the others.

"This woman, now, she has a name. Dworje. A very pretty name. The equivalent of our Dora. She must come from better stock, because some of their women don't even have a first name. I wouldn't be surprised if this child here"—he pointed—"had no name at all." He turned to Dworje. "What is the child's name?"

Dworje had been listening to him and the light of consciousness had returned to her eyes. She stretched out a long bony arm and drew the child to her. "This," she said in the Yiddish jargon, "is my Fehgele."

"You see," said Sapponyi to Melita, "she says that is her little bird. The child has no name. Do you recognize the word *Vogel* out of which her dialect makes *Vehgel* and the diminutive 'le'— *Vehgele* . . . Fehgele . . . little bird. Pretty, isn't it?"

"Yes," said Melita. "But isn't the way they distort the German language funny? Fehgele. If you hadn't told me it came from our word *Vogel*, I wouldn't have known it." She laughed and Sapponyi felt the same resentment as when Thérèse had turned up her nose at the cherries in the ghetto.

Then Melita suddenly asked, "What is to become of them?"

Sapponyi looked at the woman and the child for quite a few moments before he spoke, and then it came from him harshly. "I shall give them sufficient money to continue their journey home. Dworje," he addressed her in an authoritative voice, "where is your home?"

She shrugged her shoulders.

"Where were you bound for?"

She made a visible effort to co-operate with him. Her parted lips let out the hoarse word, "Roumania."

"Through the Burgenland?"

She nodded.

He felt for his wallet. "I will give you sufficient money to take you there by train."

Her eyes widened. Didn't he know that she couldn't travel by train without the necessary documents which made one a citizen of this world?

"I know, I know," he said, impatiently. "You can use the trains occasionally, and walk across the borders as you are accustomed to doing. But the money will help you to get there more easily and more quickly."

Again she shook her head. "Thank you, good gentleman," she said. "But there is fighting in the Burgenland. Without Moishe . . ." Her voice trailed off.

Sapponyi laughed. Did she think that Hungary's rapacious act of aggression was still being fought? "That was last year, Dworje," he said. "There is no fighting in the Burgenland now."

Dworje's eyes became slits, and she said in a hollow voice, "How can one tell, good gentleman, with the *Goyim*?"

Sapponyi experienced a feeling of exultation. The Jewish woman had recognized him as one of her kind. "Good gentleman," she had said trustingly, in the precarious position in which she found herself, and had given him, as thanks for his compassion, a pearl of wisdom such as only the lowly of their kind could formulate. The *Goyim* . . . the Gentiles. Yes. They were always fighting.

And he found himself saying to her, "We need another woman in the laundry. I will give you the job."

They buried Moishe in a corner of the cemetery without any rites and with nothing to mark the place where he was buried. The latter fact disturbed Melita, not because she was pious, but because her soul, burning with the desire that all people should be treated as equals, resented Moishe's shabby interment. Until all graves were bare, let the Jew have some monument too. So Melita called to the child to follow her, which the child did after a moment's hesitation, and they went off together to find something with which to mark the grave. Dworje they left in Schreiner's anteroom, where she had taken to rocking back and forth again, her hands covering her face, a sing-song moan issuing from her lips.

Meanwhile Sapponyi was saying to Schreiner, "I have a patient at Strubl who is expecting a baby which she cannot give birth to.

She has a slight cavity in the right lung and infiltrations in the left lung. A thoraco-plastic operation is therefore impossible, and she certainly cannot carry or bear the child. I would like you to perform the operation."

This was not quite true. Sapponyi did not like the fact at all that Schreiner was to perform this minor operation. In similar cases in the past, Sapponyi had not dreamed of calling in the district doctor. A first-class obstetrician had been sent for from Vienna. But in this case the patient had insisted on having District Doctor Schreiner. Why? Sapponyi couldn't imagine except for the fact that Fricka Reuther was a trying patient, the most trying he had ever had.

"Who is the patient?" asked Schreiner.

"Frau Fricka Reuther."

Sapponyi failed to notice the gleam of recognition in Schreiner's eyes. He went on, "She is very reluctant to give up the child. It took great persuasion on my part to get her to do it."

Schreiner said, "And you think it is absolutely necessary?"

Sapponyi stiffened. "I have just told you the condition of her lungs, Herr Doktor," he said, refusing, as usual, to address Schreiner as *Herr Kollege*, Mr. Colleague. "Doesn't that convey to you how serious the woman's condition is?"

"Yes," said Schreiner, "but I happen to know Frau Fricka Reuther too, and I know that she is very anxious to take the risk."

Sapponyi was taken aback. "I didn't know you knew Frau Reuther," he said.

Schreiner said nothing to that. He was not going to do Sapponyi the favour of telling him that he had not met Fricka Reuther socially, but quite by chance one afternoon, at the inn between Strubl and Pritnitz, which was as far as she was allowed to walk. There she had to wait for Strubl Franz with the freight cart to drive her back up again. On one of these afternoon excursions, which she loved because they took her away and out of sight of the Sanatorium, she had met Schreiner drinking beer at the inn, and they had started a conversation.

Schreiner saw in Fricka Reuther his Nordic ideal of womanhood.

She was a Valkyrie; she was a kindred spirit. He was not in love with her; he worshipped her as a goddess.

It maddened him to know that she was a patient of the Jew. "Of course you know," he said, "that the child can be born perfectly healthy."

"Who is thinking of the child?" said Sapponyi impatiently. "Her husband is very much in love with her and will not hear of endangering her life, as this would if she went through with it."

Sapponyi couldn't imagine why Maurice Reuther loved his wife Fricka. She was repulsive to him, the blonde, stalwart Brünnhilde! He shuddered a little and at once controlled himself sharply. "She is taking it very much to heart," he went on. "I don't see why. She has one child. And a very sweet child." The sight of the seven-year-old Anne-Marie Reuther with her halo of baby golden hair curling round her head, her transparent white skin, pink cheeks, and big blue eyes rose up before him as he had seen her walking beside an adoring father a few weeks ago.

"A girl," said Schreiner.

Sapponyi's irritation was increasing. "What's wrong with a girl?" he snapped.

Schreiner shrugged his shoulders. The Jew Sapponyi couldn't understand the German woman's hot desire for a son. "I will come tomorrow morning and examine Frau Reuther," he said. "Now, if you will excuse me, I have a patient waiting."

He left Sapponyi, who, with a brief glance at Dworje and a shake of his head, went out to see what had become of the teacher and the child. He had wasted enough time.

It was Melita's intention to find some sturdy stick that might serve as a temporary monument until she could forget the Jew. "The little bird" walked beside her but refused to take her hand. After a while she wandered off by herself.

Melita let her go. She knew that the way to win the child's confidence was to watch her but let her be.

Soon the child came back to her side with two sticks which she had laid on top of each other to form a cross. They were the thin dead branches of a birch tree, and the child had skilfully wound some long grass round the cross at its crux so that the sticks would keep their place in that position. Now she showed Melita what she had done, looked up at her and smiled as she had smiled at Julie. Again the row of pearly teeth and the dimples showed. How did her mother keep her teeth so white? thought Melita. Even in the village, where a certain amount of hygiene was taught, the children's teeth were yellow. And Melita thought, as the others had, that the child was pretty. And she laughed at the cross which the Jewish child had made for its father's grave.

What did it matter? The mother would not see it, and if Moishe could from where he was, it should not rankle. Melita took the cross. "Why," she said, "that's beautiful, Fehgele! Come. We must go back." And they retraced their steps to the cemetery.

Melita dug a hole, and they set the cross in the ground. Its wood was slightly flattened on the small beam that lay crosswise. "We could write something on it," said Melita, sitting back on her heels and looking at it. "Shall we put your father's name on it?"

The child seemed to think a while, her eyes on the cross. Then she spoke for the first time, in a deep, clear voice. "*Vater*," she said.

Melita took out her pocket-knife and cut the word *Vater* into the cross of birch-wood. The child smiled, then suddenly she lost her self-consciousness completely and jumped up and down on both feet, clapped her hands, and chuckled as she repeated the word again and again, "*Vater, Vater, Vater . . .*" They had packed him up in such a beautiful box. . . .

She laid her dirty, chubby hands on the freshly turned black earth and patted it. "Beautiful," she said, distorting the German word "*schön*" into "*schain*."

When they came back to the house they found Sapponyi standing beside the open door of his car, his watch in his hand. "Come on, come on," he said, Dworje standing apathetically behind him. "Where have you two been?"

"What are you going to do with the child?" asked Melita. She would very much have liked to take her, for company and help.

"What can I do with the child except take her along?" said

Sapponyi, vexed that she would think him soft, and he wasn't doing this because he was soft, nor out of charity, he was doing it . . . he was doing it . . . He was damned if he knew why he was doing it!

"I would love to take her," said Melita.

"No!" something cried out to Sapponyi from inside him. "You can't separate the child from the mother at a time like this," he said, leaving the question open. That was as good an answer as any, and certainly did not betray his feelings. . . .

"Of course," said Melita. The Herr Medizinalrat was right. She watched regretfully as the mother took the child by the hand and got into the back of the car without a sign of emotion.

Sapponyi sat in front with the chauffeur. The child, seeing her mother's indifference, was reassured. She clambered up on to the back seat and knelt there, looking out of the back window.

"Good-bye, Fehgele," said Melita.

The child turned and looked back at her seriously, Melita waved, and Fehgele's lips curved faintly in a smile.

"I think we're all set," said Sapponyi.

"The pack," remembered Melita suddenly. "The Jew was carrying a pack." But it was nowhere to be found.

"Come on, come on," said Sapponyi. "That was stolen long ago. They won't need the stuff anyway. All right, Fritz. *Auf wiedersehen*, Fräulein Lehrerin."

Melita came round to the side where he was sitting to shake hands with him. He wished she hadn't done so but had been satisfied with a formal nod, which was all that he had intended. This incident had brought them more intimately together than he liked. He didn't want to get on intimate terms with anyone.

The car spurted off in a cloud of dust. It was nearly supper-time, his whole afternoon had been upset. Andrea would be wild. He looked back and saw the child's back as she stared out of the rear window, her two little hands flattened against the pane—dirty hands except for the right thumb, which was bright pink from being sucked. The mother sat morosely, her unseeing eyes staring straight ahead. Nice thing I've started, thought Sapponyi, and he tried to feel vexed.

The road rose as they left the highway, and suddenly all of Pritnitz could be seen huddled in the valley, its roofs red, the church spire pointing like a needle to the sky. The sun was setting the heavens on fire above a silhouette of hills. "*Schain*," said the child again, and this time it was Sapponyi who winced at the way she pronounced it.

Chapter Two

T HE road took a sharp turn, and Pritnitz was blotted out. As they progressed toward Strubl, the countryside took on more and more the aspect of parkland. There was no dividing line to show where Sapponyi's property began. The land on either side of the road gave the appearance of an estate.

The mountains ran down to the edge of the valley and there ended abruptly. Smaller valleys branched off into the hills, cutting their way in like little rivers whose beds they once had formed. Now farmhouses nested on the stony ground. Here began the houses of the Fichtenbachers. At this time of evening the shadows in the valleys were deep purple and the trees emerald green. A few houses stood in the flat land of the broader valley through which the road wound its way. Dogs ran out and barked at the car. Sapponyi knew them all by name and called out to them, which was more than he did for the villagers.

The peasants came to the door when the dogs barked because it was the time of day when they were not working, and the children ran to the edge of the road when they heard the car coming. News had already reached them of the Jew's death. Now they saw the child's face framed in the back window of the car. The children gasped and cried out, "Did you see ? The Herr Medizinalrat took the child with him !" and there was envy in their voices. None of them had ever ridden in a motor-car.

The car passed the little inn which belonged to Fichtenbach and the schoolhouse. The brook beside the road and the rivulet formed by the melting snow on the other side grew narrower and shallower as they drove on and the grade became steeper. The road crossed the brook on a wooden bridge. On the banks grew yellow primula in profusion. Another bend in the road, and Strubl lay ahead of them.

"Look up," said Sapponyi to the child, and she turned and bent low to see what he was pointing at. Her mouth fell open.

Strubl stood on a promontory with gently sloping lawns that ran down to neat red gravel paths. The house itself was of cream stucco, five stories high and very broad, built like a Dolomite hotel, a mixture of grand manor and chalet. Its roofs were gabled brown, the balconies framed with the same wood in a rustic criss-cross pattern. A low, long pavilion jutted out at one side for those poorer patients whose rooms faced the north where there were no balconies, where the aspect of the house was stern, straight up and down like a commercial hotel. But they were approaching Strubl from the south. The dying sun made diamonds glow in every window, and the light stucco walls were tinged with pink.

The car swung round the drive and came to a halt at the front door. Out rushed a slim, light woman, dressed in stiffly starched white, a bunch of silver keys jingling from her belt, her long, thin, serious face hooded by a nun's white cap tied in a bow under her chin. The bow trembled with her agitation.

"Really, Herr Medizinalrat has been away too long," she said, then caught sight of the two in the back and words failed her— even her! Her sharp, beady black eyes grew big under their bushy brows, which she raised as her narrow face seemed to swell with astonishment.

Sapponyi, with a mischievous smile, got out of the car as though it were the usual thing to bring gipsies home with him, for that was what Sister Andrea thought they were.

"Where . . ." she stammered, "why . . . where did Herr Medi-zinalrat . . . why did Herr Medizinalrat . . . ?"

Sapponyi helped her out, not because he felt sorry for her in her confusion, but because he was in a hurry.

"This is the wife of the Jew who dropped dead in Pritnitz," he said, "and his child. They had nowhere to go. I thought we could use her in the laundry. Fräulein Spaeth said we needed another woman there."

"Yes," said Andrea. "All right. But what about the child?"

"What about the child?" said Sapponyi angrily, more afraid of Andrea's disparagement than he had been of Melita's. "What possible difference can a child make to an establishment as big as ours? Put her with her mother. There's room."

Andrea remembered that the Herr Medizinalrat had thought differently a few months ago when one of their waitresses had suddenly become pregnant. Just as Andrea was about to mention this, Dworje, who had managed to preserve consciousness throughout all the vicissitudes that God had chosen to let descend upon her, found the sight of this wiry dervish too much. She uttered a little moan and slipped to the floor of the car in a faint.

"Now Mother's dead," said Fehgele in a matter-of-fact voice.

"But not a trace of it!" said Andrea, which was her pet phrase. She propped the woman back into a sitting posture and passed a thin, white hand over her forehead, brushing the untidy hairs away from a face that really looked like death. The hand was astonishingly gentle and good to look at.

Then Sister Andrea called: "Hannes!" in a most efficient voice, and when the porter appeared, told him to get into the car and drive down with them to the cottage where the servants whose duties did not lie immediately in the house itself lived. Without another word or look in Sapponyi's direction, Andrea got into the car from the other side, and Fritz drove off with them all.

Sapponyi looked after them and his shoulders shook. That was Andrea for you! She would rant and rave, but she would act.

Andrea had been his head nurse for five years now. She had come to be assistant nurse, had taken over the head nurse's place when the latter had succumbed to a serious illness, and had remained in that position ever since. She managed the entire house without assistance. She had wanted it that way, and had proved that she could do it. If she didn't mind growing old before her time from overwork, that was her affair, thought Sapponyi. She grudgingly allowed him to call for a special nurse from Vienna for the bed-ridden patients and for operations These special nurses came from the same Bethesda Organization of deaconess nurses from which Andrea came, and their presence at Strubl always irked Andrea. She did not like to be constantly reminded, as she was by their habit, of the community to which she belonged.

Sapponyi often wondered why Andrea had chosen nursing as a profession and, an even greater mystery, why she had become a deaconess. Although they certainly enjoyed far more freedom than their Catholic sisters, still, these Methodist deaconesses were Protestant nuns, there was no getting round that, and why Andrea should have chosen to enter a community that imposed restrictions on her, Sapponyi could not fathom. Certainly she made up for it by imposing restrictions on everyone at Strubl, including himself. Why did he keep this frustrated demon as his head nurse ?

Because she was so reliable. Before Andrea, rest from responsibility had been impossible. That was it, he thought, as he walked slowly toward the wing of the house where he lived with Thérèse. That was it. She was as good as a doctor. He could at times forget Strubl and know that it was not forgotten, and lately he had frequently wanted to put Strubl aside. He was growing old, and he was tired. He was finding it increasingly difficult to breathe. "Angina pectoris," they called it. He didn't think it was only the ailment. There was something suffocating about the air that hung over Strubl—over all of Austria, for that matter.

He entered his immaculate suite of rooms, which lay on the second floor in the left wing of the house, over the large dining-room. Not that the main part of the building was not immaculate —Strubl was a model sanatorium where no corners collected dirt or germs, spotlessly clean with its highly polished linoleum floor-ing, shiny leather-upholstered chairs, glossy wood furniture, tiled fixtures, gleaming nickel gadgets, dazzling white linen—nobody could say that Strubl was not immaculate. But Sapponyi's suite, mirroring Thérèse's way of life, was not only immaculate, it was static, as though no one lived there. Every piece of furniture, every ornament, stood in the position most becoming to it, whether it was useful there or in the way; and there it stood year in, year out. Nor were the rooms inhabited by dust or insect, by fly, moth or butterfly—no animal was allowed to enter them. The grand-children, when they came to visit, behaved as the house demanded; even they fell under its static spell. They had their own cottage on Strubl's grounds to "live" in. And in these surroundings, Sapponyi lived with his wife, Thérèse. This was his home.

The odd part of it was that he felt at home in it. His wife suited him. She was a woman who never wanted you to get on intimate terms with her. That she wanted to be a saint was her affair. She did not let it interfere with their life together; she did her duty as wife and mother, and that was all that mattered. But sometimes he found himself watching her with sly amusement. Would she make the grade?

To be a holy child of Jesus, a pure woman of God, with the reward it implied and in which she implicitly believed, was Thérèse Sapponyi's one aim in life. To live a life of love—that is, a truly Christian life, was alien to her; she did her good deeds methodic-ally, as she told the beads of her rosary, one by one, like stepping-stones to her desired goal, coldly and calculatingly. There was the rug she had woven for the altar in church, twenty years of evening labour, finished now and to be consecrated this Corpus Christi. There were the alms she gave to the needy and to the Church, the food she gave away, the clothes she sewed for the poor—all done precisely, without a vestige of inner warmth.

She had married Sapponyi, not because she was in love with him, but because his plans for a house dedicated to the sick appealed to her as a superlatively good deed. Another gold star on her record for heaven. Sapponyi was a gentleman, he owned land like an aristocrat, he could have bought her a title but she rejected the idea as too worldly. With stoicism she endured a harassing conflict with her mother, who, if Thérèse must marry a Jew, at least wanted the recompense of a title. But the Comtesse Thérèse von Walden und Zugstern became plain Frau Medizinalrat. Another gold star . . .

Now, as Sapponyi entered the room, she was embroidering a fine altar-cloth in white. She had to hold the minute work close to see, even with her pince-nez on the bridge of her delicate little nose. As Sapponyi told her how he had spent the afternoon, she listened quietly; sometimes she shook her head from side to side. Her needle shuttled back and forth. She turned the cloth and finished off a thread, cutting it with a pair of little silver scissors. He wished he might once see her bite the thread.

"What a strange experience!" she said, laying her work on her knee and looking up at him. Her brown eyes were serene and innocent like a child's. She wore her brown hair in an old-fashioned way, with a pompadour and a small knot nestling in the nest formed by it at the top of her head. It suited her. She was ten years younger than Sapponyi, just past forty-five, and her face showed only the faintest lines when you came up close to it, but who ever did? And her face was pretty, like a doll's, underneath her quaint hairdress. She wore an ecru lace fish-bone collar to cover her neck, and a jabot of ecru lace; for the rest she was always dressed in black.

"A man and a woman and a child on their way to . . . where?" she went on. "I wonder. Who may they be?"

Sapponyi, seeing her lapse into one of her mystic moods, said hastily, "Oh, he was just a pedlar on his way to Bruck. The sort of people who are always on the move. Heaven knows where they originally started from. Some obscure place in Roumania or Poland . . ."

"I want to see the child," said Thérèse. "Will you have her brought to me, Manfred?"

"She's very dirty," he warned.

Thérèse hesitated. "Well, we'll have Andrea clean her up, and then I would like to see her. Do tell Andrea now, Manfred."

Sapponyi obediently called Andrea on the house phone. She answered, "I have looked the child over, Herr Medizinalrat, and it will take me a good hour to clean her up. I have no time to do that till after supper. I will bring her to the Frau Medizinalrat as soon as she is clean."

42

CHAPTER TWO

Two hours later, Andrea stepped lightly into the room which she had assigned to Dworje and her child. The woman lay stretched out on the bed, conscious now but still staring out of unseeing eyes. The child was sitting on the floor, playing with the paraphernalia of the washstand, which she had spread out around her—the pitcher, the bowl, the soap-dish.

Andrea stood looking down at her, and the child stared at the nurse's highly polished black shoes with the pointed toes that had a little pattern of holes in them, at her thin ankles in their black cotton stockings, at the pretty folds of the full white stiffly starched skirt of her uniform that rustled when she moved.

Andrea shook her head, bent down and picked up the chinaware. "Those aren't to play with," she said severely, although she had just told herself in the hall that she must be charitable, and not start off by scolding. "I'll teach you what they are for, but first I'm going to give you a bath. Come."

The child did not stir. Her eyes continued to travel up the deaconess's enchantingly strange figure, past the white belt to which was attached the bunch of keys that jingled when she walked, the belt that gathered in the folds of her skirt, letting them out again to make full the blouse of her uniform and hide her firm, very slightly rounded breasts as effectively as her full skirt hid her slim hips. No one could guess how perfectly built was Andrea under her uniform. She herself was only aware of the fact that her skin was hatefully white, due, probably, to the fact that no part of her body except her face and hands, which were tanned, ever saw the sunlight. At her throat, where her stiff celluloid collar met in two curves like a reversed upper lip, she wore a brooch with three signs, a cross, a heart . . . the third thing Fehgele had never seen before. "Come," said Andrea again, less patiently now, and held out her hand.

The child rose to her feet and patted down her dress. Then she pointed to the brooch, and her eyes looked from it into Andrea's.

Andrea's stern features relaxed. She knelt down so that the brooch was level with the child's eyes and pointed to the heart.

43

"Love," she said. Her fingers groped for the cross. "Faith," she said. And for the anchor. "Hope. And now, come."

The child followed her down into the basement, to the bath. She watched Andrea take a sponge and washcloth and a big towel from a closet in the wall. "Can you undress yourself?" asked Andrea.

The child gave no answer. "Do you understand me?" said Andrea. "Answer me so that I'll know you understand me."

Still the child gave no answer. "What is your name?" said Andrea.

The child's deep, reluctant voice said very slowly, "Fehge," with which solemn pronouncement she discarded the diminutive "le" and thought she had thereby gained in stature.

"How old are you, Fehge?"

"I don't know," said Fehge, and the words came from her with the same reluctance.

Andrea sighed. "I am going to undress you, Fehge," she said, and began to peel the black dusty clothes from the child's body.

Fehge let Andrea do as she liked without resisting. Underneath her dress she was wearing a woollen garment, damp from sweat and grey with dirt. She wore no drawers. Her stockings were held up with string which had cut red rims into her soft flesh above the knee. Andrea clucked her disapproval. Now Fehge stood before her naked. It was warm in the little bathroom and steamy from the bath. Fehge's skin was pink, but on her hip was a festering sore. Andrea examined it, then went out and came back with something in a bottle and a wad of absorbent cotton in her hand. "Now," she said briskly, "this is going to burn a little, but you must bear it. If your mother had kept you clean, you wouldn't have this sore." And she applied the stuff, quick and firm.

Fehge's eyes grew large, her mouth quivered, her lips drooped, and two big tears rolled down her cheeks. But she uttered no sound.

"Why, you're a good girl!" exclaimed Andrea, and patted her on the shoulder. A flash of fear came from the child's eyes, but Andrea did not notice it. "When you've bathed, we'll put some cotton and adhesive plaster on it, and if you wash yourself all over every day you won't have any more sores like that."

With a comb she tried to straighten out the child's matted hair. With the first tugs she realized that it was impossible, stood up with a vexed sigh and looked down at the child. "What are we going to do with you?" she said in despair. "I can think of only one thing."

She took a long pair of scissors out of a case in the large pocket of her uniform. How they gleamed! Fehge looked straight and unflinchingly into her eyes. Andrea laughed. "I do believe you'd stand there and let me do anything to you," she said, and her voice sounded pleased.

In ten minutes Fehge's hair lay on the floor, and what was left on her head curled stubbornly and stiffly. Andrea laughed and handed Fehge a mirror. The child took the glass and became absorbed with her image. Suddenly her lips curved, her dimples and her fine white teeth showed, and she chuckled, then laughed, and Andrea laughed with her.

Then Andrea picked Fehge up under the shoulders and lifted her above the bath's edge and let her down gently into the warm water. Fehge drew in her breath sharply and held it until her eyes bulged and her face was crimson. "Breathe!" said Andrea sharply. "Breathe!" When the child did not obey, she slapped her gently on the cheek so that Fehge had to exhale. "Now don't cry," said Andrea. "It isn't going to hurt. Sit down."

Fehge made herself stiff. Andrea couldn't make her rigid body bend. She stepped back and stared at the child standing upright in the tub and had to laugh. "Please," she said, "please . . . little one, sit down. Look, take hold of the sides, there, now, gently, see? It doesn't hurt, does it?"

Fehge's small behind was in the water. Thus far she got, then jerked up again into the same rigidity as before. She would not sit in the water. She would die first!

So Andrea washed Fehge standing in the bath and did the best job she could under the circumstances. Her short hair she washed, first with turpentine to kill the lice, then with soap and water, and

finally she poured pitchers of fresh water over the child from top
to toe. Fehge submitted. She only gasped and spluttered when she
breathed in the water.

The child had nothing to wear for the night. Andrea had fore-
seen that, and Hilda, the third-floor maid, had said she would
bring over one of her old white summer blouses with short sleeves.
Andrea had hated to accept the offer from the easy-going, loose-
living girl whom she despised, but she was not one to nip charity
in the bud, however objectionable the donor.

The Prussian head nurse and the Austrian maid did not get along.
To Andrea, Hilda's flamboyant charm meant nothing; she had
eyes only for the maid's slovenliness. But the patients, who found
comfort in the everyday sight of Hilda's robust health and blatant
sensuousness, liked to overlook her slipshod ways; that was why
Sapponyi had always intervened on her behalf and Hilda had been
kept on. And here she was now, with the blouse, curious to see
the mother and the child about whom there was already much talk.

Andrea took the blouse from her. "Thank you," she said.
"Have you done your dishes?"

"No," Hilda replied, and laughed. "I was much too curious to
see the child. You should hear what they're saying . . ."

Andrea didn't listen to servants' gossip. "Go and finish your
work," she said, and motioned the girl out of the room. Hilda
waved, Fehge smiled at her. "Why!" cried the friendly girl,
"she's human!"

Andrea clucked angrily. What a creature! She held up the
blouse. It would do until the right things could be provided for
the child. Andrea knew who would provide them. This was a
case for Thérèse Sapponyi, and Andrea was surprised to find herself
jealous of the woman who could spend as much as she wanted to
on charity. It was not always easy to *act* charitably, which was all
that lay within Andrea's power. She grew tight-lipped whenever
she thought of Thérèse Sapponyi, because she felt instinctively
that somehow or other Thérèse's devoutness was not entirely holy,
but she couldn't put her finger on just what she meant. Andrea
had a very hard time living a Christian life, cursed as she was with

46

a violent temper, stubbornness, and an almost unconquerable desire to dominate. Dreadfully she envied Thérèse Sapponyi her placidity.

"There," she said now, and stepped back. "Why!" she cried out, "you look like a boy!"

Fehge did look like a little Roman boy, with her short hair curling all over her head, her cheeks rosy from steam and excitement, and her compact little body gleaming through Hilda's thin blouse. The neck-line was so wide on her that it bared her two tiny pink nipples.

"That will never do," said Andrea. She went away and came back with white cotton tape and a bodkin. She drew the tape through the neck of the blouse, and pulled it up to the child's neck which brought the impromptu nightgown to just above Fehge's knees. Andrea looked her over again. "No. That won't do either," she said, and remembered a pair of shabby play trousers discarded by Sapponyi's grandson who was just about the same size as the little girl. They had been given to Andrea to give to the poor. She fetched them now and dressed the child in them. "We haven't got a skirt for you," she said, "so we'll put you in trousers. Now you will really look like a little boy," and she fastened the Tirolean braces securely.

Then she went into the next room, which belonged to the *Oberwäscherin*, or head-washerwoman, where she found a shawl which she wrapped round the child. The shawl was bright blue and made Fehge look like a cherub out of a holy picture. "Come now," said Andrea. "We have to pay a call."

She carried Fehge out of the cottage and across the narrow vegetable garden into the main house to the Sapponyi's rooms, where she handed the child over to Thérèse's maid, Mitzi, and went back to the untidy bathroom. She gathered together Fehge's clothes, took them to the back of the house, and set fire to them. Then she went upstairs to clean up the mother.

Half an hour later Mitzi brought the child back. Dworje, clean now too, was sitting in a chair dressed in one of Andrea's nightgowns. Her features were resigned with weariness, and her hands lay clasped peacefully in her lap. Andrea was standing beside her, talking to her earnestly, when the child was brought in. Fehge went up to her mother and climbed on to her knees.

Andrea said to the maid, "Well, how did it go off?"

Mitzi, with every curl in place round her forehead, her long hair done up in a tight, neat bun, her dress, her apron, her shoes and stockings as spick and span as the house she served could demand, answered in the whisper which she had accustomed herself to use, "The *gnädige Frau* was quite taken with the child. She will buy everything that is necessary for her in Vienna tomorrow." Then she went away on tiptoe.

Andrea was torn out of her contemplation of the pretty way Mitzi walked—there was a girl, neat enough even for her, but what a liar!—by the sound of a struggle going on behind her. She turned and saw the mother's hands at the child's throat, where Fehge's hands were too, and the struggle was for something the child was wearing round her neck, clutched now in her tight fist which the mother was trying vainly to open. In a jargon that Andrea could barely follow, the invectives poured back and forth.

"Give it to me, wicked child!"

"I won't! I won't! It's mine!"

"It's the devil's. Give it to me, child of the devil!"

"I won't! I won't! The lady gave it to me! I didn't steal it! I didn't steal it! It's mine! It's pretty! *Schain!*" she was screaming, "*schain!*"

Andrea separated them with a firm hand. Fehge retained what she was clutching in her fist. Andrea could see that it was attached to a thin silver chain round her neck.

"What is it?" said Andrea. "Go on. Show it to me. I promise nobody will take it from you."

Slowly Fehge unclenched her hand. Cupped in her pink little palm, which she held under her chin, her eyes seriously raised to Andrea's, was a little silver medal. A tiny Christ was nailed on the cross on one side, and the Virgin of Mariazell carrying her child was on the other. "See," said Fehge, "the dolly," and she pointed to the Virgin lying uppermost.

"Yes," said Andrea, and turned the medal round. "And see? The Saviour."

Her face was grim. How like Thérèse to tie her label on the child at once! Andrea held the charm in her hand and turned it over from one side to the other. The Holy Mother and the Saviour. She looked at Fehge. Which would she choose?

Firm resolve was born in Andrea's mind to win this child for her God. "Let her keep it," she said, turning to Dworje. "It won't do her any harm. She is better off here than on the road, and so are you."

Dworje moaned. "Ay, ay, ay, where will this all end? What will become of us?" But she let the child clamber back into her lap.

Andrea regarded them for a moment. Good heavens! she thought to herself, they *are* savages! For the moment, however, she had to let them be. There would be time enough during the following weeks to take the matter of these two strays in hand.

But this matter God took into His own hands. Dworje never did take up her occupation in the laundry. She died fourteen days later of nothing more complicated than starvation.

Nobody noticed, until it was too late, that she was not eating enough to keep body and soul alive. When Andrea discovered that Dworje was wasting away, she sat down at Dworje's bedside and tried, sternly, to persuade the woman to eat and regain her strength, if not for her own sake, then for the sake of her child. And why, Andrea wanted to know, did she refuse food? It was good food, better than any she had eaten in her life before.

Dworje explained. The food that was eaten here was *Trefe*, and she couldn't eat it, she would rather die.

Andrea didn't know what she was talking about. Haltingly, Dworje translated the word to her, and Andrea recognized the laws of her own Bible in the food laws that the Jewish woman described. Only, Andrea did not adhere to them.

She looked down at the woman who would obey her laws and die rather than break them, and she admired her. There was nothing heroic-looking about Dworje, but in Andrea's eyes she was a heroine.

This time Fehge was not alone with death. Andrea had her arms round the child when Dworje died, to comfort her, not realizing that the child did not need comforting. Fehge, as she saw her mother breathe her last, did not connect the event with the loss of the only comfort she knew. Just as she had not realized when her father had dropped dead that, with him, had Sapponyi not so strangely intervened, went her food and drink and all the poor material advantages she enjoyed, she did not now understand what had taken place. Her mother had been so ill and so unhappy. Now she looked peaceful, and Fehge was relieved. They would put her in a fine, sweet-smelling pinewood box, as they had her father. *They* were certainly well off, packed up safely under the protecting earth.

Andrea, however, was greatly moved. "*Ach, Gott!*" she kept saying, "*Ach, Gott!*" And the two spots of high colour came into her gaunt cheeks as always happened when somebody died.

Dworje died on the morning when District Doctor Schreiner came up to Strubl to operate on Fricka Reuther. Andrea, who met him at the entrance, told him to make out the death-certificate. Schreiner pretended not to remember who Dworje was and had to be told the whole story again, and throughout the telling he showed his distaste by the curling contempt of his lips.

"The child had better be sent to a Jewish orphanage in Vienna," he said.

"No," said Andrea hastily, "the Herr Medizinalrat says she can stay," and the tone of her voice betrayed the part she had played in this end.

Thérèse had been as persistent as Andrea in her persuasion of Sapponyi, with whom the decision lay. He had understood Thérèse's reasons for wanting the child to stay in the valley, purely mystic ones—she rarely had any others for doing anything. But Andrea's eagerness to keep Fehge amused him. To give this Prussian spinster a Jewish child—it was ironic! Besides, Fehge would make no difference to Strubl's budget nor to his private fortune. Some of Thérèse's charity would be diverted to her—that was all. She would go to the village school, learn to wait at table or clean vegetables in the kitchen, to wash or iron or scrub the stone steps. If the village ever forgot her origin, she might even marry. Anyway, he would be investing practically nothing in the almost certain acquisition of a good and faithful servant. "Yes, Sister," he had said, "the child may stay."

Schreiner shook his head at Andrea. "The Medizinalrat does not consider the fact that she will have to go to school with our children."

"Why shouldn't she go to school with the children here?" asked Andrea indignantly. "She won't do those louts any harm!"

Schreiner shrugged his shoulders. "For a German woman," he said, "you have peculiar views, Sister."

Andrea's fury mounted. Who did he think he was, this little quack doctor? "What does the Herr Doktor know about German women?" she said tartly.

Schreiner drew himself up to his full height and said, "I am a German."

Andrea said nothing more. What was the world coming to with this Austrian riff-raff classifying itself as German? Rabble! thought Andrea, for the nth time this day, as on every other day she spent here. Rabble!

An hour later, Schreiner was standing beside Fricka Reuther, feeling her pulse. On the other side of the bed stood Andrea. Between them lay Fricka, slowly recovering consciousness, her face still pink and slightly moist from the heat of the operating-room, one braid of her golden hair lying over each shoulder and covering her breast. The austere white nightgown she had worn for the operation made her look like a prisoner. She looked very young and pretty, and when she opened her eyes they were pale blue and vacant. As they regained vision the colour deepened, and her lips became petulant. She saw Schreiner and started to say something, her dry lips parted. Then she saw Andrea and closed them again. "I want to speak to the Herr Doktor alone," she whispered.

Andrea rustled briskly out of the room, not offended in the slightest. She was much too sure of herself to care whether a patient asked for her to come or go. And she had so much to do that she was always glad when her presence in the sick-room was not needed.

Fricka Reuther and Schreiner were alone. The sun flickered on to the dark green linoleum-covered floor as the wind moved the branches of a tree outside.

Fricka liked Schreiner. He shared her views and, in the society she had moved in since her marriage, there were not many men who did. She had been married off to Maurice Reuther at the age of seventeen by a frail but very firm mother who thought that by this marriage she would save her daughter's soul, which she might have done if her daughter had had a soul. But Fricka Reuther, *née* Krausewitz, had none.

She had not been upset by the fact that she was not marrying for love. A love-match had no place in her philosophy. The "man of steel" did not "love." Fricka was as much an arranger of life as was her delicate little mother, but her plans lay in a diametrically opposite direction. They were plans which had been instilled into her as a child by her father, who was not entirely to blame for their taking such deep root in his offspring, for Fricka was by nature pre-eminently disposed to a creed of assertive superiority and domination. When her father died of apoplexy she was left stranded and yearning in her adolescence, at the mercy of a gentle mother whom she despised but whom, convention-ridden as she still was in those days, she felt she must obey.

Fricka's mother had hoped that social life in the cultured city of Vienna would make good the harm that Königsberg had done, or perhaps it was unfair to blame the city and not the father who had distorted the philosophy of Fichte to fit into his chauvinistic German mind.

Fricka had no objection to balls, banquets, and teas, to opera, concerts, and good theatre, and to travel in foreign lands; but she could not stomach her decadent husband—that was how she saw him—who could delve into history, which he had at his finger-tips, and with cold, contrary facts shatter her dream of the rights of the Germans to the entire world. She hated him when he did it, and when he taught their daughter, Anne-Marie, the kindly, humble gospel of Christ. How could she ever hope to counteract the soft teachings of the child's father?

Maurice had taken Fricka away from Germany where lived the men after her own heart, the heroic men who could endure. Schreiner was not her ideal, but he was at least actively working for the glorious German future her father had taught her to dream about, a dream she would never outgrow. What was more, he was showing her ways in which she could actively work for that glorious future, and she was very grateful to him. She had discovered, in the course of their friendship, that the heroic man was not exclusively her type after all. The frustrated man, the man with a chip on his shoulder, the bitter man, was too—the man like Schreiner. She could poke her fingers into his wounds, metaphorically speaking, and make them bleed afresh, an effect that stimulated her. She loved rousing people. In this, too, Maurice had always thwarted her.

There was no desire mixed with her feelings for him. Fricka Reuther's sensibilities were entirely sublimated and had their ecstatic outlet in her dreams of, and now, thanks to Schreiner, in her activities for, the great German future. She groaned with displeasure when Maurice took her, and would have been as disgusted with the love-making of any man, even one she admired. The act was to propagate, and to have children she would let it happen to her again and again . . . to have children . . . to have sons. . . .

Her lips parted. The words came softly from them, and Schreiner had to bend low to hear. Instinctively he knew what she was going to say. "Was it a boy?"

"Yes," said Schreiner, "it was a boy."

One large tear welled up from under Fricka's closed lids and rolled down her cheek. Schreiner said, "Please accept my sympathy."

Fricka drew in a deep breath that was a shuddering sigh. "I will never forgive him," she whispered; and as Schreiner wondered if she meant her husband or Sapponyi she gave him the answer, "The swine-dog . . . the Jew . . ."

Chapter Three

ANDREA, dressed in her Sunday-best black alpaca gown and cape and the black silk cap with the hemstitch edging covering her stiff white hood, took Fehge by the hand as they left Strubl to accompany Dworje for the last time. The black dress that Fehge wore for her father now had to do for her mother too.

Thérèse watched them go from behind the lace curtains of her window. No one could see her, but she could see Fehge walking beside Andrea. No one knew of the jealousy in her heart as she saw the Methodist nun leading the child—no one except Sapponyi, who was an amused spectator of this struggle for the child's soul. But there was one thing he had yet to do, and now was as good a time as any to get it over with.

He called Thérèse from the window and asked her to sit down. "There is something I want to say to you," he began, and she gave him a friendly, encouraging smile.

"I have been thinking about the child," he said.

"So have I," she answered, "ever since that evening . . ." Her voice took on the dreamy quality he feared. He did not want her hobby to become a curse and drive her over the edge of sound religion into insanity.

She was thinking: He found the three by the roadside, an old man, a woman, and a child. She had been told "a girl," but Andrea had brought her a boy. Oh yes, she knew now that Andrea had had nothing else to put on the child but Ferdy's discarded old trousers, and had cut off her hair because of the lice; still—it was an omen, and that night, in her dreams, the three had been transformed into the Holy Three, Joseph, Mary, and the Child, and an angel had appeared to her and said, "Care for her." Whenever she saw the child Fehge now, she saw the Child Christ. Thérèse Sapponyi was preparing to earn another gold star. Fehge had become a part of her way to God.

Sapponyi knew exactly what was in her mind, and he was determined to nip this idea in the bud.

"I don't think we should interfere with the child's religion," he said, coming bluntly to the point. "I think, if you will excuse my saying so, my dear, it was a mistake on your part to hang that thing round her neck on her first night here. It upset her mother quite a lot, so Andrea tells me. Poor thing. Now she's gone, I shall have to think what would best be done for the child. I don't think we have any right to interfere. We shouldn't . . ." She let him talk on and on. "Don't you think I'm right?" he finished lamely. He wished she would give him some answer.

She did. "I think the child should be baptized and brought up in the faith," she said.

Sapponyi braced himself. It was the first time he had ever crossed the path Thérèse was treading on her way to heaven. "No," he said. "She must decide for herself when she grows up."

"Decide what?" said Thérèse, her face unmoved.

"What faith she wants to follow, my dear."

"There is only one faith," she said. "You know that, Manfred." Her voice sounded anxious. Was he really devout?

"We think so," he said, "but she may grow up to think differently."

"Then she will sin, and ours will be the greater sin for failing to guide her on the right path."

"No," said Sapponyi, "I don't see it that way. It would be taking an unfair advantage of her to baptize her now."

"I don't understand you," said Thérèse. "Did you feel that you were taking an unfair advantage when you had your child baptized?"

How long ago that was, thought Sapponyi, and thought: My child? The girl had always been hers. He had not wanted a child. He did not need a child. He needed no one.

"It is our duty," she said firmly.

"No," Sapponyi persisted. "I can't help feeling enough obligation to my race to want to give the girl a chance to choose, at least. You forget that I am a Jew."

Her eyes grew big. She said, "How unlike you to bring that up."

He laughed, and to him it sounded a short, bitter, unhumorous laugh. "How pretty you are, my dear, when you open your eyes wide like that." He went over and kissed the top of her hair. "I won't bring the matter up again. I confess, I hadn't thought of it for years. The sight of the man brought it back to me. Humour me. The child shall decide for herself. And," he smiled down at her, "I am sure she will choose the faith you want her to choose."

Melita came to the door of the schoolhouse as Andrea passed by with Fehge. She knew that the child was going to stay, and was glad. She still wished Fehge could live with her. Perhaps that could be arranged now.

She came out and stroked Fehge's hair. "Don't worry," she said lightly. "You are not alone."

Andrea said briskly, "Fehge knows that her father and mother are watching her from heaven and won't let any harm befall her."

Melita had her doubts about that. She would like to have taken the child by the hand and strolled down to the cemetery with her and found a cross for Dworje's grave, as they had done for Moishe's, but Andrea looked forbidding and possessive. Melita sighed as she looked after them. It would be a pity if the old dragon took over the child and made a bigoted Methodist of her. But if the priest took her over, the priest who gave religious tuition in *her* school, something she had to tolerate—something her beloved Republic had not yet been able to abolish . . . It really didn't make much difference. It was a pity the child couldn't grow up naturally, as all children should, with a moral code rather than a mystic one.

That night, for the first time, Andrea prayed aloud before Fehge. She called it "holding devotional exercises." It was a very simple procedure. Andrea did not kneel; she simply sat in the one comfortable chair in her room, Fehge on a stool beside her. She folded her hands in her lap and closed her eyes and told Fehge to do the same. But after a few seconds Fehge opened her eyes again, just a crack, and, seeing through her long lashes that Andrea's eyes were closed, dared to open hers wider and watch the nurse's stern features, the way her short black lashes quivered as people's do who are pretending to be asleep, while she prayed, in her own words, to an invisible Being whom she addressed as "Dear Saviour."

As Andrea sat with her hands folded humbly and her long, aesthetic, sallow face with its regular, austere features, the long aquiline nose with its flaring nostrils, the firmly set red lips and prominently rounded chin, she looked like a bloodless woman from an old Flemish painting.

The words she spoke were mostly of thanks, with a few small requests at the end and a blessing on them all. The room was very still. Never had it been so still and the night outside so black and quiet! Fehge sat without stirring, and the chills ran up and down her spine until she turned cold. Andrea, this big, stern, all-powerful, all-knowing Andrea, was talking to someone she couldn't see, who was therefore undeniably *there*, talking to someone who disposed of the beauties of nature, the good health they enjoyed, the good food they ate, who could heal the sick and, wonder of wonders, protect the dead and, of course, the living, from evil and harm. *Why had no one told her this before? Why had no one ever told her that such a Being existed?*

Fehge felt as though chains round her body had burst. She breathed deep and her heart beat so that she could hear it. The tears stood on her lashes and rolled slowly down her face. Her breath came in little shudders. She was so immensely relieved.

"Amen," said Andrea, and opened her eyes and saw the child's emotion, which pleased her.

She took her Bible and read the twenty-seventh psalm aloud: "The Lord is my light and my salvation; whom shall I fear? The Lord is the strength of my life; of whom shall I be afraid? When my father and my mother forsake me, then the Lord will take me up. . . ." Andrea could find the right answer to every need in her worn old Bible.

When she had put Fehge to bed, she said another prayer for the child's soul which had found its way to God. Now there remained only to lead the child to His house on earth, the church, which, in Andrea's mind, was the Methodist Church. That, too, would come.

Chapter Four

IT was Dennis Seymour's first day out on the balcony. He had been in bed for six weeks. Today he was going to lie out of doors for two hours, and from then on longer and longer every day until he could go downstairs—at first for midday dinner, then for supper. Later he would go for walks, at first for ten minutes on level ground, then for half an hour, then for an hour, then up a slight slope, and in the end up into the hills he was longing to explore, where—so he had been told—the clearings were carpeted with royal-blue gentian at this time of the year. This spring he would not see them, but next spring . . . When you knew as much about the disease as he did, you learned to calculate like that, by years, with an equanimity according to your temperament. He knew pretty well how things would develop unless he was suddenly and unexpectedly snuffed out, as was sometimes the case, because the heart grew tired. The lungs could take it so much longer than the heart could. This he had learnt from years of convalescence, and he knew that each case and cure were different. None of his lapses had been alike or taken the same time to heal. So he didn't worry. His heart, he knew, was fine.

Dennis wanted to get well. With each relapse his desire to get really rid of the disease, to be a healthy man, had grown. This new operation, now. He hadn't hesitated for a moment to take the risk, even though the rather stodgy old specialist in London had been noticeably sceptical. It might make him completely well. Of course, it might kill him right off, too. It hadn't, though. Here he was, standing on his own two feet, facing the hills, his warm flannel dressing-gown loose over his pyjamas. He took a rare, deep breath and felt well. He wished his father were here now to see him walk so much more securely, to see his firm flesh and fine colour, not the heightened red of fever, but the slow all-over bronze of returning health.

Poor Dad. The finest football coach in England, and his only son a consumptive. Dennis could feel for his father, who had never been sick, who had never felt weak, who had dealt in his daily life only with athletes and had had to see the two people he loved most suffer from a disease that, to him, seemed diabolical and uncanny. It had killed his wife; a few years later it had attacked his son.

At that time Dennis hadn't minded being ill. His father had thought he was just putting up a front, but in time he had come to realize that Denny really didn't mind, a fact that never ceased to astonish Jasper Seymour, to whom a man lying on his back was a man cut off from life. But for Dennis it had, at first, been a relief to lie down and not have to do all those things which a young man his age was supposed to do, to have instead as much time as he liked for reading, writing, painting, and contemplation. His illness had made him free.

Ever since he could remember, and this point of view went back to his earliest childhood, freedom had seemed to gleam like a far-away and delectable light. Complete, individual freedom. He could remember it at first as the palpable urge to have a room of his own, a wish granted to him comparatively late in life, considering how well off they were and how many rooms the fine old house on Clapham Common had. But his mother was one of those warm-hearted impulsive, animal creatures who had not outgrown her dormitory days and couldn't bear to be separated from those she loved day or night, and in emotional matters her husband was her slave. But in the end Dennis's wish was granted. Then came the urge to shut himself up in that room, to shut himself in to be free, and to fit his room with things entirely of his own choosing— no sports trophies, no school pennants, but a Greco Christ all alone on the wall over his desk. This was not because Dennis was pious, but because the wild light in the picture pleased him and aroused his first desire to see tortured Spain. He liked to keep his own room clean at such an early age that it had been comical. His mother had laughed when she'd told his father how Dennis had said to her, "Mother, I've dusted my room. Please don't let Meg into it." Meg was all right. He was very fond of their temperamental Scottish housekeeper. But she didn't put things back in their places, and after she'd cleaned he invariably found the atmosphere he had been at great pains to create destroyed.

It was not always possible to retire to the freedom of his own room. He could recall stumbling embarrassedly through the drawing-room that was always full of his hospitable little Irish mother's guests at tea-time, full of people he couldn't see clearly because he was so short-sighted. One had to go in and say, "Hello." No, not hello—"How do you do. I'm very well, thank you." The words slithered off your tongue mechanically, even if you weren't feeling well at all and had a stitch in your side. Mother would have been hurt if he hadn't gone in, if he'd used the back entrance, which would have been so simple, and one couldn't hurt Mother's feelings; she was one of the "musts," to be considered ahead of oneself. This freedom had to be achieved without hurting people, at nobody's expense. It was only to be acquired after treading paths unstrewn by spiritual corpses, and if one had to wait to be a hundred it would be worth it. Any other freedom would be without peace. So one traversed the drawing-room, making a stiff little bow; one even handed round scones and tea-cakes. How he had flushed when one of the ladies had said, "Cathy, I do believe the boy's short-sighted!" He should have been grateful to her, for shortly afterwards he had received his first pair of glasses, and the world became clear. Terrifying at first, but worth it, well worth it! He had been able to see, and his hands had stretched out—metaphorically speaking—aching to reproduce what he saw now so suddenly, so late. Not the people, but the landscapes, the flowers, inanimate things; above all, colour, colour, colour! Painting came into his life. But he dared not show he loved it more than football. That would hurt his father.

Having been born with a heart full of consideration, one had to be very careful, on one's way to the shining objective of freedom, not to hurt those people from whom one was gently, ever so gently, trying to extricate oneself. It might take a lifetime to do it that way, but that was the way it had to be done. One's father and mother did not constitute the only entanglements. The nets that wrapped one round at birth and were made stronger by fate didn't begin and end with parents; they went on and on throughout life. There was the net of religion, for instance. That had been a very subtle net; he had not been able to make up his mind for or against it for a long time. To see his father on his knees, a big, grown man—it had always made Dennis squirm. But his mother looked sweet telling her beads; it was the only time he could remember her in repose (he had not seen her sick), and could observe her lovely features (he was not with her when she died). But you couldn't judge religion by the fact that it suited one person well, another badly. For Meg, religion was a decidedly healthy outlet. Without religion, Meg would be as mad as a hatter. But for him? No. He clambered out of that net too, probably because it was another net, a community of people. He didn't want to belong to any community of people, not because he was unfriendly—he had a reputation for friendliness and kindliness and understanding. Dennis Seymour was always ready to listen and give you of his time. But this matter of belonging to a group—how could you see them clearly or preserve your objectivity if you were standing in their midst? To get above them, without any idea of superiority, just to be able to see them all clearly. To take sides? Not yet. Not for a long time. Not until one was wise, and would that ever be? Was it within man's reach?

Jasper Seymour had visited his son three weeks ago. He had sat, feeling helpless, at his boy's bedside, folding and unfolding his hands, looking incongruously robust in the sick-room, the sun gleaming on his bald red pate with the silver hair still growing thick all around the edge. His face was ruddy from fresh air and strong liquor, his eyes restless in their frame of wrinkled flesh, his cheeks still as smooth as a child's, his mouth firm, with the lines of laughter betraying his good humour. With his good broad face and stocky build he was a strange contrast to his rangy son sprawled in the bed.

"Are you glad you came up here, Denny?" he'd said. "Seems to me an out-of-the-way sort of place after those Swiss sanatoriums you've been to before. Awful lot of foreigners here, too."

Jasper had no idea of the humour in this remark, that he, the alien on foreign soil, should be complaining that there were too few of his kind and too many natives whom he called "foreigners." Dennis had laughed and pointed out the error in viewpoint to the old man, who had laughed with him. "I guess you're right there," Jasper had said. "But I hope you're not going to be lonesome."

Dennis had had to smile at that. Funny, how your own people could know you so little. Lonesome? No. He was only going to be free, free of another enveloping net . . . the so-called British atmosphere. It would be good to be rid of it for a while. Those Swiss places he had been to before—they were so full of English people, you might as well have stayed in Brighton. Here, he could tell, everything was going to be different.

He had caught glimpses of some of the patients on his weekly excursions down to the fluoroscope, exotic people, the like of whom he had never come in contact with in the sanatoriums he had visited before. There were people from the Balkans, and from Asia Minor, for whom civilization was still centred around Vienna in spite of the collapse of the Austro-Hungarian monarchy.

He always met the patient who had been weighed and "looked through" before him, as he stepped out of the lift on his way to Sapponyi's office once a week, and he met the man whose turn was after him when he was through and ready to go back upstairs again. He saw these strange beings, their figures lost in the nondescript folds of their dressing-gowns, their gait and stature distorted by the way they held themselves in this state of undress and had to shuffle in their bedroom slippers, so he had only their picturesque heads to go by. Thus he had seen the old Turk, on whose emaciated, swarthy head you missed the fez; the queer-looking pimply son of a famous Roumanian statesman; the fabulously wealthy

Hungarian landowner who looked like a giant gipsy—no, a lion-tamer! That was it! A lion-tamer! Dennis had been racking his head for days to think what it was the big burly black-moustachioed man reminded him of. And the tall, handsome Rabbi from Galicia with his squat, ugly little wife who wore a wig and had a mouth full of enormous gold teeth. He had thought at first that she was the Rabbi's servant and had wondered why he had chosen such an unprepossessing one. How the lift reeked of garlic when they had been in it before him! Some people probably hated them for it. Some people could hate because others smelt different. Why? It was absurd.

Hannes, who ran the lift, proffered all kinds of information, and by the way he spoke you could tell exactly who gave the best tips. Of the Rabbi and his wife he spoke with contempt and told how she kept food between the storm windows of her room and how it stank to high heaven! When asked if there were no lady patients, he had answered loftily that *they* had "check-up" on another day.

Now Dennis stood on his balcony and looked about him. Three balconies, his in the middle, jutted out a few feet from the side of the house. They were matched, about six balconies farther along, by another three which jutted forward in like manner. Both chairs to his right and left were unoccupied, their mattresses gleaming white in the bright sunshine. Dennis was glad that his left-hand neighbour, the garrulous old Pole, was in bed for that day. What a scramble there had been yesterday to find his mislaid false teeth! Dennis had finally spotted them, gleaming white and ghoulish on the tin roof that projected like a shelf at the foot of the balconies, on which the rain tip-tapped sometimes, rhythmically and pleasantly. The jolly maid, Hilda, had retrieved the teeth with a mop, and they had all had a good laugh, even grim Sister Andrea.

The old Polish *Grossgrundbesitzer*, or Greatlandowner (as though that were a profession!), was pleasantly mad. He had leaned over the railing between his and Dennis's balconies one bright afternoon and stuck out his bald, shrivelled old head on its long neck until he could see into Dennis's room. This uncalled-for gymnastic feat had made the old man cough. The head had been withdrawn like a turtle's into its shell, but, nothing daunted, the old boy had tried the stunt again, more cautiously this time, and had been able to say in a conspiratorial whisper to Dennis, who was watching, fascinated, to see whether he'd make it, "Hello there!"

Poised in this precarious position for a few minutes every day, the silly old man had managed to relate to Dennis a surprising amount of his life-story, surprising in volume and content. "I have so many children and grandchildren," he said one day, as though in conclusion, "so many . . . I don't know how many. I've slept with so many women in my life . . . so many women . . . I don't know how many . . . all the women on my lands. And they all have children, children of mine. Now, I have three legitimate children and they're all no good. But there's one boy, a son of mine . . . his mother is a fine peasant woman with a very good character. He was a smart boy, so I sent him to college in Warsaw, and now he's a dentist. A very good dentist! Now. Young man, I ask you. Shouldn't I leave all my castles and money to him? Eh? He is so much more worthy than my own children. But what will God do to me if I sin like that and leave my own children destitute? Eh?" He shook his head mournfully. Oh, he had his problem!

Before troubling himself too much with it, Dennis had checked up on his wild stories with Sister Andrea. He understood German, or thought he did, but the old boy had spoken with a dreadful accent, and his tales were so strange and confused that he wasn't sure he'd heard right.

Andrea clucked her disapproval when Dennis, with the swinging English drawl added to his faulty German, repeated the old man's tales. "Tsk, tsk," she said. "To think a man like that has so much power and he's crazy!"

"Oh," said Dennis, "he *is* crazy. Then it's all not true?"

"It's true, all right," said Andrea grimly. Yes, indeed, he did own all that land, and he probably had all the children who were haunting him now. Andrea had reddened when it had come to that point, and Dennis was sorry to have hurt her sensibilities.

"What can you expect of a Pole?" she had said, and that seemed to settle it for her.

Dennis had told his father about old Father Goose, as he had nicknamed Grossgrundbesitzer Sabatsky, and had laughed. He didn't see anything wrong in the fact that Sabatsky had spread his seed about so promiscuously. But his poor, devout father, so uncomprehending in the face of life as it was lived beyond the conventional borders of Anglo-Saxon territory, had been shocked. "Why!" he'd cried out, "they're heathen, that's what they are!"

Dennis wiped his glasses, put them on, and looked around him at the panorama which he could see now for the first time. On the top of the low hill opposite stood a crag, a lone piece of black rock embedded in the hillside like a hollow tooth, which was what it was called "*der hohle Zahn*." Behind it a mountain rose to a height of three thousand feet. To the right and left the hills were considerably lower. Here, leaf trees intermingled with the pines, the firs, and the evergreens, the way Dennis liked it. Down to the right ran the road, just now void of any sign of life, white in the late noon sunshine that tinged the very sky itself with gold. To the extreme left, the mountain called Schwarzenberg began its ascent as if born out of the womb of the Fichtenbach Valley. On the cleared and steeply rising land stood small cottages with ploughed garden plots framing them geometrically, looking incredibly tiny from Strubl's balconies. The earth was black, the seed freshly sown. These patches of laboriously cultivated earth gave way every now and then to rich, green clover fields, fodder for the cows and goats that were grazing. There were no herds—nothing as affluent as that—just three cows here, two goats there. Billowy, fat complacent clouds hung stationary in the sky. The sun was giving its first warmth, and the stillness of after-lunch siesta hung over everything. The peasants had left their work and retired into their houses to eat their frugal lunch, leaving their outwardly neat little homes the only sign of man's hand in a valley that was otherwise still practically undisturbed by civilization.

Dennis thought: You can relax here. You don't feel you're living next to one of the world's seven wonders, as you do in

Switzerland. You don't have to look all the time. You can forget all about those mountains when you feel like it. They won't intrude themselves on you, and when you want a rest, there they are . . . so green . . .

He wondered whether he shouldn't have a try at the hills as they were today with the fresh green of spring standing out yellow among the dark evergreens. It wouldn't be easy. But if he muffed it, it didn't matter. He painted for his own pleasure exclusively—the luxury of the true amateur. Yes. He'd make a stab at it.

Andrea suddenly appeared from nowhere to help him into his sack. "I'd like to paint that hillside," he told her. "Would you be so kind as to hand me my things?"

"Now, you don't want to paint on your first day lying out," Andrea said firmly, as though speaking to a child. "You'll be very glad if that's your one activity for today, just getting out here and back into bed again. I'll be back for you in two hours."

Dennis was breathing quite fast after crawling into the sack, and he had to admit that she was right—he couldn't have painted anything now—but he felt irritated by the way she had said it, telling him, "Now, you don't want to," as though she knew what he wanted, telling *him* what *he* wanted. . . . But his irritation soon melted in the soft spring breeze that was wafted up to him, rich with the smells of farm and freshly awakening life. Dennis closed his eyes and fell miraculously asleep.

He was awakened by the quaint chanting of a child's voice. He raised himself to a sitting posture and looked over the side of the balcony. From there he could see nothing, but when he crouched low in his chair and looked between the laths of the railing he could see the child who was chanting the sing-song which had awakened him. She was dancing clumsily, her arms stretched out stiffly at her sides, all five little fingers spread, lifting her legs as though they were heavy, her toes upturned.

It was a year to the day since Dworje had died, and Fehge had on her first coloured dress. In spite of Andrea's indignant protests, Thérèse had kept the child in black for a whole year. What could Andrea do? It was Thérèse who clothed Fehge.

The coloured dress, together with two others, had been waiting for this day for the last two weeks where they had been stored on hangers in Fehge's room, and Fehge had sat adoring them in her free moments. There was a red dirndl with tiny white spots and a blue dirndl with little rosebuds for every day, and a white dirndl with rosebuds, like the blue one, only in finer material, for Sundays. All three dresses had little puffed sleeves, narrow velvet ribbon stripes around the bottom and neckline, and the Sunday dress had white bobbin lace around the neck. But the most miraculous thing of all was the little red woollen jacket with gentians and edelweiss embroidered on it and a draw-thread of chain stitch with a thick white tassel at either end. It was a warm day, but Fehge had on the red dress and the red jacket, and as she danced, the tiny beads of perspiration gathered above her eyebrows and over her upper lip. She was in a trance of happiness.

Dennis's loud "hello" broke the spell. Fehge stopped dead, and her stiff little braids trembled on for a while. They were at a very unbecoming length, barely touching her shoulders, and Andrea braided them so tight that they stuck out straight, as though wired. Her hair was so harshly scraped away from her shining, clean face that it pulled her skin a little, and this made her screw up her eyes tight every now and then in an effort to loosen the grip of her hair. This funny way of winking with both eyes had become habitual with Fehge. She did it now as she looked up at Dennis. And she put her hands up and scratched her head where the taut hair made it itch at the temples. Then her thumb wandered towards her mouth until, with a startled gesture, she withdrew it, made a fist, and put the fist firmly in her pocket. She cocked her head to one side and blinked up at Dennis, the sun in her eyes; and what she saw there seemed to inspire her with confidence, for she answered, "*Grüss Gott.*"

Fehge had gained confidence ever since the remarkable revelation of an invisible, protecting God, but she had not yet discovered His house on earth. Thérèse never crossed Sapponyi in anything. She had done her best. Let it be on his head. Andrea, of course, would not take Fehge to the church in Pritnitz. The "heathenish" display of altars and holy pictures was enough to mislead any child. She had asked Sapponyi if she might take Fehge with her to Vienna where she spent every fourth week-end in the mother house, so that she could take Fehge to *her* House of God, which was, of course, the only one she approved of. But Sapponyi had said to her what he had said to his wife, "Let the child choose for herself."

Andrea, with a queer feeling of loyalty to the dead Dworje, had acquiesced. Probably the Herr Medizinalrat was right. After all, she, Andrea, was there to see that Fehge chose the right thing when the time came.

Fehge's school-teacher, Fräulein Bahr, was certainly the last person to show Fehge the way to God's house. On the contrary, it was she who kept Fehge from the one person who might have done the trick without any inhibitions whatsoever—the village priest. Sapponyi had not forced the child into a religious groove, and Melita admired the Herr Medizinalrat for this exhibition of firmness. She was determined to be as forthright. That was why she excused Fehge on the afternoon once a week when the priest came to the schoolhouse to give religious tuition.

Meanwhile Fehge was perfectly satisfied with God ever-present in the air she breathed. It never occurred to her to house Him. Her outside world had so far co-operated with Him in helping to dispel her fears. In school, Melita had crushed firmly at the outset all signs of anti-semitism, and the children had almost forgotten Fehge's origin. They were not friendly—that they did not know how to be—but they ignored her, and their indifference was far more than she had ever hoped to receive when she realized that she had been "left behind" in the valley.

Except for Walter Reischer, who, together with his shamefully guarded fears, nursed as shameful a feeling of pity for the orphaned girl, the children with whom she went to school were not the ones who had seen her father dead on the road. They had nothing more to forget than the gossip of their fathers and mothers, and Fehge soon ceased to interest those adults since no one ever came to see her who might have kept their interest alive. Fehge had become a fixture at Strubl. She was the Strubl Fehge, as Poldi was the Brandstetter Poldi and Lisl the Ströcker Lisl.

"What's your name?" said Dennis, thinking inwardly, Why can't grown-ups ever think of a better way to approach a child? But now the banal phrase was out.

The child said, "Fehge."

"Fehge what?"

Fehge didn't know what he meant by that, so she said nothing. Her newly acquired confidence tended to melt in the face of strangers. Besides, she knew she was out of bounds. She was not supposed to use the gravelled paths and open spaces reserved for the patients, but today was a red-letter day. She had thought of the round open space, in front of the balconies, that the gipsies used when they came by with a dancing bear and tambourines, and she had decided it was the only fitting setting for her in her splendid new attire. She hadn't thought for a moment that the gipsies got pennies thrown down to them from the balconies, and that she might too. There had been no calculation of that sort in her decision to do her clumsy little dance just there, so when one of those little packets of *Groschen* wrapped in paper flew down to her from a balcony above Dennis's, she did not even move to pick it up. She was very busy thinking that here she was, where she shouldn't be, caught in the act by this stranger whose face she could not completely see, since pieces of it were hidden behind the laths of the railing. But she could see his spectacles glistening.

Fehge wanted to run away, but Andrea had taught her that she must answer when spoken to and never go until she had been dismissed. Since nobody ever thought of dismissing her officially, it often happened that she stood stolidly by when she was no longer wanted, until the magic words, "Now run along, Fehge," or "Go on, child," were spoken, whereupon she would trot off docilely.

There was something almost stupid in her blind acquiescence to things. Often it angered Andrea, who felt rightly that a child's upbringing should meet with some opposition. From Fehge she got none. Andrea, who loved a scrap, missed this opposition.

Dennis got none either. Fehge remained standing where she was, every now and then blinking with both eyes.

"Who's your father?" said Dennis, wondering if she were the chauffeur's daughter or something like that.

"Father is dead," said Fehge.

"What does your mother do?" asked Dennis then, thinking: Washerwoman's daughter.

"Mother is dead," said Fehge.

Really, this was grim, thought Dennis. "So poor Fehge is all alone."

The surprising child answered him with the words, "Fehge has God."

Dennis stared for a moment, then he leaned back in his chair and looked up at the sky and tried to digest what he had just heard. In his mind's eye he could see the words in gold lettering spanning the mountains like a rainbow. "Fehge has God." It was a jolly fine sentence, he thought. He closed his eyes for a moment. When he opened them again, she was gone.

Chapter Five

WHEN Andrea came back two hours later, Dennis asked her first thing about the child.

Andrea's lips formed a thin, mean line and she said, "Fehge? She had no business to be out there."

Oh dear, thought Dennis, sorry that he had given the child away.

To get Andrea's mind off the thought of punishment, Dennis repeated his question about Fehge. Who was she? Andrea told him the child's history curtly. All the time she was busy bustling him back into bed, and when he got round to asking her whether Fehge couldn't come up and see him, he was in a horizontal position again.

"No, I don't think I could let her do that," said Andrea, poised in businesslike fashion at the door "That wouldn't do. You must understand that." And she gave him a penetrating look from under her beetling eyebrows.

Dennis didn't understand. The thought of infection never entered his head; he couldn't see any reason why he shouldn't see the little girl who interested him at closer quarters.

He turned over on his side to sleep, a luxury he had been able to indulge in again only since yesterday. "Would you please wake me in an hour?" he said, his back already turned to her. "I am expecting a visitor and would like to make myself presentable."

"A visitor?"

Dennis was dropping off, and Sister Andrea was keeping him awake. The out-of-doors had made him sleepy. His voice was irritable and drowsy as he spoke with his eyes already closed and the covers up to his nose. "Yes. The teacher from the village. Doctor Sapponyi has arranged for her to help me improve my German."

"*Tick-tack*," it clicked in Andrea's mind, who had known nothing of all this.

"I have called off the lesson," she said. These were the white lies one told for another person's welfare; they were not chalked up against one in heaven. "You have done quite enough for today. Tomorrow is another day."

Dennis, groping for anger, gave it up. He was too sleepy and too contented to rouse himself sufficiently to say to her what was hazily on his mind, that she had no business cancelling his engagements without consulting him.

Andrea said, "Now, is there anything else I can do for you?" rearranged his shaving things over the washbowl so that they stood in an orderly row according to height, wiped a speck of dried shaving-soap from the wall . . . *ach*, that girl Hilda! Then, in answer to his mumbled "No, thank you," she nodded her head absent-mindedly, her thoughts already on the next room she had to visit, and left him. What she had to do to Fehge was safely pigeon-holed in her mind. It would have to wait until she had made her rounds.

When Andrea had seen to it that every patient was where he should be at that hour, she hurried down to the kitchen. She never had the patience to wait for the lift. She took the shallow stone steps lightly and quickly—it was delightful how gracefully she sped down them, but there was nobody to see. Once a patient who had had to interrupt his rest period had seen Andrea sliding down the highly polished broad banisters frontways. That was how she had used to take the stairs when she had thought herself to be alone until the day she was caught at it. Oh, how angry she had been with the poor man who had been rewarded for having the stomach-ache by seeing a deaconess slide down the banisters! She had had no understanding at all for his dilemma, only chagrin for hers. She had never slid down the banisters again.

Andrea found Fehge, as she had known she would, in the big kitchen which lay on the north side of the house where Strubl had an extra floor because it was built on a steep incline. The cellars, which took up the smaller part of this basement, had only transom windows at the top which were level with the ground on the sunny south side, opening out on to an alcoved walk. But the kitchen had large glass windows that let in plenty of light, if very little sunshine. Here Fehge was busy slicing noodles.

The pastry-cook had just spread the thin dough on the board for her, and had sprinkled it with flour. Now Fehge, her small fingers neatly held against the edge of the flat roll, lightly, so as not to squash it, was slicing the noodles fine with a long sharp knife. Every now and then she peeped without lifting her head to watch the pastry-cook spreading the strudel dough, first letting the slithery mass drool down over her two clenched and closely upheld fists, then spreading it gently from the middle outward over the big, clean, wooden table that was covered with the strudel sheet, until the dough was transparently thin with never a tear in it. A breathless business!

"Go on with your work," said the pastry-cook in a kind voice, flattered by the girl's fascination.

How could she see that I was peeping? thought Fehge, who could only do one thing at a time, and she began slicing again. One

day she would let the thin dough dribble over her hands like that
and spread it thin, like the material fine ladies' dresses were made
of, over the table and sprinkle it with the apples that smelt like
heaven and the bread-crumbs and the yellow melted butter.

"Fehge!"

The girl started so that she almost cut herself.

"What were you doing on the grounds that were reserved for the
Herrschaften?"

The *Herrschaften*—that word for which the English language has
no adequate equivalent, a word coined long ago for the serf to use
when speaking of his master, his master's family or guests. On the
continent of Europe it had not yet become obsolete.

Andrea was hard! The pastry-cook tore a hole in the dough
sheet. Andrea was a devil!

"He who will not learn must feel," she said, and slapped the
child hard on the cheek. Her hand that she could cup softly to
lay on a fevered brow had turned to stone. Then she said, "When
you have finished what you are doing, go down to the schoolhouse
and tell the Fräulein Lehrerin that the Englishman is too tired to
have a lesson this afternoon. She should come a week from today."

"There's enough salt in the dough without your tears on it,"
said the pastry-cook when Andrea had gone, but she let Fehge use
her handkerchief.

"The old Prussian!" she said, and hated Andrea, as all the
Austrian servants did.

"But she's right," said Fehge wearily, her voice still hiccoughing
with sobs. "She's always, always right."

Fehge walked down to the schoolhouse with the red on her
cheek, where Andrea had slapped her, fading. As the road steep-
ened she dropped into a little skipping rhythm—step, step, step and
skip, step, step, step and skip, and by the time she reached her
destination both cheeks were equally aglow.

It was the afternoon when the priest came to the school, and
Melita had to leave her field to him, which never failed to vex her.
Apart from the fact that he taught misleading things, she thought
he gave very poor lessons and the children were obviously bored.

Were they more interested in what she taught? She brushed aside the disturbing thought.

Fehge arrived at the schoolhouse just as the priest was leaving. The children had already dispersed with the alacrity they always showed when school was out. The priest paused in the doorway to look down at the child about whom he had heard much.

Fehge looked up into the pallid face of a very tall man. So this was he of whom she heard the children say, "Today comes the Mr. Clergyman," or the "*Herr Kapprater*," which in their dialect was supposed to mean "the Mr. Co-operator," or the "*Herr Kaplan*," the "Mr. Chaplain." They could not seem to agree on his title. But whatever they called him, it was always said with a disrespectful grimace. Why? He looked lovely.

"Who is dead in your family?" she asked him as he blocked her path and made no move to go, giving him no title, playing safe.

The priest smiled. "Nobody has died in my family for a long time, God's mercy be thanked," he said. "Why do you ask?" He had a heavenly voice!

"Because you're dressed all in black," said Fehge. "I was, until today, because my father and my mother died." And she patted her bright new dress with renewed delight.

"I shall wear black," said the priest, "until I meet my Father in Heaven."

"Did God tell you to do that?" asked Fehge.

"I do not receive messages from God," said the priest. "The laws of my Church tell me what to do."

Melita, hearing them speak together, hurried to the door. "*Grüss dich*, Fehge," she said. "What brings you back here?"

The priest lifted his huge round black hat and said "*Grüss Gott*," and walked off in the direction of Pritnitz, his soutane flowing so gracefully behind him that Fehge, at first, did not answer Melita but watched until he was small and undefined in the road.

"What are you staring at him for?" Melita asked her.

"I'm watching," the child began, and now she spoke in the dialect of the children of Fichtenbach, her Yiddish accent gone, "how beautifully his robe . . ." She stopped suddenly in her description because she could not find the right words for the swishing wavelike motion of the long-legged man's black robe as he strode away, and, since the words failed her, she made the motion with her hands.

Melita had to smile. What a sense of beauty the child had! She had never watched the priest go with anything but disapproval in her mind. She was sure that even the children who were supposed to enjoy his visits had never paid attention to the picturesque *swish-swish* of his medieval garments—and she felt a little abashed in the face of such natural and unadulterated appreciation of a figure spoiled for her by the knowledge of how these romantic-looking men deceived the people.

Fehge gave her message and hurried back to Strubl. On her way she thought of some means by which to mollify Andrea. There were all Andrea's black stockings to mend, the stockings that had been darned so many times already that practically nothing of the original foot was left. In its stead was a foot as fine, woven by Andrea with black thread. She had taught Fehge to make darns like weaving. If Fehge hurried through the work still waiting for her in the kitchen, she would have time for Andrea's stockings. Terribly serious was the expression on her face and she was breathing fast and sweating when she got back to Strubl. Skip, skip, skip and a jump couldn't be managed uphill.

Melita had watched the child go until she was nothing but a blood-red spot on the landscape. It was Melita who had established Fehge's age. Since it would never be known when and where she had been born, Sapponyi had said that the teacher should decide how old the child was according to the work she did at school. Melita found that Fehge had a rather one-track mind but, given one thing to do, would do it well. According to her intelligence rating, Melita decided that Fehge must have been approximately six years old when her father had died on the road. So six she was then, and seven she was now, and her birthday, Melita had added with a laugh, might as well be set as the day Sapponyi had taken her up to Strubl, but Sapponyi had not even smiled at that. There was something solemn about the way he took the child.

Melita was very satisfied with her year in Fichtenbach—on the whole. She had decided, right from the start, not to waste her time on the adults; it was the children who counted, she thought, thinking that she and those who stood for the same thing would live to see a nation grow up which they had tutored in their ways.

She had observed the children dispassionately throughout a bitter winter, bitter climatically and emotionally—had watched how the girls and boys fought among themselves, fights that often ended with one or the other in the hospital at Wiener-Neustadt. She recalled the horror she had felt in the face of their callousness toward the dead Jew. Now she saw that they behaved the same way toward one another. She came to believe that if Conrad had been lying dead in the road they would have cried out "Hi, look! Conrad's dead!" and robbed him of his change when no one was looking. They were not anti-semites, they were anti-human!

In this lonely year of revelations in the Austrian provinces, Melita was reminded again and again of an incident in her childhood which had, until now, been blotted out by the teachings she had absorbed in her adolescence, teachings that stood on the fundamental ground of "we are all brothers"—we, the people, of course, not the capitalist, not the great landowner, not the priest. They were not "people."

It had happened in the last year of the great World War—1918. The cities were starving; in the country butter and eggs and milk could still be purchased by the assiduous, so their mother had taken them to the country.

Perhaps they had not been assiduous enough; they had been able to buy very little. But there were the wild berries in the woods which their mother sent them out with tin pails to pick. While they had been thus busy, their backs bent, their fingers knocking the berries off their brittle little stems, letting them roll pungent and dry into the pail, the peasants had come and thrown stones at them. "Go home where you belong, city scum!" they had yelled.

Melita and Anton had had to run for their lives, and the berries had dropped out of their madly careening pails. Melita had said to Anton at the time, "Now I *do* believe that they wash their hands in milk every day so that the city folk won't get it!" which was what was rumoured in Vienna. Anton, with his firm ideal of "the people" had, even then, with a bump on his forehead the size of an egg, refused to admit that "the people" could be beasts, and when Melita, in an agony over his hurt head, had shown no mercy, he had started on a eulogy as to *why* they were thus and so. All right, Melita had agreed, they are poor and overworked . . . why doesn't it make them depressed or cowed or . . . or . . . "Because they are a strong, good race," Anton had said. "The reaction of the strong man to injustice is hatred. Would you rather see them whine?" "Yes," Melita had sobbed, "anything rather than hatred!" "*Pfui*," Anton had said, "how like a girl!" And, because she worshipped Anton, she had steeled herself.

Now, her feet firmly set on the path which could always find a social excuse for the shortcomings of "the people," she tried hard to put this wartime memory where it belonged, into forgetfulness, for was not the peasant a part of "the people," who were all worthy and who were unfairly treated by capitalist, landowner, and priest? The people whom she must love. No. Whom she did love. But did she love those who could laugh at the miserable death of another poor man? Who had stoned her brother and herself when they had been starving? She put the thought aside. It upset her ideology.

It had not been easy going to begin with. The children were not stupid. It would have been so much simpler if they had been. But they were bad. For once Melita did not take time off to reason why they were bad. She set her mind straight toward the goal of bettering them. They were able and they had energy. The thing, therefore, that she had to do was to conduct their vehement energies into constructive channels; in other words, keep them occupied. This she had tried to do.

She had started them building a dam, so that the water from the brook might be directed closer to the schoolhouse. She had explained in answer to their sullen acquiescence that this was to their advantage, since they had to fetch and carry the water for the schoolhouse and, with the water so near, they could move the pump closer to the building and have no distance to carry it at all. They had brightened up at the thought that they were going to labour to their own advantage, and their parents had grudgingly spared them for the time required. Now the dam was built and Melita had set them to turning the little vegetable garden that belonged to the school into a garden for medicinal herbs, about which she knew a great deal, and which could be sold to bring in a tidy sum if managed systematically. Yes, she was satisfied with her year in Fichtenbach and felt sure that she had found the solution to the problem of the recalcitrant provinces—education toward a constructive end. It was as simple as all that. What she needed now was time. What she quite overlooked was the fact that physical activity was not what these people lacked. Their lack was a spiritual one.

Chapter Six

MELITA walked into Dennis's room a week later in answer to his "*Herein*," and said, "*Grüss Gott*, Herr Seymour. I am Melita Bahr."

Dennis, who had been dozing, couldn't at first imagine who this smiling young girl with the serious eyes could be. Then he remembered. The teacher.

In Switzerland Dennis had always shied away from any attempt to perfect his German because of the rather attractive Swiss singsong accent, the deep gutturals and queer idioms. It was fun to listen to, but not something he wanted to acquire with any effort. Now, he thought, when settled at Strubl, here was his chance to become fluent in a language he could read and write, but speak only haltingly. Sapponyi had suggested the teacher, had said she was a nice young girl, and here she was. Dennis invited her cordially to sit down.

CHAPTER SIX

Melita's ever-ready smile changed to an expression of solemnity that made her look even more attractive as she set herself to observe this lanky Englishman ill in bed before her. The fact that he wore glasses did not in any way detract from the beauty of his features which, had he but known it, he had inherited almost intact from his mother. Only the pronounced jaw was not hers, and it was that which gave the necessary masculinity to a face which would otherwise have been too tender.

Melita's first thought was that he had a fine face, the kind of face she liked, not fleshy, the planes and shadows formed by its bone structure. Like Anton's, the jaw jutted forward a little. The mouth was prettily curved and sensitive; the cheeks long, the cheekbones high, the forehead finely modelled. His hair grew long for a man's—ash-blond and shaggy, like Behrendt's, which looked as though it were never combed. His rimless glasses were becoming to him. Through them Melita could see that Dennis's eyes were hazel colour, a shade darker than his hair, which his pale brows and lashes matched. A sandy-coloured man, she thought.

He was tall and thin; the long angular lines of his body showed clearly under a white feather counterpane which he had managed to crease considerably. She saw how he moved his legs restlessly and punched his pillows into odd shapes. They bulged forth on all sides of him like turbulent waves. Now he sat up and held his head forward slightly so that the whole man gave an impression of eagerness which she found very appealing. He reminded her of Anton; he reminded her of Behrendt—the two men she loved. He was the aesthetic, the sublimated, the philosopher type, yet he was different. He was something new. The British atmosphere that Dennis had come to this Austrian backwater to be free of for a while was making itself felt.

How kind his face was, thought Melita, as kind as the gentlemanly gesture of his long, white hand that offered her a chair as he waited with great interest for what she would now do or say.

But she did not say anything. She was tongue-tied. She thought to herself that she needed to take in this strange young man more thoroughly before saying anything. But was he young? Dennis had a timeless face and build. He could have been twenty-six or forty-six. Actually he was thirty.

"Would you like to read?" Melita asked him. "I have brought along a grammar."

"I don't think we'll need it," said Dennis in his stilted German and with his appalling pronunciation. "I'm not a beginner, you know. I read philosophy at Cambridge, and you can't get by philosophy without learning to read German, can you? In philosophy they are big," he added, proud of the colloquialism "*sie sind gross.*" "But I would like to be able to speak the language," he went on, groping, now, for a word.

"*Fliessend,*" she helped him out. What a generous smile he had!

"Yes," he said, "fluently. I thought I couldn't find a better way to occupy my time while I'm laid up here."

She liked that, the fact that he wanted to keep busy even when he was laid up. Probably a hard-working young man, she thought, and was greatly mistaken. Dennis was merely putting in time, now that he was almost completely free of entangling obligations to people. Had Melita but known it, Dennis was, according to her ideals, the parasite, *par excellence*, a type found almost exclusively, to such perfection, in England.

Now he took an old black pipe from the table beside his bed and began to suck it. It was not filled with tobacco—he was not allowed to smoke yet—but the sucking of the beloved old stem and the lingering taste of good tobacco which the pipe would never lose were consoling.

Finally a flow of prosaic conversation started between them, Dennis speaking hesitantly at first, but surprised, as he proceeded, to find how quickly he achieved the transition from a literary knowledge of German to conversation.

The little teacher wasn't too interesting, but, for the purpose, good enough. And she was very pleasant to look at in her white blouse and shoulder-strap dirndl. He rather liked the quaint, old-fashioned way she wore her hair, bobbed and parted on the side, curling naturally, soft and golden, and fastened back off her face with a cheap amber barrette. Refreshing, the way you could tell a mile off that she'd never been inside a hairdresser's.

Melita was not at her best on this first visit. The sight of the young man affected her strangely. She felt light-headed, rather foolish, and could not speak freely. After twenty minutes had passed, she came to the embarrassing conclusion that she was falling in love.

It was quite a new feeling, she discovered to her surprise—she who had thought she was in love with Behrendt, who was so happily married to a woman whom she considered not at all suited for the role of a great political leader's wife. Hedwig Trattner-Behrendt was beautiful, womanly, motherly, devoutly Christian, and totally disinterested in politics. Yet her Jewish husband, Moritz Behrendt, worshipped her.

Now Melita knew why her unrequited love for Behrendt had not made her unhappy. She had never been in love with him at all! In the ten years she had known him, he had never excited her like this. And why this strange young man should give her such a new feeling she could not fathom. Her efforts to explain this strange new emotion to herself, while at the same time correcting his German, proved to be so great that she knitted her smooth pink brow into a little frown that made her face look petulant, a characteristic she certainly lacked.

"We have *Föhn* today; don't you feel it?" she said, referring to the warm wind from the south that made everyone in its path feel limp.

He agreed with her. The sky was laden, and in between sharp gusts of warm air the leaves on the trees hung static. It was because of the *Föhn* that he was in bed today with a slight temperature, a fact he had so far been able to keep from Andrea, otherwise the lesson would have been postponed again.

Melita thought what a poor impression she was making, and it confused her still further. The room was hot, or was she? This was an unpleasant condition she found herself in.

She faced it squarely. All right, she thought. The young man attracts me. What have I to offer that I may attract him?

Melita knew that she was nice-looking, but she guessed rightly that that wouldn't make much difference to Dennis. What had she to offer? And as she groped about her, spiritually, she could see only one thing, her faith. "Tell me," she said to Dennis, "are your slums in London really as dreadful as one hears?"

Dennis couldn't say. He didn't know much about the slums in London, no, nor why nothing was being done about them. "Such a wealthy nation as Great Britain," Melita said reproachfully, and made him feel uncomfortable, as though he had been sitting on Britannia's money-bags.

Dennis said, "I take it you are interested in politics. I suppose you all go in for that sort of thing much more than we do."

Go in for that sort of thing! He spoke about the welfare of mankind as though it might have been archaeology or botany. The red of indignation heightened the colour in Melita's cheeks, and the petulant pucker on her forehead was gone. She began to talk to him about "her" Vienna, about her Party, about its new fiscal policy, which included government housing, their plans to tax wealth, luxury, and pleasures in order to build magnificent dwellings for the poor which could be let cheap to both employed and unemployed, to make provisions for their welfare, and to provide the best and most modern education and care for their children. Her soft eyes glowed and darkened as she spoke.

Dennis flattened out in bed and lay still, listening to her. She took great pains to explain it in simple words, asking him every now and then if he could follow. Oh yes, he told her seriously, it wasn't so difficult to follow.

Yes, she said, it sounded simple, yet where was it being carried out except in Austria? And were these not the fundamentals without which no nation could hope to succeed?

She paused for breath. "You're a Communist, aren't you?" he asked her, with the naïveté of the lay Englishman to whom politics is not a matter of life and death.

"I am not!" she answered vehemently. "I am a Social Democrat!"

Politics. At once it rushed to his mind that this was the net most assiduously to be avoided if the freedom of peace were to be achieved. But her cheeks were still flushed with anger. "Would you mind explaining to me the difference?" he asked.

"The name implies the difference," she said, as though speaking to a child. "We Social Democrats are democrats. We believe in working for the welfare of mankind by the means of democracy. The Communists have established a dictatorship in Russia."

"But it's the dictatorship of the working-class, isn't it?" he said. "Your class."

"That doesn't make any difference," she told him. "We do not believe in dictatorship, not of one person nor of one class. We believe, like the Communists, that the means of production should be in the hands of those who produce, but that is all. Our methods to achieve that end are totally different. We hope to achieve everything through legislation."

Dennis's back ached, and he slid down farther in his now thoroughly disarranged pillows. His eyes were filled with amusement as he looked at her. He began to note a certain fondness for this young girl with the ton-weight beliefs, such big beliefs for such a little lady. If only he did not tire so easily. "Is there a lot of Communism in Austria?" he asked her.

"Where Social Democracy works," said Melita, "Communism is never powerful. No," she went on relentlessly—as though bitten by a bug, thought Dennis—"we suffer from no Communist menace here in Austria. It is the Black Ones who hamper us so terribly."

"Who are the Black Ones?" Dennis wanted to know.

"The clericals," she said. "They run this country. In Germany their party is called the Centre. That's so's they won't have any difficulty falling in either direction, whichever is the most advantageous for them."

"And what are they called here?"

Really, the young man was abysmally ignorant! "The Christian Socialists. Have you ever noticed how every faction nowadays borrows the word 'Socialist'? Because you can't palm off any political creed without it any more. The National Socialists in

Germany have done the same thing. National Socialists. Christian Socialists. And they none of them know the meaning of the word socialism!" Her face was angry again, and because she was young, it did not spoil it.

"And why do you let these Christian Socialists run this country if you so heartily disapprove of them?"

"We are in the opposition," said Melita.

"Because you have not got a majority."

"Neither have they, nor any of the other parties," she cried. "But in one thing they are all united—their hatred of us. For that they get together."

"For hatred you will always find people getting together," Dennis interrupted her, but this little bit of philosophy didn't register. She was too deeply immersed in her chronic beliefs and went on:

"We stand alone. We will not compromise, not even if we happen to hate the same fellow as the other. And we will get our majority and be invulnerable. You will see. We have only to win over the provinces." She paused.

"Aha," said Dennis, "I see. That is why you are here."

She flushed because she knew he was teasing her, and it hurt her physically in the region of her heart. "I am doing my bit," she said softly, and it cut him with the same pain, but for shame.

"The people in the provinces are very ignorant," she went on.

"And is it difficult to enlighten them?"

"Very."

"Then you will have to be clever enough to find a way to attract them before you enlighten them," he said.

"That's what the *Hakenkreuzler* do," she said, and looked pensive.

"Who are the *Hakenkreuzler*?" he wanted to know.

"The National Socialists."

"I thought you said they were in Germany."

"Some of them are everywhere," she said, "spreading their propaganda. But they do not worry us. The *Heimwehr* is our real enemy."

The *Heimwehr*, she explained to him, was the civilian army of the Christian Socialists.

"And I suppose you Social Democrats have your army too," he said.

"Yes," she answered quite seriously. "They are called *Schutzbündler*."

Truly a formidable array of antagonists, thought Dennis. The *Schutzbündler*, when translated, proved to be Protective Bundists; *Heimwehr* meant Home Protectionists, and the Nazis, or *Hakenkreuzler*, had taken their name from their symbol, the swastika. National Socialists, Christian Socialists, Social Democrats, Communists . . . He could see the entire little country at battle, and it was a wearying spectacle.

He turned from it to the young girl sitting opposite him, her healthy build, her fresh young skin, and clear, unwavering eyes. "Don't you have any private life?" he asked her.

Melita blushed because now, for the first time in her life, she seemed possessed of just that. "How can anyone think of themselves when humanity is in the appalling condition it is in today?" she said.

Dennis shook his head and put aside his pipe, which his arms were tired of holding. "I have always had a very strong feeling," he said slowly, "that we should concentrate on the improvement of our own private lives—not materially, of course, or, let us say, not only materially. In that way we may do more for mankind than if we turn our attention too much to the problems of its condition. They are such gigantic ones. Very few of us can grasp them without being adequately educated for it. Whereas, we should each one of us be able, if we make a very great effort, to keep ourselves in hand."

Melita, he could see, was eagerly waiting for him to finish. Then she went off at a tangent. "Before people can behave right," she said, "they must be housed, fed, and clothed right." She added, "You have never been poor."

Dennis, hearing the old reproach of the Socialist, answered her, "Yes. That often riles me."

At that moment Hilda came in with the supper-tray. Melita jumped up abruptly. "Oh," she exclaimed, "I have stayed too long."

She had. Dennis was in a sweat now, from exhaustion, a little from vexation too, but he was going to go on with this German-political course, perhaps just because the way she thought and felt irritated him. It was stimulating.

"Not at all," he said.

They agreed on a price of 3 *Schillinge* the hour and Melita shook hands with him as she said good-bye. It was going to be all right. She was going to see him three times a week. The thought satisfied her momentarily, but as she left Strubl behind her and walked back to the schoolhouse she felt depressed. She had fallen into waters in which she could not swim. And, suddenly, there in the oppressive grey of twilight, she understood what she had never been able to understand before—how Behrendt could have fallen in love with and married a woman so disinterested in what he had dedicated his life to. The one had nothing to do with the other. Love had no consideration for taste or inclination. But of what Hedwig had to offer Behrendt *instead* of a similarity of goal, of what kept them so happily united that they were more talked about in a city notorious for its unhappy marriages than the most scandalous divorces—that Melita still could not fathom. And her lack of comprehension on this score made her apprehensive for her future.

When Melita had gone, Dennis remembered that he had meant to ask her about Fehge. He would next time. Meanwhile, as Hilda arranged his things for him on his bed-table, he asked her about the child.

"*Ach*," said this completely pleasant creature, with her buxom body too tightly clad, "there's a sweet child for you! I take her with me on my free days. She's just as crazy about the country as I am. And I didn't go to the old dragon for permission either. I went to the Herr Medizinalrat, and he said it would do her good."

"Is the old dragon in charge of the child?" asked Dennis, knowing very well that she referred to Andrea.

"She thinks she's in charge of everything," said Hilda. "Now, Herr Seymour, have you all you want?"

Dennis looked the tray over. Hilda wasn't neat, but she never forgot anything. "I think I have everything, thank you," he said. "Why do you take the child with you on your free days?"

"I don't know," said Hilda, striking a pensive attitude. "I don't like children. But Fehge is nice to have around. And," she added, as she went out of the door with the empty tray balanced on her upturned hand flattened out backwards, "when I have her with me, the men leave me in peace." And she gave him a look and was gone.

Chapter Seven

DENNIS recovered rapidly, and on his first walk out he at once left the park with its gravel paths reserved for patients and wandered, without asking for permission, to the back of the house, in search of Fehge. Again they were to meet on forbidden ground, but this time Dennis was the trespasser.

Summer was dying in a welter of heat that dried the leaves which would soon be falling. Fehge was in the vegetable-garden pulling up carrots. Like all the children here, she had no time for play, nor did she have any toys. Her many duties kept her busy in kitchen and garden, and every evening sent her up to the summit of the mountain called Schwarzenberg, at whose foot Strubl nestled, to fetch down the "drinking milk" for the patients.

She had a good climb of twenty minutes to get to the top, where stood an inn whose keeper let her drink cheap soda when it was hot, in exchange for the pennies she gave him. Fehge had loved to watch his wife transporting the milk down to Strubl in winter, sitting on her sled frontways, balancing the two hermetically sealed cans adroitly on either side, steering with the heels of her stout boots, her skirts billowing so that they showed her black-stockinged legs and her black woollen bloomers, the snow spurting away from her heels and the sled's runners like spray. It was such a jolly sight! It had made Fehge laugh until the tears had come, tears that had frozen on her cheeks, so cold it had been. She was looking forward to doing this herself when the snows came again, on the sled Sapponyi had given her last Christmas.

Physically she had developed immensely. Now she was sturdy, with none of the unhealthy, flabby chubbiness of a year ago, big for her presumed age of seven.

Dennis found her barefoot. She was wearing the blue dirndl, now as faded as the clothing of other children. I would like to paint her, thought Dennis. It might be awful, but she wouldn't mind. She was the first human creature he had ever wanted to paint.

"Hello," he said. "Don't you remember me?"

Fehge stood up straight and let the carrots she had just uprooted drop in a heap at her feet. She was working in the hot sun, and her face was wet.

She wiped the sweat from her forehead with the back of her arm and blinked at him from between half-closed eyes. No. She did not remember him. She shook her head from side to side slowly.

"My, you're hot," said Dennis. "Why don't you go and wash your face?"

"I'm not finished yet," said Fehge.

"Won't you come for a walk with me?" asked Dennis. "Go on. Wash your face," and he pointed toward the pump. "I'll take the blame if there's any to take."

She didn't move. "Who are you?" she said.

"I'm a patient from up there"—he pointed to the bleak northern side of the Sanatorium—"and I'm out for my first walk. I'd like a little girl, like you, to show me the way."

"I'm not allowed over there," she said, pointing in the direction of the park.

"You aren't? I see one of the village girls walking with a little girl patient in the park every day."

Fehge stared at him, expressionless. "She's a little girl," she

88

said. "You're big. You don't need anybody to walk with you."
Then she added contrarily, "You'll have to ask for permission."

"Whose permission?" said Dennis.

"Sister Andrea's."

"I am grown up," said Dennis haughtily. "I don't come under
Sister Andrea's jurisdiction."

She shook her head. "Only the Dear Lord doesn't have to obey
Andrea."

This made him smile. "Come on"—he stretched out his hand
—"I won't let anything happen to you."

Slowly she made up her mind, turned her back on the carrots
and walked over to the pump. Dennis was surprised at how
meticulously she washed herself, digging under her nails to get
the black earth out from under them. He walked over and stood
beside her. She wiped her hands and face on her dress, and the
wet showed in patches as she let it down. She looked up at him
seriously and showed him her clean, sweet face. Then she winked
with both eyes as he had seen her do before because her braids
pulled at her skin.

Dennis turned her round and began to undo them. She let him.
"I've been waiting two months to do this," he said, and rebraided
her hair, loosely, so that it no longer tugged at her skin. "There.
That should make things easier for you. Life in a strait-jacket must
be unpleasant."

He saw how she wrinkled her brow with relief and said, "Can
you wiggle your ears?"

He showed her what he meant. She tried. She could do it too.
She had never known that she could wiggle her ears. It amused
her and she did it again. When she laughed now, she showed a
gaping hole where her two front milk teeth had fallen out. The
second ones were slow in coming. It made her look very droll.
There was no resisting that smile. Nothing he had experienced
here had cheered Dennis half as much. "Come on, now," he said,
"let's go."

"Would the *gnädiger Herr* like to go up the Schwarzenberg?"
asked Fehge.

"Don't call me 'gracious sir,'" said Dennis. "I hate it. My name is Dennis."

She stared for a moment. "And what else?"

"You didn't tell me what else, Fehge, that time. Remember?"

"I have no other name," said this strange child. "But everybody else has two."

"As far as you're concerned," said Dennis, "I also have only one name."

Fehge repeated her first question. "Would you like to go up the Schwarzenberg?" she said, giving him no title, but not calling him by his first name either. She hadn't caught it.

"I would love to," said Dennis, "but we'll have to do that some other time. Today we must choose the flat places to walk in because my breathing's not too good yet."

Fehge said, "Does it hurt?"

"No," said Dennis. "You'd be surprised how sometimes the things that don't hurt can do the most harm."

Fehge mulled over that one. Things that didn't hurt you could harm you too! What a treacherous world! Bad enough were the things that hurt, like Andrea's hand, like the darning-needle that pricked you, like the potato-knife that gave you calluses, like the handles of the full pails that gave you blisters, like the indifference of the children with whom you went to school.

"What doesn't hurt you but does you harm?" she asked.

"Germs."

"What are germs?"

"Little things that eat their way into you unawares and try to kill you."

"Will they kill you?"

"No," said Dennis, "because I'm fighting back."

"Will they kill me?"

"You haven't got any," he said, and held out his hand.

She took it and found that it was slightly moist and hot, so she let it go again, wiped her hand on the side of her dress, looked up at him, and smiled apologetically. He flushed and looked straight ahead, and they walked slowly side by side, their arms dangling. She reached to his waist.

They rounded a corner, and there was Sapponyi, Andrea at his side. They were coming from rest-cure hall; Sapponyi had just ended his morning tour of inspection. He and Andrea saw the pair at the same time, and Sapponyi stopped, Andrea a step behind him, as the two approached.

"Well," said Sapponyi, "how did you two find each other?"

He had not seen Fehge since Christmas, when she had come to the present-giving at his house with the other servants. Now he found that the sight of her gave him more pleasure than the sight of his own daughter had ever done, the daughter who had looked, even when a child, like a miniature version of Thérèse, and who had grown up to be as bigoted as Thérèse, without her mother's alleviating mysticism. He felt more kin with this child looking up at him now. Blood is thicker than water. . . .

Dennis said, "I have been anxious to meet this little lady again ever since I saw her first two months ago. So I went to look for her, and I found her uprooting carrots behind the house. I asked her to walk out with me, and I'd like to hire her for this purpose every day. May I?"

Andrea looked vexed. She opened her mouth to speak before Sapponyi, who put out a hand behind him to stop her. He could tell by her sharp, indrawn breath that the incident had angered her. "Why not?" said Sapponyi.

Andrea said quickly and sharply, "Fehge goes back to school soon. Then she can't go walking in the mornings."

"Then we'll walk in the afternoon," said Dennis blandly. He propelled Fehge past the two and nodded his head in farewell. "Grüss Gott."

Andrea watched them go, then she hurried after Sapponyi, who was strolling on ahead, deep in thought which her brusque words, "You're not going to let that child walk out with him every day!", disturbed.

"Why not?" said Sapponyi again, hoping that he would be permitted to continue his train of thought. But he was not.

"I don't think it's right," said Andrea. "After all, I have all the trouble of bringing up the child—"

Sapponyi interrupted her. "Sister," he said, "there are an extraordinary number of people who would gladly relieve you of that burden. I don't know why there are, but there are. There is Melita Bahr, my wife would like to have the child, and there you see . . ." He waved in the direction Dennis and Fehge had taken.

That was just what Andrea was afraid of. "The Herr Medizinalrat knows I don't mean it that way," she said. "What I mean is, I wouldn't like to have the good I've done undone by Fehge's getting into contact with . . . with the people up here."

"You are afraid of infection?"

Andrea wasn't thinking of the germ of tuberculosis. She knew very well that at Strubl, with its extremely hygienic management, one was as safe from that germ as anywhere in the world. No. Andrea was afraid of the germ of Catholicism. She did not know Dennis well—knowing patients was not on her schedule, however long she remained in contact with them—and Dennis was a Catholic. She knew that by the way his father had behaved when he had been there, by the fabulous sum of money he had left at the Pritnitz church for a Novena for his son, about which the entire village, even Thérèse, had been agog. For Andrea, the Catholics were not a religious group, they were more than that—they were a race. And she didn't trust them. Although Dennis had so far shown no signs of piety, she didn't want to see him influence the child.

But Sapponyi's words had given her as good a way out as any. So she answered, "Yes, I am."

Sapponyi said, "Nonsense! What can happen to her if they walk out together in the fresh air? I'm surprised at you, Sister! Mr. Seymour has been a very good patient. I am glad to oblige someone with so few whims."

With so few whims. Sapponyi knew Dennis well, and had him sized up correctly. Dennis appealed to him, who also yearned for peace but without any hope of attaining it, because Dennis seemed so sure it was attainable. The sick man had the effect of a tonic on his doctor. A pity there weren't more people like the young Englishman, but there were not. Of course, there were physical reasons for Dennis's concentration on a spiritual goal—there always were physical reasons for everybody's attitude. You could usually trace it down to a glandular condition, prosaic as that might seem. And nowhere was that clearer than here, at his side, in Andrea. "You have nothing to worry about," he told the spinster, just to calm her down, not because he believed it, "he'll soon be bored with Fehge."

Chapter Eight

BUT Fehge did not bore Dennis. From then on, every afternoon, they walked together to a little summer-house in the park. From here they could see through the trees convalescent patients taking their coffee on the balcony, receiving visitors, visiting each other to play cards. The empty balconies with the door to the room open like a black maw was where the bedridden patients lived; and where a balcony was empty and the door closed, the room was untenanted. There were very few empty rooms.

In time Dennis and Fehge had their names for those they saw daily: "the Goddess" next to Dennis on the right—Fricka Reuther was big and golden like the sun—and the "Baron" on Dennis's left. Father Goose had died a few weeks ago, after actually bequeathing his vast estates to the illegitimate dentist, a will his legitimate children were now bitterly contesting.

Then there were those who passed by the summer-house—"the lady with the red parasol," whether she had this fascinating gadget with her or not, and old "Tante Spielmann," as she wanted to be called, who had the balcony above theirs and who grunted as she walked along, bent over her stick. Why did they make her walk?

Why didn't they let her be bedridden? How could she impress her son Maxl if she wasn't in bed?

Old Tante Spielmann was fat, ugly, and heartbroken because her good, her only son Maxl had married a Gentile girl! And this Gentile daughter-in-law, who had nursed her through her first months of illness like a slave, she treated like a servant, and she tried very hard to cough up blood so that she might send for Maxl again, a trick Andrea soon cured her of.

She would stop and stare at Fehge from under her beetling eyebrows and say, "Yes, yes, and he had to go and marry a Gentile girl . . ." She liked Fehge. When she walked on again, she forgot to grunt.

Then there was the frail-looking girl who had been a ballet-dancer and who died one morning of heart-failure while trying to do an arabesque in front of the mirror, just to see . . . just to try if she could still lift her beautiful leg into the right position. "I can! I can!" she had cried, and then just crumpled up on the floor in front of her horrified mother and died.

Dennis and Fehge missed her, the way she had walked past with her back so straight, her young shoulders so square, her narrow waist-line and shapely legs. And there was the tiny black-haired, black-eyed woman from Greece whose name was Thalia, "Muse of Joy," Dennis told Fehge, so they called her that, although she looked anything but joyful. She was very ill. And there was the young conductor with a thatch of red hair who talked with his hands, and the scraggy lady who wrote books and was nervous and irritable as she smoked forbidden cigarettes in the sanctuary of their summer-house, and the bank director who looked like Goethe. "Here comes Mr. Goethe," Fehge would say, as his silver shock of hair, growing out of the back half of his head, rounded the corner of their path. These people were all a part of the pageant that passed them daily as they took their coffee in the little summer-house—milk for Fehge—with crescent rolls, butter, and jam. When it rained, Fehge came and sat with Dennis on his balcony. They never missed a day.

And Dennis did paint Fehge. He dug into the bottom of his

trunk for his easel and set it up in the summer-house, and Fehge sat for him in the red dirndl, which was her favourite, full face, her hair loose—that had been her idea—her hands folded simply in her lap.

Oh, it was good to smell the paints again and to have the colour stick under his finger-nails, dyeing them rainbow colours! And when it was done he stood back and looked at it and thought: Wrong! He should have painted her in an imaginary burnous, its cloth white against her brown skin, and for a background the white sands and golden sunshine of Asia Minor where her kind, in their natural setting, were most beautiful.

But, on the whole, it pleased him, his first portrait, and Sapponyi said it was "not at all bad." Andrea laughed and said, "Wild colours, aren't they?" But then, she had no judgment on things artistic and, anyway, she was jealous.

Fehge was his severest critic. She said nothing, but covered her mouth with her little hand, from behind which she spluttered her laughter. That was all. He hadn't felt worse under his ragging in prep school. Now he knew why he had had to undergo that purgatory—to be able to laugh back at this child's disrespectful mirth in the face of his masterpiece. "Go away," he told her. "You don't understand a thing. It's not half bad!" And he hung it up in his room, opposite the bed.

He read aloud to her, *Alice in Wonderland* and Kipling's *Jungle Book*, translating as he went along, which he found wonderful exercise. There were some things, of course, that were untranslatable, like "'Twas brillig and the slithy toves did gire and gimble in de wabe . . ." He had always wondered if Carroll had meant it to be pronounced "ghire and ghimble" or "jire and jimble." Now he asked Fehge to choose, and she chose "jire and jimble," and she laughed until she hiccoughed over the silly words. How did she know that those words were adorably silly.

"Dearly beloved"—how translate that? He didn't. He taught her the phrase in English and discovered that she had a parrot-like aptitude for the language, so he taught her other phrases. She asked him to teach her an English prayer, so he taught her the

Lord's Prayer and "The Lord is my shepherd," and she said them aloud to Andrea, who could not approve, even if the words were devout. The child was being taken from her.

Dennis learned more German with Fehge than with Melita, but he had long since ceased to look upon the lessons with the teacher as German lessons. He was being initiated into the whirlpool of Austrian politics, and in this sense they were of interest to him. But he enjoyed the time he spent with the child far more. There was an intangible feeling of affinity, based, according to a conclusion he had recently arrived at after much perplexing thought, on the fact that she had been privileged to begin life in the state he hoped to arrive at in time, that of complete freedom from shackles. He was very anxious to open her eyes to this fact, to make her aware of her favourable position. But the first few times together had sufficed to show him that it was much too early for any such discourse. He learned just how unphilosophical the mind of a seven-year-old child can be. Characteristics he could find, plenty of them, determined, irrevocable ones, but no powers of abstract thought. She might catch the idea from him, though, and become aware of it in time, in a long time, of course. And whence came this feeling that they would be together for a long time? He had read Thomas Mann's *Magic Mountain*. The net of sanatorium life was the last he was going to let himself be caught in. Yet he was counting on this child's companionship into the distant future. Why? He couldn't tell.

Sapponyi found the development of Fehge under the tutelage of "the mad young Englishman" one of the most entertaining things it had ever been his privilege to observe. This girl who, by rights, should develop into a peasant, was receiving the spiritual education of a lady. Would she become a lady? It intrigued him. It roused him out of his apathy. He took more interest in it than in his daily paper.

One day the Prelate Schädelmeyer came to visit a colleague of his who was a patient at Strubl. Meeting Sapponyi in the hall, he brought the conversation round to Fehge. He asked what was being done for the child's religious life and whether she would not be baptized. "I think," said Sapponyi, "that my wife is going to take that in hand in time."

"I wondered why she had not already done so," said the Prelate, who knew Thérèse Sapponyi.

"I'm sure I don't know," lied Sapponyi suavely. "Thérèse's ways are strange. I never interfere with her in such matters."

The Prelate bowed slightly, as though accepting this bit of information for what it was worth. Then he said, "I have heard a great deal about this Englishman, Seymour, and what he is teaching the child and about her amazing aptitude for a foreign language. Is she so clever?"

"No," said Sapponyi, "I don't think she is clever. She learns like a parrot. It seems to me that the child would make a very good medium. I am sure that she could be easily hypnotized, and I think that what the young man does with her comes under that heading. It is certainly interesting to see how she falls in with the things he reads to her and tells her."

"*Hm*," said the Prelate, and then repeated, "*Hm*." But he did not ask to see the child. He felt strongly that he did not want to see her.

Sapponyi went on, "She is extraordinarily acquiescent, yet I think she is possessed of a rather unfathomable source of strength. I mean, no great act of violence on her part would surprise me. For instance, if this placid creature should one day commit a murder, I would believe it possible. I would consider her capable of any sudden outburst."

"What makes the Herr Medizinalrat come to such strange conclusions?" said the Prelate, feeling dislike for the man who, with his psychic probing of his fellow-men, seemed to see much more than he, Schädelmeyer, saver of souls, could see. He liked to believe that Sapponyi was mistaken.

"With a certain knowledge of psychology," said Sapponyi, "it is easy to see that the girl Fehge is a psychopath. She is hysterical."

"Hysterical?" said the Prelate. "But you just said that she was placid."

"Yet she is a hysteric," said Sapponyi. "Wait and see. Time will prove me right."

"If you think the child is such a bombshell," said the Prelate, "why do you keep her? Why don't you send her to an orphanage?"

Sapponyi pursed his lips. "I don't know," he said. "But I don't think anyone would send Fehge away."

The Prelate shrugged his shoulders angrily. "Ridiculous!" he exclaimed, "this cult around a Galician Jewish child!"

Sapponyi said, "Our Church, Monsignore, makes quite a cult of another Jewish child."

"That," said the Prelate sharply, "is blasphemy!"

Sapponyi drew in his sails. "I have no intention of letting a cult develop around the child. It was your word, Monsignore, if I may be so bold as to remind you. I look upon the child as most of us do, as a sort of talisman, a mascot, that is all. We just pretend that she brings us luck. How do you find Brother Peter?" he went on, thus bringing the conversation about Fehge to an end.

Thérèse Sapponyi learned nothing of the Prelate's interest in the child. Sapponyi knew that she was in Vienna visiting her daughter or he would not have lied so glibly. Had Thérèse been there, the Prelate would have called on her and then the fat would have been in the fire. Sapponyi did not relish a coalition against him in this matter. But Thérèse was away and the Prelate didn't come again because Brother Peter was soon removed to a Catholic home for convalescence, and the mystic aureole which, in Thérèse's mind, had hovered over the girl Fehge when she had come to Strubl was permitted to continue to grow dimmer and dimmer, as Sapponyi wanted it to do, since he did not see it there.

The dream of the Holy Three was fading. Thérèse still provided Fehge with everything she wore, but not in the same mood. It was not any more like sewing tiny pearls on the Holy Virgin's new dress; it was just another act of charity for the poor. Thérèse had placed Fehge in her mind as a servant girl. She was much too natural and healthy to be a celestial messenger, and once this matter of religion was settled, Thérèse would be through with her; there

were always new omens ready to crowd into her mystic mind.
Meanwhile she preferred to see the child fall under the sway of
the "poet"—as she rightly classified him—Seymour; she preferred his influence to that of the ascetic, Andrea. Seymour would
bring beauty into the child's life, and that would not estrange her
from Catholicism; whereas the teachings of Andrea might implant
an austerity which would for ever close the child's mind against
the sensuous mysticism of the religion Thérèse was still determined
that Fehge should embrace, be she servant, lady, or angel from
heaven!

Chapter Nine

AT Christmas Dennis asked and received permission for Fehge
to sit at table with him in the big dining-room for dinner.
A Christmas tree, so high that its crown touched the ceiling, stood
at the far end of the big room, the lights of its wax candles reflected
in the silver nuts and tinsel with which it was decorated and in the
highly polished maroon-red linoleum of the floor. As though
that were not enough, each table held a miniature copy of the big
tree, a little fir with tiny silver nuts and loops of tinsel. A gramophone hidden behind the big tree played "Silent Night" and "Oh,
Tannenbaum," and everybody wore evening dress.

The year before, Fehge had stood with the other servants and
peasants at the big window outside and looked in, stamping her
feet as they had done on the cold, hard-packed snow that had
gleamed white and blue in the moonlight, their breath coming
from their mouths in puffs of transparent white smoke. With the
others she had envied the waitress, Rosl, who had the Ströcker Lisl
and the Hirschegger Annie helping her, for being inside. This
time she would be inside too.

She was delighted. She had no idea that this would be just

another nail in her cross of unpopularity. "*Frohes Fest*," the peasants she had met had cried out to her, even to her, only that morning, the morning of December 24, 1925, a Christmas when many Germans all over the Reich were able to give the first edition of *Mein Kampf* to each other as a Christmas present. "*Frohes Fest!*" Fehge had answered in her clear, deep voice. A happy feast, indeed! Peace on earth and good will to all men.

They would not wish it her again for a long time. Their good will was at its lowest ebb. For the village had become jealous of Fehge. Their first reaction to her had been envy when she had driven up to Strubl in a motor-car the year before, something they had never done and could not conceive of ever doing. Now their envy found fresh impetus, first of all in the different position Fehge enjoyed. Fehge didn't stay in school to learn her catechism as their children did, Fehge didn't go to church; Fehge had no beads to tell. Melita had buried one spectre—anti-semitism—only to raise another, paganism. "A heathen!" she was in their eyes.

Then there was the superior position she enjoyed. There was the food she ate. When their children came out of school, a piece of dry black bread awaited them. Fehge would go home to hot chocolate, white bread and butter . . . butter . . . something they never saw in their own homes, for lard was the only fat they knew.

Then there was the fantastic tale of the Roumanian patient, spoilt with presents, who had sent to "the little girl he could see coming down the slope on her sled sometimes and whom he liked to watch," a basket of fresh strawberries in midwinter! It was one of six that had arrived from Vienna, packed in absorbent cotton so that they should not freeze . . . absorbent cotton . . . of which there was never enough when their wounds had to be dressed in Schreiner's office . . . to wrap strawberries in . . .

Fehge slept in a well-heated house and could open her windows at night. Her cheeks did not go grey in winter as theirs did. And she slept alone, in a room of her own. Not that any of them would have liked that. How they would have missed the feeling of safety that emanated from a warm body lying next to theirs, the sound of other bodies turning in their beds, the sounds of their children, of father and mother, had they been forced to sleep alone! Yet Fehge's own room served as another lever to pry her loose from the village.

But most of all they were jealous of the young Englishman's interest in Fehge and of the fact that he had taught her to speak in a foreign tongue, which was what the few words she could speak in English had become in the mouth of village gossips. It seemed like witchcraft to them. They had all been up at Strubl at some time or other on some pretext and had seen strangely dressed men and women walking slowly as though there were nothing else in the world to do, not hunted as they always were by another and another and yet another job to be done before nightfall, walking with sticks, talking in foreign tongues, like beings out of another world; and now Fehge could speak like that too. Fehge was becoming one of the *Herrschaften*. Their indifference turned to hate.

Peace on earth, good will to men.

That Fehge was eating Christmas Eve dinner inside, instead of stamping her cold feet with them outside, was the proverbial last straw. Dennis looked every now and then at the stolid faces grouped in rows behind the big window, and they made him feel uncomfortable. Damned unsocial, that they should look in like this at them all eating *pâté de foie gras* and stuffed goose and—the final miracle yet to come—the *Bombe*—a tower of varicoloured ice-cream with a curlycued décor of whipped cream. Fehge had described it to him, and the Leaning Tower of Pisa could not have elicited more admiration from anybody.

What would Melita have had to say about this class division? When Dennis thought of it, he was glad that she was spending her holiday in Vienna. His father was to have come and spent Christmas with him but had succumbed to the influenza. Meg had written one of her rambling letters which he could never quite unravel, much as he wanted to do full justice to what this faithful housekeeper of theirs had to say. Dear old Meg . . . How delighted Fehge had been with the Christmas card she had sent Dennis— home-made cut-outs pasted on cardboard in scrapbook array, terrifying in colour. Meg's taste was poor, but her heart was in the right place. Too bad about Dad, but Dennis couldn't really miss him. Fehge was such good company.

The faces out there . . . unmoving. They looked in like that on moving-picture night too. It had made him squirm then. There were movies in Pritnitz on Saturday and Sunday, but none in Fichtenbach except those privately shown at Strubl for the patients on every Tuesday evening. It was then that he had seen the faces outside first. Medieval . . . no, feudal . . . that was the word he wanted. Feudal, it seemed to him.

He had spoken to Andrea about it. "We can't let them in," she'd said. "That just isn't done. Besides, they'd smell."

He supposed that they would. Well, then, wouldn't it be kinder to let down a curtain, a real dividing line, over which they couldn't look and feel envious?

Andrea had shaken her head impatiently. "Don't bother your head trying to satisfy them," she said. "It's waste of anybody's time."

"There now," Dennis had said to Melita, when telling her of the incident. "She's never been rich, but she doesn't seem to have much mercy with the poorer classes."

"She is a Prussian," Melita had said. "They have no mercy with anyone."

She is a Prussian. He is a Pole. How positive they all were! How categorized everything was! Were there no just plain human beings? Without a label? Were there no individuals?

Peace on earth, good will to men. Dennis had given Fehge a little fur coat for Christmas, to wear when she sat out on the balcony with him. They had tried it on that afternoon, and she had sat, as she had done throughout the autumn, in her favourite place on the low wicker table with her feet on the arm of his long wicker chair, her knees hunched under the coat to keep them warm. The coat dropped down to her ankles that way, and she was snug inside it. On her head she wore a Red Riding-hood cap in wool which Andrea had taught her to knit in her free time, and the gloves that matched it she wore on her hands. The thumb she had had to rip three times. After all, she was only seven years old, going on eight. . . .

There she had sat, happy in her new finery, and had stared at the white curtain which the Goddess had had put up between the balconies, "for privacy, I suppose," Dennis had told her. He couldn't think of any other reason. The white curtain always scared Fehge a little until Dennis took her mind off it by some story.

Andrea had given her a Lutheran Bible, Thérèse a blue and white and gold Madonna and Child that stood on a black pedestal. Such a pretty doll! Fehge, who had never had a doll, had no urge to do anything with the beautiful little lady except that which was the proper thing to do with her—stand her up in the niche above her bed where, until now, she had kept wild flowers in a cheap glass. The Bible lay on the little table beside her bed, brooding down there in black, while the lady with her child was such a pretty, bright spot that you were constantly driven to look at it. The Bible was very hard to understand. Sapponyi had given her skis. And the third-floor Hilda, her very best friend, without whom she would never have discovered the miracles of Nature— in short, the world—had given her a sack of feed for the deer. Now she could go to the crib that stood in a clearing of low blue firs on the top of a round hill in the park, and the deer would eat out of her hand, and she would at last feel the soft wet touch of their dear little black noses. She was allowed in the park now. Dennis had opened its gates to her, and she had no idea that, as she entered them, the doors of the village had closed behind her.

Peace on earth, and good will to men. Today was the Saviour's birthday. Fehge knew all about it from Andrea. How Thérèse had longed to take the child to Pritnitz to show her the manger, all of whose dolls were of her giving and dressing and arranging! The Fichtenbach innkeeper Riess had made a very imaginative background for it. Quite an artist, this Aloys Riess, in his primitive way. But she had mastered her desire until now it only burned inside her. She had given Fehge the Madonna. That was as much

THE OUTNUMBERED

as she dared to do, and Sapponyi's smile as the child had taken it had been quite inscrutable.

Peace on earth, good will to men.

Fehge sat at Dennis's table on a cushion so that she should be big enough to eat nicely from the dazzling white table. Her breath came thick and fast, and her heart fluttered with excitement. How festive everything was!

Almost everybody was downstairs. Only those who would never walk again stayed upstairs in their beds. With the Baron were his wife and his pretty seventeen-year-old daughter, the Comtesse, who was dressed very simply in navy blue with a little white lace collar. She crossed herself before she sat down to eat. Fehge had already said grace as Andrea had taught her to do, "Come, dear Jesus, be our guest, and what Thou hast given us, please bless . . .," faster than she had ever said it before. Now the big golden Goddess was coming in, and she had visitors too. They walked in behind her, a lady looking pinched, and . . . an angel-child!

Anne-Marie Reuther walked into the dining-room filled with curiosity but determined not to show it. These silly sick people! Her mother was going home soon. Her mother would never be sick again. Anne-Marie could not be as ashamed of her mother's sickness as she might have been, because her mother looked so well. Anne-Marie wondered if she had really been sick at all. When Papa was sick he looked green, and when she was sick she vomited. Anyway, she, Anne-Marie, was never going to tell that her mother had been ill. She had already told so many fairy-tales about her mother's absence from home that she was beginning to lose track of them.

Now she sat down at the place her mother designated and found herself across the room from a girl about her own age, whose skin was very smooth and brown, who wore her black hair loose, as Anne-Marie did, with a ribbon round her head, tied in a bow at the top where the parting was, exactly like Anne-Marie. We're like Rose Red and Snow White, thought Anne-Marie, and the thought pleased her. The child smiled to her and dimples showed.

Fehge smiled out of her radiant good-humour and regretted it the minute it was done. Anne-Marie was about to smile back, when her mother laid a firm hand on her soft arm and said, "Don't smile! Don't look at the child! She had no business to be here!"

Anne-Marie's big eyes looked up in astonishment at her mother, who, she now noticed, was in a towering rage. "Just a minute," said Fricka Reuther, and got up. "I will be back immediately."

She returned a few minutes later, the high red of anger blazing in her cheeks. "It is inconceivable!" she said, addressing the governess, but speaking well above her head as though she were scarcely there, speaking, obviously, only to relieve her outraged feelings. "But what can you expect when you come to a place run by a Jew!"

The governess did not know what the *gnädige Frau* was talking about, but she was anxious to acquiesce just as soon as she could.

"The child has no business to be here," Fricka Reuther went on, refusing the soup with an angry gesture of her hand. "Yes. You must have some, child," she said to Anne-Marie, and made her sit in another seat, so that she would not be facing Fehge. "I'm just too upset to eat," she went on. "Not only is the child from the village—I wouldn't object to that. But she is a Jewish child . . . a Polish Jewish child, one that just strayed by. Anne-Marie! I told you not to look at her!"

"But she is beautiful," said Anne-Marie, to vex her mother. "And she has a lovely dress on. I have never seen a child like her."

Fricka Reuther's Christmas was spoiled. "There will come a day," she said with bitterness, "when we won't have to put up with this sort of thing!" And she really felt deeply injured.

Anne-Marie did not look at the Jewish child again. She and her mother hurried through the meal. But Fehge never took her eyes off this golden creature.

"We'll find out if she's staying," said Dennis. "Maybe you can play with her."

Fehge gave him a piercing look. "No," she said. "She won't play with me."

"Why not?"

"You'll see."

"The Goddess hasn't been very friendly, but then, goddesses never are!" Dennis said. "They have to be cold and aloof. But the child looks friendly enough. She was going to smile over to us when the Goddess must have thought of something she'd forgotten, because she went out of the room very angry. Didn't she?"

Fehge nodded.

"Shall we ask her afterwards if you can play with the little girl?"

Fehge said swiftly, in an agony of fear such as he had never seen in her before, "No! Please don't!" Then she went on in a calmer voice, "Besides, I haven't any time to play."

"Can't we have the week off," said Dennis, with whom this was a sore point, "seeing it's Christmas?"

Fehge shook her head. "They're busy in the kitchen," she said, "you can see," and her little face gestured in a motion that seemed to embrace all the eating people. Dennis was reminded of how hard her little fingers had worked to help to produce what was now so rapidly being swallowed up. Damnable, the way she had to work, and how she seemed to thrive on it!

Fehge and Anne-Marie came face to face, however, on Christmas Day, through no fault of Fehge's. It was Anne-Marie who wandered to the back of the house on the look-out for the Jewish child, to whom she was determined to speak. She wanted to be able to brag about it at the very select school she went to and in the kitchen at home, especially to the parlour-maid, Pepi, who had told her that the Jews murdered Christian children and drank their blood.

Fehge had just removed the debris of Christmas from her own and Andrea's rooms and was carrying away the papers, straw, and boxes to burn them. She was looking forward to building a fire. She loved the dancing flames, the glow, crackle and the smell of them. She was thinking of this when she saw the angel-child, whom she did not greet. She lowered her eyes and was going to pass her when Anne-Marie spoke. "You had no business being in the dining-room last night."

Fehge didn't answer. The angel-child stood in her way. "Did you hear me?" she said, and her voice was high and sweet like a bell's, and her breath made a pretty little cloud as it came from her parted lips. She was dressed in a pale-blue coat and cap to match. The coat had a little cape of fur. She wore white leather leggings, and she stood with her legs close together and a white muff was slung round her neck by a white silk cord. Fehge wondered what the muff was for until the angel-child put her white-mittened hands in it. Pretty.

"Did you hear me?" the angel-child said again. "You had no business being there. I'm not allowed to play with you," she went on, "because you're a Jewish child," and she added, echoing her mother, "a Polish Jewish child that just strayed by."

Fehge said nothing.

Anne-Marie stamped her foot. "Why don't you answer me?" she screamed, her voice rising until it was harsh. "Answer me! Answer me!"

"You didn't ask me anything," said Fehge, and she looked through the girl, at the hills behind her. Here was one of the things that you couldn't see that hurt you. Anne-Marie, the angel-child, was a germ.

"*Ahhh!*" shrieked Anne-Marie, her feet trampling in her rage. "*Ahh, ahhh, ahhhh . . . awahhh!*" And the governess heard her and her mother heard her, and they came hurrying to the back of the house.

"What have you been doing to my child?" said Fricka Reuther, planting herself rigidly beside Anne-Marie. The governess stood meekly behind them.

Fehge did not answer.

"I'll have you run out of this village," said Fricka. "You have no business being here."

The things Fehge was carrying trembled with her agitation. She must not drop them! She must get by somehow!

At that moment Dennis came. "Well," he said, "that's funny! I was going to ask you, *gnädige Frau*, if you would let your little girl play with my little girl."

"Your little girl!" said Fricka Reuther, and she could scarcely speak for her indignation. "Your little girl! That heathen child of a Jew! You are a foreigner, Mr. Seymour. Do you think it is fair to behave as you are doing in a country where you are a guest?"

Dennis was stunned. This was something he had never come in contact with before, that he had not believed existed. We read about things, he thought, hear about them . . . we don't realize them as they are. Not at all!

Dennis thought he was going to be fighting mad for the first time in his life; he thought that must be it, the way his teeth suddenly ground together hard until it hurt him, the heat behind his eyes, the way he had to hold them wide open and the way a thousand words were crowding to his lips so that he was in great danger of not being able to speak at all. Then he looked into Fricka Reuther's pretty, vapid, doll-like face and realized that he was face to face with a mad woman.

His anger melted and was gone. "I think the *gnädige Frau* is exciting herself unnecessarily," he said. "If the *gnädige Frau* would think it over quietly, she would know that I have done nothing to deprive myself of the right to visit this beautiful country."

Fricka Reuther was beside herself. "This cult," she spluttered, "this cult that you have built up around this dreadful child . . ."

"If we must continue this conversation," Dennis interrupted her, "then, please, not in the presence of the children."

"I have nothing to say to you," said Fricka. "Nothing, Mr. Seymour. You are degenerate, like everything that comes from England. I only want you to see to it that for the few remaining days which my child will spend here, *your* child, as you so crazily see fit to call her, does not molest her."

"Fehge wouldn't molest anybody," said Dennis. "It is not in her. If your girl leaves her alone, I don't think you have anything to worry about." He put both hands on Fehge's shoulders from behind. "Good day," he said, and took the things Fehge was carrying.

Fricka took Anne-Marie by the hand and swept her away. The

governess lingered for a brief moment. She was a mouselike creature in grey, with her dark hair scraped off her head and knotted into a bun, with no colour, no light in her eyes, no distinguished feature whatsoever. Her nose was so narrow and pointed that Fehge wondered how she could breathe through it; her cheekbones were high, her skin taut over the broad, bony frame of her face, her lips scarcely showed. She whispered across to Dennis, "I am so sorry. You must forgive the *gnädige Frau*. She has changed so in the year she has been here. What will the *gnädiger Herr* say? She is not herself."

Dennis said, "I don't think you have to worry about that. She's herself, all right. I never saw anybody as natural. I know her kind."

The governess shook her head and tripped away.

Fehge looked up at Dennis and said primly, "That was a dreadful experience."

"The little girl's no angel, is she?"

"No," said Fehge, and they built the fire together. "You said, 'I know her kind.' What did you mean?"

"Her kind?" said Dennis, making the fire smoke. "The kind that loves to hate."

"Are there a lot of her kind?"

"Most people," said Dennis, and the red flame broke through, and the smoke turned from blue to white.

Fehge sniffed. "Smells good," she said. "I don't hate people."

"Neither do I," said Dennis.

"I don't like people either," the child went on, looking into the fire, her arms akimbo.

"You don't?" said Dennis, looking up at her from where he was hunched.

She shook her head. "I try not to think about them. If you ask me, there needn't be any people."

To Dennis it seemed an appropriate sequel to "Feghe has God."

Chapter Ten

THE Baron who occupied the balcony on Dennis's other side was the Freiherr Wolfgang von Trent und Freibürgen. The Republic permitted him to use the title of Freiherr, or Freeman, to which he had been born, in place of the pre-war label of "Baron." To a plain and simple "Mr." they could not sink, because the people who made up this republic had been too deeply steeped in feudalism.

When the Baron went to Holland on business, as he often had to do, he signed in the hotel registry as plain Mynheer Trent. But here, at Strubl, thanks to Sapponyi, who would not swerve from accustomed things, the Freiherr was still the *Herr Baron*.

He had not been here as long as Dennis this time, but he had made several visits here before, and he would be back again. He was ill, and had been ill for years, according to Sapponyi, who said that if he would once, just once, stay long enough to make a complete cure, he might never have to come again. But the Baron couldn't do that. He explained to Sapponyi that there was no more rest in him. Now, in his old age, rest had left him, peace had left him— the peace he had guarded jealously and been able to preserve throughout a turbulent social and business career.

The Baron lived in a picture-book castle on the Danube. It was listed in Baedeker, with its grey stone turrets, ivy-overgrown walls, and moat. The drawbridge was let down for his big Mercedes-Benz to pass over, just as his forefathers' horsemen and carriages had passed over it in their day. His wife was the daughter of a German industrialist without whose money the Baron could scarcely have kept up the castle with the staff it required. But he did more than his share in caring for her vast fortune. He managed her affairs better than her own brothers would have done, who understood nothing but the art of making war. His German father-in-law had recognized his Austrian son-in-law's business acumen and had given him enormous powers, which his disgruntled sons were not able to shake off after the old man's death.

The Baron's wife, *née* Elfriede von Dahn, loved her husband. After the uncouthness of her brothers, he had seemed like a veritable Prince Charming. He had never ceased to enchant her, not even now, when she was fifty and he well on his way to sixty. It was she who had insisted that their headquarters be in Austria, who had forbidden that their children visit Germany, and had had them taught and brought up in the finest Austrian clerical schools.

But, as Sapponyi was so fond of saying, "Blood is thicker than water." At the age of twenty-one their son had suddenly shown his colours. He had broken out of bounds in the Austrian Jesuit School to hear the new German Führer speak in St. Pölten in 1923, and, again, to attend the Führer's party rally in Salzburg in the following year, when he had become ardently attached to Stabschef Röhm and had received his uniform—a brown shirt and cap and a swastika arm-band which, however, he was told to keep hidden. As chance, or fate, or Providence would have it—certainly not God —all this happened on his twenty-first birthday. With the swastika on his arm, the future Baron Rüdiger von Trent und Freibürgen came of age.

He and several of his comrades had moved to Munich, where they ran through a lot of money and were very busy, in what capacity his mother never could find out. Indeed, she was afraid to find out. She had nursed Rüdiger at her breast, had touched his soft hair gently with her fingers, not daring to stroke his baby forehead, so delicate did the fine skin and bone seem to be. She had held his tiny hand and let the perfect little fingers clutch her forefinger with surprising firmness, and had felt how helpless he was and how much in need of her love and protection. She had not yet learned to disassociate the baby she had fondled from the grown-up man, and she was afraid that the sight of the man at his strange activities would awaken her rudely, perhaps heart-breakingly. So she did not go to Munich.

The boy and his parents had become estranged, but every now and then he came back to Austria with friends of a type that horrified the Baroness Elfriede. They took possession of the castle, and it shook with their revelries and their "meetings." From all parts of Austria came youths like themselves, and they went into conclaves, to what end Elfriede could not fathom. One thing she was certain of—it was not to be taken seriously. Nothing so stupid was. It was only something to be ashamed of. Here Wolfgang did not agree with her. It was more than that. Elfriede saw the thing mirrored in her husband's reaction, an emotion she had never seen in him before—fear. And that sobered her more than anything else.

Now the Baron listened to Dennis telling him what had just happened between himself and Fricka Reuther. "Aha," said the Baron as he listened. "Aha."

He was tall, broad-shouldered, handsome, clean-shaven, with not a grey hair to betray his age and only a few lines in his fine brown skin. His head was a little too small for his body, his features aesthetic. His eyes, not large and of the most piercing blue, were cold, hard, and shrewd. He wore the green *loden* with the deer-horn buttons.

This was the time when he should have been lying down, but he had no intention of doing so. He had been pacing his balcony like a caged beast when Dennis had begun speaking to him. He did this often, until the patient downstairs complained. He would not rest, he could not lead a horizontal life! He would go home as soon as his temperature was within bounds and his breathing easier so that he could sleep at night. He was on the verge of this half-cured condition now.

He stood against the railing between his balcony and Dennis's. When Dennis had finished, he said, "Mr. Seymour, if you but knew it, you are not only in a consumptive house, you are in a consumptive country. A germ is creeping in on us, and we are quite unaware of it. Only two men in Austria can see it, Sapponyi and I. What a rare mind is his, and what a poor spirit! But who am I to talk? Have I more spirit? Why don't I get up and do something about it? Why don't I?"

Dennis saw that he had started something, not only in the Baron.

At last, in him too a spark had been ignited, the spark Melita had been so anxious to fire. Fricka Reuther had done it. Why? Why hadn't Melita, with her more positive creed, been able to inspire him? Why had the example of what he did *not* want to see rampant on this earth so inflamed him? Right should be more potent than wrong. But it had not been. There must be something amiss with the right Melita had been propounding. Perhaps it had not yet been correctly formulated. But the wrong of Fricka Reuther was glaringly, effectively evil! And it was involving him. Definitely he realized that he was being drawn with the heat of passion into something that would carry him away from the splendid isolation he had been tending toward all his life. This tide was forcing him to take sides . . . which side he did not know . . . he only knew which side he was against—the side on which Fricka Reuther stood.

He did not call it a "net," this thing he felt himself being drawn into. It was something much bigger than that. It was a tide against which all opposition was futile; it was as inexorable as fate because it involved ethics, or a lack of them, and ethical obligations Dennis had never intended to renounce.

"Don't let this issue of anti-semitism mislead you," the Baron was saying. "That's as old as the hills. It is only a side-issue of the general menace, blown up to do just that—distract your attention from what is really rolling along. German barbarism. Watch it devour Austria!"

"But," said Dennis, braced by Melita's schooling, "as far as I can make out, you all want union with Germany. The Social Democrats want it, your clericals want it. Who's against it?"

"I, for one, was always against it; but that is neither here nor there. When it comes, none of them will want it. But then it will be too late. When it comes, it will be union with a Germany about which they know nothing, blinded as they are by the thin veneer of German capability and diligence. It will be union with a monster, the monster you just met with in the form of Fricka Reuther."

"But she is an Austrian!"

"First of all, she is not an Austrian. She is a German woman from

East Prussia. But that is also neither here nor there. When I said 'German barbarism' just now, I used the word German as an adjective to denote everything despicable, as our friend Nietzsche once advised the world to do. What I am speaking of, the member of any race can be. He must have certain attributes." He counted them off on his fingers as he spoke. "He must be brave. He must be energetic. He must have no scruples, no morals, no love in his heart, least of all love of a good life. He must be the suicidal type. And he must be ambitious for intangibles." The Baron coughed. He had been describing his son Rüdiger. "Excuse me," he said. "This excites me."

"I am sorry," said Dennis.

"The day when our Austria is joined to that Germany," said the Baron, and he pointed a vehement finger across the hills, "on that day, Austrian history ends!" And with that he went into his room with strides that would have taken him across a larger space. That evening he ran a temperature of a hundred and three.

Chapter Eleven

ONE day during the following spring, after school, because Dennis had been invited to the Baron's tea-party, Fehge was free. There were a thousand things she should have been doing, but the first humidity of an approaching summer made her drowsy, and, in a strange mood of relaxation, she began to walk down the road in the direction of Pritnitz instead of up the hill back to Strubl.

The dust lay thick on the green that grew near the road. The fields needed rain. Fehge looked up at the sky like an old farmer. Not a sign of it. The primroses were done. The violets still gleamed purple against the brown earth. Up on the hills the gentians were blooming to form a carpet of royal blue. How Dennis had enjoyed it! His strength had grown so that now he could walk down as far as the schoolhouse with her, and lately even up to the inn on Schwarzenberg's summit, taking the steep incline very slowly, taking three times as long as Fehge would have done alone.

She closed her eyes and drew in a deep breath of ecstasy. Then she wrinkled her little nose. Horse's dung steamed on the grey dust. A cart had just turned off into one of the valley cracks where the Bruckner farmer lived. All this was still in sight of the schoolhouse. Now she turned a corner and was in unaccustomed territory.

She hadn't been beyond the schoolhouse since they had buried Dworje. She did not know the village of Pritnitz, she had never been inside its church, she had forgotten its cemetery. She knew only the road from Strubl to the schoolhouse, but of that every curve, every stone, and she knew and loved every *Marterl* on the road and on the trail up to Schwarzenberg's summit. These little wooden altars were her landmarks on the paths that ran through her little world.

They stood erect, sometimes a little aslant, on weather-beaten posts, framed on all four sides by protective wooden boards that jutted forward, most of them topped by a small gabled roof. Inside was a picture of the Virgin and Child or of the Virgin alone, and on the wooden shelf formed by the frame beneath it stood little glass jars full of wild flowers or *Immortellen*, the autumnal-coloured straw-flowers that lasted for ever, which the children picked and put there.

In the inn opposite the schoolhouse, in a corner over the bar, stood the prettiest altar of all, a Madonna with her child set in a wreath of painted field flowers. She had a face like a doll's, and she simpered a little in what the children thought was the most beautiful smile.

But Fehge's favourite *Marterl* stood on the trail up Schwarzenberg. It was one of the reasons why she loved her daily excursion up the mountain. She liked to greet God there. The *Marterl* was a carved wooden crucifix without any protection from the sides, with only a narrow gabled roof over the top of the cross on which the snow piled high in winter. The figure of Christ had once been painted in colours and gilt; now the porcelain-white of His body was grey from weathering, and the blood that poured down His forehead and out of His hands and feet and side was dark brown with age. Only the blue of the background seemed to have preserved its eternal glow.

His head hung sideways as though His neck had been broken, and His eyes were upturned heavenward in their agony. When she looked up at Him for any length of time, Fehge would be forced to her knees. The poor Saviour . . . the poor Saviour . . .

For Fehge's strongest feeling was compassion. It was out of compassion that she loved the Saviour bleeding on His cross more than the Mother who carried her child and always looked contented. She knew more about the Saviour, too, because Andrea was interested only in Him and not at all, so it seemed, in His Mother, who was glorified in every other of the little altars along the road.

Twice Fehge had celebrated His birthday. Now, for the second time since she had come to Strubl, the time of His suffering and crucifixion was approaching, and her life's background was troubled by the almost constant consciousness of His tortured body. She understood very little else about it except that nails had been driven into His hands and feet, that the flesh of His forehead had been torn by a crown of thorns, and that a spear had been driven into His side. Her body hurt when she thought of it, and she wriggled with the imaginary pain so that Andrea would tell her to sit still. "Oh," she often said, "it must have hurt Him so!" The very idea of crucifixion of the live body was almost more than she could bear.

"He suffered and died for us," Andrea told her, but that Fehge could not comprehend. She remained with her own thoughts and said, as her mother so often had done, "Ay, people are bad."

The houses she was passing now on this unfamiliar stretch of road were very plain structures of wood and stone. Never had she been inside one of them. She passed by the morose glances of the grown-ups working in the fields, and the unfriendly barking of their dogs; she felt their animosity, and it made her shrivel inside.

"If you ask me, there needn't be any people," she had said to Dennis last Christmas Day. To Fehge the world in itself was beautiful, the mountains, the fields and the hillsides in every season, the cattle browsing, the dart of a dragon-fly, the lone cry of a cock at dawn, the owl's *too whoo* at night, the chirping of the crickets, last butterflies fluttering in a waning sun, the birds winging south—the people spoiled it.

The people were bad and she feared them. How she feared, for instance, any sign of anger or strife between human beings! However beautiful the mating fight of two male robins might be, accompanied by their wild cries, as she had seen it only the other day, she found it detestable when human beings fought among themselves. The slightest form of argument seemed to her to be a quarrel, and she shrank from it. The scene with the angel-child and her mother last Christmas Day had been a foretaste of hell. Outwardly she had been calm, but inside her she had been all a-tremble so that she had thought she would fall apart.

If Fehge's tongue had been taught to speak philosophically, she would have said, "God is harmony." She could sense discord in the air as soon as her surroundings were peopled. On that last Christmas Day, Dennis had given words to her own instinctive fears, and she had not forgotten it . . . the majority of the people in this world loved to hate. Dennis, Andrea, Sapponyi, Thérèse, Melita, Hilda—yes, even Hilda, who only showed her wonderful things and otherwise let her be—all those who had done her only good, never harm . . . all those who did not hate . . . what were they when you stood them up against the cruel rest? The kind were outnumbered.

As she walked on under a sun that pricked her skin, a sure sign of an approaching thunderstorm, she thought what a good thing it was that a protecting God was in the heavens to see to it that the kind were not inundated by these others as by a second great flood.

Now she passed the open space where the gipsies sometimes

camped, charred holes in the grass showing where they had built their fires. She reached the place where the road merged into the highway, where her father had dropped dead. At once, before her, in her mind's eye, rose Conrad, whom she had not seen again since that fateful day—Conrad, who had gone to live with his aunt in Munich, so Andrea had said, "and a good thing, too, for the boy to get away from a place like this to such a beautiful city as Munich." Accordingly, Schreiner had gone up in Andrea's estimation.

Of all the persons who had gathered at the roadside when her father had died, only Conrad remained clear in her mind, the personification of everything evil. Conrad had gone away, but Fehge still feared him more than anything else in the world. It was because of Conrad that Fehge sometimes ran off the beaten track into the sanctuary of the woods, driven by a wild, inexplicable fear that an approaching person whom she could not recognize from a distance might be he. He might have come back. And she would run until steps and voices were left far behind.

"Fehge," her mother had called her, "Fehgele," and "Fehgush," and sometimes only "Gush" for short. "Gush, gush, gush . . ." the trees seemed to call after her as she ran.

It was only the wind soughing in their branches. But she thought she could hear her mother calling her to stop, her mother, who was with God in the air—she knew that from Andrea—and she would stop and look about her, at the still forest, at the pine-needles on which she stood, at the age-old roots gnarled on her path, waiting to trip her. There was nothing to be afraid of. Slowly she would retrace her steps.

But some day Conrad would come back. . . .

She turned the corner where the inn with its little beer-garden stood, and walked straight into Julie, dressed in her Sunday best and on her way to church, although it was a week-day. Once a week the idiot girl went there when she could be alone, which she liked best. She cleaned the brasses, dusted the altars and woodwork, refilled the vases with flowers, and always wore her Sunday best. It was her life. Nothing else in the world existed for her;

even her tight-lipped mother, who was sometimes kind, was only a hazy dream.

Suddenly Fehge, the first human being whom her dim eyes had seen clearly, the magic child, was standing before her. Julie's crooked mouth curved into a strange smile and she stretched out her arms.

Fehge walked up to her and let the grotesque creature fondle her. All the time she stared at the girl's strange face and the beautiful golden hair. Julie finally stretched out her hand and indicated that Fehge should go with her. And Fehge went.

Thus they walked through the village of Pritnitz. Everybody whom they passed stared at them. Who did Julie have with her now? Heinrich Grabautschnik, who came to the door of the Lamb just then, was able to enlighten them. He did his best to cast an unfavourable light on the child Fehge, since he approved of her as little as did his next-door neighbour, Kurt Schreiner, and for the same intangible reasons. But the child's reputation was vexingly good.

Grabautschnik's wife, Clotilde, came to the doorway too, but her husband's huge body filled it. She was small and frail, and she peeped at the two children whom the talk was about from behind his back, between his arms, which he held akimbo. Her eyes bulged hungrily. Heinrich, her husband, had forbidden her to go to church.

The two girls reached the old Gothic building whose steeple had been burned down several times and each time been more shabbily replaced, but whose foundation and nave were good from the artistic standpoint, the windows not too highly arched, with stained glass endowed by Thérèse Sapponyi, by the fabulous Count, by his ancestors, and by rich farmers in the past.

Julie motioned to Fehge to take the kerchief from round her neck and tie it round her head; and when Fehge complied, both girls entered the church. Julie dabbed the holy water on her forehead and made the sign of the cross with it on Fehge's. Julie's heavy boots clattered on the cool flagstones, but Fehge's bare feet made no sound.

"Oh," said Fehge, "the big Saviour!" She stopped dead to

stare at the gigantic figure of Christ, carved and painted by a modern artist, that topped the altar. His body ran down a flat, central column, and His arms, tied to the cross, stretched out from side to side. His head hung limp, His eyes were closed, the lids puckered as in a Roger van der Weyden picture; the artist must have been influenced by that melancholy Flemish master painter. His body was yellow and bloodless, with the dark red blood coagulating on His brow where the thorns pricked into His flesh, on His hands, on His feet, and gushing from His sides above her. It was a horrible sight.

"Oh," breathed Fehge again, and squirmed where His wounds hurt her. "Oh."

Above his head were inscribed the words, "Come unto me, all ye that labour and are heavy laden, and I will give you rest," in big, black Gothic letters.

Underneath this gruesome figure and in strangest contrast to it was perched a Madonna carrying her child, resplendent in white satin embroidered with tiny seed pearls, as exquisitely clad as fairy-tale royalty. Thérèse had dressed them. They glowed and smiled, perpetually oblivious to the agony above them.

Julie knelt down to pray. Fehge began to walk along the sides of the church from altar to altar, admiring, not praying. It was all perfectly beautiful. The paintings in their bright colours, the wood-carved tableaux of the life of Christ, the statues, the beatific Thérèse of Lisieux holding pink roses against her soft brown cassock, the gentle St. Francis of Assisi, the lady saint with the difficult name of Creszentia . . . but Fehge returned again and again to the big Saviour who said "Come." To her, obviously. Did she not labour? Was she not often heavily laden?

It was the most exalting experience of her little life. Fear was gone. And there was something entirely new in its place—security, and with this new emotion came happiness. Fehge stared up at the ceiling, arched, and higher above her head than any ceiling she had ever been under. And suddenly it dawned on her why she was thus overwhelmed. This was God's house! Oh, indeed it was fitting!

She skipped lightly across the stones of the centre aisle like a dancer, back to where Julie was kneeling in prayer. "Oh," she said, interrupting the girl rudely with a push against her shoulder, "I am so happy!"

Julie opened her eyes, smiled her crooked smile and nodded her head, mouthing what she meant to be words. Fehge had no idea that the girl's vocal cords were giving forth their first sound. "Don't speak so silly," she therefore said, with utter disrespect. "Why don't you try it slowly?"

Julie looked at her and began again. "*Ich . . . I . . .*"

"Go on," urged Fehge.

"*Ich . . . seh! . . .*"

"You see," said Fehge. "What do you see?"

"*Weiss' Licht,*" said Julie, pointing to behind Fehge's head.

Fehge turned round. "Where do you see a white light?" Then she looked down again at the girl. "You mustn't talk silly. Tell you what," she said then, very matter-of-factly, "if you want to come up to Strubl sometimes—the evenings are the only time I have—I'll teach you to talk."

Julie stared uncomprehendingly. "Oh," said Fehge impatiently, "you are dumb!" Then she stopped herself, then she grinned. There was no one else in the world she would have dared be so rude to. It was a very pleasant sensation. From that moment she looked upon the idiot girl as her friend.

Julie rose and began to go about her business. The sunlight threw coloured patterns on the stone floor. Fehge watched them. It was cool and damp in the church, and she felt refreshed. It was still, and she felt what she had never felt in her life before—powerful.

By the time Fehge returned to Strubl she was late, and Andrea was anxious. When Fehge told her where she had been, her anxiety turned in another direction. So it had come!

"The church," said Fehge, "is the House of God, isn't it?"

Andrea said, "Yes."

"It *is* pretty," said Fehge dreamily, her mind on what she had seen there. And in her awoke, for the first time, the urge to belong to a community, the community that worshipped in this house, for whom all the empty benches were; those people who, she knew, washed themselves and dressed in their best every Sunday to enter it. She had seen them. The people she feared became something else in her mind when she could classify them as worshippers in God's house. It might be a good thing to be a part of this neat, subdued, transformed community of Sunday people. At any rate, it was worth trying.

"I want to go to church like the other children do," said Fehge. "Will you take me? Why don't you ever go?"

"I go to church," said Andrea, sounding very haughty because she was very hurt, "but I don't go to that one. Don't you want to wait until I can take you to my church?"

She would like to have added, but her training in religious tolerance forbade her, "It is much nicer." And she realized that Fehge would never like her church as well as the one she had just been to with its ornate beauty. What child, left to herself, would choose Andrea's austere house of worship in preference to the pretty haven offered by Catholicism? The children in Andrea's church were led there by the hands of their parents.

"No," Fehge answered, "unless your church is prettier."

"It isn't a question of whether a church is pretty or not," said Andrea wearily. What was it a question of? Sincerity. Obviously. But why couldn't one be as sincere with incense and gilt? What was it a question of? Certainly nothing she could explain to an eight-year-old child.

"Oh, but it is!" Fehge cried out, consternated. How could Andrea say such a thing, Andrea, who had introduced her to God? "God's house must be the most beautiful house in the world. Anyway," she went on, in her matter-of-fact way, "yours is too far away for me to go to," and she thought how practical it was that God had houses within easy reach of everyone.

Andrea said she would do something about it and didn't, hoping that Fehge would forget. But Fehge did not forget. When Sunday came, she was up and ready to go to church at seven o'clock in the morning. Andrea looked at her in despair.

"If you can't take me," said Fehge in a most determined voice, "I can go alone. Most of the children do."

Andrea said, "Wait," and hurried to finish her dressing.

"I don't want to miss it," said Fehge.

"You won't miss anything," Andrea snapped back at her.

When she was dressed, she took Fehge by the hand and led her across to the home of Thérèse Sapponyi. Thérèse was up and ready to go to early-morning Mass, as she always did. Andrea said, "Frau Medizinalrat, Fehge wants to go to church. I thought you would like to take her."

It was as simple as all that. The gigantic tussle between the two women over the technicality of which road Fehge should tread on her way to heaven was over. Andrea thought, as she always did when she was defeated, and never without great bitterness, "God's will be done." Thank God she rarely had to resort to Him that way. She rarely lost.

Thérèse's eyes narrowed in her triumph, and Andrea reddened with humiliation. "So!" said Thérèse. "But that pleases me!" And she drew her petite little body to its full height. "Certainly I shall take her."

She stretched out her little white hand to the child, who only stared at her. This was more than Fehge had bargained for. She had thought that Andrea would take her, or that she would go alone. To go with the "porcelain lady," which was the nickname she had given Thérèse because she looked as though she might easily break, made her heart beat wildly with fear. Why couldn't she go alone? She would much rather go alone.

"Come," said the porcelain lady, her hand still outstretched.

"Go with the Frau Medizinalrat," said Andrea, and added bitterly, properly brought up as she was, "It is a great honour."

Fehge changed hands.

Andrea made no move to go. Thérèse stared at this undoubtedly well-meaning woman who yet was doomed to end in hell like any heathen. Incredible creature, to stick so pertinaciously to a path of sin when so obviously cut out for good.

Still Andrea lingered. "I hope she will be all right," she said softly, a quite different Andrea from the one that faced her work. "I hang very much on her," and she meant that she was devoted to the child.

Thérèse was not so thick-skinned that she didn't sense this moment of the deaconess's vulnerability. "Why don't you let the child lead you to heaven, Sister?" she said. "It may be a sign for you."

Andrea flushed and came to. The nerve of the woman! "We shall all see heaven if we live righteously on earth," she said tartly. "It doesn't make any difference in which house of God we worship! Before God we are all alike!" And she turned and went away.

The little tiff gave Thérèse a slight spasm in the region of her heart. How right she was to keep away from the mundane contacts of this earth!

She told the child to wait in the hall where there were two large antique chairs with rounded seats and a brocaded velvet strap for the back. They were very uncomfortable to sit on. But Fehge did not have to wait long. Thérése reappeared again, this time with her hat and coat on. Except for her sturdy boots, she was dressed elegantly, as though she were going to St. Stefan's Cathedral in Vienna, instead of a little country church. Now she came over to the child, who had risen when she entered, buttoning her black kid gloves, which snapped sharply as she fastened them.

"You are going to church with us," said Thérèse, "but you know that is only the beginning. You must join the church."

Fehge's breath came fast. It had not been her intention to "join" anything; in fact, she didn't know what the lady was talking about. The house of God was there. The people went to it. So, she thought, would she. "Must I, Frau Medizinalrat?" she said, and curtsied.

Thérèse said, "You must want to," and found it difficult to impart to the child what she must want, as though a hopeless abyss yawned between her and mankind. Vaguely, her inability to inspire the child came to her as a reproach and made her angry with Fehge. "The priest will explain it to you," she said curtly. "And now come."

They met the Herr Medizinalrat downstairs. He had been to see those patients who could not wait till after Mass. He raised his eyebrows when he saw Fehge, and Thérèse hastened to explain, not without a trace of triumph in her voice, that it had been the child's idea.

So they all drove to church together. Fehge sitting in front with Fritz. Sapponyi covered Thérèse's and his own knees with the rug and smiled an ironical smile. Then he sat back, literally and figuratively speaking, and sighed. So it was over. He could almost feel a breath of relief roll across the land as it subsided after this spiritual battle for the child's soul, which Thérèse had won. . . . But had she? He had certainly put her *hors de combat* right from the start. He wondered if the gold star would not, after all, go to Fehge, who seemed to have found her way to God's house all by herself. He knew nothing of Julie's hand in the matter—a good thing too, or in his cynical way he might have said something very inept about it.

Fehge sat with the Sapponyis in the pew reserved for the *Herrschaften*, apart from the villagers. She looked around her at the kneeling figures and bowed heads. How right she had been! Here, in the house of God, even the savages behaved themselves.

That amazed her perhaps even more than the priest resplendent in white and gold, going through his strange ritual of reading in a large book that was first on the right side of the altar, then on the left, his crooked elbow close to his body, his hands held in a queer position of blessing. To Fehge it looked more like gentle supplication, with thumb and forefinger touching each other. He moved his hands, making signs over the big book, then he turned and made the same signs in their direction, whereupon the people curtsied and bowed their heads and tapped their foreheads and lips and breasts with the nail of their thumb.

But what impressed her most of all were Reischer's Walter and Pfeiffer's Gustl, who were dressed in long black robes like little priests, with short white lace dresses over them, and looked like little angels instead of the devils which she had known them to be until then. *If the church could do this to them!* In everyday life they were unkempt and none too clean. Now they were washed radiant, their hair neat, the expressions on their faces innocent. Pfeiffer's Gustl, so she had heard, had, at the age of six, kicked his pregnant mother in the stomach so that the baby had come too soon. He had once knocked Fehge down in the schoolroom and would have kicked her in the face had Melita not come in in time and intervened.

Well, that harassing affair with Pfeiffer's Gustl had been long ago. He must have changed into a good boy now, or he wouldn't be here. Reischer's Walter had never done her any harm, but he had bitten Hirschegger's Hedi in the arm, she had seen that with her own eyes, until he had drawn blood, then he had been scared when he'd seen the blood . . . and that hadn't been very long ago. Still, here he was, with Pfeiffer's Gustl, and both of them looked really good.

Gustl picked his nails every now and then; Walter yawned often. In full view of the preciously dressed little lady and the Saviour who said "Come" it didn't seem quite correct. But they always came to attention at the right moment and knelt and bowed their heads when the priest did, their foreheads touching the top step of the altar like his. They waited on the priest, they helped him, Reischer's Walter and Pfeiffer's Gustl, whom she had never seen do anything for anybody else in her life! It was they who lugged the big book on its cumbersome stand from one side of the altar to the other. *If the church could do that to them . . .*

What a lovely cloth the altar had! Fehge lost herself in the intricacies of its lace, which Thérèse had crocheted with the finest thread in the world. But always her mind and eyes wandered back to the miraculous boys. The priest had just given Walter a little glass bottle to hold, and the boy crossed his arms and held it quite irreverently in his hand under the elbow of his other arm as though it had been nothing more sacred than an inkwell. There was, in fact, nothing reverent about the boys. They behaved as though they were thoroughly at home in what they were doing. That was what made their apparent sanctity so convincing. Whatever happened in the future, she would do her best to remember them like this. It was something utterly surprising to cling to. Nothing could have converted Fehge to the Catholic Church so potently as the converted aspect of these, her rude schoolmates.

The people . . . She tore her eyes away from the boys and watched the people. They were kneeling again; so, she discovered, was she. The Frau Medizinalrat had gently drawn her into that position without her even having noticed it. The people held necklaces of black beads in their hands which they slipped between their fingers. The Frau Medizinalrat had a chain too, and hers was the prettiest of all. Her beads were white pearls with a tinge of pink in them now and then. Everybody in the church looked as though they could do nothing but good. Fehge's heart sang within her. Here nobody would harm her. Here she would always be safe. Here she belonged.

Chapter Twelve

FEHGE sat on the wicker table on Dennis's balcony. The white curtain was gone with the Goddess, who had been dismissed as cured, and the Baron was gone too. The balconies on either side were peopled now by a lady from Bombay and a surly Minister of Agriculture respectively. Neither of them interested Fehge. "I am going to be baptized," she told Dennis, who had already been told, "and I must have a name. A proper name."

Dennis nodded. "Of course you must," he said. "And high time too." His mind was not on what she was saying, but on the thought that had never left him since Andrea and Melita had told him, each bitter in her own way, of Fehge's desire to join the Roman Catholic Church. She had had her chance and thrown it away! She had been born free and chosen chains. Human beings didn't want to be free. Even he, ever since the encounter with Fricka Reuther, found that his fixed forward gaze had been deflected.

"My mother called me 'Fehge,'" the child was saying, "and sometimes she said 'Fehgush,' and sometimes she just called me 'Gush . . .'" She paused.

Dennis forced himself to concentrate on her little self. "Can't do much with any of those," he said, shaking his head. "Fehge . . . Fehgush . . . gush . . . gush . . . Gusti. Gusti is a good Austrian name." He gave it its Austrian pronunciation of "goosty," and then thought of the name from which it originated and said aloud, "That comes from Augusta."

He was sorry the minute it was out, because she snapped it up and clapped her hands and said, "Augusta! Oh, Dennis, that is a fine name!" And she had called him by his for the first time. "I knew you'd think of a fine name for me."

Dennis had to laugh. "It's rather a big handle for such a little pot," he said. "Besides, it isn't a saint's name."

But it was. The day of the Holy Saint Augustine, apostle of England, was on May 26, and that date was approaching now. Fehge would be ready to receive baptism when it came.

In the face of such an indisputable omen, Dennis gave in. "All right," he said, "Augusta it shall be. Now, what about a second name?" And as he asked the question he knew the answer. It came straight out of the feeling of affinity for her which did not seem weakened by the fact that she had been proved a deserter. "I have it!" he triumphed. "Mine!"

Sapponyi was amused. "Why don't you adopt her?" he asked Dennis, but that wasn't to the point in Dennis's mind. Their relationship was outside the realm of legalities.

They spelled it the German way, "Siemohr," and for the first time he thought of it phonetically. He didn't do things by halves either. He was godfather. Sapponyi, Thérèse, and Andrea attended.

To Dennis, Melita had said what she would not have dared say to anyone else, "So she did fall for the rotten magic!"

"What can you have against it if it makes her happy?" had been his sharp retort, no one more surprised than he to find himself sticking up for Fehge's act of desertion. "She will develop much better if she is content."

"It is contentment built on a false foundation," she had said. "They mislead the masses." And she had gone on to tell him of the many dishonest priests she knew. "It is just a business," she had said, "like any other. The most successful in the world and one of the most dishonest."

To that Dennis had said, "I would advise you not to let yourself be misled by the few dishonest men you may have managed to uncover in the business—you will find them in any business, private or state-owned—*to a false evaluation of the thing itself!*" He had leaned back in his chair and sighed. How she always tired him! "That would be a great mistake," he had added.

Of course, after that, he didn't ask her to attend the ceremony. What a fanatic she was! Fehge had let him down too, yet that didn't make them fall apart!

Fehge wore her white dress and a wreath of artificial white flowers in her hair. She wore white cotton gloves, white cotton stockings, and white shoes. Her stockings wrinkled a little, and before they entered the church Andrea straightened them.

The priest said to Dennis in Latin, "What dost thou ask of the Church of God?" and Dennis answered, "Faith."

Then the priest said, "What doth faith bring thee to?" and Dennis answered, "Life everlasting," and, really, it didn't seem to mean a thing.

Then the priest breathed on Fehge and said, "Go out of her, thou unclean spirit, and give place unto the Holy Spirit, the Paraclete." And he made the sign of the cross with his thumb on her forehead and breast. "Receive the sign of the cross both upon thy forehead and also upon thy heart. Take unto thee the faith of the heavenly precepts that thou mayest now be the temple of God."

To Fehge it meant a great deal. It meant just what it said. "And I shall be a temple of God," she had said to Thérèse, who had taken the trouble to translate the Latin responses for her.

"Yes," Thérèse had answered her, "as we all are who are baptized in Him." But Fehge had not listened to that.

The priest blessed the salt, and Fehge tasted it on her tongue.

Wetting his right thumb with spittle from his mouth, he touched her right ear and said, "Ephetha, that is to say, be opened. . . . But thou, devil, begone! Behold, the judgment of God shall draw near." And the words made Fehge tremble inside.

Then he questioned her. "Dost thou renounce Satan?"

"*Abrenuntio*," said Fehge, "I renounce."

"And all his works?"

"*Abrenuntio*."

"And all his pomps?"

"*Abrenuntio*."

Then the priest anointed Fehge with oil on the breast and between the shoulders with the sign of the cross. "I anoint thee," he said, "with the oil of salvation, in Christ Jesus, our Lord, that thou mayest have life everlasting." He then wiped his thumb and the parts anointed with wool and changed his violet stole for a white one.

The priest was treating her as he treated the paraphernalia of the altar; she, Fehge, was a part of the ritual. It filled her with such exaltation that she feared her body would not contain it. But outwardly she was able to preserve a deadly calm.

She's taking it dreadfully seriously, thought Dennis, and he felt apprehension for the responsibility he had so lightly assumed. He was only her father "in God." It hadn't seemed to mean much when he had promised it except for the giving of presents and the keeping an eye on her, which he wanted to do anyway. But as he watched her now its meaning seemed to swell to proportions he could not grasp, and he stemmed his soul against the drug of mysticism that was overpowering him.

He would not give himself up to it. He would not. He would . . . What would he do? Fehge had chosen the net, or the haven —he must try to see it with her eyes—of the Church. Andrea had taught her the story of Christ. Catholicism would give her the comfort of an eternally interceding mother. What would he give her? Godfather. And, suddenly, he had the solution. He would give her something supremely best—the philosophy of Christ, a Christian philosophy.

Something diagonally behind him caught his eye and interrupted his train of thought. He turned his head and saw Julie, who had entered the church and was kneeling at the back. It was the first time Dennis had seen the idiot girl, and he looked away again quickly. Such sights nauseated him. He remembered how, in Barcelona, the sight of the cripples with their sores exposed had made him feel faint, and all the other idiots and dwarfs throughout the whole of Spain. Funny, he thought. In our country they put creatures like that in a home.

"Wilt thou be baptized?" the priest was saying.

"*Volo,*" said Fehge.

The priest put the "white garment" on Fehge's head. The white linen cloth lay still on her black hair. Then he gave her a lighted candle. "Go in peace," he said, "and the Lord be with thee."

It was over. Fehge sheltered the light with her hand as she turned to leave, and saw Julie. The eyes of the two girls met, and Fehge's were full of love for Julie, the only person on earth whom she need never, never fear.

Julie came to the edge of her pew as Fehge passed, and Fehge said to her, "I am the Temple of God."

Andrea, who was behind Fehge, said, "So is everybody who is baptized," and this time Fehge heard.

Her face grew puzzled. "No," she said. "*I* am the Temple of God."

Andrea said sharply, "Humility is the first thing you will have to learn, my child."

Dennis began to propel the little group forward again. "Humility?" he said. "Why, there isn't anyone in the world more humble than Fehge."

Andrea had thought so too. Now she said briefly, "I'm not so sure about that."

"Fehge will always be humble in the sight of God," said Dennis. "You don't have to worry about that. If she isn't humble in the sight of man, it is perhaps because she hasn't seen him at his best."

Fehge preserved her light until she reached her room. Then,

with it, she lit the everlasting light under the Holy Mother of God that Thérèse had given her. The light swung beneath the figure, which stood on its little ledge, from a metal chain in a red glass cup. Fehge knelt before it, and her prayer was of her own making. "I am the Temple of God," she said, over and over again.

Forgotten in their graves lay Moishe and Dworje. Fehge had not thought of visiting them. Andrea had thought that, under the circumstances, it was more tactful not to mention them. Now she sat in the one comfortable chair in her room and prayed. "Dear Saviour. The mother of Fehge may please forgive us. Watch Thou over her child. Preserve her humility. She did not enter Your Kingdom through our Church, as I would have wished it. Protect her, however she may have found her way to You. Keep her from sickness and harm. Amen."

Thus was Augusta Siemohr baptized in the church of Pritnitz on May 26th, 1926, when she was presumably eight years old. Her new name gave her legally a day which she might celebrate like a birthday, when presents might be given to her, and she might choose to eat what she liked best—her name day. For here, where Fehge lived, the day of the Saint after whom a child was named was celebrated like a birthday, not the day on which she was born. But, aside from that, Fehge's new name was quickly forgotten, not to be resurrected until twelve years later when legalities entered her life again. For everyone who knew her she remained the Strubl Fehge.

Chapter Thirteen

ON Sunday, October 31st, 1926, Otto Bauer, leader of the Social Democratic Party of Austria, was to announce the party's programme at a big rally in Linz. Although the failure of her tactics was by now well proven, Melita still tended to let politics do her courting for her. "Come with me," she said to Dennis. "You have never seen such a sight in your life."

Her impetus alone would have failed to take Dennis to Linz for anything but a sightseeing trip, had he not meanwhile become interested in another ardent Social Democrat. He had not yet met Moritz Behrendt personally, but he already knew a great deal more about him than mere acquaintanceship would have made possible.

It was ten days now since Behrendt had brought his wife Hedwig to Strubl to die. The case was doubly tragic. No one had suspected the disease in her throughout the months just past, when she had borne her child with ever-failing strength. Once she had given healthy life to it she had collapsed, and the doctors had recognized the strange throat ailment from which she had been suffering for what it was—tuberculosis. By that time her powers of speech were gone, her vocal cords eaten away; she had very few weeks left to live.

In those ten days Dennis had been told a great deal about Moritz Behrendt by Melita, who was very anxious that the two men should meet, and by Hilda, who gossiped about him whenever she cleaned Dennis's room or came in with a tray. Hilda's information, although she was far less well acquainted with the man, was much more vivid than Melita's. Hilda could make you see things by the realistic way she described them. Dennis, watching her and not always listening, sometimes thought what a fine actress she would have made. But to what she said about Behrendt he found himself listening.

She told him how the impecunious Jewish lawyer had succeeded in making one of the lovelist Viennese society women his bride, a woman twenty years younger than himself. Hedwig, together with her sister, Stefanie, were daughters of the famous *Burgtheater* actor, Leo Trattner. They had had no dowry but their beauty. It had therefore been expected that they would marry for money. Stefanie, to all appearances, fulfilled the expectations of those citizens of Vienna who kept their eyes on the social column, but not Hedwig. Why, Vienna was still asking, had this lovely woman married a man neither appealing as a lover nor secure as a provider? Hilda told Dennis, "You know, in Vienna, love is the last thing people marry for." And it was written all over her glowing face that she thought the world of the Behrendts for doing just that.

Melita showed Dennis the other side of the picture, Moritz Behrendt, the political leader or—what made him more interesting to Dennis's mind—political "driver." According to Melita he was a furious but unobtrusive worker, a superlative organizer and propagandist, an unspectacular drone of Austria's Social Democratic Party. "He never speaks in public," Melita said; but it was he who made the wheels go round. The picture of the man devoting his life to a people he in no way required as an adulating audience to feed his self-esteem, this obviously selfless, this "ugly" man, as Hilda had defined him, with the lovely wife—the two versions, when brought together, were intriguing.

Melita soon discovered that the meeting of the two men was not easy to bring about. Behrendt's visits to Strubl were fraught with nothing but misery, for he realized that he was about to lose the only person who had been able to give him relief from this distressing world. Hedwig was his religion, and he was going to have to live the rest of his life without her. The thought of the crying infant at home, with its wet-nurse from the Spreewald (his spectacular father-in-law's innovation), her black lace-edged cap spreading out behind her bland face like a sombre sail, in no way consoled him. With its mother gone he felt no relationship to it whatsoever. Never again would he base his life on that of another human being. If there were any consolation on this earth, then only in total renunciation of self and dedication to the party. In this mood, in which he could speak freely and easily to Melita, he could scarcely be asked to meet a charming but otherwise utterly unimportant Englishman.

Melita's suggestion to Dennis to come to the party rally in Linz was not bound up with her desire to bring the two men together; it seemed unlikely that this could be achieved in the commotion of that event. But Dennis seemed somehow to connect the two things, because he asked at once, "Will Behrendt be there?"

"Of course," she told him.

"How can he take time off?" Dennis asked. "I mean, how can he concentrate on Linz with her dying here?"

Melita's face was a little scornful, or did he only imagine it? "A man like Behrendt doesn't belong to himself alone. He can't turn his back on Linz, whatever straits he may be in personally."

Dennis nodded his head slowly.

"Hedwig Behrendt was never interested in politics," Melita went on, "but she felt that way about him too. That he belonged first to the party. I think that's why they got along so well together."

Dennis did not think that this beautiful legendary love—marriage was a word he always avoided, even in his mind—was based on anything as cut-and-dried as freedom of taste, but he did not feel disposed to argue the point just then. He could have said what came to his mind: "He belongs to the party. They, over there in the Reich, belong to the Fatherland. No! A man belongs to himself!" But he only said, "And what becomes of the children of such half-parents as Behrendt?"

Melita retorted, "I don't think he wanted a child," and added bitterly, "he wanted only her."

"And now he loses her," said Dennis, "and has only the child," and he felt sorry for it.

But to Melita's invitation he said, "All right. If Sapponyi will let me, we'll make a day of it. And we'll take Fehge."

Melita's face fell. "I don't know whether we can get Andrea to let us do that," she said. "We'll have to spend one night in Vienna."

"Not if I take a car," said Dennis. "Wouldn't that be the best way to do it?"

"It certainly would," said Melita, "but it would be the most extravagant way too. And what will we do with Fehge during the meeting?"

"I'll show her the town," he said.

"Oh," cried Melita, "no! You must hear Bauer speak!" However, when she saw that his heart was set on taking the child, she said, "I have friends in Linz. They will look after her."

It turned out to be a glorious day. The trees were all the colours of an autumnal rainbow from palest yellow to copper brown. The birches waved their golden ducats in the breeze, and the firs were black against the fiery pageant of the leaf trees. The sun shone clear from the moment it topped the mountains and dispersed the morning mist that lay in the cracks of the valley. By noon it would be hot.

Sapponyi had given them his car for the excursion. He had been glad to give Dennis permission to spend the day in Linz. It was high time the young Englishman found his feet, preparatory to leaving Strubl, which he would surely be able to do at Christmastime. Dennis picked up Melita at the schoolhouse and Fehge, coming from church, at the crossroads where her father had died. Nobody thought of him. That had been long ago.

Fehge was dressed in her Sunday best, a dirndl with a black velvet bodice, carrying the homespun woollen jacket which she had knitted for herself in the most complicated of cable stitches. Her bright kerchief, which she usually wore on her head, was now tied round her neck, fastened with a cheap little brooch from Vienna that Andrea had given to her in defiance of Thérèse's good taste. Her black hair was braided and hung thick and long down her back to her waist. My! thought Melita, she is going to be a handsome girl!

All three sat at the back of the car and Fritz drove them like a robot. Fehge put her kerchief back on her head and made slits of her eyes as the wind slapped them.

"Put on your jacket," said Dennis, and put the rug over her.

Melita and he wore the white coat and hood of the Austrian motorist, a dress that was indispensable where drives led across miles of dusty dirt roads. Melita, on Dennis's other side, let her head fall back and closed her eyes. She could feel Dennis. In the void that the drive made in her mind, it was heart-breaking to feel him so close and so hopelessly indifferent. Why . . . why did she get nowhere with him? She knew that she was nothing more to him than a little political encyclopedia, one he wouldn't even rely on because he loved to prove her wrong. Why did nothing ever happen? Was it her fault? Maybe. She realized that she was dreadfully inhibited. But wasn't the man supposed to make the advances? If not, couldn't he at least meet her half-way? But Dennis didn't.

There was more antagonism between them than affection, and they were bound to each other by a strange form of mutual irritation. It was a tie that left her fully aware of the hopelessness of her love for him. She could not even wish for anything to come of it. And yet she did. Two tears welled up in her eyes, and the wind blew them away.

Melita was also facing the fact that Behrendt would soon be free. She had little emotional reaction to this except, perhaps, for the bitter feeling that it was her fate to find what she had longed for within reach when she no longer wanted it—power over the people as she now possessed it in the valley; Behrendt, when she had attached herself hopelessly elsewhere. She had grown wan in the past year; she suffered often from fits of deep depression. And not only because of the problems of her private life. The provinces were nibbling at her confidence in the great and glorious future for mankind. Not even the political future was secure.

Anton pooh-poohed her spoken fears that something was growing big in the provinces, and not Social Democracy. Of course, the Nazis were not to be taken seriously, but they were popular. They were more popular now, she thought, than the *Heimwehr*. And they were certainly more virile in their brutish way. Anton had been vexed with her. Virile? They, the Social Democrats, had a monopoly on that attribute. "Wait," he had said, "until we come out with our party programme on the thirty-first!" Well, now the day had come.

The car followed the curves of the mountain stream that travelled almost as fast as they did in spite of its handicaps of boulders and little round stones. They passed through a shady chasm of rocks where the sun found its way for an hour at high noon, so narrow that it left space only for winding road and brook until it widened and spilled them out on to the peaceful countryside of Lower Austria. Farms grew more frequent. The villages they passed through took on more the aspect of towns. Then they left the stream, now grown into a little river to wend its way to the capital, and turned off to the left, avoiding the city, meeting the Danube at Melk, whose monastery on the cliff drew a gasp of admiration from Dennis and Fehge.

There it stood, in its magnificent proportions, a huge, sprawling white stone edifice with lofty lines, the ornate baroque domes of its twin towers coloured by the mellow tarnished green of copper. Was Melita looking at it, or was she thinking of its benighted monks inside? Was her mind concentrated on beauty or looking for a cause for argument?

Dennis looked at her. Her mournful eyes were on the monastery. He immediately felt sorry for his antagonistic thoughts and put his hand over hers. It trembled under his. What was the matter with her lately? The poor girl was run down. He was glad he had been able to treat her to this trip in comfort. "Enjoying it?" he asked.

She turned her face to his and nodded her head. He smiled and turned away, and said nothing more until they passed a sign on the road which made him sit up straight. "I know somebody who lives here," he said. "I wonder if we'd have time to stop and say hello? I don't think he'd mind."

"Who is it?" asked Melita.

"The Baron von Trent und Freibürgen," said Dennis.

Melita's face became stony. "I certainly can't see him," she said.

"Why not?" said Dennis. "You're my friend. I don't even know whether it will be convenient for him to see me, but if it is I can certainly take you with me. I'd like to see that fairy-tale castle of his."

"There it is," she said morosely, as they rounded a bend in the road.

It stood on a hill-top, its grey stone walls ivy-grown, its shape like a toy cardboard castle you could buy in a box and put up yourself. By God! One stodgy Social Democrat isn't going to stop me from going up there! thought Dennis.

"What's the Baron done to you that makes you so mad with

him?" he asked Melita as the car entered the village that took its name from the castle.

"The Baron hasn't done anything to me," said Melita petulantly, "and I'm not mad at him. He just belongs to a class of people with whom I cannot mix."

"Oh, I see," said Dennis. "Because he's an aristocrat. What about your human equality? Aren't aristocrats people too?"

"It's not because he's an aristocrat," Melita replied wearily. "But he is a monarchist. He wants the return of the Hapsburg monarchy."

"No, he doesn't," argued Dennis, anxious to get in his penny-worth, and here he was treading on sure ground. "Do you know what he told me once? This will interest you. Somebody else was saying how fairly the Hapsburgs had managed their minorities, how they let everybody use their own language in school and worship as they pleased, how even in the Army the officers gave the commands in the language of the commonest foot-soldier . . . and do you know what the Baron said? I can see him now. He said, that was just the damnable part of the Hapsburgs, that they were so smart at exploitation! Under their narcotic blanket of pseudo-liberalism no race could ever revolt and better itself. He said that never in the history of mankind had there been a family so persistently out for self-aggrandizement. They were even ready to be liberal to attain their selfish ends."

He paused. Her serious face broke into gaiety. "You made that up," she said, and laughed. "You absurd creature!"

Dennis laughed with her. "It may be my phraseology," he said, "but he gave me the idea. What did I know about the Hapsburgs before I came here? Only that they had protruding chins," and he made his jut out still farther, reminded of the Velasquez Hapsburgs that he had seen in Madrid. "My own chin gives me a good start, doesn't it?"

Melita had to laugh with Fehge at the face he was making.

They were passing through the village. "Fritz," said Dennis, tapping the chauffeur on the shoulder, "stop here." They were on the square. "I want to get out."

"What are you going to do ?" asked Melita.

"Telephone. I suppose that cardboard castle has a phone."

He was getting out. Melita's face was stern again. The joyousness that had lighted it a moment ago had disappeared, as though covered by a swift shadow. "He won't want to see me," she said, with her usual obstinacy. "Really, he won't. You don't understand these things. I'll wait down her. Please."

Dennis hesitated for a moment. "All right," he said, then in a gentler voice. "Have it your own way."

Five minutes later he came back. Melita was already out of the car. "Get right back in again," he told her. "I told the old boy your scruples. He laughed and said you were to come up too. Now, if he can be so broad-minded, you're not going to disgrace your party by being petty, are you ?"

Melita felt the sagging of defeat inside her. "All right," she said wearily, and got back into the car.

The drawbridge was down, and the Baron was at the big front entrance to greet them, his wife standing a few steps higher up. The Baroness was what Dennis called a horsy-looking woman, with her wide skirt much too long to be stylish, her stout, brown laced boots, her mannish blouse and tie. But how gracious and womanly were her ways!

After formal greetings and introductions, they walked into the huge entrance-hall with windows at both ends, a fireplace that was high enough for a grown man to stand up in, several hunting trophies on the wall, bearskins on the stone floor, old carved benches, couches, chairs—never had Fehge seen such a large room! She clasped her hands behind her back and looked up at the carved stone ceiling with its coat of arms in every notch. She stared at the antlers, the stuffed birds, and the ancient firearms on the walls, and wondered what the big house was for.

The Baron served drinks. They asked about his health, which was—his wife wanted to say something, but he shrugged it off and said, "All right. I won't need Strubl again this year."

The conversation was formal, stilted, meaningless; but Dennis was moved, as always, by the beauty and elegance of his surroundings. Melita sat in a large chair which made her look like a child, on her face the same stony expression with which she had agreed to come.

Fehge walked over to the Baron,. who had just taken Melita's empty glass, and said softly, " Who lives here ?"

The Baron smiled. " My wife and I do, and my children when they are home from school."

" Many children ?"

" Only two."

" There would be room," said Fehge, " for a lot more."

The Baron threw back his head and laughed aloud. Dennis and the Baroness had to be told the joke, and they laughed too. Even Melita smiled.

The Baron addressed her. " I think the child said what has been on your mind ever since you came in, that this big place should be put to a more significant use than housing a consumptive old Baron and his German wife. Well, maybe some day it will be. I know that we are *passé*."

Melita felt her heart warming to his frankness and, if she had only realized it, to his charm. Perhaps some of the good things she had heard about Trent were true. Her face relaxed, and she leaned back in the huge chair and said, " Why does the Freiherr say that ? There is such a thing as keeping up with the times."

The Baron laughed. " These times are not any I feel I want to keep up with. Come," he said, addressing them all, " I am going to show you round."

What followed reminded Dennis of sight-seeing trips he had taken in France, in Germany, in Spain. The castle was not big, but it had one perfect example of every room a castle should have, from grand ballroom over the hall they had entered, with its sparkling crystal chandeliers reflected in the mirror of its parquet flooring, its ornate orchestral balcony and stone-cupided baroque terrace, to the small white-and-gold rococo morning-room with white-tiled oven and a view over a rose-garden which reminded Dennis of Sans Souci. In all the rooms they saw, no rope or railing divided them from the exquisite furnishings. You could go up to a Sèvres vase and take it in your hands. Dennis did.

The Baron was saying, "Lately I have begun to feel very strange in this house. As though it were an anachronism to be living here at all. I don't feel that way in my Vienna home. Only here. Every time I go down to the village I feel it. A walk down the hill, and I am in another world. I think I will have to move to Vienna."

"You see," said Dennis, trying to include Melita in their conversation—she was walking stiffly a few feet away from them—"the Baron favours your Vienna."

"Why does she consider it hers?" asked the Baron, smiling to soften his words.

Dennis was afraid that Melita might say something tactless. You never knew about these class-conscious workers, and he felt responsible because he had practically forced her to come. So he said hastily, "Melita always says that the influence of the Social Democrats is so much stronger in Vienna than in the provinces."

"I agree with her," said the Baron, "and I wish," he went on, addressing her directly, "that you could make your influence felt more in our village—in all the villages in the provinces, in fact. It might improve the mood of the people there, which, as it is now, will lead to no good end."

Melita started to speak, haltingly. "I am surprised to hear the *Herr Baron* say that. Isn't the *Heimwehr* very influential in his village, and in the provinces?"

"No," said the Baron. "It may appear to be, but it is not. And I doubt whether it ever will be under the leadership it enjoys at present."

Dennis could not appreciate the dig at the *Heimwehr* leader, Starhemberg, but Melita did, very well. She laughed. "Well," she said, "the Baron will understand when I say that that would be only to our advantage."

But the Baron didn't even smile. "Don't be so smug," he said, not unkindly, only sadly. "If my *Heimwehr* fails, that doesn't mean your *Schutzbündler* are going to win. A third party may come in and take victory from us both."

Melita knew whom he meant. So *he* took the Nazis seriously. It weighed on her heart like lead. It would be dreadful, inconceivably dreadful, if they should have to take the Nazis seriously too.

Politics, politics, politics, thought Dennis. You talked about them here as you talked about the weather in England. Politics were a religion. Why, even Sapponyi, when he had looked at the chart and inquired after sleep and cough, plunged into politics. Dennis could hear him doing it every day as he went from balcony to balcony. The only person he'd never done it with was the Goddess. With her his visits had been brief and mumbled.

They were standing in the middle of the Baron's study and had forgotten to go on. Fehge was very glad of the pause. Now she could look at all the lovely, useless things at her leisure, especially at the pictures, some of which told interesting stories. The landscapes and the flower paintings were not as lovely as their originals; but the picture of the Baron's daughter over the fireplace—that was lovely! She recognized the young girl at once; she had seen her often at Strubl. On the opposite wall was a dark square patch on the brocade that lined the walls, the same size as the picture of the Baron's daughter. Fehge looked from the patch to the picture, back and forth. Finally the grown-ups paused in their talk and she could ask, "Why does that spot hang there?"

The grown-ups looked at the patch, and the Baron's face seemed to go grey, or was it because he had turned away from the light? He said, "A picture of my son used to hang there. I took it down the other day because he had vexed me." Rüdiger had said, "I don't see how you could let that Jew paint us, Papa." The boy had called it "in poor taste." The greenhorn! The stupid little greenhorn! The Baron looked down at Fehge with eyes that did not see. "How do you like it here?" he asked her, to break the embarrassed silence.

She smiled up at him. "Everything is very pretty," she said. "But it must be very hard to keep clean."

It made them all laugh.

"I think your little girl is going to be an ascetic," the Baron said to Dennis, and he turned his back on the patch on the wall and led them through the next room, a little waiting-room, and on to the entrance-hall from which they had come. Here the Baroness had a glass of milk and a piece of black bread and butter for Fehge.

The Baron shook hands with Melita first. "Good-bye," he said. "I know you are going to have an inspiring time in Linz."

"Why doesn't the Baron come with us?" said Melita, and to her came the swift thought that a short hour ago she would never have conceived of extending such an invitation to the Baron von Trent und Freibürgen. It only went to show that one should not lump people together, but judge them as individuals . . . if at all. Oh, that last thought was Dennis speaking in her!

The Baron shook his head. "No," he said. "I have a meeting of my own to attend in the village tonight. That will be inspiring too, but in another way."

"A meeting?"

"A Nazi meeting. A young Austrian is going to talk about 'My Two Years in the Reich.' His name is Conrad Schreiner. You should know him because he is the son of the district doctor in Pritnitz."

Fehge was very busy trying to eat her bread without letting any crumbs drop on the fine floor. She was keeping a wary eye on the Baroness, who was smiling, but Fehge knew that crumbs on the floor might change that smile as they did Andrea's, so she was being very careful, and since she could concentrate on only one thing at a time, she did not hear what was being said.

Melita said bitterly, "So he's back. I knew when his father sent him away to Munich—" Then, all of a sudden, her mood changed and she said to the Baron passionately, "Oh, why don't you do something about it?"

The Baron threw aside courtesy and let all the sternness he felt show in his face and voice. "Because," he said, "you—yes, you —have destroyed individualism, and I am condemned to sit idle. Because where I would like to lead, my heritage damns me! There is no room in a people's movement for a Baron Wolfgang von Trent und Freibürgen, regardless of his qualifications. If I joined you—within five days your leaders, who know me, would make me a leader. And within five more days your followers—who do not—would have me booed out of office as a bloody aristocrat! No. You have built up your own undiscriminating barriers. You are narrow, you have no vision for mankind as a whole. Let that be a part of your undoing! I can do nothing to stop it."

With that his anger petered out and Melita stood shaking her head up and down solemnly as though his vehement tirade had not been directed at her. Dennis wanted to laugh. But Fehge was staring at them, her eyes dilated with horror. The grown-ups were quarrelling!

The bread was luckily safe in her stomach, but the half-full glass of milk trembled so that a few drops spilled on to the floor, and the Baroness stretched out her hand and took the glass from the child just in time. Fehge put her hands up to her face and burst into tears.

Just as all their combined assurances that nobody was going to do anybody any harm had succeeded in consoling her, a car drove up to the entrance and stopped behind theirs. It was a huge white Mercedes-Benz racing-car, with red leather upholstery and a gleaming metal tube worming out of the motor at its side like a snake. It spurted gravel as it came to a stop. They turned all eyes to the door of the car, out of which stepped a beautiful woman. Melita gave such a start of surprise that Dennis noticed it. The woman was very tall and dressed in a smart, navy-blue, tight-fitting, tailor-made suit. One slim hand held her black fur-piece in position. She wore a turquoise-blue turban well back on her head and showed a white parting in her dark hair prematurely streaked with grey. It was knotted simply at the nape of her neck like a peasant girl's, yet in her aristocratic Old-World elegance she was as far removed from a peasant girl as a queen. She said a few words to her chauffeur and came up the steps, the Baron already on his way to greet her, the Baroness a few steps behind, as they had stood to greet Dennis and his party.

Dennis saw the woman's large violet-blue eyes shine as she greeted, first the Baron, then his wife, clasping their hands in hers and bending slightly forward with the most gracious gesture imaginable. In a rich, deep voice she said, "Forgive me for surprising you like this, but I was lonely for you both," and they replied with warm expressions of pleasure, thanking her for the surprise.

Dennis felt embarrassed that they should still be there and, as the three came up the steps, he came forward to say good-bye.

"I am very glad you called," said the Baron, and then, turning to the beautiful woman, "This is a young Englishman from Strubl."

"Oh," she exclaimed, turning to Dennis with a natural friendliness, as though she had always known him, "I would ask you how my sister is, but you wouldn't know. She is very ill. She is in bed all the time. Oh," she repeated, turning now to the Baroness, "she is so ill! And they will not let her see the child. I know it must be necessary, but is it not unbearably cruel?"

The Baroness asked. "Is the child all right?"

"Oh yes," answered the beautiful lady a little impatiently, in a tone of voice as though still speaking of something desperate, "the child is well."

The Baron said, "You will tell us all about it," and this was Dennis's moment to shake hands. He took the beautiful woman's in his, and she said before he could speak, "I didn't give Trent a chance to introduce us, did I? I am Stefanie von Hohenberge."

They drove on in the direction of Linz.

"That was Hedwig Behrendt's sister," said Melita, "the Countess Stefanie von Hohenberge," and she gave the lovely lady her title with unconcealed contempt.

"You know her?"

"I know of her," said Melita. "She is considered the most beautiful woman in Viennese society. But I think Hedwig Behrendt is more beautiful than her sister. They are really as alike as twins, only Stefanie's beauty is more flashy than Hedwig's. She paints her face, and all that. I suppose that's why she's famous for it."

"And that is why you prefer Hedwig's type of beauty."

Melita's smile was disagreeable. "Perhaps. But let me assure you," she went on, "like most women of her type, Stefanie von Hohenberge is a very superficial person."

"I don't believe it," said Dennis. "I suspect that she is merely human."

Fehge had no ears for what they were saying. Now they might have quarrelled for all she would have cared. She was completely immersed in her unproblematic memories of the beautiful, gentle lady.

Stefanie von Hohenberge was like the Madonna at the inn opposite the schoolhouse, and what could be more divine than that comparison? For the Virgin Mary was proving to be a far more peaceful haven for Fehge than the tortured Christ had ever been. She was beginning to forget her favourite *Marterl* on the track up Schwarzenberg and had learned to devote herself more and more to the Madonnas, as the other children did. The Madonna at the inn she loved best of all, and Stefanie von Hohenberge was like her.

Fehge was not far wrong. If a child had tried to paint a portrait of Stefanie, she might have achieved something like the Madonna at the inn, the same demure parting of the hair, the same oval face and gentle, gracious bend of the head, the same sweet smile that seemed to tell of pending sorrow, all very crudely executed. But for Fehge, whose artistic demands were not great, they were exactly alike. For her, the Blessèd Virgin had come to life.

Chapter Fourteen

AT Linz the Danube widens like a lake, and the green hills of the Bohemian woods can be seen in the distance. The city lies on one side of the Danube with the town of Urfahr on the other.

Fritz drove first to the Franz Joseph's Platz with its Plague

Column dating back to the eighteenth century. They were all practically alike, these lumpy baroque memorials that commemorated the victory over the great medieval plague in every Austrian community that could call itself a town, rising from the ground like a series of swellings, crowned by a Madonna and Child and backed by the golden rays of an imitation sun.

They had a rendezvous with Anton at the Restaurant zum Goldnen Löwe, thin, bony, gangling Anton, who looked like a Soviet poster come to life. Dennis and Fehge knew him. Melita spent her bad-weather week-ends with him in Vienna, and Anton spent the good-weather week-ends with Melita in the Vienna woods where they went on long walks or ski-ing tours, the length of which would have made a healthy man pause.

Anton had come to Linz the day before and had taken part in the torchlight parade on Saturday evening. "The mood is wonderful," he told them, his eyes sparkling, and Dennis thought, Their eyes glow for a thing like this as another man's for love.

In Linz today it was very evident that a large liberal party which was suffering under the slow choking embrace of reaction had met to spell defiance to the reactionaries, to the Black Ones, as they called them. The city was full to overflowing. Restaurants, hotels, boarding-houses, and private homes were full to the last bed and table. The streets were decorated with the red flags of the Socialists; the *Schutzbündler* were out in their uniforms, the police force had been augmented to keep order, for there was heavy traffic in the streets of Linz. The young folks passed each other, fist held high in a triumphant greeting, and Dennis, for the first time, heard the song of the Austrian worker:

> "*Wave, then, thou flag of fiery red,*
> *Wave at our long procession's head.*
> *Vienna workers all are we,*
> *Fighting for future liberty !*"

Here, too, Dennis thought, the stress lay on Vienna. There was, indeed, a discrepancy between that great city and its sparse frame of provinces. Austria had a population of six million, and Vienna's population alone was two million. Top-heavy. Statistics were at his finger-tips now, thanks to Melita. He looked at her as she strode beside him. Good girl. She had cheered up. He took her hand, and the colour shot up in her cheeks.

Fehge clung to Dennis's other hand. The many people who filled the streets looked friendly. They smiled as they raised their clenched fists and cried to one another a fine word, "Friendship!" But they were filled with that excitement which always tended to make Fehge afraid, whether it was expressed in jollity or anger.

"Why are they all here?" she asked, staring at them as they surged past. "Where are they going to?"

"They are going to hear a great man speak."

"A priest?"

"No," said Dennis, "a political leader. They are going to a political meeting."

He knew it could mean nothing to her. The question on her little upturned face with its wrinkled nose was therefore not unexpected. "What's that?" she asked.

He thought of answering, "Nothing you can understand yet, Button," but he had forbidden himself that formula. There must be a way, he had told himself a hundred times, to bring everything down to the level of ABC. So he said, "Strubl is a big place, isn't it? Who runs it?"

"Sister Andrea."

Dennis smiled but decided to let it go at that. No use complicating an already tough issue by telling her that those who made the most fuss weren't always the most important people. "Well," he went on, "a country has to be run just as Strubl has. The business of running a country is called politics. These people here are interested in having it run this way or that way. They meet to discuss it and to hear their leaders speak. That is called a political meeting."

She said, "And do they always get so excited about it?"

"Yes," he told her, "they do."

She nodded her head. It was comprehensible now in a vague sort of way.

They took Fehge to friends of the Bahrs. The woman was delighted to have another hand to help her with the preparations for the huge dinner she was giving that night to party members. They left a contented Fehge in the little kitchen that was crowded with an unaccustomed amount of food and people. It worried Dennis, as it always did, that Fehge never got a chance to play, didn't seem to know what play was, yet that was the way all the children here lived. It wasn't right, thought Dennis, as he went off to the meeting hall with Anton and Melita, and wondered why she never worried about that.

Dennis didn't pay much attention at first to what Otto Bauer was saying. His eyes roved about the festively decorated hall. Red, red, red—the revolutionary colours everywhere—and rows and rows of backs of heads in front of him. He thought of Fehge's question, "What are they all here for?" and tried to answer it for himself. For the material betterment of their existence, of course, like every other political group.

"You have never been poor." Melita's words came back to him. Did it make all that difference? He would never find out, and he regretted that fiercely. He could do with much less. But if you had always had less? Did it make a difference? If someone came who taught contentment with the same vehemence with which these leaders everywhere were teaching betterment, wouldn't the world be a better place to live in? Christ had done that long ago. Everyone shall be equally poor, not equally rich, He had said. But today His priests kindled no fires in the hearts of their listeners, as these political leaders did.

This man, now, who was speaking—Dennis knew a great deal about him, and could agree to a great extent with his ideas because he could follow what he was saying. But how many of his listeners could do that? Even those who agreed with him? How many of the world's workers could comprehend Marx? The theory was bound to get lost in the shuffle. And there lay the great pity. For it was the theory of socialism which led, logically, to the legislation of socialism, of which Dennis could so whole-heartedly approve. Take away man's comprehension of that, and what was left? The philosophy of socialism, a philosophy that had resulted in what he saw in Linz today—the movement of socialism. A materialistic movement. Of course. Its leaders might be as idealistic as the angels in heaven, but the effect on the masses out to influence legislation toward the material betterment of their lives had to be a materialistic one. Your goal inevitably puts its stamp on you. Not that it was wrong that people should agitate to the end that everybody be adequately housed and fed and occupied. What else was a government for but to see to that? But this economic fight for the material necessities of life should not become a personal creed. The creed of socialism. That was what made such inroads on a man's spirit. Socialism had become a way of life, a belief, a religion. And it did not suffice for that.

"The Viennese workers are in peril of mistaking the position of power in Austria with the position of power in Vienna," the speaker was saying.

Dennis looked sideways at Melita and met her glance. She nodded her head and pulled at Anton's sleeve. "I told you so" was written all over her face.

"We must make this Austria clear to ourselves *as it is*!" he cried. "We have in Austria a large city with the workers in a very powerful position. We have, around this city, several important industrial centres in which the workers are very strong and where in some cases they could be very much stronger! We must not forget that, apart from these large industrial centres, the greater part of Austria is agricultural. From that fact we must conclude that no government of the proletariat is possible if we are not able to capture stronger positions of power outside the big cities and industrial centres, in those quiet Alpine valleys and in the little towns scattered among them."

And then the speaker went on to give a concise definition of Austrian Social Democracy's aims.

"We have not won democracy in order to destroy it, but in order to shape it according to the needs of the working-class, to take away step by step the production apparatus from the capitalist and the big landowners. We will have to do it and we will do it *under complete maintenance of all those civic freedoms, freedom of speech and press and of assembly, which are the basis of any democracy!* We will fight the bourgeoisie with spiritual weapons, we will fight for the souls of the majority by democratic means; but if the bourgeoisie succeeds in destroying democracy, if we are not capable of hindering this destruction, then, I will say, the proletariat will have no choice left but to take the power by civil war! *But to the way of force, only our opponent can drive us!*"

At last! The opposition had something it could put its teeth into. A garbled version of the speech was pamphleteered by the Christian Socialists. "Bauer calls for civil war!" it was headlined on the following day. But that night in Linz the Social Democrats were obviously jubilant. Otto Bauer had promised them a fight if necessary, to defend their rights, and with that the leader had dispelled all nervous tension, at least momentarily.

The woman said to Fehge, "Mr. Behrendt's here already, so the meeting must be over. You'd better get ready. They'll be coming for you any time now."

She looked down at the little girl who had been such a willing and efficient helper all that day, and her smile was as affectionate as for her own children. She knew from Melita how Fehge had come to the valley and the circumstances under which she was being brought up. In Melita's telling, Andrea's influence on Fehge was paramount, Dennis's negligible, nothing more than the dot that topped the "i." The woman looking down at Fehge couldn't suppress the thought that a Prussian upbringing was something hard to beat.

Fehge went over to the sink and washed her hands and began to take off the apron which had been loaned to her by Mitzi, the daughter of the house. Mitzi had worked with Fehge all day and was now setting the table. She was a few years older than Fehge, and she had been friendly but very dull.

Just then the swinging door to the kitchen opened and a man entered the big old-fashioned room where utensils and furnishings had been handed down for several generations. Some of the pots and pans, Fehge had noticed, were worn very thin, but they were all as shiny as Andrea could have demanded. The man seemed to change his mind for a moment and, with half his big bulk in the kitchen, stuck his head back into the room he had just come from and said in a loud voice, "Just wait and see what the opposition will make of it! Bauer calls for civil war! I can see the headlines in tomorrow's papers!" After which prophetic words he let the door flap to and came into the room to them.

He was so impressive that Fehge stopped everything to stare at him, the apron she was about to hang up suspended in mid-air. He was elderly, and he walked in a slightly lop-sided fashion sideways, like a crab, his tall back hunched a bit. He looked pale and ill, and his eyes were strangely alive. He wore a moustache like a walrus's, but it in no way gave his face a comical appearance. No grotesqueness of body could mar the dignity which came from his soul. His nose was thick-set, his forehead high, and his sparse grey hair, once blond, looked as if it were never combed. His hands were powerful and very white.

"Moritz Behrendt," the woman cried, her face wreathed with smiles of welcoming delight. "Coming to look into all the pots as usual!"

Her greeting was unusually affectionate and a little strained because she was very anxious to help him to forget that on all his former visits to her house Hedwig had been with him. He, too, was trying to make this visit appear like any other. That was why he had come into the kitchen to sniff into the steaming pans on the stove and to be given a taste of this and that, as had been his wont.

But he stopped now on his way to the stove when he saw Fehge's solemn gaze fixed on him. "That is Fehge," the woman told him. "Melita Bahr brought her here to spend the day with us. She has been a great help."

Behrendt stretched out his hand. "*Grüss Gott*, Fehge," he said. She took it gravely. It was fleshy, but it gripped firmly.

He knew about her. Melita often spoke of her. "I always thought I'd see you up at Strubl," he said, "instead of which we meet here in Linz as though we were travelled people, which neither of us is," and his eyes twinkled in a way Fehge found very reassuring.

The woman was fiddling with a black money-purse. Now she took a shiny *Schilling* piece out of it. "Here," she said, as she handed it to Fehge. "I want you to buy yourself something you like with that," and she added, "for being such a good girl."

Fehge looked down at the coin in her pink palm, at the money that was supposed to mean so much to the members of her race. She could not see what it had to do with her good behaviour.

Behrendt put his hands behind his back and looked down at her from his great height. "What are you going to do with it?"

She looked up at him solemnly and said, "I don't know."

He threw back his head and laughed and laughed. "What a classic answer!" he spluttered. Neither the woman nor Fehge could fathom what amused him so.

Then he stopped laughing abruptly, patted Fehge on the head a little clumsily, and said, "It will be interesting to see how this little girl develops away from the bitter handicaps of her racial heritage."

Then the woman thought she knew what had made Behrendt laugh, but Fehge remained completely at sea. Behrendt gave her a final, lingering look. She was going to be a beautiful woman. Her skin was a lovely olive shade, her face a perfect oval. Her eyebrows grew in one solid black curve with dark stray hairs forming a smooth shadow beneath them. Her lashes were so black, and the eyes so dark brown, that the white shone like enamel. The line from chin to neck was delicately curved, like that of the Egyptian queen, Nefretete, the coloured lithographs of whose exotic head hung nowadays in every middle-class home that made any pretence to culture. Yes, Behrendt thought, she could easily have passed for an Egyptian. He found her extremely interesting.

When the three called for Fehge, Dennis met Moritz Behrendt, who endeared himself to Dennis in the very brief conversation they enjoyed together by talking of nothing but Fehge. Melita was agog to discuss the Bauer speech, but was not able to get them off the subject of the orphaned Jewish child who was being brought up in a Catholic community by a Prussian deaconess. "If nothing comes of that!" Behrendt cried. The man was a tower of personality, Dennis thought as they drove through the night, a great, all-round person. What a discrepancy lay between the man and his followers!

The drive home was not without incident. They were taking Anton with them as far as St. Pölten, from where he would get a train to Vienna. The car was closed. Dennis had asked Fritz to put up its antiquated hood because the autumn night was cold. Anton sat in front beside Fritz, and Dennis bedded Fehge with her head on his shoulder and her legs stretched out behind Melita. Fehge pretended to fall asleep right away. What she really did was dream what she had been dreaming all the day long, between kitchen smells and the smoke of an overfilled restaurant—the dream of the beautiful lady who had said her name was Stefanie von Hohenberge. But when they passed again through the village at the foot of Trent's castle, Fehge was really fast asleep.

The castle was lit up and looked more than ever like the backdrop for a Christmas pantomime. But the village was ablaze too, with the fitful light of torches brandished by a crowd of young men. By their light it was easy to make out that the atmosphere was not gay, but belligerent.

Many Social Democrats had passed through that day on their way to Linz, and now were passing through on their way home. Here they had evidently come to blows. The sound of a brawl could be heard from the inn and a crowd had collected outside. Their car was forced to a standstill.

Anton was about to get out. "Don't!" implored Melita. "Don't get mixed up in it!" She remembered and added, "It's a Nazi meeting."

The *Heimwehr* men, recognizable by the light green of their uniforms and the dark green glistening cock's feather in their green caps, the Social Democrats' *Schutzbündler* in blue-green, their chauffeur-like cap with its visor, and a few young men wearing high boots, brown breeches, and brown shirts open at the neck, but otherwise with no marks of identification whatsoever, were in

the crowd outside the inn, and the inn itself was spewing forth
more of them until, a moment later, the doorway gaped empty.
Then a tall figure dressed in the *loden* green of the hunter appeared.
It was the Baron. In his hand he held a flag without a stick, which
he let drag on the ground. He uttered no word, and the crowd, too,
was silent. A silence fell over the entire square like the hush which
must have fallen before the guillotine's knife.

It woke Fehge. Through heavy lids, her big sleep-blurred eyes
began to see. Her mouth dropped open. None of them in the car,
she least of all, could make out from that distance what the flag was.

The Baron parted the crowd easily and strode over to his car.
He had to go round theirs to reach it. They did nothing to attract
his attention; they had lost their identity, as had everyone else on
the square in the dramatic impact of the moment.

The crowd closed in again behind the Baron, and now all eyes
were turned away from the inn toward the cars. The Baron walked
to the back of his. They could see his face, and never had Dennis
seen a man so white with rage and misery. By the flag's own cord
he attached it to the back of his car and then got into the driver's
seat. He had come alone. Now he started the car, and the flag
began to unfurl as it dragged in the dirt, and thus, for the first
time, Dennis and Fehge saw the swastika. Fehge stared at the
crooked cross as it sprawled, then curled up and disappeared in a
cloud of dust.

The crowd, now galvanized again into action, began to move,
to rumble, to roar. The *Heimwehr* men were cheering "their"
hero.

The *Schutzbündler* were silent, chagrined that it had taken a
Heimwehr man to break up the Nazi meeting. One damned
aristocrat without a weapon had done what they had been unable
to do, although they had outnumbered the enemy! He had walked
up to the platform, had pushed aside the speaker so that he had
toppled and fallen ignominiously off the edge, and told them to get
out, fast.... That was all. And they had got out. Shame. Shame
on them! The *Schutzbündler* stood silent, neither cheering nor
belligerent. But the young men wearing the khaki breeches and

the brown shirts open at the neck who had been ejected from their meeting, whose flag the Baron was trailing in the dirt, bellowed in their rage now that the strong man was gone, and shook their fists in the direction he had taken.

Their faces, red in the torchlight, all looked alike to Fehge. Then suddenly, in the front ranks, close to her, she saw Conrad, his features distorted by hatred and frustration.

She recognized at once the face she would never forget. It had come at last. He had come back. "Ow," she yelled, at the top of her lungs, with the pitiful wail of a hurt child. "Ow! Ow! Ow!"

"What is it?" said Dennis. "What's the matter?" And to the chauffeur he said, "Get us out of here, will you? The child's frightened."

Fehge had covered her face with her hands. "What is it, little one?" he asked her.

"Him," sobbed Fehge. "I saw him. I didn't ever want to see him again. I'm so afraid of him."

"Of whom?" said Dennis, first to her, then, since he got no answer, to Melita. "Of whom? Whom did she see?"

"I don't know," said Melita. "I don't know whom she saw."

The village, the lights, the belligerent cries were gone. With a few last sobs, Fehge fell asleep again. She hiccoughed once or twice, then lay still.

They drove through the starry night. The milky way was as light as any moon. Nobody mentioned the incident in the village until Dennis said, "What flag was that?"

"That," said Melita, "was the swastika flag of the National Socialists." Silence fell, then she said, "It was a rather wonderful thing he did, wasn't it?"

"Who?" said Anton.

"The Baron." Silence. "And without a weapon."

"He had a weapon," said Dennis. "His assurance." But they didn't seem to want to argue.

They dropped Anton and cut straight into the Vienna woods to their backwater.

Melita's head was leaning against the back of the seat. Now she let it fall to one side and looked up at him. Their eyes had grown accustomed to the lack of light. "Oh, Dennis," she said, "I love you."

His hand shot out to cover hers, and he crushed it hard. He was sorry, sorry till it hurt him. This was what he had always been afraid of. Why hadn't he seen it coming? Because he had been so preoccupied with side-issues, because he had let himself be diverted from his goal and become careless of absorbing encroachments.

Melita took his hand and held it up in the soft, warm groove of her neck, and then she kissed it. Still he held hers tight and said nothing. Fehge stirred. Melita had forgotten her and was leaning too heavily on her little legs. And then they were at the schoolhouse. Melita got out and was gone, and Fritz drove on.

When they arrived at Strubl, Dennis lifted Fehge out of the car. Andrea was up. That didn't surprise him. She would martyr herself like that. He could easily have put the child to bed. But Sapponyi was up too. That did surprise him. "I want to talk to you," said the doctor. Dennis handed the sleeping child over to a tight-lipped Andrea and followed Sapponyi into his office, sensing disaster.

Sapponyi handed him a telegram. "Come home at once. Father not well. Poor darling. Meg."

"Poor darling." How like Meg! He tried hard to take the immense jump out of the world that was Strubl back into the world that was his father's. Father. Not well. It was difficult. He must try again. Father. Not well. Was Meg trying to spare him?

Meg had wanted to spare him. When she had sent the cable his father was already dead. It hadn't been influenza the winter before, either, but double pneumonia, and his heart had given out.

Dennis was free. From the fine old house on Clapham Common he looked around him. Strubl and everything he had experienced there seemed like an agitated dream. He couldn't imagine that he would ever go back. He was cured. He felt confidence in his newly acquired health. Now the life he had always longed for should begin.

At his departure Fehge fell again into the mundane groove which had been hers before he had taken her out of it. Work flowed in and filled the time-space his going away left free. And with the return to normal of her daily life the animosity of the villagers began to ebb, and as the years went by she became one of them, until a strange event again uprooted her.

Chapter Fifteen

EARLY in the following spring, something happened that was to have a decisive influence on Fehge's life.

It was night, and third-floor Hilda was in bed. She was not alone. Conrad was with her, and they were very quiet. The moonlight cast a restless pattern through the lace curtain. This was the moment when Conrad felt elated beyond measure and wanted to talk, and Hilda wanted to lie still and think. Nothing made the mind as clear as what had gone before, thought Hilda, as she felt the sweat drying cold on her body.

"Hilly," Conrad whispered, "you have no idea what's going on in the Reich and what's going to happen here, to us, when the Führer's ready. . . ."

"*Mmmm*," mumbled Hilda.

"When it does, will you marry me?"

Hilda laughed, and Conrad said, "Sh!"

"Marry you," the girl said contemptuously. "You greenhorn!" And she let her hand, which was lying peacefully above his head, drop down on his shaggy hair and ruffle it.

"I'll be a great man, you'll see."

"The Baron said that all of you tramps who are running over there now won't ever be any different."

"You've been talking!"

"And what if I have? A girl like me wants to talk to somebody intelligent once in a while."

She was justified in what she said. Hilda's intelligence was far above that of the average servant girl. She had been born on a farm in Styria thirty years ago. Only the oldest son had stayed on the farm and brought his wife to live there with him. The other boys and girls, Hilda included, had wandered away, Hilda with the ambition in her soul to "see the world."

First she had been a maid in a big hotel in Vienna. Right from the start she had earned money on the side by the generosity of her large, handsome body. One day a bank director had wanted to take her with him on a holiday trip to the Dolomites. Here was her chance!

She let him buy her the appropriate clothes and a fine suitcase of pigskin leather, then they set off together.

When they reached the Italian border at Tarvis and the train stood still in the noonday heat, and she saw the alien customs officials and heard the strange language, panic seized her. She looked at her fleshy companion with his oriental features. Suddenly he, too, seemed very strange. "Excuse me," she said politely, and tried to smile as though nothing were wrong.

She took her handbag and retired to the toilet. The train was letting off steam and the milky-glass window was half open at the top. She could look out, and she saw the Austrian colours, red, white, red, on the customs shield, and the Austrian officers talking leisurely to the Italian peasant women waiting with bundles. She tried to compose herself, but she did not succeed. Terror gripped her heart at the thought of leaving her native land and entering foreign territory. The conductor called, "All aboard," and raised his staff with the disc at its end. Hilda quietly opened the door of the toilet and walked down the steps to its right on to the platform.

The door of the carriage closed behind her, and she walked away from the train as it drew away from her, her back turned to it determinedly, her steps none too steady. She couldn't help thinking of the pigskin-leather suitcase and all the fine things it contained.

Then she shrugged her shoulders contemptuously and said aloud to herself, "What matter! I'll get them again."

And so she did, but not in Vienna. When she got back to that city she was deflated. She could not have returned on the resources of her handbag alone, but a man at the ticket-office helped her out in exchange for ten fleeting minutes in a little back room behind the ticket-office. She looked at the city with eyes freshly re-accustomed to the green countryside and mountain scenery. She appreciated Vienna, but the air was flat in the city when compared with the air she had been breathing during the last few hours, and she suddenly realized that what she wanted more than anything else was bucking up, physically, by fresh country air. But how was she to see the world if she went back to rural life?

An advertisement in the *Wiener Journal* gave her the answer. She presented her buxom, red-headed self and got the position as third-floor maid at Strubl. There she had been for six years now, and she loved it. Strubl did everything for her she wanted. She could breathe the fresh country air and go for long mountain hikes on her free days, which she did. Not a track for miles around was strange to her, and her strong, stout legs carried her tirelessly from valley to summit and down again with long hours of lying naked in the sun in between.

Serving at Strubl was better than seeing the world; here the world came to you. She had learnt what she wanted to know from every foreign visitor, and had repaid in her way. Andrea sensed what went on behind her austere back, but speak of it to Sapponyi? That she couldn't do! There were certain things that were un-mentionable. If only Hilda would betray herself! But Hilda never did Andrea the favour of indiscretion. She was at Strubl to stay.

Conrad's ignorance and uncouthness bored her. She pushed his seeking hand away. "Stop it," she said, turning away from him. "I want to rest."

She was in love with the Baron, had been ever since his first stay at Strubl years ago. This did not prevent her from enjoying herself with other men; the one had nothing to do with the other.

But she loved the Baron, and she loved the way she loved him. She cherished her feelings for him as the "finest" emotion in her. It was selfless and patient and oh, so romantic! He had gone, but he would come again. Meanwhile she could catch glimpses of him when she visited her friend Mina, who was on his staff at the castle.

There she was, enjoying the love of an eighteen-year-old boy and dreaming of a sixty-year-old man. Age didn't make any difference to her. What she wanted were the finer things of life. The Baron had said once that she was a patriot. That was when she had told him the story of her escape from the bank director. She had never looked at it that way. The sight of a foreign land had scared her. Did that make her a patriot? She kept a large picture of Otto von Hapsburg on her dresser and flowers in front of it. Did that make her a monarchist? Perhaps. But she had put the photograph there because Otto was such a pretty boy. That was all.

"What are you talking about?" she asked Conrad suddenly.

"I'm not talking," he said sullenly.

"I mean, what you were saying a while ago."

"I was telling you about the wonderful things that were going to happen to us . . . soon."

"What sort of things?"

"We're going to be a part of the Reich."

Hilda turned on her elbow. "What? And that's what you want?"

"That's what I'm going to work for."

"You dog! You pig-dog!" she hissed at him. "Belong to the Reich! Be run by a lot of bloody Prussians like our Andrea here! Have to work and slave and keep our noses to the ground! No, sir! Not me! Get out of my bed!"

Conrad was livid. He was going to be believed in, by God! No Austrian slut was going to desecrate his beliefs like that. He grabbed her wrist and wrenched her to him, hurting her. "You wait," he said. "When the day comes, you'll be glad to marry me! You'll go down on your knees! You will!"

Hilda didn't want a scene. At once she acquiesced to him, and his last words died in his throat.

But their argument had wakened Fehge. She could hear the man's voice and Hilda's, protesting. Hilda was in trouble.

Fehge sat up in bed. Hilda was in trouble. Hilda, who on her free days took Fehge into the hills, along tracks that she could never have found alone, who showed her which berries to pick and which to leave alone, which mushrooms were good to eat and which poisonous, who showed her how to sun herself so that she would get no burn, how to bathe in the lake near the summit where the water was rusty brown from the iron pyrites in the rocks, who told her the names of the trees and ferns and wild flowers, who had shown her the carpet of lilies-of-the-valley in the glen where they had both thrown themselves face downward in ecstasy and lain until the scent had made them headachy—Hilda, her big, generous Hilda, who let her snuggle up close to her in bed sometimes, in the early morning, whose body was warm and soft and ample, not hard and bony and cold like Andrea's—Hilda was in trouble.

Fehge slipped out of bed and walked to Hilda's room, which lay diagonally opposite hers. She listened outside the closed door. She could hear muffled sounds, as of a sinister struggle. Somebody is choking her, thought Fehge. She turned white, and the sweat of fear stood out on her smooth, round forehead. Taking a deep breath, with the strength that is born of fear she opened the door and entered the room.

She had been quite right. Somebody was choking Hilda, somebody was trying to kill her. "*Ah!*" screamed Fehge, "*ahh, ahh, ahh!*" Then she covered her wide-open mouth with both hands because the sound of her own screams frightened her.

The man leaped down from the bed, and by the light of the moon she could see that it was Conrad.

Hilda was sitting up in bed, holding the sheet across her shoulders, her head down, shaking it as though awakening out of a bad dream. Then she turned and saw Fehge and said, "You little fool!"

She looked as though she were about to cry with rage, but she didn't. Instead, she threw herself back in the dishevelled pillows and began to laugh silently, her shoulders, her breasts, heaving under the white covers.

Conrad bared his teeth so that his lips disappeared; and Fehge, seeing the expression on his face, backed. But he was between her and the open door. There was no escape. She ached all over with fear.

He stretched out his long arm and grabbed her at the nape of the neck and stepped aside, holding her. With one hard push he threw her out of the room. She fell and slid across the narrow corridor to hit the opposite wall, where she lay still. She had suffered a slight concussion and she fainted.

"You fool!" Hilda said to Conrad, sitting up again in alarm. "What did you have to go and do that for?"

Andrea and Rosl, the waitress in the room opposite, heard the dull thud in the corridor. They both came running out of their rooms, into the passage. Andrea, with a low moan, picked up Fehge and held her in her arms.

Hilda jumped out of bed, closed the door to her room, and locked it. "See that you get out of here," she hissed at Conrad, pointing with her head to his clothes.

He began to scramble into them. "How do you expect me to get out with those hyenas in the hall?"

"Out of the window and across the roof and down the balconies. You've done it before. Don't make out you're stupider than you are!"

There was a knock at the door.

"Who is it?"

"Sister Andrea. Open the door. I want to talk to you."

"It can wait till the morning," said Hilda vehemently. "I'm not on duty now."

Hilda and Conrad listened, without moving, to hear what reaction this remark would bring. For a moment there was no sound on the other side of the door, then they could hear Andrea's light steps moving away.

Conrad was dressed. He made as though to embrace Hilda in

farewell, but she shook him off. "Haven't you made enough trouble already?" she said.

His face darkened. "What do you mean, haven't I made trouble? You haven't had anything to do with it, I suppose? Who started me coming up here anyway? You did! You! Wearing your dresses so low a man can see your guts!"

"Go on," she said. "Get out! I'm sick to death of you!"

Conrad, balked and enraged, made and unmade fists of his hands. "You'll be sorry," he said. "I'll make you pay for this!" He swung out of the window.

Hilda's lips curled contemptuously. The stupid Nazi!

She waited until there was no sound. Then she walked over to the window and leaned out, her elbows on the sill. There was a full moon. The warm night breeze fanned her cheeks and moved her hair. She breathed deeply. What a beautiful night!

She moved away from the window and found some bread and cheese in a cupboard she used for food. With it she went back to the window and began to eat. She cut a piece of bread, put a large piece of cheese on it, and ate stolidly. Poor Fehge, she thought suddenly, poor, silly, little thing!

Conrad crouched for a while in the eaves until his eyes grew accustomed to the moonlight. That didn't take long. When you looked away from the few lights cast from the windows, it was as bright as day.

The cool night air was pleasant on his forehead. It stirred in his hair. He felt calm now, and a little tired. He could see the undulating mountain-line as clearly as though it had been drawn by a sharp pencil. He loved it. It was home. He had seen a lot of the Bavarian Alps during his stay in Munich, but this very line of hills was his.

He began the descent, like some quiet jungle animal. On the third floor he paused. He had come to a ticklish spot. The balcony next to the one on which he was standing, the first one of the three that jutted forward, was partly lit by a lamp in the room. Whoever was in there was awake. And he had to pass across it. Adroitly he got up on the sill of the balcony's railing and stepped with his long, lithe legs on to the railing of the adjacent balcony, which did not project forward sufficiently to make this step difficult, unless one were inclined to be dizzy, which Conrad was not. The craggy summits of mountains had often confronted him with far more dangerous situations than this.

He lowered himself from the railing to the floor, keeping well in a rectangular space that was dark, and slowly moved his head forward until he could see into the room through its closed glass door.

The patient was not in bed, but was apparently preparing to go to sleep, for she was taking off her jewels and putting them one by one on the dressing-table next to the door. A diamond bracelet, wider than any he had ever seen. Diamond earrings. A brooch that glistened and . . . one . . . two . . . three . . . four rings. And a wrist-watch that sparkled too. Holy Mother of Jesus!

The woman was fat and ugly and dark, and her dress was black and plain, Conrad thought, with a queer, crooked neckline. He could not, of course, know that it had been bought at the Salon de Mainbocher in Paris a few months ago. The lady's finger-nails were long and blood-red. Conrad had never seen such nails in his life before. They revolted him. He looked up again, at the lady's swarthy face. A Jewess, undoubtedly, he thought, and was wrong. The patient was the lady from Bombay, the Begum Neguchi-Sah, a full-blooded Hindu and Aryan—in fact, the only Aryan in Strubl and vicinity. Conrad could see the caste mark on her forehead and mistook it for a scar.

A Jewess, of course, with all that jewellery! Stolen from the poor, hard-working Aryans! And at once, and most naturally, Conrad became determined that this jewellery should return to its rightful owner, symbolically speaking—himself. That was only fair and just, according to his schooling.

With growing impatience he watched the "Jewess" undress. But she did not get into bed. She put on a shiny lavender velvet gown with wide sleeves, sat down and began to rub creams and lotions on her face and rub them off again, for fully twenty minutes.

God! What was she doing it for? If he were totally out of luck, she'd even read when she was in bed. The Jews had their noses in books all the time.

He thought of risking the drop down to the dark balcony directly below him, the balcony of a room that was occupied . . . and let the Jewess defeat him? No. He would wait until she was asleep if he had to wait all night.

At last the "Jewish whore" was ready to go to bed. She came toward the glass door of the balcony and opened it, pushing it out and back until it shut Conrad into the triangle formed by door, railing, and back wall. She could not see him, of course. She was in the light and he in the dark. Besides, she was looking straight ahead, into the moonlight, at "his" mountains. She breathed deeply, laid a hand on her big bosoms and murmured something in a language he couldn't understand. Hebrew, he thought, and was wrong again. She was saying in Gujrati, which is almost pure Sanskrit, "What a beautiful night." Then she went back into the room and got into bed.

Would she read? She picked up a book, passed a hand over her beautiful big brown eyes into which Conrad had never looked, groped for something . . . her glasses . . . she had forgotten to take them to bed with her.

She looked toward the dressing-table where they were lying. Conrad could not know that she was wishing herself back in Bombay, where one could have many servants because a majority of the population had not yet been taught to despise the profession of waiting on another person as something unworthy of human-kind. The Begum was, of course, a reactionary. She leaned back on her pillows and closed her eyes. Her hands groped for the light and put it out.

Conrad waited until he could hear the woman's heavy breathing, almost a snore. He had hardly to enter the room to take the jewellery, which he pocketed. Then he turned slowly and quietly to go the way he had come, when the lady from Bombay woke up. She saw a man in the doorway and screamed.

Had Sepp, the head gardener, not been making love to one of

the kitchen-maids up at Strubl that night and been on his stealthy way back to his own quarters, Conrad might have been able to make his escape. But the Begum screamed, and Sepp looked up just as Conrad's figure appeared over the edge of the balcony, about to jump, and the man-hunt was on. Sepp shouted to Hannes, who slept downstairs, and Hannes rang the alarm.

The Begum snapped on her light, and other lights began to go on. . . . *Tick . . . tick . . . tick . . .* one little beacon after the other streamed out of the side of the house that had been shrouded in darkness a moment ago. They were poor little searchlights, not penetrating far into the night, but they proved to be a devilish handicap to the fleeing Conrad. His way back up was blocked by one. He swerved and started to clamber across, to the right, and stumbled into another light. The patients began to appear on their balconies in their dressing-gowns. Now there were people as well as lights to avoid. There was someone on the roof. Damn it! Fritz's voice crying "Give in! I have a gun!" Then Hannes's voice from a first-floor balcony. "Stand still! Hands up! Or I'll shoot!"

Conrad was unarmed, but he didn't give up so tamely. There were still plenty of dark spots. There was still hope.

The alarm had never sounded for a burglar before. In Sapponyi's room and in Andrea's it had rung often, but only for medical emergencies, a low, burring buzz, and a light flickering on and off behind milk glass.

That was what Sapponyi thought it was now—a medical emergency. As he got hastily into his white coat he wondered who it might be. He could think of no one. But then, in this incalculable disease, a haemorrhage might start at any time. . . . The X-ray plate couldn't show everything.

Andrea had put Fehge in her bed and was sitting up waiting for her to awaken. The child had vomited once, without really regaining consciousness. But now her colour was normal, and she was breathing evenly in sleep. Andrea thought she would be all right when she awoke, but she wanted to be there when Fehge opened her eyes. After all, the poor little thing had been through something horrible. Andrea's eyes were full of compassion when she thought of it.

She was dozing in her chair when the buzzer woke her. She thought, as Sapponyi had done, that a patient had been taken seriously ill. She got into her things and was fastening her uniform and her hood, which had a tiny, irritating button and eyelet at the back, as she hurried across to Rosl's room. The girl would be angry to be awakened again. But the child mustn't wake up alone.

Andrea knocked on Rosl's door. When the sleepy girl answered it, Andrea ordered her to Fehge's bedside. But in this world she lived in, nobody would do anything for nothing; she knew that. So she said, "You want your vacation week moved forward, don't you? I shall see that you get it. You do this for me in return," and Rosl, who did want her vacation time changed, said she'd be glad to.

Andrea and Sapponyi met in the big first-floor hall and found themselves in a madhouse. The patients who were afraid to watch from their balconies where the hunt was on were standing fearful in the halls. Andrea was told there was a burglar at large. "But not a trace of it," she said, so firmly that everyone except those who had seen the hunted man dart through a light believed her. Now she began hustling everyone back to his room. Sapponyi went to his office and got his gun out of a locked drawer.

It was Hannes who finally ambushed Conrad on the roof of the rest-cure hall, from which he could easily have jumped down to freedom had the house not by then been surrounded by the armed male staff. The boy had been all the way up and down the building and twice across it. He was exhausted and his breath came raspingly. His wet clothes were torn, his eyes bulged, his veins stood out blue, and his hands were trembling and bleeding.

They took him into the office where Sapponyi was waiting after telephoning to the Lamb for the *gendarmes*. He took the jewellery from Conrad and returned it to the Begum via Andrea, who gave Conrad a look of utter contempt that would have withered him had he been susceptible to disparagement from anyone but Hilda. As it was, he didn't even see her. He wasn't seeing anything just then. He was trying to catch his breath.

Then they sat and waited for the *gendarmes* to come, Sapponyi in his chair behind his desk with his gun in his hands, his head shaking a little. He was getting old. Conrad slumped sullenly in the armchair on the other side of the desk. Diagonally behind Sapponyi was the window.

Fritz and Hannes walked restlessly in and out of the doorway, stopping to talk now and then in whispers. What occupied them most was what Schreiner would have to say to this. They were excitedly pleased that he was going to be hurt.

The *gendarmes* took their time. An hour passed, and not a word was spoken. Sapponyi told the men to go to bed, but they wouldn't leave him. He said they might smoke, but they were reluctant to break so traditional a rule. "Go ahead," said Sapponyi. "This is an unusual occasion."

Where could the *gendarmes* be ? Sapponyi shrugged his shoulders and laughed contemptuously as he thought of all that could happen before this superlative police force could be brought into action. Rotten. Like everything in Austria's civil service. It hadn't been different under the Emperor, it had never been different, only the force of crime had never been so strong.

The atmosphere was getting drowsy. Suddenly, like a flash of lightning, Conrad leaped for the window, smashed it, and was half-way through it—the Jew, he thought, can't shoot straight, and the others had put away their weapons—when Sapponyi aimed low and fired. Conrad yelped and fell back into the room, and the blood began to trickle down his leg.

Sapponyi swallowed hard to choke down the tremendous upsurge of satisfaction that this shot had given him. Not because he had hit precisely where he had intended to, in the boy's leg, but because he had wounded Conrad Schreiner. He had not participated in the last war; he had preferred and been permitted to build and run a lazaret for the wounded. He had never drawn the blood of a human being before except with healing intent. And now . . . this. . . . Times had changed. Now, he realized, he wanted to hurt. Why? What was happening in this world to change one so fundamentally? Oh, he could find a hundred answers to that question, but his train of thought was interrupted by an idea which seemed to be imposed on him from outside. Hurt, it said, is not enough. . . . Kill! He should have shot Conrad Schreiner through the heart. Then he would have been doing the world a service. But he was not the man who could react that way. Not yet. Perhaps not ever.

Fehge woke up a few minutes after Andrea had left, and found Rosl seated at her bedside. "There," said the spry little waitress, "you feel better now, don't you?"

Rosl had to laugh again at the little innocent, as she had done off and on ever since it had happened. When she laughed, her face looked as old as she was, forty, but in repose her face was like a young girl's, so well preserved was Rosl.

Rosl was a very shrewd woman. She managed to get a great deal out of the men she went with, and the villagers said she saved every penny of it and was going to buy herself an inn, and that she would marry the young man she was going with steady now, not because she loved him, but because he was hardy and docile and would do the work of ten men, and that, at the inn she was going to buy, would come in handy. No one ever got much from her. Who ever had? Wasn't she sitting beside Fehge now, not out of kindness, but because Andrea had promised to get for her the vacation time she wanted, and she wanted it then when the innkeeper Grabautschnik took his? He was going to take her to Aussee with him, and she was counting on that trip to teach her a few things.

Fehge looked at Rosl timidly. Then, as memory of what had brought her low came back, her lips drooped and she began to shiver.

"Whatever possessed you to rush in on them like that?" guffawed Rosl mercilessly. "You little fool!"

Fehge looked down at her trembling fingers that were bending a hem in the top of the sheet. "I wanted to help Hilda," she said in a voice that was a whisper. "I thought he was killing her. He was right on top of her."

Rosl's shrieks of laughter drowned out all further sound. "Of course he was, you idiot!" she shrieked, amid splutters of mirth. "And she likes it!"

Under ordinary circumstances, Conrad would have been given a year's imprisonment for attempted burglary, but the Jewish judge who presided at the trial at Wiener-Neustadt gave him two. He did this in consideration of the fact that Conrad had burgled a sanatorium, that was to say, a house of the sick, as casually as though it had been a hotel. It made the offence doubly heinous.

There was something in the judge's decision too. The shock had been a setback to more patients than one, and affected practically all of them in a peculiar way. They had slept peacefully with their balcony doors wide open throughout the years. Suddenly, in spite of the fact that they had seen the burglar caught, they began to fear his return and wanted their doors closed at night. Sapponyi had to smile. What a psychological quirk! Not until Sapponyi hired a night watchman and bought a watch-dog did they begin to sleep with their balcony doors open again, which was so important for their sick lungs.

The first watch-dog turned out to be a failure, not because she wasn't vicious enough. She was a belligerent bitch with the Germanic name of Ute (pronounced "Oo-tay"), a Doberman Pinscher; but she became so attached to Fehge, who, it must be admitted, wooed her on the sly, that she whined at night to be permitted to go to the girl. So Sapponyi gave Ute to Fehge for a present and bought another dog who, Fehge was told, she should please leave alone, because not if he howled his head off would she get the police-dog, Bruno. Sapponyi would shoot him first.

But Fehge was satisfied and happy to have Ute, who would protect her from Conrad, for, however long two years may seem to a nine-year-old child, Fehge was no ordinary child. She had vision, and she knew that the two years would pass and he would come back.

Chapter Sixteen

*T*HIS *is my body. This is my blood. Do this for a commemoration of me.*

Fehge received her first Holy Communion in the late spring of the year 1928. Had she not wanted so intensely to grasp religion with her mind as well as her heart, she might have received it immediately following her baptism, at the correct age of eight; but Fehge had not been able to accept blindly, and it had taken these two years to prepare her for the sacrament. The priest, for instance, had had quite a tussle with her over the Holy Trinity. Did not the first commandment order her to adore one God alone? "But the Holy Trinity is not three gods," the priest told her, "it is three in one."

"In God there is but one spirit," he went on patiently, "but three Divine Persons, the Father, the Son and the Holy Ghost." And, finally, in concession to the unfathomable, "We cannot understand these great truths. They are too great for our minds. We believe them because God has told them to us."

With a sigh, Fehge gave in. And, looking about her at the vastness of the universe which God had made, she had to admit that His creative mind had realized more than hers could comprehend, more, apparently, than even the mind of the priest could fathom. From then on things were easier for the priest.

Her schoolmates who stood beside her at the altar for the ceremony were all the right age. Fehge towered over them by several inches and seemed to be their leader. To her right stood the frail Leitner Annie, to her left the dark, rosy-cheeked Pfeiffer's Serafine. The others were Moser's Creszentia, Luckner's Walter, and Postl's grandson, Stefan, who was always called the Postl Stefan after his grandfather, not the Winzl Stefan after his father, who was no good.

Fehge's full, ecstatic appreciation of her first acceptance of the Body and Blood of Christ was somewhat marred by the fact that she had to share it with these others. She could not completely lose the feeling of being hemmed in by them.

Dennis knew about Fehge's first communion through Sapponyi, with whom he corresponded about his health, but no letter of his arrived without inquiries for the girl, and Sapponyi answered them as thoroughly as he replied to questions of health, because he knew Dennis was as interested in Fehge as in his delicate lungs, and so was Sapponyi.

Last Christmas Dennis had sent money for a bicycle for Fehge, and Fehge had written to thank him. Andrea had said that that was what one must do.

Fehge did not miss Dennis. For that she had no time. But as she had taken pencil in hand on that bright New Year's Day, a phrase had come to her mind which she would have liked to use. "Dearly Beloved," she wanted to address him on the cheap square-lined paper Andrea had put at her disposal. "Dearly Beloved," as she had so often addressed him and he her, as the man in the book that they had read together had addressed the little girl he told his stories to. But Dennis had never thought of telling her how to spell the words, and about phonetics she knew nothing. Andrea, noting the hesitation with which she held her pencil, thought, quite unjustly, that she was too stupid to compose her own note of thanks and told her what to write, and as stilted a letter had resulted as any little German girl could ever have concocted. Now Dennis sent five English pounds for Fehge to "buy herself a pretty dress and have her picture taken."

Fehge wanted to have her picture taken as she had been dressed for Communion, but Sapponyi said no, and Andrea said no, too. She didn't want to see Fehge dressed up as a little bride of Jesus again. So Sapponyi told Andrea to take a convenient day off and go with Fehge to Wiener-Neustadt and attend to the matter. He gave her the money. "Why, it's a fortune!" gasped Andrea. And for what? Such frivolity!

Four-fifths of the money she put away for the child, and with the equivalent of one English pound in her purse she set out one fine day with Fehge for Wiener-Neustadt.

They drove down to Pritnitz with Franz in the freight cart early in the morning. All three sat up on the long front seat, Fehge between them, subdued as she always was with Andrea. Andrea wore the black alpaca hood with the hemstitch edging over her starched white one. Fehge looked at it every now and then and thought how pretty it was. Andrea's dress was becoming, like the priest's. A costume. It must be fun to be dressed differently from everybody else, dressed up especially for God.

They were half an hour early for the train, but Andrea needed that half-hour for a dressing-down she was to give Keppler. This was a mission she enjoyed. What had the slovenly Austrian done? One of the patients, a student of medicine, had ordered a bookcase from Keppler. As the only carpenter in Pritnitz, he sometimes did jobs like that too, less lugubrious than his usual fare of making coffins. The doctor had designed the case herself, and Keppler had carried out the measurements exactly, had stained and varnished the wood, and a good job it was when done. He had delivered the bookcase on the same day as a coffin. His only unpardonable error lay in the fact that he had put the bills in the wrong envelopes! Thus the young "Miss Doctor of Medicine," still bedridden and not yet over the shock of knowledge of her ailment, got a bill for a metal-lined, embossed coffin—one hundred and sixty *Schillinge*! It had been a great shock to her; but Sapponyi, hardly able to suppress a grin of amusement, had brought her round to the point where she, too, could laugh about it. However, with Keppler he was furiously angry and had given Andrea the welcome task of scolding the man.

Fehge said she would like to call on her friend Julie while Andrea went to see Keppler, and Andrea said she might, adding the disparaging remark, "What can you see in that idiot?"

Andrea emerged from her interview highly stimulated and feeling more cheerful than she had for weeks. It was a perfect day, and she had the child she loved with her.

The Gfrerrer Inn was on the way to the station. As she came to it, the two girls were already at the gate. "*Grüss dich*," Fehge said to Julie as she gave Andrea her hand.

Julie looked down to shut out the sight of Andrea and said in a hoarse whisper, "*Grüss dich.*"

"I thought she couldn't talk," said Andrea as they walked to the station.

"Of course she can talk," said Fehge indignantly. "She's just slow, and nobody's ever taken any trouble with her."

"And who has done that now?"

"I have."

"You?" Andrea stopped and looked down at the child. "Why?"

"Why? I should think you'd ask why didn't anybody teach her to talk before," said Fehge, not meaning to be pert. "But," she sighed as she went on, "she can't seem to talk to anybody else but me. The others scare her so. It does vex me."

Andrea looked down at the ambitious little pedagogue and couldn't suppress a smile. Fehge meanwhile was thinking that these uncouth people were enough to scare anybody out of their powers of speech and one shouldn't blame Julie too much. Patience. She must learn patience.

"When did you teach her?" asked Andrea.

"She comes . . . sometimes . . ." said Fehge pensively.

The train was practically empty, since Pritnitz was its second stop. They had the compartment to themselves, and Andrea settled down by the window, facing the direction the train was going, Fehge opposite her. "Don't sit in the sun," said Andrea. "It'll make you sleepy, and we have a long day ahead of us."

Fehge moved more into the middle of the long wooden bench. "Smooth out your skirt before you sit on it. Do you want to look like a tramp by the time you get there?"

Fehge got up and smoothed her skirt and sat down again gingerly. She was used to this kind of thing. If she had sat in the shade, Andrea would have told her to sit in the sun, it was good for her. If she ate slowly, Andrea told her to hurry, she didn't have all day; if she ate fast, Andrea told her not to gobble, it would give her indigestion; if she'd arranged to do her mending in the evening, Andrea said she'd ruin her eyes in the poor light; if she did it in the daytime, Andrea said she was wasting the best time of the day on something that didn't take any energy. Of course, Andrea was right, but she was very wearing. And there were other, unfathomable, things. If she had decided to stand for a certain kind of work, Andrea told her go sit and not tire herself unnecessarily; if she sat, Andrea told her to harden herself, to learn to stand at her work. Fehge stopped trying to anticipate Andrea's commands. She watched, waited for them to come, then hurried to obey. Obedience! It was Andrea's first commandment, years before Adolf Hitler demanded it in ear-piercing screams from a German nation predestined to obey.

Now Fehge looked at the deaconess under drooping lids. Was she through with her for the moment? Andrea was sitting back, her eyes closed. Fehge began to permit herself the luxury of relaxation. She seemed to ooze back into the wooden seat. What a wonderful day it was going to be! They were going to buy a dress. What was meant by having one's picture taken she had little idea, but she was full of anticipation.

The train jolted them back and forth and it groaned rounding the bends. There was something skittish about its creaking speed as it progressed downhill. Up to Pritnitz it chugged more slowly.

Fehge regarded the nurse, who for a few precious moments was paying no attention to her. Andrea's thoughts were running along an ambitious track, as they always did when she was free on a worldly expedition. The Medizinalrat was getting old. Who would come to Strubl in his place? What would become of Strubl when he died? What would become of her? She could not conceive of ever working again in any position that was not as completely authoritative as the one she enjoyed at present. Was this thought sinful?

Fehge could see the nurse's already stern features contract in a frown. No, Andrea thought, it was just the desire to make the most of one's capabilities. And, on the whole, she had to admit that the Bethesda Verein understood how to do that very well. The Verein knew how to distribute its nurses. The weak and stupid stayed in the Mother Houses, of which there were three, one in Nuremberg, one in Hamburg, and one in Vienna, to mend, cook, clean and launder. The sturdier ones were used for field work, for the Verein owned several farms. Only those suited for nursing were allowed to make use of their training. And those, Andrea pursued her reflections, who were cut out for administrative work were given the administrative posts. The Oberin in Vienna was old too. If God meant well with her, Andrea, the old Oberin and the Medizinalrat would both depart this life at the same time. And then? And then . . .

Andrea opened her eyes and found Fehge staring at her, and she smiled. Fehge stopped breathing. Her pupils dilated until her eyes were black. Then she was able to smile back, and it seemed to her that her heart would overflow. Andrea was in a good mood. Oh, it was going to be a lovely day!

They had to change trains in Leobersdorf. Trains were late, arriving and leaving. "Austrian slovenliness!" Andrea called that too. At last, Wiener-Neustadt, and the minute they got out of the station on to the street, a feeling of disaster in the air. The police. People standing in groups.

An atmosphere charged with political unrest is sinister, the more so when the sun shines. The acute differences seem to be fermenting in its heat. Belligerently the groups of police and civilians stand huddled, as though poised to strike.

"Now! What's up here?" said Andrea in a loud voice, unafraid, unimpressed—what could these undisciplined people be up to this time?

There were always people ready to explain. There was to be a *Heimwehr* parade. Now, Wiener-Neustadt was staunchly Social Democratic, and its citizens had petitioned their Prime Minister, the "Without Mercy" Cardinal, as they called Monsignore Ignaz Seipel, whom they hated, to forbid the parade. This the Prelate Minister had refused to do. So the Social Democrats were going to match the *Heimwehr* demonstration with one of their own!

A cordon of police divided the city in half, the one half reserved for the *Heimwehr* men and their enthusiasts, the other for the Social Democrats and their partisans. No one in uniform was allowed in the other's half.

Andrea's lips curled in contempt. This, then, was the Cardinal's solution. To think that he wasn't ashamed to demonstrate how divided his country was! Had he only stayed in the pulpit where he belonged, he might have succeeded better in uniting them!

She stood still for a moment and considered what would best be done. Fehge looked up into her face anxiously. Was something going to spoil their day? Andrea's face was vexed. With her?

Andrea saw the child's worried expression and pressed her hand reassuringly. Now that she had something else to vent her ire upon, she could afford to be gentle here. "Don't you let these silly people worry you!" she said. "Dolts! Only happy when they're bashing each others' heads in!"

These cursed republics! No order. And how could there be order when every stupid busybody was allowed to have his say? How could there be order without disciplined leadership and the leadership of discipline? And order there had to be! What would Strubl be without order? And wasn't a country just a vast enterprise like Strubl?

"Politics!" she snorted. "They should leave their fingers out of that pie!"

Fehge wrinkled her nose. There it was again. Politics! The thing that made the people excited.

She recognized the uniforms she had seen in Linz on many of the men standing around in groups, but their faces today were sullen.

Andrea hailed a taxi. She hated to do it, but the street cars weren't running, and they couldn't walk. She didn't want to tire the child, and she didn't want to get into any trouble, either. "To the centre of town," she said, and very soon they were there. She gave the man a good tip. What had to be done, had to be done.

The same ominous atmosphere hung over Wiener-Neustadt's main thoroughfare. The shops were practically empty, and the salespeople had their eyes on the street. Many of them stood in the doorway and only returned to the counters reluctantly when they were called. What were they waiting for? For shots to be fired, for the running of feet and the scuffling of a street fight, ever more often recurring events in this, as in every other provincial town in Austria. More and more, private life was being submerged, as in wartime. "*Ja*," sighed the young girl whom Andrea asked to wait on them. "It's just that there isn't anybody strong enough to keep order. There just isn't anything you can really believe in." And she went drearily about the business of showing Andrea dresses in Fehge's size.

They bought a dress which was obviously Andrea's choice—cheap, durable, yet fancy in an old-fashioned way. Andrea considered herself really frivolous when she decided that Fehge might have this party dress. It was white, with a thin pale-green stripe and pale pink dots in between every other stripe; it had full elbow sleeves and frills round the yoke, on the edge of the sleeves, and round the tight-fitting neckline. The skirt had two flounces and fell several inches below the knee. It was a size too large for Fehge, but the ones that fitted her round the waist were too tight for her across the shoulders, and too short, thought Andrea, just below the knee. In this dress Fehge looked thin and frail, neither of which she was. But Andrea liked her to look frail. She thought the child had never looked so sweet. And the dress reminded her of one she had worn as a child, which was exactly what it looked like, a dress of thirty years ago. Andrea nodded her head. All her love of lay clothes, which she had not worn for over fifteen years, surged up in her as she contemplated Fehge in this dress which might have come out of her past. She bought it, although it cost more than she had intended to pay. On the way out they passed through the hat department and they both saw it at the same time—a large straw with two little green plumes and a black velvet ribbon that went round the edge and far down the back from a neat bow. It was the hat for the dress.

To buy it, Andrea had to dig into her own resources. Of course, there was four-fifths of the money Dennis had sent for just this purpose at home. She was only borrowing from her own money;

still, she couldn't understand why she was so extravagant. She shook her head at herself.

Fehge was pleased with both purchases. Nothing could spoil this day now. She saw the dress, not as an old-fashioned monstrosity, but as something the like of which she had never owned before. Its elaborateness pleased her, and she looked down at it every now and then as she walked along. A light breeze caught the brim of her hat, and she had to hold it. This was the first real hat she had ever possessed, and she felt transported in her new glory. Her feet in their fine new patent-leather shoes, a present from Thérèse, barely touched the pavement. She looked up from under her hat and smiled to herself, but passers-by thought she smiled to them and smiled back. She did not see them, but the sight of the carefree little girl in her quaint, pompous get-up walking out with the deaconess on a day so full of foreboding set many a heart to beating normally again. Children were a blessing, like the beauty of Nature, like the sun that continued to shine over any tragedy and the rain that would continue to fertilize the fields, however ravaged.

Andrea had asked the girl at the department store for the best photographer in Wiener-Neustadt, and they walked to his studio. The best photographer was the right one for Fehge in the dress she was wearing. His studio had a tiled floor, and his old wooden camera stood on three wooden legs and was covered with a black cloth. It had a cap over the lens, which he removed in hushed silence when he took the picture and replaced again as quietly. He took a photograph as though he were stalking an animal. He was small, stout, with very little red hair left and a bristling red moustache, and so near-sighted that his glasses had the thickest lenses Fehge had ever seen. You could not see his eyes at all behind them, but you felt that he could see through you. Fehge cringed when she saw him, very little, but he noticed it. "You needn't be afraid of me, little girl," he said, and smiled, and when he smiled he looked unspeakably cruel.

He turned to address himself to Andrea. At the back of his neck, above the old-fashioned shiny white collar, lay three rolls of red fat. "A bad day for us," he said, and began to get his plates ready.

He was incredibly slow about it. He reminded Andrea of something very unpleasant.

"It all seems to me to be foolish nonsense," she said. "Why don't they do as they're told, all of them, and mind their own business?"

"Most of them haven't any business to mind," said the little photographer. "Unemployment is the scourge of the Republic. But there'll come a day when they'll have plenty to do." He stopped, a big black metal plate in his hand, and leaned forward with a leer. "You, a German, will understand that."

Andrea didn't understand. She didn't know what he was talking about. "How did you know that I was German?" she asked, because it had always interested her that they knew this, here, at once.

"Oh, by the way you speak," he said, "and by the *Abzeichen* there," and he pointed to the silver brooch she wore with its cross and anchor and heart, which he had just called a badge as though it belonged to some military organization. "Bethesda nurse?" he asked, and she said, "Yes."

He nodded. "An aunt of mine is."

"Are you German?" she asked.

"Of course. Of course," he said. "After the *Anschluss* we won't have to ask that any more."

Anschluss. It was not the first time Andrea had heard of it. She read her paper every night before her Bible and with much more intensity, especially the murders, of which there were many, mostly in the Balkans, where they were very bloody and incestuous. The one, for instance, where the seventy-year-old man had been brought to court for the rape of his eleven-year-old grandchild, whose mother, his own daughter, was still lying in her shroud on her death-bed. In the same room. Incredible! The neighbours had seen, through a crack in the blind. . . . What had the photographer been talking about? *Anschluss.* Well, he was very stupid if he thought Germany would ever saddle herself with such a poor, ignorant country as Austria. It wasn't much better than the Balkan countries. Andrea didn't make the mistake of the Viennese

Socialist. She judged the land by its provinces, by its majority of four million.

"Now," said the photographer, and his tone became brisk, "where does the little girl want to have her picture taken? In the boat? Or with the Alps at the back of her? Or at this pretty little gate?"

The backgrounds in his studio did, indeed, include all of these things. There was a rowboat with a seascape behind it, an Alpine landscape with a chalet painted on it, and a real bench to sit on in front of the chalet.

Fehge said, "I'd like to stand at the gate, if you please," because she thought she would like to have something to hang on to, and she didn't want to sit because she wanted her dress to show.

The little piglike man photographed her at the gate. When he peered at her, his hands covering the cap he was about to remove as though it were a gun that was to shoot her down, terror was in her eyes. "What are you afraid of?" said Andrea. "He's not going to shoot you!" And she laughed as she realized that the child was terrified. "Heavens!" she said, "there's nothing to be afraid of. It all happens without your feeling a thing."

Fehge knew there was no escape. She put on her bravest, brightest expression, and with her hand clung to the silly little gate. She stood there as though facing a firing-squad.

"That's a good girl," said Andrea, and it was over, and she really hadn't felt a thing. All the same, she was dizzy from strain.

When they left the photographer, he shook hands with them both. "Good-bye, little girl," he said to her, and to Andrea he said, "*Grüss Gott, Schwester. Heil Hitler.*"

The greeting annoyed Andrea, who answered tartly with an old folk-greeting she seldom employed, "*Gott befohlen.*" It implied, in its Old-World way, "May your spirit be commended to God."

They came out into the sunlight, which blinded them for a moment. They were in that part of the city which had been partitioned off for the *Heimwehr*, and Andrea found the people here pleasanter to look upon than those they had seen in the other—nice, clean, respectable, better-class people, not a lot of working men and women. Her father had been a street-car conductor, but he had never looked like a Bolshevik!

There were emaciated beggars, of course; no city street in Austria was without them. Sometimes you couldn't escape looking into their hungry eyes, and it gave you the creeps. It was like looking into a volcano that was bound to erupt. Andrea gave a little to everyone who asked; it was a rule of her Order. She hated complying with it here. In Germany it was different. In Germany, if a man was begging, it was because he couldn't find work; here it was because he didn't know how to work.

At a street corner some enterprising man had put up an old merry-go-round for children. Andrea said, "Do you want a ride?"

Fehge couldn't believe her ears. She could only nod. Andrea gave the man a ten-*Groschen* piece, and Fehge got in, mindful of her dress, careful of her shoes. She sat between other children all younger than herself so that she looked big on the seat that ran all round the primitive little circling machine. She held tight to the thin railing with one hand and to her hat with the other. Andrea had offered to take it, but she had refused. She nearly swooned with joy as the merry-go-round started creakily to circle round and round. She was having a good time. Like . . . like . . . like nobody she knew. Like these children here? No. They were town children. They had been on a merry-go-round before. Like no one else.

She closed her eyes. The little roundabout spun faster. She began to feel a little sick, but she didn't care. Slower. Slower. Stop. It was over. She had to wait a few seconds before her legs would support her.

"Did you like it?" said Andrea as she helped her out. "Look out! Mercy, child, has it made you as dizzy as that?"

"Oh yes," said Fehge, in answer to everything. "Oh yes." And Andrea felt immensely pleased with herself.

They went to a cheap beer cellar and had sausages with sauerkraut and boiled potatoes. They both liked spicy food. Fehge drank milk and Andrea coffee. She would have loved a glass of beer. It was not forbidden. Nothing was forbidden. It was just not done.

"Sister Andrea," said Fehge, and as she said it, Andrea thought how rarely the child addressed her by name, how rarely, altogether, the child spoke before spoken to. Had she been too strict with her? Was she repressing the child?

Torn, as she was today, out of her accustomed, rigorous routine, Andrea was defrosted.

"What is it, *Kleines*?" she said. There! How rarely did she call her "little one."

Fehge swallowed and said, "Am I a German?"

"No," said Andrea. "you aren't yet. But you heard what the man said. There's going to be *Anschluss*. That means Germany will take over this country in which we live. Austria. Then you'll be German too. Then you'll be a Bethesda nurse as I am," Andrea went on enthusiastically. Why not? When she reached the age of reason, the child would see reason. As she grew into a woman, her demands would grow more mature. She would draw away from the sham tinsel of Catholicism towards the sincere austereness of her, Andrea's, religion. There was no reason, especially if there were *Anschluss* and the purifying German spirit could permeate this rotting land, why Fehge shouldn't choose the right religion in the end, and then she could be a Bethesda nurse like herself.

"Fehge," she said, "you are ten years old, old enough to begin to learn something worth while. I don't want you to work in the kitchen any more. I am going to teach you how to help me to keep the doctor's office clean and the operating-room and the X-ray-room. How will you like that?"

Fehge hesitated. Out of the kitchen. Away from the vegetables she loved to handle, the dishes neatly stacked, the shining metal of the pans, the good smells, the clean way the cook cut the meat, the sleekness of batter, the supreme moments when the cake received its icing . . . away from all that . . . upstairs to where the instruments of torture were kept, the operating-room, bloodstains, pus, cold gleaming scissors, the memory of pains and groans . . . "But may I still do the stairs?"

What a queer child she was! Now, why did she want to continue to wash those low, marble steps every day?

It was a good thing Andrea didn't ask the question out loud, because Fehge would have had to tell her the reason, and Andrea's amiable mood would have been shattered. Fehge had made up for herself a little game for the steps. There were five flights of fourteen steps each, to be washed on every week-day. Now, these five flights matched the five decades of her rosary, she had discovered—you could spread your prayers over them and come out right just as you did with the beads. The contemplation ... Our Father ... ten Hail Marys ... the final prayer ... five times and you were done. She said the Joyful Mysteries of Annunciation, Visitation, Birth of Christ, Temple Presentation, and the finding of Christ in the Temple by His Mother on Mondays and Thursdays, as was the correct thing to do. On Tuesdays and Fridays came the Sorrowful Mysteries of the Prayer and Bloody Sweat, of the Scourging, Crowning with Thorns, the Carrying of the Cross, and the Crucifixion; and the Glorious Mysteries were reserved for Wednesdays and Saturdays when she recalled the Resurrection, the Ascension, the Descent of the Holy Ghost, the Assumption into Heaven, and the Coronation of the Blessed Virgin Mary. It would be better if Andrea did not know that the steps had been turned into the stations of the Rosary.

"Of course you can go on doing the steps if you want to," said Andrea. "Fräulein Spaeth will be only too pleased. Anyway, you do them before I get up. You must be very careful," she went on, mindful of the costly apparatus which Fehge would be called upon to handle, "not to break anything. You would like to be a nurse, wouldn't you?"

"Yes," said Fehge, having no idea what was implied by being a nurse beyond what Andrea had just offered her—the job of cleaning the doctor's office, the operating-room, the X-ray-room, and the medicine-cabinets with their shining instruments. Of what actual nursing Andrea did in the sick-rooms she went into, Fehge had no idea.

The photograph was a great success with everyone except Sapponyi. It showed Fehge at her brightest as far as her facial expression was concerned, yet in the cramped position of her hand as it clutched the absurd little gate lay all her suppressed fear. But the tilt of her chin, the determined firmness of her lips, showed her growing self-confidence, perhaps even latent defiance, to a world in which, whatever she did, in spite of God, His Church, and its well-behaved community, she still felt out of place.

One copy was sent to Dennis. A second copy Andrea kept for herself as a reward for the trouble she had taken getting it made and because she wanted it so badly. Sapponyi said he didn't want the third, he'd rather take a good snapshot of the child, which he did, and sent that to Dennis too. So Andrea gave the third copy to Fehge.

Fehge had not dared ask for it, but her hand trembled with suppressed eagerness as she took it. She looked for a long time at the reproduction of herself. How it all came true, what the priest said! Now she was immortal. Here she stood, dressed in her best, and would never die.

She said to Andrea, "Is there enough money left to buy a frame?"

"Yes," said Andrea, "you can frame it if you like."

"I would like to take it down to my father and mother," said Fehge, "so that they can see what their little girl has grown to be like," for with her knowledge of the fourth commandment had come the wish to honour her parents. It was difficult, though, to honour the dead. The priest had said the best thing she could do was to grow up to be a credit to them. To put the picture on their grave, however, seemed something tangible that could be done right away.

Andrea said, "You can please yourself, but to me it seems a silly thing to do. They can see you as you are. They don't need a picture."

Fehge knew all that. "I know," she said. "It's just a symbol. Like we know the Blessed Virgin is there, and yet we have a statue of her. It helps."

So, on the following Sunday, Fehge had the picture under her arm when she went to Mass. She had left time to find the graves and say a prayer beside them. They were wildly overgrown with weeds. Fehge left them as they were. Some of the weeds had pretty flowers in the spring. There was high thick clover among them. She nailed the picture in its frame to a stick, which she embedded in the ground. Then she stood back to see the effect and was satisfied. She knelt down and patted the earth. Yes, they were very well off beneath it.

Chapter Seventeen

ANDREA kept her promise. Fehge advanced, as Andrea considered it, from kitchen to operating-room, X-ray-room, and doctor's office in Strubl's left wing on the second floor.

One summer's morning, four years later, Fehge was putting the finishing touches to the Herr Medizinalrat's desk. She had just finished waxing the floor of the office and the long strip of corridor that led from it to the operating-room, all her territory now. The wax-polishers were heavy, in spite of her strength, which was as much as a man's any day. That was why Franz took her down with him to fetch the freight. And she preferred shifting the freight to the meticulous and, what seemed to her, senseless way she had to put back the things on the doctor's desk exactly as they had been before—the long scissors level with the top of the blotter, the inkstand, the calendar, the notebooks, the clock—just so.

Andrea was in the office with her, putting the large black X-ray plates back into their folders.

"Do you want to see something interesting?" she asked. She was holding an X-ray plate up to the light so that she could see through it.

Fehge, duster in hand, went and stood behind the nurse. She

could see the plate with its strange shadows like smoke, its skeleton-like rib bones clearly defined, and, where Andrea's finger was pointing, a little black object. "That," said Andrea, "is a bullet."

Fehge clucked with her tongue. Well, of all things! "The person is dead?" she said.

"No," said Andrea. "This is a picture of the lungs of Mon-signore Seipel, who is dying upstairs. And he isn't dying of the bullet, either. He has been carrying that about with him for eight years." Fehge shook her head. "Here." Andrea pointed to round, dark shadows framed by the rib bones. "Cavity, cavity, cavity . . . more lung gone than left him, for years back. And he never stopped working."

The tone of her voice was full of admiration for Austria's former Prime Minister.

"Who shot him?" said Fehge.

"A Socialist," said Andrea. Then she remembered that Fehge, as far as politics were concerned, was "an unwritten page," and added "An undisciplined hooligan." (The Monsignore, at the time, had called his assassin simply "a misguided man.")

It was a terrible thing to shoot a man, thought Fehge. He might die. Thou shalt not kill. How few people kept the command-ments! How did they dare disobey them? Where did they find the courage? She would be afraid to. She was more afraid of breaking a law of God than of man himself.

Andrea put the plate carefully back into its folder, and Fehge went on with her work, the thought of the great man's pitted lung still on her mind. She remembered the day, the fourth of July, when they had brought him to Strubl to die. He had not retired to his bed, which any other man in his condition would have done years ago, until he had supervised the arrangement of a little chapel next to his room. Here he conducted Mass for himself and his nun-nurses every day. One of them had a sweet, waxen face that haunted Fehge in her dreams. She hoped one day to be privileged to speak to this nun, although what she would say to her she didn't know. Perhaps she would merely be permitted to walk beside her through the countryside, as she had dreamed she had done a few nights ago. In the dream they had been walking through a field of golden corn that reached to their waists, like Jesus and His apostles in a picture she had once seen. But there wasn't a field of corn in the valley.

"There is a rim round the stopper," said Andrea, and she pointed with her long fingers to the washbowl.

There was always a rim. The water here was chalky, and it was hard to get the rim off. It wasn't dirt, Fehge had once protested. But it looked like dirt, Andrea had said, and it had to come off, however much your arms ached, your wrists throbbed, and the perspiration stood on your forehead.

The wide-open windows let in not a breath of air. Outside, nothing stirred. "*Ach!*" Andrea's harsh voice was saying now, "those long forceps should be behind the short ones. But I told you that yesterday!"

Fehge looked up from the washbowl, and for the second time watched Andrea arrange the implements in the medicine-chest as they should be, symmetrically, like soldiers. She didn't fear the head nurse any longer when she snapped at her. Fehge had made the discovery, perhaps on that day in Wiener-Neustadt four years ago, that Andrea's bark was worse than her bite. There were times, though, when Andrea so consistently barked that Fehge's patience wore thin and something inside her snapped. Then she would cry, with big, convulsive sobs that almost made her ill, and for hours nothing could stop her. Invariably, of course, Andrea was sorry. But the devil drove her, and there was no one but this girl on whom she could let him out. Once she had almost said as much to Fehge, who thought about it for a long time and decided that, if she could act as a receptacle for Andrea's devil, well, perhaps that was what she was there for. She certainly did not feel him enter her. The nurse's violent outbursts of temper only confused her.

Fehge's daily routine now, in the year 1932, required that she rise at half-past five. With a warm cup of malt-coffee and a piece of black bread and salted lard, which she preferred to butter, inside her, she first of all did the steps. Then she breakfasted with Andrea, after which she fetched upstairs from cellar to kitchen the foodstuffs that were needed for the day. Lydia Spaeth had said she couldn't dispense with Fehge for that. Who else could lug as many bushels of potatoes up the stairs in one trip? Crouched on one knee, she got the heavy sack on her shoulders, and then it was just a matter of taking the stairs with one's back at the right angle so that it didn't strain one's stomach, and it was easy. After that she was ready to do her cleaning for Andrea. There was always something to do "thoroughly" every day. Then came lunch, after which she went with Franz for the freight. The rest of the afternoon was spent in disposing of the freight and helping wherever help was needed, in the operating-room again if there had been an operation, in the laundry if she was needed nowhere else. Before supper she fetched the milk down from Schwarzenberg. After supper, she mended for Andrea and herself. At nine o'clock she went to bed, pleasantly exhausted.

There was never any time for rest or recreation. It never occurred to her to ask for any during the working week. After all, God had rested only on the seventh day, and so did she.

Her day of rest commenced at seven o'clock with morning Mass. Ever since last Whitsuntide Sunday, it was also her dearly loved duty to ring the bells. This had come about in the following manner:

On the Sunday before last Whitsun, Fehge had come early to Mass. Reischer's Walter, fully eighteen now and very sturdy, whose duty it was to ring the bells, had asked Fehge if she would like to come up with him to see how they were rung. That this invitation was tantamount to a quick act of love in the belfry, for which Reischer's Walter considered the fourteen-year-old girl completely ready, Fehge did not know.

She went with him up into the belfry whose broad beams and cross-beams cut fantastic patterns and threw long shadows, where it smelled of warm wood and dust, where spiders had woven nets of all sizes, filling in the corners with grey veils. Walter explained the bells to her, since she seemed really interested in them. She had touched all the ropes and looked up into their metal jaws, her lips parted prettily with excitement. You could hear them all the way to Strubl when the wind was blowing in the right direction.

Then Walter had gone into action and had had his arm round her waist and his rough hand feeling for her breasts before she knew what was happening. A second later, however, Walter was spiralling down the belfry stairs, and he landed so clumsily that he broke his arm.

He lay on the lower landing bellowing like a bull. Fehge leaned over the rough wooden banister, and looked down at him as she adjusted her dishevelled blouse, and what she saw there made her laugh. But his yells were a horrible sound to be issuing forth from a belfry on a Sunday morning! She went over to the bells and rang them as Walter had explained they were to be rung, and their sound drowned out the bellows of the injured peasant boy, who was helped down by two of his friends.

The priest had gone up into the belfry then, and watched Fehge. She was strong, all right! The bells were heavy, and Walter Reischer no light weight, but she could handle them both. "That's enough," he'd told her, and she had turned a glowing face to him. "Oh," she had said, "may I do it again?"

"If you like," the priest had said. "But you'll be straining yourself. It's a man's job."

"I'm used to doing a man's work," she had answered.

"Why did you come up here with the boy?" the priest had asked her then. "Didn't you know what he wanted you up here for?"

"No."

"Well, now you'll be more careful, won't you?"

"Yes, Herr Kaplan," she had said, "but I'm not afraid of *him*."

The priest had smiled. "With your good right arm," he'd told her, "I am sure you don't have to be afraid of anybody." And she had rung the bells for early Sunday morning Mass ever since.

Church over, she would wander off into the woods for flowers, berries, or mushrooms, according to season. In the spring all Strubl's public rooms were bright with the flowers Fehge brought down from the mountains in her knapsack. Sapponyi had said once that the law forbade the picking of Alpine flowers, but that was a silly law, and Fehge ignored it. She never pulled them up by their roots. In the summer, she and the other servants would feast on the berries she had picked, in the autumn on the mushrooms she had found standing erect like miniature umbrellas under the leaves of bushes still wet with recent rains, the brown-capped, white-stemmed *Steinpilz*, or boletus, the orange-juicy, greenly tinted *Reizker*, or orange agaric, and the pale yellow, pleated-skirt *Pfifferling*, or chanterelle.

On these days she would often walk fifteen miles or more by herself. Since the incident with Conrad, there had been a cessation of the outings with Hilda. The two had not quarrelled; the outings together were simply not resumed. Neither one ever mentioned them. When Fehge and Hilda met now, which was not often, since Strubl was so big and, by its floor system, so divided that one could easily keep away from anyone whom one did not want to meet, there was a slight veil of embarrassment, mainly on Hilda's part, who knew very well what she was blushing about. Fehge, who still did not know what had happened, felt less embarrassment. She refused to listen to those who would enlighten her, because she herself was vexed about the whole thing. She had evidently done something foolish. She wanted to forget it.

Her attitude toward all this eagerly proffered enlightenment had already earned for her the status of a prude among the staff. "Fehge wants to be a saint," they said. This spring's incident in the belfry had been no help. The story had spread like wildfire, and Fehge was labelled queer because she didn't want to make love. They'd had a girl like that in the valley before, who hadn't let anyone near her, but she'd had relations with her father and hanged herself when he'd died. Not that there was anything like that about Fehge. She was just queer, and since her extraordinary strength was by now a well-established fact, she was safe from further molestation.

At two o'clock on an afternoon in August, Fehge was seated as usual beside Franz on the freight cart and they were riding down to the station with the sun on their faces. She was burned brown.

He was red and ageing now, the long moustachios that hung down on either side of his mouth turning grey. He liked to have the young girl with him. She was always pleasant company and the best help he'd ever had.

They passed the schoolhouse and could hear the drone of children's voices. Fehge had finished school that year. Melita had suggested that she should go to a secretarial school in Waldeck, where she could learn something more and aspire to something better than a servant. Melita had said she would write to Dennis, who would surely and gladly provide the money. But Fehge had balked at the plan. She could see nothing better in learning to write very fast in signs or on a machine than in cleaning. You weren't even writing your own thoughts, which, if you had any worth putting down, would be a noble thing to do.

"You can earn much better money that way," Melita had said.

Fehge had been slow in formulating the obvious reply, "I have all I need." No, she didn't think that was the work she had been cut out for at all.

"Well . . ." Fehge had groped in her mind—it was always so difficult to explain things and the grown-ups were always probing —"I want to do something . . . that I can get right deep down into," and her hands had made the motions of digging and grasping earth. You could almost see her standing knee-deep in a ditch, so expressive was her gesture.

Melita had given up. She could not make this girl class-conscious!

Now they were passing the Pfeiffer house, and into the still afternoon air was carried the sound of a low moan, a sound so full of pain that Fehge put her hand on Franz's arm. "Listen," she said.

The horse snorted and the cart creaked. "Oh, stop the cart, please!" she cried.

Franz stopped the cart. There was the sound again, floating out into the stillness of the hot summer's day.

Fehge jumped down from her seat. "We'll miss the train if you stop here," said Franz.

"I must see," said Fehge, and ran into the house the door of which stood ajar.

A few minutes later she came back to the door and called out to him. "I must stay. I'm sorry, Franz. Frau Pfeiffer's very ill."

"She's only getting a child," said Franz impatiently, but Fehge shook her head. "She's ill, I tell you. And before you go to the station, tell Schreiner to come up here," and she went back into the house.

For eight years, now, she had lived in the valley and never been inside one of these homes. She had never been asked. Nothing but a cry of pain such as the one she had just heard would have driven her into one of them, and into the Pfeiffer house at that. Pfeiffer was one of the few men in the valley in whose mind her origin had never died. Everybody hated his wife, Ludmilla, because she was Slovak . . . and she was dirty. You only had to look around you to see that. The bedding was grey and the dust lay thick on the furniture. So Pfeiffer got his own back wherever he could. One way was to hate Fehge, whom he always referred to as "the Jewess." He never answered her greeting on the road, but glared at her from under his bushy brows, especially when he was drunk, when he even went so far as to take his long pipe out of his mouth and spit belligerently. The Pfeiffer girls were the only ones in school who had persisted in ignoring her to the end. And from Ludmilla she had never heard anything but unfriendly words; for instance, when Ute had snapped at one of the Pfeiffer girls—you couldn't expect such a fine dog not to sense the antagonism toward her mistress. Since then, Fehge had had to keep Ute muzzled whenever she took her out of Strubl's bounds. Fehge would have made a long detour to avoid having to pass and say "*Grüss Gott*" to any of the Pfeiffers, but today she had run into their house without a trace of hesitation. The moan had sounded so desolate. It was quite clear that someone was in pain and alone.

The first room Fehge entered was small enough, with stove and table and two cots against the wall, but it proved to be the largest in the house. There was no one in it. A slight smell of something burning came from the stove. Cooking had obviously been interrupted. Fehge went over to the stove and took off the pot, which had been seared by the flame. There it was again, the sound. It came from a little room to the left.

Fehge found Pfeiffer's wife, Ludmilla, lying on her side, hunched and groaning. Her feet were drawn up so that they were hidden under the ample folds of her skirt. Her hands were tautened into fists with which she beat herself on the forehead in her pain; she was biting her lips, the sweat was pouring down her face, and her eyes were closed tight. Fehge knelt down beside her. "Can I help you, Frau Pfeiffer?"

The woman didn't answer, but went on groaning with sounds forced out of her like grunts. It was then that Fehge ran out and gave Franz the message to get Schreiner.

When she came back to the little room, Ludmilla Pfeiffer was sitting, hugging her knees, rocking back and forth. Where had Fehge seen a woman rocking back and forth like that before? Her mother, Dworje. In the face of death. This woman was going to give life, and was moaning in just the same way about it.

"Can I help you?" said Fehge again, and she clasped and unclasped her helpless hands as she stood over the woman. "Shall I go and get the *Herr*?"

The woman opened her eyes, but her brows remained knit and the look she gave Fehge, was full of agony. "*Den Mann*?" she said. "He's gone to Neustadt to see a vet about the cow."

Fehge knew the story of Pfeiffer's cow. They had talked about it in the laundry only yesterday. The vet in Pritnitz had prescribed a salve for a sore on her back, and she'd licked it off and since then become sick. The vet had no right to sell a salve to be administered externally that could make the cow sick. The vet said it wasn't the salve. Now Pfeiffer had gone to Neustadt to find out, because his cow was more important to him than his wife, who had had six children already. What was there to get excited about this seventh, even if it did come today, as Ludmilla had said she felt it would? Women always started moaning days ahead of time. The cow made much less fuss about it.

"Schreiner's coming," said Fehge. "I told Franz."

The woman crumpled up on her side again and closed her eyes. "You stupid fool," she said, "sending for Schreiner."

"You look ill," said Fehge.

"I'm just going to have a baby," said Ludmilla, and her breath came short and raspy. "You don't get the doctor for that. You get the midwife. And she wouldn't get here in time. Because it's coming this very minute." She hunched her knees as high as her laden belly would permit it. "I can feel it."

She knew the feeling. It had happened to her again and again and again, and it would go on happening, although the doctor had said last time that she wouldn't live through the next. She hoped this would be the last time. Life was too hard to bear.

She opened her eyes and stared straight ahead at the hard wooden boards she was lying on. "You'll have to help me," she said to Fehge. "I'll tell you what to do. First help me to get on the bed."

She meant that the girl should put a supporting arm under her shoulders and help her to rise and hobble to the bed against the wall. In the small room there were four cot beds against the available floor space that was left free by the large old peasant commode, the only other piece of furniture. To her great surprise, the young girl put her arms under her worn-out body and lifted her as easily as if she had been a child.

Fehge lifted Ludmilla Pfeiffer, helpless in her pain, and discovered that she was no longer in the least afraid of her. On the contrary, she noted a feeling of great warmth in her toward this woman who was now entirely at her mercy, with whom she could do what she pleased. What she pleased to do was to help, to give of her own great strength to this woman who was momentarily robbed of hers. It seemed that people had to be very ill before she dared approach them. She held the heavy woman in her arms a little longer than was necessary as this profound revelation came to her. Then she laid her down gently on the bed.

"My, but you're strong," said the woman, and her voice sounded relieved and friendly.

As Fehge put Ludmilla Pfeiffer down on the bed, her eyes

fell on a Pietà which stood on a shelf above her bed, the dead white Christ with His bloodless side-wound agape, on the lap of His sorrowing Mother. Fehge crossed herself. The dear Lord help the woman through her ordeal, the sorrowing Mother have mercy.

Ludmilla Pfeiffer was breathing heavily. "They hate you and they hate me," she said, "so we should be helping each other like this," and her face was distorted with a smile.

"Shh," said Fehge.

"Now," Ludmilla began; then she rolled her eyes till only the whites showed and a rattle came from her throat. A little blood seeped out of her mouth, and she lay still. Her pregnant stomach stood high and round as she lay there flat, on her back and quiet.

My God, thought Fehge. What shall I do now?

As though in her sleep, the woman began to stir. She drew up her legs, and her skirts seemed to hamper her. Fehge drew them up. Without opening her eyes or speaking, she showed Fehge by plucking at them, that she should remove her black bloomers. Fehge did, and could hardly suppress a scream as she saw how far things were. She felt faint and swayed on her feet, and in this moment of utter helplessness she saw, in the speckled, misty mirror over the commode, the waxen face of the nun she adored. Sister Angelica was standing in the doorway.

Fehge turned. "Oh," she gasped. "God be thanked that you have come!"

Sister Angelica was the night nurse for the great man Seipel, who was dying at Strubl. She usually slept until two or three in the afternoon, then, after prayer, she went for a little walk. This was what she had been doing when Franz had passed her on the road and told her of the predicament Fehge was in and asked her to go and help the girl.

Angelica had run all the way to the Pfeiffer house, which had given her pale cheeks a faint glow and made her unusual, slanting eyes shine. As she hurried across the room now to Ludmilla's bedside, Fehge noticed her beautiful white hands raised gently, ready to administer help, like the hands of the Madonna of the Sacred Heart in church. The big cross swung from her waist.

Sister Angelica told Fehge to make up the fire and to boil water in two large pots and one small one. She told her to look for white cloths and a pair of scissors, and to boil the pair of scissors, which were blunt and had first to be sharpened on a stone outside. In one of the large pans Fehge boiled all the cloths she could find, and by opening the iron door of the stove she could dry them almost at once. The heat from the fire blistered her cheeks. The sweat rolled down her body. The whole house became unbearably hot, and the perspiration made a little damp rim stain all round Sister Angelica's white coif.

Meanwhile, the most incredible things happened. The child was pushed out of the woman's body by her own violent efforts, and Sister Angelica started to wash it in the bowl, after slapping the baby, which startled Fehge far more than cutting the cord. The baby cried. But the nun kept her eyes on the woman all the time, and suddenly she handed the baby to Fehge because . . . because the woman was giving birth to something else. It was dark-red and flat, and veins ran all over it like little rivers. It was the placenta, Sister Angelica told her, and Fehge thought, "What a pretty name!"

But then even Sister Angelica lost her calm, because Ludmilla bled. She bled profusely and persistently, and Fehge could see by the expression on the Sister's face that it worried her.

Fehge was holding the dry and slightly wriggling infant in her arms, wrapped in a white towel. What a little red worm it was! And in her grew a feeling of awe for God, who let the infallible grown-up commence life in such ridiculous shape and fashion. They came, like that, out of any woman's body. And then they grew up and blew themselves up and were Hofrats and Ministers and Nationalrats and Professors and Prelates and Chancellors and Vice-Chancellors—since the great man had come to Strubl she had learned titles—and they all started out like this! She held the infant easily, the whole of it, in her two hands, its head slightly raised, facing her. It wriggled and grunted and grew purple in the face. Then it opened a round, empty little red mouth and cried. Fehge forgot Sister Angelica and the sick woman and began to laugh.

"We must find clean cloths," the nun said in a desperate voice, "we must find more . . ."

Fehge put the baby down on one of the beds and began to hunt. They had used up everything. Blood-stained rags lay on the floor. The bed was a sight. There was nothing in the commode, there was nowhere else to look, and the Sister was looking at her piteously, her hands trying to stem the flow of the woman's blood with a rag that was already soaked red.

Fehge lifted her skirt. "I put it on clean this morning," she said, and took off her petticoat.

"It will have to do," said Sister Angelica. "Tear it into pieces."

Fehge did, and handed them to her and watched how she changed the rags, how she knelt beside the bed and with her free hand, which she had asked Fehge to wash, stroked the hair off Ludmilla's forehead, took another piece of the fresh white cotton and wiped the sweat off her face and gazed into it. She did all this with such tenderness and love in every motion that Fehge was reminded of the Pietà on the wall, of the sorrowing Mother, as though Sister Angelica were the sorrowing mother of this woman too. She thought of everything that Sister Angelica had done since she had come into that room, of how everything would have gone wrong if she had not been there, not only of what the Sister had done, but of *how* she had done it—with so much love for the sick woman whom she did not even know. That was nursing! And that was what Fehge wanted to do. At last she had found a relationship toward human beings which would enable her to live contentedly with them on this earth. She had found her vocation.

Ludmilla Pfeiffer ceased to bleed.

"I wish we could move her to a clean bed," said Sister Angelica, "but we will have to do it very carefully. Let us pull her away from the wall, and then you get on the other side . . ."

She got so far when Fehge stepped between her and the bed and lifted the woman in her arms as she had done before, only this time she was aware at once of the thrill of satisfaction that it gave her.

Sister Angelica said, "Oh, you mustn't lift her alone. She's bigger than you are. You'll strain yourself!" But Fehge was already across the room with her burden.

"My," said the nun, "you are strong!"

At that moment Pfeiffer came home, his shoulders sagging with defeat. Yes. There had been poison in the ointment; the cow would die. He could sue the vet, of course—or the apothecary, if the vet tried to put the blame on him. Sue. That meant spending money, trips to Neustadt, a lawyer. The idea of the lawyer finished it. A lawyer was an insurmountable obstacle for a poor tree-tapper. He wouldn't sue. The cow would die. He took in the entire room with his desolate eyes. There was another child squawking on the bed; that damn nosy Sister telling him his wife wouldn't be able to work for quite a while, she had had a haemorrhage . . . what did she mean? Bleeding. Well, why didn't she say so? The cow . . . he couldn't buy another cow. Not in his lifetime. And his eldest son was no good. Ran off with the *Heimwehr* last time he got out of jail. Never heard of him since. Wait till the second one was big enough? Ha-ha! He had consumption. Then came the four girls, who did nothing but eat the food out of his mouth. And now the wife couldn't work. If she'd only died! You could get another wife, but you couldn't get another cow.

Fehge kept a wary eye on the sullen peasant. He didn't go over and put a gentle hand on his wife's forehead as Sister Angelica had done. Ludmilla was looking at her husband out of fearful eyes. Sister Angelica took the baby and laid it in its mother's arms, but the mother turned away from the child. "I don't want it," she said. The damp smell of it sickened her.

Then Pfeiffer became aware of Fehge. "What's the Jewess doing here?" he said.

The nun stiffened angrily. "You can thank the Lord she was passing by and was here to help. Otherwise you mightn't have found your wife alive."

So the Jewess had preserved the life of the woman on the bed.

God damn the Jews! She had probably cast a spell on the baby, who would grow up an idiot. She had made his wife bleed. Now his wife couldn't work! His hands became fists, and he advanced on Fehge. Sister Angelica grasped his arm with surprising firmness, and brought him to a standstill. "Have you gone crazy?" she said very quietly. Fehge grasped this moment to run out of the house.

Outside, she met the two oldest Pfeiffer girls. They were both still schoolgirls, and they stared with mouths agape at the Jewess coming out of their house. Fehge ran past them. When they heard, a few minutes later, that Fehge had officiated at the birth, they ran for the priest to baptize the child at once, and they made a great business of scraping together their meagre savings to pay for this much more expensive emergency baptism. But if they didn't see to that, the child might die with the curse of the Jewess on him.

They paid the priest, but they didn't pay the doctor. Schreiner was furious that he had been called instead of the midwife. This was the kind of thing that happened to him, while the swine-Jew up there in his castle had patients like the ex-Prime Minister of Austria, Monsignore Ignaz Seipel—not a man he admired, but nevertheless a man who had made history. Just you wait, pig-dog up at your castle! They made Conrad a captain in the Austrian Legion today over there in the Reich . . . the boy you shot in the leg when he was unarmed and defenceless . . . and he's coming back!

That night Monsignore Seipel died. As many famous visitors came to see him dead as had come during the entire six weeks he had spent dying at Strubl, and the staff was kept busy running to windows and oh-ing and ah-ing at the celebrities whom Fehge could no longer think so much of since she had seen how they all began.

That pretty little man, for instance, called Dollfuss—his title was Chancellor. What a fuss they made of him! Of course, he was doing great things, superhuman things, when you came to think of it. He was steering Austria—so Fehge had been told (and at once she could see him at the helm of a tossing ship, steering them all through a wild sea)—away from Germany, toward Rome. "The Lausanne Protocols," whatever they might be. If she had only gone on listening, she might have heard about a new Allied loan to Austria in exchange for a promise not to enter into a customs union with Germany.

Fehge looked out of the dining-room window with the others and watched the little doll man with the moustache and the round fat cheeks like wax. They should have been rosy, but they were unhealthily pale. He had dissolved Parliament, whatever that might be, and was ruling by decree, and he had started off in life no different from the rest of them. That was so puzzling, to what different destinations life bore different people. But the little man out there certainly had courage. He had dissolved the mighty Nazi Party too, and that did impress Fehge. For she had learnt to tell them apart—the *Schutzbündler*, the *Heimwehr* men and the Swastika-ites—first of all by their uniforms, then, more subtly, by the atmosphere that she could feel went with them—the firm friendliness of the first, the flabby shiftiness of the second, the strength filled to the brim with animosity of the third. There were more of the Swastika followers than of all the others put together.

This little man, now, after doing away with the others, had founded a gang of his own called the Fatherland Front and had incorporated the *Heimwehr* into it, and he dragged an anaemic child in his wake called the Catholic Action, "a still-born child, by God!" But they didn't have a uniform yet, they didn't have a flag, they didn't even have a badge! How far did they think they'd get that way?

In the kitchen and laundry Fehge heard nothing else. It was as though the great man's visit and death had plunged them all into the whirlpool of political madness. It didn't mean a thing to her. The Pfeiffer baby didn't die. Ludmilla Pfeiffer was up and about much sooner than the doctor had said she would be, and what an admirer she had grown to be of the girl Fehge! No more the sow-Jewess. When Fehge had lifted Ludmilla Pfeiffer up in her arms, she told everyone, "Our dear Lord couldn't have felt safer on the shoulders of the Holy Christopher!" There was Ludmilla for you! The Slavs were all crazy!

But Ludmilla Pfeiffer had the right to vote, as her husband had and as her children would have when they grew up, as Conrad had, and Schreiner, and Hilda, as every Austrian had. Their fine Republic had given them that. A fine thing, this voting, a fine, fair thing!

Only Fehge hadn't the right to vote. Fehge wasn't an Austrian. Fehge hadn't a country. Fehge had nothing but her burning personal desire to become a nursing nun like Sister Angelica. Her eyes would become luminous like a seeress when this thought overwhelmed her, as it so often did these days. At last she had found her place on God's earth and, at the same time, something she could get deep down into. She would help to heal the sick, not because she had learnt to love the people, who, in their unfriendly, belligerent way, were still as unfathomable as God's mercy, but because God had created them in His image. This uplifting thought, however, soon had to give way in her honest little mind to the less glorious truth, that she was choosing to be a nurse because she was not afraid of man when he was sick, with which sorry admission, much of her inspiration would leave her.

Chapter Eighteen

THE Countess Stefanie von Hohenberge was considered not only the most beautiful, but also the most tragic woman in Viennese society. Not that anything so immensely heartrending had happened to her. No children, an unhappy marriage, love-affairs that didn't last. It happened to so many other women. But it somehow did not go well with Stefanie, who seemed totally unsuited for the luckless fate that dogged her.

The Countess did not use her title, and once, after she had left her German husband, von Hohenberge, and quarrelled with her father, had even worked as a model in a smart dress shop in Berlin under the name of Stefanie Hohenberge. This had been very embarrassing for Oscar von Hohenberge, with whom she refused to live but who would not give his wife a divorce because he would not grant her the chance of finding in a second marriage the peace which she had not found with him.

The modelling proved so embarrassing to Hohenberge that he took time off for a trip to Vienna, where he had a long interview with Stefanie's father, with the result that the ever-impecunious Leo Trattner was able to make so generous an offer to his daughter, Stefanie, that she could not refuse to return to Vienna to live the life she had been cut out for—that of a society woman. She had no idea that she was doing this on the money of the man whom she loathed so that it physically sickened her to think of him.

Now she had come to Strubl to die. The flush in her cheeks and the feverish lustre of her eyes made her look more beautiful than ever. She was stricken by the same disease that had killed her sister, and she had listened to the disastrous news as a welcome release from a life that had brought her nothing but unhappiness.

She refused to show any signs of her malady. Therefore, when she was short of breath, which was especially the case on those days when a new pneumothorax filling had squeezed her lungs together so that she could hardly breathe, she would walk with her head slightly bent and her back very straight. After trying out everything, she had found that, in this way, she could draw the necessary breath for the walk from her room to the dining-room and even, on occasions, into the sunshine of the flat gardens just outside the house.

With her lovely head thus bowed in what seemed to be humility, her way of walking had an added graciousness. She wore silk gowns that clung. Sometimes she would lean against one of Strubl's big entrance doorposts, her arms crossed behind her back, as though she were about to run down the hill like the wind, she, whom it took every bit of fifteen minutes to get from the door to the lift and from the lift down the corridor, past five doors, to her room again.

She had many visitors. Her social life went on as though it had never been interrupted. Nobody minded the trip out to see her, and social activity was so much a part of her life that she would have missed it had it ceased. Her room was crowded with flowers and presents, and the chairs in her room did not suffice. A couch was brought in and an extra armchair, and Andrea shook her head when she threaded her way through the scant floorspace remaining. But even Andrea said nothing against it. She, too, had fallen under the beautiful lady's spell.

The days when Stefanie's father visited her were distracting. He would come with her two wild young brothers, the twins, who had been given the absurd old German names of Ingo and Ingraban. (There were some things one could only just barely forgive Papa for!) Eighteen they were, the sons of a second marriage. They came in a long white roadster with a loud klaxon, and they came during rest hour, regardless of rules. The klaxon would wail from afar off and awake not only the sleeping patients but the mountains too, which re-echoed the sound. The car would take the curves at high speed, Trattner at the wheel, and would come to a stop with a jarring of its brakes and a spurt of gravel. Out would tumble the menfolk, Trattner the youngest of them all, as young as only an old man can be, his sons as blasé and "old" as only hopelessly spoiled young boys can be. For them it was all a lark, even visiting a sick sister; and, anyway, she couldn't be very ill, she didn't look any different, she was a bit slower, but then . . . cheer her up, cheer her up . . .

The waitress, Rosl, and the maids who could leave their floor, and the girls from the kitchen and the cook would rush to the windows. "*Der Trattner*, look, *der Trattner!*"

It was the famous old man they were ogling, not his young sons. To his dying day he would be the unrivalled centre of attraction. It was what had made his path to fame so incredibly smooth.

"He isn't so old that he should have such white hair."

"It's always been white. Since he was seventeen. He used to dye it blond."

"With his children he hasn't any luck."

The Trattners would storm upstairs, burst into Stefanie's room, Stefanie in bed resting. They joggled her bed when they sat on it and didn't notice how she winced. They all talked at once. Trattner said, "I'll have a nap out on your balcony. The boys can sleep on the couch. They haven't slept all night. And at four o'clock we'll throw them to the females!"

Roars of laughter. It hurt Stefanie to laugh. The beads of perspiration stood out on her forehead with the pain. But she laughed with them.

The boys had brought her lute. They put it on her lap, on the white bed-covering, and she laid her long, beautiful fingers over the strings as though silencing them for ever. How sweet they were, not realizing that she had hardly enough breath left to talk, much less sing. "After tea you must sing for us," they said. She nodded her head, the tears near, for she loved her lute. With it she had flown away from many a mammoth German drawing-room, from people whose cold, gossiping eyes she hated, away to a world of her own. She said she would, and then let them forget it.

They brought cake with them from the finest *Konditor* in Vienna and a box of pralines from the finest candy shop, and a gramophone, and they played it very loud. A record called "Miss Otis regrets . . ." Trattner, ignorant, had to have the words translated for him. And Stefanie could do it just like the negress who sang "Miss Otis regrets . . . she's . . . unable . . . to lunch . . . today . . ." The sobbing pauses were cut out for her who had to draw a fresh breath for every third word anyway.

They had brought other presents too. American silk stockings. Stefanie held them up to the light. "Light gossamer," she sighed, her lips making a pretty round "o" of delight. Nail polish. "I can't wear it that red, Ingo. I'll look like a whore!"

"In Vienna the best people are doing it."

"*Are* there any best people in Vienna?" Laughter. How silly they all were!

"Look what I can do, Steff!" Trattner, the sixty-year-old man, could do a handstand from the floor on to the table.

"Papa! You'll have a stroke!" But he didn't. His face just reddened, and he sprang lightly to his feet again. "Tomorrow I go hunting," he said. "Count Palini has promised me a thirty-two *ender*!" He accepted such munificent gifts as a matter of course. Wasn't he one of God's chosen? But with his children he had no luck.

"Ingo's going to join the German Air Force," his brother interposed. Silence. Trattner was changing a record, Ingraban was cutting the cake. But Ingo's attention was not distracted from his sister's face. "Why, what's the matter, Steff?" he asked her.

"You wouldn't do that," she said, and drew as deep a breath as she could. "You wouldn't do that?" And she drew another breath. Damn the pneumothorax! Why did they pester her like this? It wouldn't save her. Why didn't they leave her alone so that she could have this out with Ingo? That was more important than that she should live another few months.

"What's the matter with it?" asked Ingo, whose face had never changed since he had been ten.

The music started. "Turn it off, Papa," she said sharply, and he acquiesced with a dumbfounded expression on his face. What was the matter with Stefferl? She looked so angry, and she was so pale except for the high colour in her cheeks, round red spots, like bad rouge. Trattner stopped the gramophone. "With whipped cream or without?" asked Ingraban, flourishing the cake knife.

"You can't do it!" said Stefanie. "You mustn't do it. There will be war, and you mustn't be messed up in it! Ingo! Why don't you go away? Why don't you two boys go to America?"

"I'm not a Jew," said Ingo. "Why should I go to America?"

"Don't make a joke of it, Ingo! Why should only the Jews be saved?"

Ingo said, "Now, Steff. Just because Hohenberge was a boor, you don't have to condemn the whole race."

Stefanie leaned forward. "I thought Germany had no air force," she said. "Aren't you being very indiscreet?"

The boys laughed. "Oh, everybody knows, and nobody gives a damn!"

Stefanie said, "Treachery! Typical German treachery!" and she had a fit of coughing.

Trattner said, "Really, Stefferl, when are you going to stop being melodramatic?"

But Stefanie could say nothing more. She was sitting up, exhausted, her knees hunched, her right elbow resting on them, her aching forehead cupped in her right hand, her other hand listless on the bed beside her. She looked from one to the other. She was so weak. And, suddenly, she wanted to be strong again. Would life never let her go in peace?

"I wouldn't fly," said Ingo's more pallid half, "if you paid me. I'm going to Berlin. I've had a good offer."

"With the Ufa," said Trattner proudly. "It's a small part in the next Wessely picture, but it's a beginning."

Stefanie leaned back. Papa, she thought. He never could take care of any of us!

"Let Fehge serve tea," she said wearily.

Fehge came into the room from the balcony, where she had been sitting in the brilliant sunshine, which she could always bear without a head covering. She had been running ribbons through Stefanie's exotic lingerie. Now she got the cups and saucers out of Stefanie's little cupboard that they had bought for her and inserted in the wall. Fehge was Stefanie's maid.

It had all been thus ordained by a benevolent God. Fehge had not even had to ask for it. She got fifty *Schillinge* a month from Stefanie, more than twice what Strubl had paid her, and she needed the money to buy herself a decent winter coat. At any rate, Andrea said she needed it. The shawls she wore, Andrea said, were unworthy of such a fine girl and made her look like a peasant, which she was not. Andrea, who on the trip to Wiener-Neustadt had discovered that she could let loose her imagination on what Fehge should wear, envisaged one with a little collar of rabbit fur. A daring idea! To that end, the salary paid by Stefanie would be helpful. Andrea had been reluctant on only one score.

"Wash your hands with Lysol in the water," she warned Fehge. "Never touch your face with your fingers on duty. Never accept food. Don't bring anything out of the room into your own room, no books, no papers. The Frau Gräfin is very ill."

It was not the kind of work that Fehge felt she was cut out for; it didn't include getting deep down into anything. It was very easy. But she looked upon it as a little luxurious gift of God, this "soft" job, serving someone whom she adored, not only because she was physically beautiful, but because she was gentleness personified, and such a lovely, kindly light shone from her. Yes, this was her interim gift from God, before she embarked on the arduous life of a nursing sister. A superlatively satisfied Thérèse had promised her that she might enter a convent when she was twenty years old. She was now fifteen.

On the day after Ingo's revelation, Stefanie asked Sapponyi to release her from the pneumothorax treatment. "It is the only thing we can do to help you," he began.

"It won't make me well," she said. "Will it?" When he didn't answer, she repeated, "Will it?"

He knew she didn't want to hear him say yes, so he told her the truth and said, "No."

"There you are. So what's the use? I don't care if it shortens my life. I want to be free." She shook herself. "Free of this chain round my chest. I must breathe, Herr Medizinalrat. For these last months I need all the breath in me."

Her life was her own. Sapponyi gave in. But all the breath in the world would not have deterred Ingo from the path he had chosen. He was, after all, a Trattner too. He went to Germany, and Stefanie mourned for him as though he had died.

One day Stefanie was expecting a visitor early in the morning. Fehge tucked her into her chair on the balcony. It was a perfect spring day. Stefanie was grateful for her breathing, which was certainly better since the chain round her heart had been removed. Her temperature was higher in the afternoons, and the cough in the morning more violent; but she didn't care . . . she didn't care.

Fehge stacked away the breakfast dishes, took the bed apart, stood the mattress up edgewise on its three parts, washed her hands, and left the room. The maid would clean it.

When the visitor came, Stefanie rang for Fehge; she wanted her to prepare coffee in the Turkish coffee machine as she had taught her to do, and prepare white goose-liver sandwiches with the crust cut off . . . yes, with the crust cut off. The crusts Fehge crumbled and gave to the birds. She spread the crumbs out on the railings' sill, and the finches who seemed to stand eternal watch in the near-by firs swooped down and picked them up.

Olga Retschnichek, the visitor, was a resplendent woman, tall, full-bosomed, with a deep melodious voice and a profusion of golden hair gleaming under her large black hat. She wore many jewels and a fox fur-piece. The two fox heads over her right shoulder seemed to be biting into her flesh. She leaned back in the wicker chair, her hands moving all the time, one foot jiggling back and forth on her crossed knee. She showed a fine leg up to her thigh.

"This is Fehge," said Stefanie, pointing to her. "I advise you to get on the right side of her and take her with you when I no longer need her. I'm sure she'd go with you, wouldn't you, Fehge?"

Fehge smiled and shook her head. The Frau Gräfin loved to make fun.

But Stefanie thought she had had an idea. "Wouldn't you like to work for Frau Retschnichek when you have done all you can for me? In Vienna? I am sure she would pay you much more than I do, and you would make a fortune in tips, for she is always having visitors." She turned to her friend. "Fehge is the most *serviable* little creature in the world. She seems always to have an eye on your needs. I can highly recommend her."

Olga Retschnichek beamed. Maids from the country were much sought after. Stefanie turned back to Fehge. "Well, what do you say?"

Fehge reddened and hesitated. How to explain it and not be rude? Both women were looking at her so kindly. Olga Retschnichek was thinking what a prepossessing girl Fehge was, with her beautiful dark skin and rounded features, with her calm, beautiful, Biblical face, like a Miriam; and Olga Retschnichek thought, as so many women her age did, how long ago it was since the skin round her eyes had been so smooth, an effect you could never create with cosmetics. Fehge was so disarmingly young, and innocent looking, thought Olga Retschnichek, who had practically never been innocent.

"I am going to be a nursing sister," said Fehge, "when I am twenty."

Stefanie raised her eyebrows. "A hard life you've picked out for yourself, Fehge."

"It doesn't seem hard to me," said Fehge. "I want something I can get deep down into. This . . . this is no work for me," she went on, using the phraseology she had employed when Melita had wanted to guide her on more professional paths.

Both women laughed, and they were still friendly. "Then why do you do it for me?" said Stefanie.

"Well, I'm not twenty yet," said Fehge, in her matter-of-fact way, "and"—she blushed—"I think the Frau Gräfin is so beautiful. I want to be near her."

Olga Retschnichek laughed again, but Stefanie was silent, and the tears stood in her eyes as she looked away from the girl's sincere face. No one could be further removed from the characters of the women she associated with than this girl, Fehge.

Olga said, "Well, I'm certainly glad you're being so well taken care of by such a faithful girl."

"I will not take up much more of her time," answered Stefanie lightly. "I am going to die, Olly, and you know I am glad."

Olga looked away into the hills for a moment and was still, hands and legs. "It's so damned unfair," she said, and her voice was very low, "that you should have to say a thing like that, and I can't say you should feel otherwise. Why did you have to marry Oscar? Oh, what a fool your father is!"

"You're doing Papa an injustice," said Stefanie. "He didn't force me to marry Oscar. In fact, he would have had a hard time stopping me. I was so afraid of life after Mother died and Hedy married. I felt so alone, and my admirers harassed me. Didn't yours ever harass you?"

"No," said Olga, and laughed.

"Oh, I was harassed. By their numbers, their presents, their demands. Offending them. Not offending them. It was terrifying. I wanted a friend so badly. And that was what Oscar seemed to be. A friend. He was so reserved and aloof. So disciplined. I knew I attracted him, and I admired it so in him that he didn't want to maul me about constantly. Really, Oscar drew me like a magnet. There's no other way of expressing it. I would fly to him from their emotional demands. What a relief it was to dine and go to the opera or to the theatre with him!"

Olga raised her eyebrows. "Don't tell me you married your ideal?"

"I think he must have been proceeding according to some sort of plan when he was courting me," said Stefanie, not as an answer, but more to herself, "for as soon as we were married he was completely changed. I was acquired; I didn't count. You hear a great deal about the calculation of the German militarist. The German industrialist is made of the same cold, hard steel. Olly, it was like being part of a machine. Perhaps, if I had been able to stick it out, he might of his own accord have discarded me, you know, as a man changes the oil in his car, to make it run more smoothly. But suddenly, one day, I had touched his honour. His honour! I told him that I would never bear his children. Propagate that strain? No. And, it was strange—from that day on his hatred seemed to bind him to me more than his love had ever done. He won't divorce me. He hangs over my life like a big black shadow."

If Olga had not sat so silently, Stefanie might not have gone on. "Let me tell you something typical of the man. You remember Kleibner? You've heard of him. He invented a chemical that could be used as a cheap fertilizer. It proved to be a sensation in the field of agriculture. His wife, who was a scientist too, understood his invention and warned him that it could also be used for destructive purposes—to make poison gas. Kleibner pooh-poohed the idea. Now Oscar was a friend of the Kleibners and Kleibner's wife used to talk to Oscar about her fears and he would quiet her. Meanwhile, Oscar's chemical firm had acquired the rights to Kleibner's invention and all the time, while he was quieting Kleibner's wife, Oscar was making poison gas based on the Kleibner invention. Those gases were used in the last war. When Kleibner found out, he killed himself."

"The German," said Olga, her leg jiggling again, "can turn everything into a weapon of destruction."

"I detest them," said Stefanie. "I would have them all . . . all . . . every man, woman, and child, killed, to the last man. But that is no solution for people like us. Out here I have been trying to think of one. It is very confusing and difficult. There are so many of them. They are so stupid and so diligent, so long-suffering and so selfless and so ambitious for things that have not hand or foot . . . that are neither here nor there. . . . It is such a wicked combination."

Olly said, "Well, one thing is certain—we Austrian women should never marry a German. We speak their language, but that is really all." To which Stefanie replied, "I wouldn't say Austrian women, just like that, Olly. Austrian society women—yes. But think what an infinitesimal fraction of Austrian women that covers, and the others . . ." She paused.

"What about the others?"

"Aren't different from the others everywhere else."

Suddenly her delicate little nose sniffed. "Fehge," she said, "I think you've ground that coffee into pulp."

Fehge started. She had been listening. Now she hastened to fill the little copper pot and make the coffee, one cup at a time, as Stefanie had shown her. In a few seconds the black brew bubbled and she skilfully poured out a cup and handed it to the resplendent lady, who thanked her with an absent-minded nod.

"If only I had a child," Stefanie said, and Fehge for the first time heard her voice break with the grief she always seemed to personify. "People with our ideals should have children, children, children! That is what *they* are doing. If we don't do the same, they will soon outnumber us."

"I think they do that already," said Olga, and her gaiety seemed completely gone.

"If I had a child of my very own, to bring up according to our ideals. . . . It seems silly, it would be only one amongst so many others. But it would give me hope. I would live, Olly, and I could live if I wanted to. But I am going to die, quite wasted."

She shivered. "Get me my jacket, please," she said to Fehge.

When Fehge came out of the room with the red suède jacket lined with soft lamb's wool, both women were looking through the balcony's railing at a man who, in an English golf suit, pipe in mouth, was walking rapidly down the curve in the road that led toward the village. Stefanie said, "Look, there goes the Englishman. He used to be a patient here. Now he has come back to live. He has rented one of the cottages on the estate and fixed it up. You should see it, Olga. It is charming. He is a nice young man, not really so young, but, you know, one of those people who are eternally young. I like him very much."

Chapter Nineteen

"DEARLY BELOVED," said Fehge to Dennis, "how does a child come to be born?"

She was cleaning his shoes in the early morning, sitting on a hassock as he breakfasted. It was still so cold that they could see their breaths. A fire crackled on the hearth. The chimney grew up out of the centre of the house so that every room built round it could have a hearth fire. They could see the thin blue smoke spindle away in the distance against a clear sky. The hearths had been

Dennis's idea and the breakfast-room, which had replaced a large, bare pantry because the sun struck here first thing in the morning, and the dark wood panelling looked warm and brought the forest into the house.

Dennis had come back for a few tangible and many intangible reasons. Because the house on Clapham Common was too damp to live in and too full of cloying memories; because Bramwell Heath, up on a high hill where the air was clear, and with a splendid view of the Thames Valley, still could not compare with Fichtenbach; because the English people were so dull, he was so accustomed to them, they would do nothing untoward; because Paris had grown dirty and sluggish and belligerent; because the Swiss seemed suddenly so stodgy, the Balearic Islands too enervating, and Germany a place he would never go to again of his own free will; and because Fehge so obviously didn't care whether he came back or not.

Her bright little face had looked into his day after day from out of the absurd photograph taken in Wiener-Neustadt, and had seemed to challenge him. Melita, he had heard, had been transferred. His decision to return to the valley seemed to date from that knowledge, which, however, proved to be based on a misunderstanding. He found Melita still there, a changed, withdrawn Melita whom he could never get completely out of his mind although he very rarely saw her. She was the only person who had ever made him feel cruel.

To the peasants in the village he was an enigma. He was, of course, no aristocrat. It wasn't his shabbiness that made them come to that conclusion, but the fact that he had no residence in the sense that an Austrian aristocrat had, however shabby. He was not rich, that was evident by the simple way he lived and cooked his own meals—a queer sight, indeed—nor could he be poor, for he never did a stroke of work and yet seemed to be able to keep a roof over his head, food in his mouth, and clothes on his back. He painted, of course, but that was not work.

Fehge didn't bother her head about the social implications of Dennis's presence in the valley. She was very grateful for it.

Now, had he suddenly gone away, she would have missed him. He was her wise man, her own private encyclopedia. She needed him.

Stefanie's routine, that of a woman used to living her life by night, was not so easily broken. She slept until ten. This left Fehge time to clean Dennis's cottage every day after she had done the steps, and to prepare his breakfast. He had suggested that she breakfast with him, but she had said that it was not the proper thing to do.

"You ate Christmas dinner with me eight years ago," he challenged her.

"I was a child then, and didn't know any better," she said. "I'm grown up now, and I know my place."

He had thrown back his head and laughed and laughed, and when he had been able to speak again he had said to her, "Many a young lady in her teens has told me that she was grown up, because she was hopelessly and unhappily in love, or because nobody understood her, or because she knew exactly what she wanted to be—usually something she was totally unfitted for; but you're the first young creature I know of who has followed up that statement with positive proof of its accuracy."

Of course she hadn't known what he meant, but she had laughed aloud with him because his laughter was irresistible.

Now this accredited grown-up sat before him and asked, "Dearly Beloved, how does a child come to be born?"

"Why," said Dennis, "you know all about that," and, of course, she should, a fifteen-year-old girl living in the country.

"I don't know anything much," was her answer.

"Well," said Dennis, thinking that a woman should be telling this story, but rather glad that Andrea had not done so, or Melita . . . Melita, he was sure, would have made a very dry thing of it; "you have seen Pfeiffer's cow calve, haven't you?"

"Yes," said Fehge, "and Pfeiffer's wife nearly died when Hansi was born."

"Of course," said Dennis. "Why, you were in on that! You were with her when the child was born."

"Yes," said Fehge, "and Pfeiffer wasn't nearly as upset about his wife as he was about his cow that had licked a bad ointment off her hide. She died."

"The wife?"

"No. The cow."

"Well," said Dennis, "you know all about how babies are born. What more do you want to know?"

"I want to know how babies start."

That was exactly where Dennis had hoped to be able to end his story. Queer, that she didn't know. Most girls around here her age already did, by experience. Of course, she lived a very secluded life, guarded by a dragon. Still, it was supposed to stir in you so that you found a way.

He sighed, and sipped his coffee. He wanted to make a beautiful story of it. She had every right to expect that of him. Everything that had happened between them until now had been poetic. He put down his cup, sat back, and, gesturing with his open hand toward her young body, said, hesitating as he spoke the words, "That is where women carry the seed which grows and becomes a baby child at the given time."

"And what is the given time?"

"The given time is when the seed of the man joins with the seed of the woman as it tells you in the Bible." And he was glad that, thanks to him—and, an afterthought, Andrea—she knew her Bible. "Then the baby starts to grow," he finished.

"Where does the man carry his seed?"

Dennis walked over to an old cabinet that stood against the opposite wall and took paper and pencil out of a drawer. He made a fairly good and quick drawing of Michael Angelo's Adam, which, to him, had always seemed the most aesthetic drawing of a man. He had sketched the figure often, and it came to him easily.

Fehge's lips parted in the effort to grasp what was being explained to her. In one hand she still held the brush, in the other Dennis's large shoe. She closed her mouth, nodded her head and said, "I see. And now, please show me where the woman receives the seed."

Dennis drew for her the woman's body and explained its functions. During this anatomical lesson the coffee grew cold. "Shall I warm it for you?" she asked him, as he sat back and started to drink again.

He shook his head. "I like it cool."

Fehge looked at the drawings, her forehead knit in a frown. "Does it hurt?" she said.

"No."

Suddenly her face fell. "So a woman cannot have a child without a man?"

"That's right," said Dennis, "and it wouldn't be fair otherwise, would it? The child would be all hers."

"No," said Fehge regretfully, "I suppose it wouldn't."

"And the man and the woman should love each other," Dennis went on.

"Why?"

"Because then the child is born good."

"Do you think," said Fehge, "that you could love the Countess Stefanie?"

Dennis, about to fill his pipe, laid it down again. Fehge finished brushing the shoe and put it beside its shining partner. "Why?" said Dennis.

"Because she says that if she had a child she would live. It would save her life. Now, if you could love her and give her your seed, she could have a child."

Fehge had obeyed her commandments since she had learnt them. The sixth commandment told her, "Thou shalt not commit adultery," and the Catechism further specified, "We are commanded to be pure in thought, word, and deed." It never occurred to her that, in what she had just suggested, she had committed an act of impurity.

But Dennis couldn't share her placidity any longer. He felt the heat of embarrassment rush to his head and could suddenly feel his heart beat faster. The whole conversation had, for him, been carried on in a sort of vacuum. His hands had turned quite cold. How perverted we are physically, he thought. Couldn't man do anything better with his spiritual powers than use them to pervert his physical attributes? He was angry and ashamed at his unnatural approach to such a natural matter. So much for fundamentals. But it would never do to let this viewpoint sway him here where a stranger seemed somehow to be involved.

"Fehge," he said, and could have shaken himself, so pompous did his voice sound all of a sudden, "have you spoken about this to the Countess Stefanie?"

"No," said Fehge, "I wanted to discuss it with you first."

"That was quite right," said Dennis, and now he wanted very much to laugh.

"Well. Will you?"

"If you promise never to mention this whole matter to anyone else in the world, especially not to the Countess Stefanie—I promise you to think it over."

Fehge smiled happily. "Oh," she said. "You always help."

Chapter Twenty

HER conversation with Olga remained with Stefanie long after that flamboyant creature had gone. She thought of her sister. Hedwig was dead, but her child was alive. Her boy was strong, all his organs intact. His mother's womb had shielded him from the disease that was devouring her.

The last time Stefanie had seen Eugene Behrendt he had been racing his colt down a steep hillside on her father's estate near Bad Ischl. Trattner had looked after him and said, "If Hedy could see him! If Hedy could only see how well he's doing!"

The boy was all Trattner's. Eugene adored his jovial, spectacular grandfather and was shy of his morose and preoccupied father, with whom he spent less and less of his time. Stefanie's lips curled with contempt as she thought how easily Moritz Behrendt had relinquished his child to a grandfather who was undeniably great fun but no spiritual guidance whatsoever. The Party would always come first. If she had a child, she would relinquish it to no one. It would grow up to be like her, like them; it would grow up to *be* something, not to stand for something, and that was what counted now, she thought. If she had a child . . . And why shouldn't she have a child?

Next morning, at eleven, Sapponyi came and she was not up; which surprised him.

"I am still in bed, not because I feel bad," she cried out gaily, "but because I want to speak to you." On the balcony, voices carried.

Sapponyi said, "Oh, that's it, is it?" and Andrea went quietly out of the room.

When Andrea had gone, Stefanie told Sapponyi that she was going to have a child. He said nothing for a moment, but looked at her piercingly. Then he said, "If you are going to have a child, we shall have to take it from you."

"Why?" cried Stefanie. "Eugene is alive and well!"

"Yes," said Sapponyi. "But Hedy is dead."

"And I must die, so . . ."

"You will not die any more quickly than any of us if you will live carefully . . ."

"Like this?"

"More or less like this."

"I would rather be dead."

Sapponyi said nothing. He couldn't blame her.

"If I can give life to a complete human being, not half a human being, as I am, would that not be better? Herr Medizinalrat, I will not let you take the child from me!"

"Who is the father?" said Sapponyi, who knew that it could not be Hohenberge.

"I can't tell you," she said.

"And if I refuse to continue treatment under these circumstances?"

"You wouldn't do that?"

Sapponyi smiled. "No," he said. "I wouldn't do that."

Stefanie repeated what she had said to Olga. "People like us, people with our ideals, should have children, children, children . . ."

Sapponyi looked at her for a moment, then he said, "The Countess has been lying to me. She is not going to have a child," and Stefanie laughed. Sapponyi said nothing more, but he did not leave. He looked out of the window and tapped with his pencil into the palm of his hand while the tears stood in Stefanie's eyes.

Then he said. "Don't do it. It would be madness."

"If it should happen," she said softly, "you will take care of us?"

"If it happens. You are of age. It is for you to decide."

"And you will take care of us?"

"Yes," he said, "I will take care of you," and he used the plural, "*euch*," as she did.

He left her alone, and she lay for a long time without stirring, watching the shadows cast by a noonday sun move fraction by fraction of inch across the room. When Fehge came to serve luncheon, she asked the girl to bring her pen and paper. "The Frau Gräfin, her lunch will get cold," said Fehge, twisting the sentence in the village dialect which she now used less and less frequently. Parrot-like, she was picking up the "high" or pure German she heard from Stefanie.

"I don't care," said Stefanie. "I'm not hungry anyway."

Fehge was used to that, but not to what followed immediately after. "Wait!" said Stefanie. "Bring me that tray. I will eat."

Fehge stopped and stared. Stefanie laughed. "Don't stare like a fool," she said. "Bring it here. I will eat." And she did, the first hearty meal since she had come to Strubl to die. It was hard work; she had to eat very slowly, but she went through with it and she drained the glass of milk which she had formerly never touched.

Then she lay still to keep the precious food down. It was a disagreeable feeling to be so full. She could never remember having eaten so much in her life. When she felt that what she had eaten was down to stay, she reached for the paper and pen which Fehge had left on the table at her side and began to write a letter. Her beautiful brow furrowed with earnestness, and her breath came short with excitement. She wrote fast, read what she had written, addressed the envelope with handwriting that flew but was distinctly legible, and sealed it. Then she fell asleep and slept until Fehge brought her coffee on a tray. "I want to go out on the balcony," she said.

Fehge had to ask Andrea. Andrea phoned through to Sapponyi, who ordered : "Let her do anything she likes."

Chapter Twenty-One

PETER ALTERN let the slow-moving train rattle him toward Pritnitz and Strubl, undisturbed by its jerks and groans. He had asked for a second-class ticket and paid for it—all this at the ticket-office of the Südbahnhof in Vienna. When he reached the train, he discovered that it had no second class, only third. He went back to the ticket-office. "Why, for God's sake, do you sell second-class tickets when there's no second class on the train ?"

"The gentleman asked for a second-class ticket," said the moustachioed old clerk indignantly, and began slowly to go about changing it. That was Austria for you. A moth-eaten land. If inefficiency was a harbinger of doom, then this Austria was certainly doomed. *Doo . . . oomed, doo . . . oomed, doo . . . oomed*, the train seemed to say, and made him think of Stefanie. What could she want with him ?

He sat back, his eyes closed, his feet crossed on the empty bench opposite. He and a forester in a green *loden* cape with the pointed Tirolean hat and brush, a long pipe hanging down over his chest, were the only occupants of the compartment.

The wooden seat creaked, the windows rattled, the train breathed laboriously as it wound its way up into the hills between dark firs that cleared every now and then to reveal a view of the valleys.

Peter wore no hat. He was tall and broad, and he looked twice the size of the forester, whose long moustache trailed down both sides of his full red lips. You always expected a man's moustache to hide his lips, but this one's didn't, and the effect was startling.

Peter was big, but very perfectly built. His skin was smooth and looked as though he did not have to shave often, this in spite of the fact that he was very dark. His eyes were bright like black cherries and quick, his features very even, his face, as it was now, in repose, not clever. When the train stopped and the conductor cried out from the ground below, "Pritnitz!" Peter opened his eyes with a start and said, "Jesus Maria! Don't tell me that we've arrived!" And he threw a "*Grüss Gott*" at the immobile forester, who answered with a grunt.

Two hours later these unanimated features were aglow with animation. Peter was talking to Stefanie, and his delight at seeing her again had enlivened his face. It sparkled with the brightness of his eyes and the flash of his smile. As he moved restlessly back and forth, Stefanie regarded him lovingly from her chair. She was up and dressed every day now. She looked fatter and stronger than she had done for years. They had told him that she was seriously ill. He had never seen her looking better in his life.

"Why did you send for me?" he asked her. "What's up? I haven't seen you for ages. And do you know, this is the first time you've resorted to our childhood pledge?" The childhood pledge to come to each other from the farthest corners of the earth if the one or the other should need it, a pledge given after a romantic afternoon of playing a game of knights and ladies, she, Hedy, Peter, and another girl—he couldn't remember the other girl's name. "Fricka something or other," he said. "I can't remember her last name. She was an awful German brat, but her mother and your father were friends, so she was staying with you. Imagine calling a girl Fricka! Like a Walküre! I wonder what became of her."

"She married an Austrian," said Stefanie. "I don't think she's very happily married, although you can't go by gossip, can you? The Viennese love to think people are unhappily married and happy only in their affairs."

They both laughed. "Well. Why did you send for me? I didn't come from the other corner of the earth, but in my financial condition Paris *is* the other corner of the earth. It took all my savings!"

"Don't tell me you're living from hand to mouth?"

He put his hands on either arm of her chair and his face close to hers. "Do any of us ever do anything else?" And he kissed her eyes.

The full moon rose like a ball of fire over the hills. "Isn't it beautiful!" she said.

"Don't hedge. You're up to something. As usual."

"Let's go out on the balcony," she said, "and talk in whispers."

He laughed. She had always loved to talk in whispers, even when they had not been conspiring.

She stretched out on the long chair, and he sat in an armchair beside her. The moon rose high and paled. It cast its light across the smooth grass before the house. The trees that ringed the lawn stood in solid black with deep purple crevices where the moonlight could not enter. The mountains were silhouetted sharply against a dark-blue sky.

The mood affected them both. Peter grew calm and Stefanie felt stronger. "Now," she said. "I will tell you. I want a child. Your child."

Peter's heart beat fast. How hard it was to breathe when one was excited.

"Why?" he said, when he saw that she was going to say nothing more.

"Because you and I are so much alike. I would like to have had this child all by myself, really, all on my own . . ."

He laughed. "How like you, Steff!"

She laughed now, too, very low. "Yes, isn't it? But since this was impossible, I thought its father must be one with me. And you and I are one, more than anyone in my family is one with me, more than any of those I have loved have ever been. You know what I mean?"

"Oh yes," he said, and he did. He understood her perfectly. It had always been like that. They had thought alike, felt alike, squirmed over the same things, delighted in the same things, had the same ideals and the same passionate hates . . . ever since he could remember.

Stefanie looked at him. "Agreed?" she inquired.

He laughed and put his arm round her, lightly, like a brother. But it trembled a little. "I'll have to think it over later," he said, "whether I should be flattered or not. Would it, for instance, be more complimentary if you desired me, or is this the great thing, that you should want me to be the father of your child?" And his eyes ceased to dance and looked sombre.

She smiled. "You'll have all your life to think that over."

He *was* like her. He said nothing practical now, as to whether she ought to have a child. He made no mention of the future. He only asked her, a while later, whether it was a daughter she wanted or a son.

"Oh," she sighed, "I don't care. I only want a child of my own, like me, like us. There are so few like us left."

He asked her, "What do you mean? Like us?"

She said, "Gentlefolk."

Chapter Twenty-Two

AT just about this time, in the spring of the year 1933, Fricka Reuther suffered a serious relapse of her former ailment. When she was sufficiently recovered to be transported to a sanatorium, to her husband's great astonishment she herself suggested Strubl. Maurice Reuther said nothing, but Fricka noticed the raising of his eyebrows. "I know my way around there," she said, and spoke the words as though chagrined.

CHAPTER TWENTY-TWO

Her husband shrugged his shoulders. "I wouldn't know where I would rather have you be." She knew that, but it was not the reason she had chosen Sapponyi's sanatorium.

She knew her ailment well by now, and realized she would have to spend at least a year at Strubl. Anne-Marie was seventeen and had finished school. She had turned down the offer of a university education. Her interests didn't lie in that direction. Neither her father nor her mother could make out what she wanted, and neither of them trusted her. She was an unfathomable creature to them. Therefore, thought Fricka, if I leave her so long alone with her father she may fall under his influence. I will take her with me.

Maurice was relieved. He knew his daughter well enough to know that she would never fall under his influence. He had dreaded watching her with her mother gone; he hated to watch anyone. He would have liked to let her be free, as he himself loved to be, as free as he left his wife, Fricka, who abused that freedom. But you had to do your duty to your child, up to a certain age anyway, so, with Fricka gone, he would have been forced to keep a strict eye on Anne-Marie. When Fricka, therefore, as surprisingly relieved him of that loathsome duty as she had relieved him of the problem of the sanatorium, he was pleased.

Fricka rented a cottage on the Strubl estate, one not far distant from Dennis's, and she brought Anne-Marie and the girl's governess with her—the same timid, mouselike creature who had tried to placate Dennis seven years ago. She had acquired no more stamina in the years that had gone by; in fact, she was now a shadow of that shadowy former self, and as for being governess to the girl— she had no authority over that young lady whatsoever. She was nothing more than lady's maid to young Anne-Marie Reuther, who was disgusted at being buried alive with her mother in the backwater of Fichtenbach.

They arrived, and Fricka took to her bed, not to leave it until two months later, when she began to take walks, short ones, then longer ones—she was making a remarkable recovery. It was on one of these walks that she met Stefanie.

227

The women recognized each other; both knew that the other was at Strubl. Stefanie's childhood memories of Fricka Krausewitz had not been enhanced by what she knew of Fricka Reuther. She had heard of Fricka's strange political convictions, and they shocked her. Fricka, on the other hand, had no use for the decadent Austrian aristocracy with whom she classified Stefanie spiritually if not physically, and rightly so. The meeting of the two women was cool and formal.

They bowed and shook hands. Stefanie wore her social smile. "How do you do, Fricka, and how are you?"

Fricka, who could not put on airs, as she called it, though what she really lacked was poise, smiled in spite of herself, an unpleasant little grimace that gave her face no light. "Hello, Stefanie. I'm surprised to see you up."

"Oh, I am ever so much better," said Stefanie. "My temperature doesn't even rise in the afternoon any more. I hardly cough in the morning, and I have grown fat, haven't I?" She spread her arms apart, lifting the stick which she used to walk with, to show her girth.

It was all quite true. She had had her dresses let out, she coughed not at all during the day and very little in the morning, and Sapponyi had taken her temperature himself yesterday afternoon because he could not believe that it was normal.

Fricka did not congratulate her. Some people have all the luck! she thought. A useless woman like Stefanie. And she'll probably get well, at that!

Fricka was on her way to meet Schreiner at the inn opposite the schoolhouse, and Stefanie von Hohenberge was the last person she wanted to accompany her. But now there was nothing to be done about it except try to shake her off.

They started down the road together. It wound between shrubs and fir trees and past occasional open fields which were thick with wild flowers at this time of the year. A girl with flaming red hair was turning the wet hay in a distant field. She was wearing a brown dress. Stefanie was enchanted with the colours.

"How long have you been here?" she asked Fricka, knowing

quite well, since new arrivals and departures were announced by maid, waitress, porter, shoe-boy.

"Too long," said Fricka bitterly. "He keeps us here just to make money out of us."

Stefanie said sharply, "Sapponyi doesn't keep people here any longer than is necessary. Ever!" And she told Fricka the story of the woman whom Sapponyi had forced, against her will, to go home, and who had now, a year later, given birth to a child, a healthy boy.

Fricka grunted. "I suppose she was a Jewess."

Stefanie wrinkled her forehead. "I think she was," she said. "But what has that to do with it?"

"A boy," Fricka went on. "He would! A Jewish boy. One more. *Ach*, it *is* a conspiracy!"

Stefanie raised her eyebrows and had all she could do to keep from laughing out loud. Suddenly the objectionable, priggish child that had been Fricka was walking beside her. "What are you talking about?" she said gaily. Fricka, just like a little girl, sulked and didn't deign to answer.

Suddenly, in a complete outburst of joy, and because she found the other woman's attitude so unbearably ridiculous, Stefanie said, "Be consoled," and she used the "*du*" that they had used as children, "not only Jewish children are being born. I am going to have a child."

Fricka started. "You?" she said, and turned her head sharply to stare at Stefanie. "You can't have a child."

"Why not?" said Stefanie, still laughing, not seeing the hatred in the woman's eyes.

"When they know, they'll take it from you."

"When who knows?"

"Sapponyi."

"But he does know," Stefanie said, "and he isn't going to take it from me."

"So!" said the other woman, and stopped dead. "So! He isn't going to take it from you. But he took mine! A boy."

Stefanie laid her arm on the other woman's shoulder, who shook it off furiously. "I am so sorry," Stefanie said gently. "I had no idea that you had been through anything like that or I wouldn't have spoken about it."

"It *is*, it *is* a conspiracy," Fricka went on. "I always knew it!" And she shut her lips like a trap.

"Conspiracy?" Stefanie repeated. "What are you talking about? What conspiracy? Sapponyi wouldn't have done anything like that if you had not wanted it."

"He made me . . ."

"Oh, he couldn't have!" Stefanie interrupted her, angry at the woman's unreasonableness. "Sapponyi never makes his patients do anything!"

"I don't mean Sapponyi," Fricka said. "As if I would let myself be dictated to by a common Jew!" and Stefanie winced. "No. It was Maurice! My husband!" And she spat out the words with contempt.

Stefanie stood bewildered in the face of the woman's strange emotions. It was she who started them walking again, slowly, as though the motion might calm the temper of their discussion. "Perhaps he loves you," she said quietly, trying to remember what Maurice Reuther, Viennese society host, looked like.

"Yes," said Fricka, the contempt in her voice changed to mockery, "he loves me!"

"You have a daughter."

"I want a son!" cried Fricka. "I want a son!" And her voice had nothing human in it, nothing gentle, nothing that one could associate with a mother, not even with a lioness.

"Why do you want a son?" Stefanie asked into the hard silence that followed, and the answer came from Fricka like a hiss.

"I want sons for our Führer, Adolf Hitler."

There it was. Stefanie had never believed that there were people, people out of her own level of society, who followed that man and believed in him, the way Fricka Reuther believed in him. Fricka, the child she had played with. "Of course," she said softly, "I forget. You are German."

Fricka stopped again, drew a deep breath, drew herself up to her full height, and said in a resounding voice, "Yes. I am German."

Why did they puff themselves up so about it?

"Shall we go on?" said Stefanie coldly, wishing the walk ahead of them were not so long. Her breath was coming short again. How this conversation had excited her! She had not felt short-breathed like this for weeks. She wondered if she could still make the schoolhouse. She knew that she could not retrace her steps uphill, so she would have to make it. She walked now as she used to do, with her chin in, her eyes on the road, leaning more heavily than usual on her stick. She was afraid. Fricka Reuther had succeeded in frightening her, and that made her very angry.

There were things she hadn't taken into account when she had embarked on this greatest of all adventures, that she had not realized were here, in this backwater, amidst the unalterable beauties of Nature, the eternally rhythmically recurring moonlight and sunshine, the static mountains and valleys—things like Fricka Reuther and what she stood for. When she got back she would have to write to Peter. What if something were to happen to her? Perhaps, after all, the child would need a man's protection.

They rounded a curve, and there was the schoolhouse, lying still, hiding its lively burden. The garden was alive with foxglove, delphinium, and hollyhock; they could see the tall bright flowers above all the others and, as they drew nearer, the darker, golden-brown faces of the sunflowers, drooping because they still stood in the shade, waiting for the sun to round the house and touch them. Stefanie remembered how she loved to bite into their seeds. She sat down on the bench outside, in the shade, leaned her weary back against the cool stone of the house and closed her eyes. She was in every sense exhausted.

Lessons were over, but the priest was putting the children through their Catechism, and their uneven voices, the girls' high-pitched and clear, the boys' low and rough, floated out of the open window to them. Fricka was walking up and down like a caged lion.

"Why don't you sit down and rest?" said Stefanie indifferently, without opening her eyes.

"How can I rest when I am so agitated?" said Fricka.

"And so discontented," said Stefanie. "And so ambitious. No. I see that you can't rest." And she thought: I am being rude. For the first time in my life I am being rude!

". . . *und die heilige Jungfrau Maria*," chanted the young voices, the first words, hurried and high-pitched, then a quaint, very low intonation of the "ri" in Maria . . . "*und-die-hei-li-ge-jung-frau-ma-RI-a.*"

The voices ceased abruptly. A few low words in a man's voice, and then, like the sudden roaring of a cannon, the clapping of wooden desk boards, the scraping of heavy boots on the wooden floor. Bedlam. Shrill voices. A clapping of hands and silence, the silence of a group of children holding bated breaths, broken now and then by the scrape of a shoe, the rustle of a dress, a sniffle or two. They were standing at the top of the few wooden steps that led straight to the front door, and they were lined up two by two. Then, "*Grüss Gott*" chanted Melita's voice, and in a chorus "*Grüss Gott*" replied the children. School was out. A mad scramble down the stairs and into the sunshine.

"I am going to the inn," said Fricka as the children surged around them and stopped to stare. She said it in a voice that did not invite company. Still, again back in her customary routine of courtesy, Stefanie murmured, "I will wait here. Franz may not stop if he sees nobody waiting."

Melita came to the door. The past years had wrought little change in her. She had seemed to shrivel up and harden after Dennis had gone away. He had answered her warm letters coolly, making her wait so long for his replies, and it seemed to her that she had remained thus, unaltered, ever since.

Her failure to win him and his going away had thrown her back upon herself to a life with no illusions of private happiness. The Behrendt myth had been shattered completely, and no one else had come her way to whom she could transfer her warmth. All this had not served to make her physically more attractive, but there was still a wholesome freshness about her which made her pleasant to look upon. And she fitted perfectly into her setting.

The children, the whole village, for that matter, looked upon her as a comrade. She had won this status for herself by her stability throughout the sentence she had thus far served in Fichtenbach—almost ten years—by her capacity for being always there, ready to help, a capacity that had grown tremendously since she had been balked in her desire to give her warm, roused love to Dennis. The Fräulein Lehrerin was always the same, a Rock of Ages, a thoroughly reliable asset. They had learnt to appreciate her, and she hugged this appreciation to herself greedily because it was all she had.

"*Grüss Gott*, ladies," she said, and, because she had heard their last words, "Franz always stops. He brings the mail."

"And if you have no mail?" said Stefanie.

"I may not have any mail," said Melita, "but there is always the paper."

"What paper do you subscribe to?" asked Fricka, and there was something greedy in the way she said it.

Melita accepted the challenge and said, "To the Workers' Paper."

Fricka flashed a knowing glance at Stefanie. What do I care what she reads! What she is! thought Stefanie.

You should care, you should care, you should care, an inner voice told her, when people like Fricka care so much!

The children that still stood around, agape, attracted her attention. They were a prepossessing lot in their wild, sturdy way. She made slits of her eyes and tried to visualize them well groomed. Fine feathers would always make fine birds. That pale child —her features were aristocratic, and very vivacious was the little rosy one standing beside her, her thick black hair parted so straight that it looked like a doll's wig. "You have good material there," she said to Melita. "You should put them in a play."

"We do, at Christmas," said Melita. "Run along now and don't stare."

They bobbed curtsies and began to move away, slowly, some of them backing, unashamed of their curiosity. The pale child with the aristocratic features picked her nose.

In the mind of the actor's daughter, politics were at once forgotten. "Oh! You must let me help you," she said. A play, by children, for grown-ups had always been a hobby of hers.

"Well," said Fricka stonily. They had forgotten her, and that would never do. Stefanie's lack of respect for her and what she stood for was disturbing. She had wanted to be alone at the inn. But she was not yet through with Stefanie. However, Stefanie said, "I'll wait here," and closed her eyes again. There was nothing left for Fricka to do but go alone to the inn that lay diagonally opposite.

Stefanie could hear her footsteps recede. She opened her eyes. "How unbending she is," she said. "Nothing can shake her, however mistaken she is. She is a real German."

"She is a real Nazi," said Melita. "There are not many like her. The bitter little man who thinks he can do better if he changes sides —once we have him in our ranks, then the Communists get him, then he runs over to the Nazis—he is only human. But she, with her desire to see the Germans dominate the whole world, she is a real Nazi."

Stefanie remained silent. She had closed her eyes again.

"And I wish more of us were like her," Melita went on bitterly. "If only all of us believed as vehemently as she did, that we, only we, were right! That's the conviction that wins!"

"And leads to injustice," said Stefanie. "Nobody can believe in what is right as unrelentingly as in what is mistaken. It is as though, when you have vision enough to see the truth, you lose the vindictiveness which the man who is mistaken carries, like a weapon, to defend himself."

"Against what?"

"Against the truth, which would upset him."

Stefanie felt less tired now, and hungry. This surprising hunger! She rose. "I think I will go to the inn after all, and have something to eat. Good day, Fräulein Lehrerin. I shall not let you forget the play."

She found Fricka seated in one of the window niches, her round arms resting on the scratched wooden boards of the table, leaning against the straight high back of the wooden seat. In repose like that, her eyes resting placidly on the view outside, her clear-cut features expressionless, she looked as innocent as Faust's Gretchen. Stefanie shuddered, and she could feel her stomach give a little turn of revulsion.

Stefanie asked the *Wirtin* to whip some butter. "Ever since it happened," she said, sitting down opposite Fricka, not caring now if her words hurt the German woman, "I've been so hungry. I eat and eat. I've gained ten pounds. It can't all be baby."

"It is all quite clear to me now," said Fricka quietly. "It was the duty of the Jew to see that this German child was not born."

Stefanie leaned forward and gently laid her hand on the other woman's arm, and she spoke as she would have done to a sick man. "Now, we've been through all that before. You are really quite wrong. You are on the wrong track." She repeated herself purposely, her voice taking on a hypnotic quality. "Sapponyi had no intention of harming you. If he took life from you, it was to preserve yours, not to kill a German child. Sapponyi would kill nothing. Don't you realize that he has dedicated himself to the preservation of human life?"

Fricka stared past her. "I should never have let Maurice persuade me to come to a Jewish doctor," she said.

Stefanie sighed. It was a stone wall. I must write to Peter, she thought again. I must write to Peter.

She looked across the room at the little altar in a niche over the bar, at the simpering Madonna, whom she didn't know Fehge associated with her, in sweet embrace with her Child. Candles flickered at its base. Wild flowers stood in glasses on a little stand beneath her. Dear Mother of God! What unholy mothers there were in this world!

The *Wirtin* brought the freshly whipped butter which she had slapped into shape, small milky drops of whey still on it, and slices of fresh black bread. Stefanie spread the butter thick. Fricka helped herself grudgingly but greedily.

"Would the ladies like some cheese?" asked the *Wirtin*.

Stefanie nodded. "And a glass of milk."

"The ladies should come down next week," the *Wirtin* said. "We're going to stick a pig, and there'll be blood sausage."

Stefanie felt her stomach turn again. Fricka. Blood sausage. Odd. They brought forth the same reaction. Should one perhaps let one's stomach judge? It might do better than the brain.

"Franz is late," said Stefanie. "Won't Andrea be vexed when she doesn't find me on my chair at afternoon inspection!" She laughed when she thought how her easy-going way of life irked the Spartan nurse. "Will you come back with me?"

"No," said Fricka, "I shall stay here a while longer."

If Schreiner would only come when Stefanie was gone! He would cringe before Stefanie, and Fricka despised his servility.

The door opened, and the district doctor stood on the threshold, one hand still on the handle, his other removing his hat. "Good day," he said in his Reichsgerman way. He never used the greeting, *Grüss Gott.*

Hesitating slightly, he advanced toward the table where the two women were seated. Fricka introduced him.

Stefanie knew the district doctor by name and by political reputation, and she wished she had stayed outside. Fricka she could put up with; Fricka was of her own set, however renegade. This man, this little bourgeois radical, she did not have to put up with. Schreiner flushed as she did not offer him her hand.

It never occurred to Stefanie to wonder how Fricka knew Schreiner or to consider their meeting here anything but chance. Political conspiracy, to her mind, took place only in operettas. She looked out of the window and did not listen to the words the two exchanged, the man still standing. Her attitude was so distant that not even Fricka dared ask Schreiner to join them. She nodded her head at him, her eyes giving a message that said "Later," and Schreiner went over to the bar.

Franz came and stood in the doorway and bowed his head to indicate to the Countess that he was ready to take her back to Strubl, Stefanie called, "Frau Wirtin, I would like to pay."

She laid the coins on the table. "*Grüss Gott*," she said to them all in one. Fricka answered, "*Grüss Gott*," and watched her go. The door closed after her.

Schreiner and Fricka were alone. He left the bar and sat down opposite the German woman. In a little while the *Wirtin* joined them. Their heads were close together, and they spoke in whispers although there was no one to listen. Gone were class distinctions. National Socialism had united the innkeeper's wife, the academic man, and the society woman as no other creed had ever been able to do.

Chapter Twenty-Three

BEFORE Stefanie could write to Peter to tell him of her fears and to voice the many different solutions she had thought of in the few days, she received the news of his sudden death in a letter from his wife, Louise.

DEAR STEFANIE,

I must write to you. I held one of the dreadful little cards with their black edging in my hand for a long time, and then I realized that I couldn't send it to you. I must write to Stefanie, I thought. She is one of us. Of course, I had always been afraid that this would happen. Peter did so many reckless things, didn't he? First there was the auto racing, then that mad, long sail on the *Peer Gynt*, then the *Wasp* and his miraculous escape when it crashed, and, in the end, it had to be the glider. Of all the mad, careening things he rode, I feared the glider least of all. She seemed such a quiet thing, she rested so easily on the wind and came down to earth so gently. *Louise*, he named her, after me. She fell into the sea, and we none of us can fathom why Peter did not get out and swim away, but she sank and took him with her. I cannot seem to adjust myself to life without him. As though my heart, too, had ceased to beat, as though he had done all my living for me . . .

Stefanie put the letter down. So she was to be alone with her child—as she had wanted to be. But she could not recapture at the moment the joyous anticipation that had been hers throughout the past months. It was blotted out by this grief that came with the feeling that she would never see Peter again, that he was gone. It left a gap that pained immeasurably.

Not until weeks later did the pain become dull and the old joy begin to penetrate and glow again. But by that time her resolution had weakened. What had been her final decision before this blow had struck? France. She had wanted to go to France to live. But now, with Peter gone, she remembered a place she had loved in Switzerland, a village just above Arosa called Prätschli, where the air was rarefied and little chalets nestled at the foot of a rounded mountain peak that wore a white velvet cap when the snow was on it, unbroken by trees or boulders, as smooth as cream. The dark firs began to grow thick just below the village, which seemed perched on the top of the world.

She wrote to her father, who was playing a guest-star role in Berlin, too busy to visit her. She did not tell him about the child. She said that she would like to take up permanent residence in Switzerland, rent a little chalet there, keep house. She was so much better, and it would be cheaper than the way she was living now.

Trattner read the letter with his mind only half on it. It didn't seem feasible to him. He referred the matter to Hohenberge, who answered that he wouldn't pay a further penny if Stefanie left the country, and what was more, he couldn't! He couldn't send money out of Germany, and he had no intention of squandering his foreign exchange on Stefanie. The money he had in Austria was different. It was only a matter of time, now, until the two countries would be one. Yes, yes, thought Trattner, who read this letter, too, with only half his mind. Why didn't they leave him alone? Didn't they realize that he wasn't Trattner any more, that he was absorbed in the monstrous effort of becoming Lear? At last, at last he was going to play Lear! Forty years he had had to wait for the part, and now they came from all sides and addressed him as "Papa" and "Trattner," reminding him of his private existence. It was most irritating. It was more than that—it was positively detrimental to his work!

He wrote Stefanie an abrupt, unkind letter, that if she left Austria she would have to fish for herself, and *basta*!

By the time this answer reached Stefanie, the conversation that had given her the idea of flight had retired to a visionary background. It had been a nightmare. So be it, she thought, back in her reliable dream-world again. "I will be your fortress, not only now," she told her stirring child, "but always. This thing shall not penetrate to you. We will live in a world of our own."

One evening she told Fehge that she was going to have a child. That the Frau Gräfin was getting well and was happy, Fehge had already noticed. So that was the reason! When her work was done, she went down to the cottage to thank Dennis for "helping."

It took him some time to grasp what she meant. Then he said, "Well, then, everything's all right. But listen! This thing is to remain a strict secret between you and me."

"And the Frau Gräfin."

"No. Just between you and me."

"But she . . ."

"Now, listen, Fehge," he said, as severely as he had ever spoken to anyone. "I can't explain it to you, but you mustn't ever mention it again. Promise me."

"But if she mentions it?"

"She won't."

"She may."

"If she does, all right. But I don't think she will. Now, promise."

"I promise," said Fehge, very reluctantly. "But it doesn't seem right. It seems peculiar."

"It is peculiar," said Dennis. "Very peculiar!"

Chapter Twenty-Four

IT was Fehge's free afternoon, and she was going to spend it out of doors. She had to leave Ute at home. The dog was in heat, a time when Fehge was always sorry for her because she whined and was full of a longing Fehge could not let her fulfil.

Fehge took the familiar path up the Schwarzenberg, but turned off to the left shortly before the road curved in to the inn to find the rusty little lake where she loved to bathe. The water was shallow, but you could not see the bottom for iron dust, and your body gleamed golden in the water. When the sun shone on the lake it was brown.

Fehge undressed. "Ah," she sighed, as her overheated body slipped into the cool water, not as cold as it would have been in the morning, warmed now by an all-day hot summer's sun.

Fehge could not swim. She moved her hands and arms to feel the water move against her body and closed her eyes. When she opened them, a man was standing at the edge of the wood watching her. It was Conrad. Before she could draw breath to make a sound, he said in a pleasant voice, "Well, Jew-girl, you've done well by yourself."

Fehge stopped the scream welling in her throat. With a bound she was on the ground where her clothes lay and had picked them up. Then, hugging them to her, she turned her back on Conrad, who had not moved, and ran into the woods, away, away from him.

Gush, gush, gush, the trees called out after her as she ran from Conrad, who was close behind her, who had always been close behind her, on her heels, ever since she could remember, uphill, downhill, leaving a zigzag path like a deer. At last she reached her destination and dropped like a dead thing in the bushes behind it and lay still on the ground, her body wet with perspiration, the little twigs and pine-needles sticking to it. The ground was warm. She panted.

She wanted to listen for his footsteps, but her heavy breathing drowned out all other sound. If only she could stop breathing like this! Before she did, however, she fell asleep.

The martyred Christ, baking in the sunshine, His back turned to her, spread His arms wide and seemed to guard her as she slept. He had been her favourite destination once upon a time, her favourite *Marterl* on the road from Schwarzenberg to Hilpern. She had run to Him instinctively now.

When she awoke, she was breathing evenly and there was no other sound. She scrambled out of the bushes and walked back a part of the way she had come, to a place she knew well, where a brook was held back by large boulders and formed a pool. Here she washed herself and shook her clothes out and, when the heat of the day had dried her, dressed and went back to the *Marterl*, neat and clean now, and knelt down before it. "Dear Saviour," she prayed in the friendly way she had learnt from Andrea, "I thank you that you watched over me while I slept. Be ever with me . . ."

Her whispering voice faltered, and she gave up the dignity of prayer. "*Ach*," she sighed, and slumped down into a sitting posture on her feet, "why must we suffer so, you and I?"

Conrad had made no move to follow her. He had seen her body as it left the water and the lithe way she had run, like a hunted animal. He sauntered over to the pool, picked a long straw on the way, which he sucked as he took off his shoes. Undressed, he proceeded to bathe in the waters she had just left.

Conrad, now a trained member of the Austrian Legion formed by Hitler out of those Austrian youths who had escaped from the dictatorial Dollfuss regime and wanted to fight their way back into their land under his flag, had returned to Austria on a "special mission." Before going into action, however, he had asked for and been granted a few days' leave, to get his affairs straightened out. His affairs were, chiefly, Hilda. Not that he had anything concrete to offer her yet, no salary that they could live on, nor any stable position, but he had plenty to tell her, and when the day came . . .

Der Tag! There was always a *Tag* to live for. The *Tag* God had given them today never seemed to suffice.

Conrad had called up from Pritnitz and been told that this was Hilda's day off and that she had gone away for the day, and the Fräulein in the office had added, "The staff does not receive telephone calls," and hung up before she could hear his belligerent words, "Tell your swine-Jew he won't have a telephone much longer!"

Conrad thought he knew where he could find Hilda. But at the pool he had found only Fehge. Hilda's way of life had evidently changed. He thought about Fehge again, as he cooled off in the water, and remembered her beautiful brown body. A pity she was a Jewess.

He dressed and walked down to Strubl. He inquired for Rosl, the waitress, and asked her where Hilda had gone. "Oho," she said tauntingly, knowing well how vulnerable was the youth who stood before her. "You'd better find yourself another girl. Your Hilda is in love!"

"She'd better stick to me," said Conrad, his face darkening. "I'm on the right side of the fence!"

"So's she, my boy, so's she," said Rosl. "Only higher up than you'll ever get! Would you like me to tell you who it is?" And she told him the name of Hilda's new lover.

It gave her great satisfaction to do so, for she, too, was frustrated. Not that her plans included Heinrich Grabautschnik—she wanted an inn of her own; but she could not be pleased about the third-floor maid's conquest of the successful Pritnitz innkeeper. Grabautschnik, in his virile, sensual way, had been a lover she had enjoyed.

Conrad blanched with fury. Yes. Heinrich Grabautschnik was on the right side of the fence all right, always had been, and a good five lengths ahead of Conrad. *Obersturmtruppführer* was Heinrich Grabautschnik, and a candidate for the post of *Gauleiter* of Lower Austria. Damn Hilda! Damn her to hell!

He stumbled off, and Rosl noted his broken walk with satisfaction.

Chapter Twenty-Five

FRICKA walked down the road with her daughter. Anne-Marie's golden hair was finer and lighter than her mother's, hovering over her head like a halo, and she had her mother's light-blue eyes. She walked lightly, indifferent to the beauty of her surroundings, bored with the valley and the uncouthness of the people. Bored, bored! Fehge, whom she was not allowed to associate with, was the only girl in the village who interested her, because she had been born contrary and because Fehge went in and out of the cottage inhabited by Dennis. This Anne-Marie would like to have done too, and was prevented from doing by two people—by her mother, who did not want her to associate with foreigners, and by Dennis, who had rebuffed her on the two occasions when she had risked her mother's furious reprimands and visited him. Now she could see Fehge in the distance, coming toward them, heading for the Sanatorium from which they had just come. The Jewess was carrying a pailful of something. Her dog on long, thin legs was prancing beside her.

She's only a servant girl like any other, thought Anne-Marie, and yet she knew very well that Fehge wasn't like anyone else at all. It was far beyond Anne-Marie's comprehension to state what Fehge was like, even though in her own mind the Jewess seemed "different."

Now a man was turning into the road that crossed theirs, between them and Fehge, and he walked up to the Jewess and said something to her. She shook her head and tried to pass him, but he barred her way. The pail, that evidently needed steady handling, hampered her. He took it from her, she letting go reluctantly, and now they advanced toward Fricka and Anne-Marie together. As they came face to face, Fehge cast down her eyes and said nothing, because she had once greeted Fricka Reuther and received no answer, but the man was about to say something, "*Grüss Gott*" perhaps, when Fricka stopped him. "Conrad Schreiner," she said, "why do you carry the pail for the Jewess? Is that what they taught you in the Reich?" The dog that was muzzled growled and moved restlessly from one fine leg to the other.

Conrad flushed and stood indecisively. Fehge took advantage of this moment to take the pail from his uncertain hand and hurry on.

"Don't make a fool of yourself, Conrad," said Fricka, as she saw him glance after the girl in spite of himself. Then she turned to her daughter. "Anne-Marie, this is Conrad Schreiner. Dr. Schreiner's son. He has just come back from the Reich. He will come up some day and tell us about it, won't you, Conrad?"

Conrad paled at the honour, and Anne-Marie stretched out her plump little hand and dimpled. Pudgy her hands were, and the rest of her quite thin.

At the touch of her hand Conrad gave Anne-Marie a look which she answered with alarming frankness. He had seen this type before in the Reich, ready to go into any dark corner, but he was surprised to find it here in the daughter of such a fine lady. He grinned and seemed suddenly at his ease. He knew more about Anne-Marie Reuther than her mother did. In fact, he knew all there was to know about her. Like a whore, he thought, thinking of the look she had given him, and out of those innocent eyes, with a halo of hair like that. He wanted to laugh. Suddenly he felt good.

"I'll come," he said, touching his fingers to his forehead, and went on in the direction Fehge had taken. On his way he snatched a long green grass and chewed it.

"Everybody makes a fuss of that girl," said Fricka, "and I can't for the life of me see why. Quite apart from the fact that she's Jewish."

"Oh, Fehge's queer," said Anne-Marie, "and people love what's queer. They say in the village that she has healing powers, that the Countess only got well because Fehge laid her hands on her, and Ludmilla Pfeiffer says . . ."

"Nonsense! I'll thrash the stuffings out of you if you start picking up their ignorant superstitions!" said Fricka, and the girl flinched a little, because her mother still hit her. "The girl has no

244

business to be here," said Fricka, and the matter of Fehge was, for the moment, closed.

Anne-Marie smiled to herself, mocking her mother's fanaticism, which she thought was silly. She didn't share it. She hated Jews because she liked to hate; she wanted to marry and have children because she wanted to have someone in bed with her, to lie close to and feel good with, and children seemed to result from that. She was tired to death of satisfying her own craving body. Further she did not think, she could not think, she was not equipped for thinking! She could feel, and that was all she wanted to do, feel, feel, feel! Feel hunger and quench it, any kind of hunger. She was emotional to such an extent that she loved the hunger as well as the satiation. There were certain things she liked to eat, that gave her the most satisfactory feeling when she ate them—sweets, and certain kinds of spicy foods. She would crave them, and when she got them, eat them with avidity, immersed in her pleasant sensations. It was an odd sight to see this ethereal creature consume a huge meal. It vexed her mother, who would not have minded if Anne-Marie had been fat, which, in spite of all she ate, she was not, but who objected to such undisciplined greed.

"What would you have done during the war?" she often said to the child, remembering the years of starvation, the grey bread made of unmentionable ingredients, out of which she had sometimes pulled bits of string and hard seed, the sickly sweet jam, the potatoes and beans without end, and sometimes not enough of this humble fare to satisfy you. "What would you have done?"

"I'd have got myself food somehow," the child would answer with her mouth full.

The sight of Conrad had aroused a craving in her, and she knew exactly for what. Suddenly her stolid mother walking beside her irked her, and she would have liked to run after Conrad. She could have screamed. "Mother," she said harshly, in a strained voice unlike her own, "how can you live such a long time without Papa?"

Fricka was taken aback. "Well," she said, after a moment, "we write to each other every day."

Strangely enough, they did; Maurice because, however much she tortured him, he considered Fricka his responsibility as if she had been his child; and she because she enjoyed the outlet of writing. Their letters were not friendly.

"Oh," said Anne-Marie passionately, "I don't mean that way!"

"What do you mean?" said Fricka impatiently, her mind on something else.

"I don't know," said Anne-Marie, vexed that she had spoken at all. You couldn't talk to Mother.

Meanwhile Conrad had caught up with Fehge. The interlude with the Reuthers had improved his mood, which had been sullen ever since he had come home and found Hilda inaccessible. In the past few days he had carried out several of the expeditions for which he had been returned to the Ostmark, expeditions which entailed a great deal of personal danger and for which he got thirty *Schillinge* if they were successful, which, so far, they had been, but it was shabby pay considering the risks involved, and it wasn't even fun any more. Nothing was fun for long. And now there was this thing tormenting him, this girl, this Jewess, whom he had seen naked that day and desired ever since. He realized that it was disgraceful to want her, but that didn't make him want her less, and to go hungry for a Jewess seemed more disgraceful still. He'd better have her and get it over with.

"Fehge," he said, when he caught up with her, "meet me down at the coach-house tonight when you've finished your work. I want to talk to you."

Fehge turned and looked at him and didn't answer. The shape of his head was good, his face was lean, he had a smooth, high, white forehead from which the hair stood up, not bristly, but soft, slightly wavy and blond. His eyebrows were very straight, his lids strangely uncurved, dropping almost straight down from his brows. His eyes, however, were slit-shaped, small and cruel. His nose was thick-set and straight, his lips in their expression merciless, yet they were full and sensual. He had a good, square jaw. He was by no means ugly, but she thought he had a very frightening face. She looked away from it again, straight ahead of her.

"I'm afraid of you, Conrad," she said. "I've always been afraid of you, ever since I can remember. I wouldn't meet you alone anywhere. Any time."

"You won't be able to help it," he said. "I'll hit upon you some time. You'll see."

Of course he was right. She knew that some time this brutal thing would catch up with her. She had been running away from it all her life, but in the end there would be no escape from it.

Since there was no escaping it, she must fight it. The realization came to her with dreadful impact. Fight. That from which there was no escape had to be fought. One must prove oneself the stronger. Only then would one be left in peace.

The hard process of thinking made the beads of perspiration stand out on her upper lip where the slightest trace of dark down grew now. Fight. But with what?

She was strong. With her bare hands? The thought of touching him, even in a tussle in which she, in all probability, would be victorious, revolted her. Her mind's eye jumped back over the intervening six years, and she could see Conrad locked with Hilda in that strange struggle. No. Not with her bare hands.

Ute danced from one side of her to the other, nervous, feeling her mistress's distress, and every now and then growled in her frustrated anger. But she was muzzled. Ute. It would be so simple to meet him and take an unmuzzled Ute with her. But then the dog would have to be shot. They had shot Pfeiffer's dog for just biting a man. And if Fehge said the word, it wouldn't end with just a bite for Conrad. Ute would kill him. No. That was not the way out. She must have a weapon.

They were passing the coach-house. Its big door was open, and Fehge could see into its dark maw, the hay in the loft, the empty space where the freight cart stood at night, horse's dung drying on the grey stone floor and, in the corner, near the door, Franz's long whip that he didn't use any more, standing upright.

Fehge looked at it, then at the old barn that stood a little way up the hill, unused now since Sapponyi had given up all forms of agriculture. "If you like," she said slowly, "I'll meet you up there at the barn tonight, at nine o'clock."

Conrad's face lighted up with frightful gratitude. "Thank you," he whispered, suddenly servile, forgetting that she was anything except what he desired at the moment, a good-looking girl with a body he'd seen and could not forget.

Fehge told no one of the tryst. It never occurred to her that her procedure for coming to grips with this thing was not guiltless of treachery. Long-accumulated fear and the unaccustomed decision to action blotted out every consideration of fair play.

She was at the foot of the hill well before the appointed time. The coach-house door was still open, the freight cart now in its place, its shaft trailing. The horses were in their stalls, and Franz's new whip stood beside the old one she had seen that afternoon.

She picked them both up, one in each hand, and tried them. The new one was shorter. She chose the long one she had seen as she had passed by that afternoon, and left the new one leaning against the wall. With the whip in her hand, she walked the few steps to the top of the hill, to the door of the deserted barn. Here she leaned the whip against the inside of the door, carefully, so that it should stand steady. Then she looked about her. From here she had a good view of the road as far as one could see in the early evening light. It would be a black night; the moon would rise late. She could see no one.

She turned her back on the scene and walked across the barn, which would always smell of hay, although it had long been empty. At its other end a sliding door was open, and there was a sheer drop into the courtyard below where the weeds grew high between cobblestones. This courtyard was flanked on its three sides by the barn. Here the horses had been kept in the days when Sapponyi had kept horses. It was Fehge's favourite place because it was so deserted. It calmed her now.

The swallows that nested in the eaves took flight at her steps. They swooped up and down below her, in the courtyard, not leaving their homes, only agitating around them. Pigeons flew up in the air with a whirring sound, unlike the silent, long-winged, lilting swallows, and settled down again on the roof of the barn, letting their wings flutter restlessly, ready to fly again. Fehge made a cooing sound, and they responded. The swallows showed flashing white breasts, and then their dark-blue top feathers merged with the light of evening. A little brown hare came out of the dark recesses of the stable with cautious hops and sat hunched, his nose twitching with sniffs to the right, to the left, and up in her direction. Fehge stood quite still. Then she heard steps.

She flew across the barn, like a bird herself, and gripped the whip in her right hand. With it beside her, she went and stood in the doorway that faced the way he was coming, up the path that lovers had trodden into the long grass.

She could see his figure lumbering toward her in the gloom. A soft mist made the outlines of the trees and figures hazy. The hills had disappeared. It was now quite dark.

Fehge tightened her hold on the whip. Its lash lay in the dust at her feet. She could hear his breathing, laboured with eagerness. "*Grüss Gott,*" he said in a husky voice before he reached her.

She said nothing. When he was about two feet away from her, she lifted her weapon and struck him, once, twice, and then again and again, aiming for and finding his face. Startled and blinded by the first lash, he stumbled and gave a cry of rage. He raised his arms to protect his face, the biting lash cutting his hands and reaching his face again as he withdrew them in pain. Blood trickled from one eye, then his nose felt the brunt of the lash, and he sank to his knees. His ears, his eyes again, as he covered his face . . . they all burned like hell-fire.

Get away from the lash, he thought, and began to run down the hill. At the bottom he stood, panting, and looked back. He could see no one in the doorway of the barn. She might have vanished into thin air, as though she had never been there. . . .

Nonsense!

He thought of running back, of looking for her, chasing her, killing her when he found her. Then he began to cry as he hadn't cried since he could remember, and blood and tears and saliva ran down his face and chin. He breathed in and vomited. No. In this condition he could track down and kill no one. He shambled back along the road the way he had come.

Slowly he took a handkerchief out of his pocket and wiped his face and blew his nose. This started it bleeding again. He knelt down beside the brook and washed his wounds until they felt soothed and he no longer bled. He would have his revenge!

Down by the cottage where Anne-Marie lived with her mother, the light streamed from an upstairs window. In its path he stopped to look at himself in a pocket-mirror. Not a pretty sight. He would have to think of a good story before he showed himself in this condition. "I'll pay her back," he kept muttering to himself. "I'll pay her back if it's the last thing I do."

Anne-Marie heard his feet moving on the gravel underneath her window and she looked out. "Hello," she whispered when she saw Conrad. "What's the matter with you?"

Conrad didn't answer, but he looked up and the light fell on his bruised face. "Oh," gasped Anne-Marie. "Wait. I'll come down."

Conrad didn't particularly wait for her. He would have stood for a while, anyway, to get his shaking limbs under control. But suddenly the young girl was standing before him, and she had nothing on but her nightgown.

Her governess was at the big house playing checkers with Andrea which had become a Wednesday-night ritual. Andrea would not permit herself games more often than once a week. Fricka was entertaining visitors in the drawing-room of the big house. At nine-thirty this would be over. It was a quarter to nine now. Anne-Marie, every sense alert, had looked at the clock before she had run downstairs, while she had been putting on her dressing-gown and taking it off again, her mind finally made up that she would go down just as she was. Her nightgown had puffed sleeves with baby-blue ribbon threaded through them, tied in rosettes, a draw-thread of blue with rosettes at the neck and waistline, and a ruffle at the bottom like a Biedermayer dress. The gown was transparent, and she could feel Conrad's eyes piercing it and touching her body like fire.

"Are you alone?" he said, not taking his eyes off her.

"Yes." She smiled at him. "Mother's got visitors, and she won't be home for another hour, and Fräulein will come back with her. She's playing checkers with Sister Andrea. I was reading in bed." She put her hands up to his face and lightly touched the welts. "Who did that to you?"

He mistook her gesture for tenderness and it irritated him, but her voice was lovely, clear as a bell and high-pitched like a ten-year-old girl's. He looked into her eyes and saw the sensuousness in them, and then, as in the afternoon, he had to smile. There was a bond between them. He felt more friendly toward this mad girl than he had to anyone else in his whole life. That was why he could tell her the truth without feeling ashamed. "The Jewess! The sow! Fehge did it with a whip!"

Anne-Marie's pretty little faced grew big-eyed. "I think she is a witch," she said. "You shouldn't have anything to do with her."

Conrad, his eyes on the girl, felt tired, and suddenly he couldn't remember why he had bothered about Fehge. In a state of relaxation into which he now fell, Anne-Marie's sensuousness reached out to him and slid over and down him like a sweet shower of rain.

"Come upstairs," she said. "I'll wash your face for you."

When they got upstairs, she couldn't seem to wait. She pressed her body greedily to his, her back rounded, her arms all round him, her cheek on his breast where the open shirt left it bare. Then she threw back her head, and he kissed her mouth and she never let go of him again. It was like a burning devil alive in her, as though the avidity of all hungry women were concentrated in her young body.

When Fricka and Fräulein left Strubl, Conrad was on his way to Pritnitz again. There was a girl he would like to live with, he thought! To marry? Yes, to marry. As though a man could marry with his prospects, which had looked so bright in the Reich! Damn it all! His hour with the girl hadn't satiated him. How had she known when it was time for him to go, when he had lost all sense of time? He felt as restless as a hungry wolf.

He passed by the valley crevice in which stood his mother's farm. He hadn't seen her since he had come back. God, how he hated her!

He turned and walked up to her house, where all the lights were out, the house in which he had spent a miserable childhood. He began to hurl invectives at the darkened window in such a loud voice that he could be heard all the way to Strubl.

Toni awoke, and her husband, Seppl, did too, and they lay still and listened. Then Seppl raised himself on his elbow, but Toni put a quieting hand on his arm. "It's only Conrad," she whispered. "He's drunk."

The foul words poured in on them. Seppl made another move to get up. Again she restrained him. "Let me get my gun," the big farmer said. "Just a shot over his head. I promise I won't hurt him. He'll wake the dead."

He could see by the light of the moon, which had risen at last, how she shook her head and the tears glistened in her eyes. He had never seen Toni cry before. "Don't, man," she said, as though he needed any further persuasion than her tears. "Don't. He can't help it. He was born bad."

That night a swastika burned in the "hollow tooth" on the mountain-top. Its great cavern, as from decay, seemed predestined by Nature for such a flaming fanfare. Conrad enjoyed the climb in the black of night and the building of the huge cross. It calmed him. The flickering of its flames put him to sleep.

Thérèse woke Sapponyi to see the swastika, and he watched it with unblinking eyes. It looked like a sign in the heavens, for the outline of the hill on which it burned was blotted out by night. Sapponyi slept no more that night.

Fehge, too, saw it burn, the crooked cross, the cross of the devil— Fehge, who also could not sleep but lay tossing about under her feather counterpane. Fehge had never slept badly in her life before, but to fight, to fight physically, had made her feel disrupted, disordered, mad, as she had not dreamed she could feel. She, too, watched the swastika-branded sky and thought, To fight is more horrible than to be submerged. And I have not defeated it. My great effort has made no difference. It is still there. It will come, catch up with me, kill me. There is nothing I can do to prevent it, and I shall never try to do anything to prevent it again.

She turned over on her side, her back to it, and to her came the afterthought: Nothing like that, anyway. There came no further clear idea to her of what other way of defence there might be, because she suddenly found herself calmed and fell asleep.

In the morning Conrad did not go home. He didn't feel like seeing his father. He had a job to do, a job he would have relished had not so many mortifications battered his spirit yesterday.

He took the train for Vienna. Opposite him sat a priest who cast many a compassionate glance in his direction, but Conrad gave him no encouragement. He looked away, out of the window, and closed his eyes, his face a sullen mask. He had had very little sleep the night before. Now he slept. His mouth fell open and he snored.

In Vienna, Conrad proceeded to headquarters, received his equipment, and walked the few blocks to the Mariahilferstrasse. There he found the shop he had been assigned to, a little jeweller's shop owned by an old Jew called Futterweit, which means "wide lining," one of those names Moishe had never acquired. The Jew's shop lay between a school and a church, which gave it a threefold suitability for the purpose.

Conrad waited until the street was very crowded, then he threw his grenade, and in the confusion of the explosion and flying dust and rubble made the easiest escape in the world. He didn't even have to run. He slipped through the crowd, then stopped and became a part of it.

The crowd moved, in the main, toward the scene of the accident, except for those who were frightened or who had children with them, who herded the latter away in front of them, saying, "Come, come! There may be another! You never can tell these days!"

Conrad now joined these frightened ones for a few moments, but soon left them behind. At headquarters he waited around all day. The job had been well done. The Jew Futterweit had been in his shop and had been blown to bits, the shop completely wrecked. There was great nervousness in the city and extra police. Conrad took his thirty *Schillinge* and walked out, still not satisfied. What he needed was a change! That evening he joined the Austrian *Heimwehr*, the civilian army of the Christian Social or Clerical Party, where he was received with open arms.

Chapter Twenty-Six

SIX weeks later, when Anne-Marie's period of menstruation was several weeks overdue, Fricka did not worry. Anne-Marie had started to menstruate years too soon, at the age of nine, and had always been irregular and suffered pain. Why the girl should be so worried now, her mother could not understand, but when Anne-Marie became persistent and said that she must see a doctor, her mother said, "Very well, I will take you to Vienna." Fricka was so far recovered that a trip to Vienna was now allowed on her programme.

"I don't need to go to Vienna," said Anne-Marie. "Sapponyi will do just as well."

How pale she is, thought Fricka, and what a will of her own!

"Isn't it enough that one of us is being treated by a Jew? I will take you to Vienna, or you will go to Schreiner, although I would rather not go to someone with whom we are friends."

She wasn't worried, not in the least. It never occurred to her that there could be anything to worry about. But a slight feeling of shame arose in her at the thought of her daughter being examined by a man she knew as well as she knew Schreiner.

"If you don't take me to Sapponyi," said Anne-Marie, "I will go to him without you.

Fricka took her.

Anne-Marie told Sapponyi her story. Before examining her, perhaps just to annoy Fricka in a harmless little way, Sapponyi asked the child the question to which he could expect only one answer.

"You have, of course, no reason to be worried at this interruption . . ."

"If you mean that I might be pregnant," said Anne-Marie, "I might."

Sapponyi felt his knees turn to water and his tongue stick in his throat. He did not dare look at the girl's mother. How terribly embarrassing for her, and in front of him of all doctors! When he had recovered his composure, he said, "Well, then, I had better examine you." And he finally looked at Fricka.

She was sitting up straight, leaning forward a little, her eyes shining with fanatic excitement. Sapponyi thought, Now she has really gone mad!

He put out his hand in a quieting gesture and said, "Please don't let this upset you too much and retard the splendid progress you have made. If it is so, and it may not be, the child can be taken from her. She is so young . . ."

Fricka interrupted him. "No," she hissed at him. "No! You will not repeat your miserable performance! She will have her child, and, God willing, it will be a boy!"

Anne-Marie had been on the verge of tears. The last weeks had been an ordeal for her—first, her searing longing for Conrad, which had started almost the moment he had left her, a hunger that she could not still; then the fear of pregnancy and all the "trouble" it would get her into. Anne-Marie didn't want to become a mother all alone, like this. Now, at her mother's words, her face was turned to stone for a moment. Then her body tensed, and she burst into shrieks of wild, uncontrolled laughter. The tears rolled down her cheeks, she covered her face with one of her plump little hands and shook from top to toe as it rocked her. "Oh," she gasped. "Oh, Mother! *You are so funny!*"

Fricka Reuther stood before her husband in the drawing-room

of their house in Vienna. The fine old crystal chandeliers shivered as they always did when anyone was in the room, for a breath could disturb them. This was called the Renoir room because six of the master's paintings hung on its walls. A serenely smiling French lady in a poke-bonnet with feathers was looking straight at Fricka. Fricka's feet sank into the pile of a priceless Chinese carpet. Its blue-and-yellow scrolls crept snakelike from under her feet across the floor. For the rest, the room was furnished in Louis XV style, and a magnificent old Meissen tiled stove stood in the corner. The room was very light. It was Maurice's room, Maurice's house; there was no trace of Fricka Reuther in it. It was the house her mother had dreamed of as the setting for her daughter.

"It is a great thing to have you back," said Maurice. "I hope you will be pleased with how you find things. Marthé and I have done our best to have everything in as fine shape as when you left it."

The fool, thought Fricka. Doesn't he know that I know that Marthé ran this house before I came and will run it after I leave? I do not fit into this house. I have been wasted here long enough!

As these thoughts passed through her mind, she slowly drew the gloves from her hands and looked at him out of her blue eyes like a lynx. Her white Angora cat came and rubbed its back against her legs. She bent down to stroke it. It raised its beautiful pink-rimmed amber eyes to hers and mewed.

"I have something to tell you, Maurice."

The tone of her voice filled him with dread.

"It is about Anne-Marie."

"Is she ill?"

"No," said Fricka, "she is very well. She is going to have a child."

All the colour left his face. His hand stopped midway to his forehead, and with a queer clicking sound in his throat he dropped to the floor. Fricka's lips curled contemptuously as she went over to the old bell-pull and rang it.

That evening Maurice asked for her. He was lying propped high in his bed, as the doctor had ordered. A glass of water was already gathering beads on the table at his bedside. A box of pills and a delicate little old French clock stood on the table. It had been a present to him from Fricka's mother, Wanda. He had been in love with Wanda Krausewitz, a gentle woman, a married woman, mother of eight children and ten years older than himself. He had been in love with Wanda first, last, and always. She had guided his love to her eldest and most difficult child, Fricka, and he had accepted Fricka because he could not have refused his love anything. He was glad Wanda was dead and could not know that she had given birth to a fanatic.

Now he wasted no time on preliminaries. "What are we going to do about it?" he said.

Fricka was surprised. Maurice was a devout Catholic. She had not expected to face this problem with him as well. "What do you mean," she said, "what are we going to do about it?"

"She cannot have this child."

"Of course she can. And she will. Don't be so squeamish, Maurice. She is old enough and strong enough."

"Does she want the child?"

"I don't think Anne-Marie knows what she wants. She doesn't think much."

"Who is the father?"

"A young man called Conrad Schreiner. She met him in the village."

"A peasant?"

"No. His father is a doctor. He is a very intelligent young man. He has been trained in Munich. He is one of us." She did not tell him that Conrad had not been seen or heard of for over six weeks.

"She must marry him," he said.

Fricka laughed, and made the discovery that this total rebellion against the conventions of the civilization into which she had been born gave her a pleasant feeling of excitement. Suddenly she realized that she was free, free of all fetters, free to take part in the world that was being born on the other side of the border. She was a new woman. Her eyes shone.

"Where Conrad comes from," she said, "the men wait to see what kind of children their women bear before they marry them!"

She is mad, thought Maurice, and closed his eyes to shut out the sight of her.

"You will leave my house," he said.

"And I will take her with me."

"Of course," said Maurice. "You belong together."

He watched her go, watched her straight, proud back. She looked so strong. Yet the disease is in her, he thought, not in me. Inside, she is rotten!

He closed his eyes again and implored Wanda to come to him. She came almost at once. "You see," he told her, "how wrong you were?" "I see," she said, in her gentle voice, "I beg your forgiveness." And she took him in her arms and he seemed to sink into a bed of rose-leaves. He wanted to ask her to let him read Shakespeare's sonnets aloud to her again that evening, but he was too tired to form the words. He thought he heard her say that there was a new book out, by Löns, and that he was Germany's greatest contemporary writer. "Poet," he corrected her, but her cheek was on his mouth and her soft hair on his closed lids. He kissed her parted lips softly, and she wound her arms round his neck. After that she never left him. It was therefore a quite unimportant part of Maurice Reuther that guided him to the drawer where his pistol lay and blew out his brains.

His vast estates, his still considerable wealth, went, according to his conventional last will and testament, to his wife, Fricka Reuther. Of this he had not thought, because, when the end had come, he had been unable to think coherently at all.

Chapter Twenty-Seven

ONLY a few weeks with the *Heimwehr* were needed to prove to Conrad that this civilian army was no place for him. He found that an extraordinarily large proportion of the men there were petty thieves and thugs with reform-school and jail records like his own, but they lacked other things which he possessed—courage and vision among them. He had, however, not yet thought of a way out.

When he read of Maurice Reuther's death in the paper, he went to see Fricka and offer his condolences. He thought this would be the cleverest way to approach again the girl who had made so pleasant an impression on him a few weeks ago. Before he knew where he was, and without any conscious volition on his part, the girl was his wife; and the first thing his mother-in-law did was transfer him back where he belonged—to the N.S.D.A.P. Here he found his position greatly enhanced by the fact that the Reuther fortune stood behind him.

Anne-Marie and Conrad were married twice. Schreiner, curiously enough, refused to consider Fricka's plans for a New German marriage on the Schwarzenberg adequate. The two were therefore married first in a registry office in Vienna, then again in as bizarre a ceremony as anything the valley had ever seen.

Dennis could hear their full, harmonious voices before he could see the lights of their torches twinkling snakelike as the party wound its way from the Strubl valley up to Schwarzenberg's summit. He knew what was going to happen there tonight. He had had no intention of going to see. But now the lights drew him like a magnet.

It was a dark summer's night; the moon would rise late. The dew had fallen, the air was dry, and a gentle breeze blew down from the mountain. He left the door of his cottage open and walked in the direction of the flares, leisurely, as though he had no intention of going far. He went all the way to the summit.

He still had to take the mountain slowly, and the festivities were already under way when he arrived. The citizens of Fichtenbach and Pritnitz formed so thick a ring that he could see nothing but the backs of their accustomed figures, and the glare of the fire rose up from their midst as though they were standing round the live crater of a volcano.

The glare lit up the forest. The trees stood proudly, their trunks copper-coloured, their branches strangely black, towering to heaven, disproportionately high. If there were stars, the fire blotted them out.

In the gloom not far away he could make out the figure of a girl. He knew her by the way she stood. "Fehge," he said, "did it draw you too?"

Slowly she turned her head, and he went over to her. In her dark-blue dress, high at the neck, without the relieving white of the apron she usually wore, she looked very austere. "I would like to see," she said.

Dennis looked around, then he pointed. "There." A few paces away, lightning had felled a tree, which lay like a sloping bridge against another. Hand-in-hand, like two conspirators, they crossed over to it. Fehge went first, placing one foot squarely before the other until she could see above the peasants' heads. She held out her hand to Dennis, who was not so sure-footed, and he came to stand close beside her.

The singing had ceased. The forest's deep silence was now interrupted by nothing but the sharp crackle of the fire whose flames leaped so high that its smoke began to spiral far above their heads. In its light the faces of the people around it were all the same copper-red colour, and their eyes shone wildly in their otherwise stolid faces.

Dennis and Fehge now enjoyed a bird's-eye view of the entire macabre proceedings, of which the peasants were not the only spectators. But they formed a semicircle at least four deep up to a pine-flanked knoll which completed the round. At its foot burned the fire; on its summit stood an evergreen-draped altar on which lay a sword and a book. Behind this altar, impaled on a post, stood a tremendously enlarged photograph of a man. The fire lighted up his chin first and distorted it, making it seem very large. Above thin, set lips grew a little moustache. The nose was very straight and the eyes piercing, the whole face stern and, in the position to which it had been elevated, formidable.

Down the knoll, on each side of the altar, stood a group of

strangers—Fricka Reuther's guests. Most of them had come from the Reich at her express invitation to attend this unique ceremony. They were dressed in pre-war East Prussian style. The women wore long, shapeless silk dresses or made-to-order suits that would outlast the wearer, big, beribboned hats, fishbone collars, mesh gloves; and they stood firmly on the ground in their high-laced mountain-boots. The men stood proudly, exaggeratedly erect, their moustaches, monocles, pouchy chins, and puffed little eyes making at least a dozen replicas in mufti of Generals Hindenburg and Ludendorff.

These fathers and mothers had loaned their daughters for this ceremony. Six girls dressed in white, with garlands of field flowers in their fair hair, shining and innocent in appearance, held hands between fire and altar. In front of this virginal semicircle stood a striking young girl, dressed in nothing but a white tunic, her legs bared and very brown, as brown as her neck and arms and the exquisitely clear-cut features of her face—a sun-baked Artemis. Under her scant garment she was smooth-breasted, and she wore her fair hair close-cropped like a boy's. "Frouja" was the name she chose to go by.

She was a professional arranger of New German marriage ceremonies. She had coached Anne-Marie and the six little virgins for this ceremony, to whom she had given the old German names of Veleda, Ganna, Thorgerd, Aud, Waltraute, and Siglinde. Her journey from the Reich and her fee were costing Fricka Reuther a small fortune, but she had it to spend.

In front of this high-priestess stood Anne-Marie and Conrad. Never had Anne-Marie looked so beautiful. She was dressed all in white as for confirmation, and she wore her golden hair in braids. On her head reposed a thick wreath of field flowers, blue and pink and yellow, clustered in summery profusion round her forehead, with little ears of corn making the wreath as feathery as a halo of light.

Anne-Marie clung to Conrad, her pudgy little hand holding his as in a vice. If only she didn't faint, as she so often had done recently! If she did, Mother would think she was doing it on purpose to spoil this ceremony, which Anne-Marie thought was perfectly ridiculous.

Conrad did not share her bitter emotions. He was a very proud groom. He was wearing the forbidden S.A. uniform, and his eyes were shining as he grasped the hand of the girl he loved . . . who was now his own, together with the child which she carried beneath her heart. The thought softened all his features. He could have wept.

A semicircle of his closest friends, all of them in the forbidden uniform, stood between the peasants and the fire, their limp swastika flags firmly planted on the pine-needle-covered earth. Fehge recognized every one of them, boys from Pritnitz and Fichtenbach, Reischer's Walter looking more alert than he had ever done at the altar. But the peasants had not as clear a view of the proceedings. They had to crane their necks round the S.A. men, the banners, and the uncertain fire. Thus, as the ceremony gathered momentum, they recognized on one side of the altar Fricka Reuther; on the other side, Kurt Schreiner and Heinrich Grabautschnik, both in full S.A. regalia.

Then the high-priestess gave a signal, and her girls began to sing:

> "Oh, fiery flame!
> Shine with thy brightest glow,
> Out to all parts . . .
> Burn at this sacred marriage,
> A German hero's courage
> Into our hearts!
>
> "For Nordic freedom's urge
> Will bear no spiritual scourge
> Never, oh, nevermore!
> Freed of all alien ways,
> True to itself always,
> German for evermore!"

When they had ceased singing, the high-priestess spoke in a melodious voice that carried like a singer's:

"Nature, in all its forms of expression, in the grandeur of its starry firmament, in the beauty of its landscape, in its various forms, blossoms and leaves, in the inevitableness of its laws, in the drama of its thunder and lightning, in the wildness of its storm-tossed seas, in the peace of its still summer days, this whole Nature—in which we people stand as an integral part—*we call it God!*"

Her voice was tremendous, as though she were speaking into a bowl. It must carry, thought Dennis, all the way to Strubl.

"What does Nature teach us?" Frouja went on. "Nature teaches us first and foremost that the idea of equality is madness. There are no two things alike in Nature, and therefore no things equal in quality. Look at the leaves of the oak! Not one leaf is exactly like the other. Compare the leaves of the oak with those of the lime tree. They are different within themselves also, but they are completely different, again, from those of the oak, in colour, in shape—and in quality.

"Thus it is with the races of mankind. They, too, are different! It is their sacred duty to preserve that difference; otherwise they sin against Nature—that is to say, against God!

"And of all the races on this earth, the German race is the best. This has been revealed to us by our Saviour and Führer, Adolf Hitler, who was sent to us by God to give us this life-giving, soul-restoring, eternally valid message. The German race is God's chosen race! Do you, Conrad and Anne-Marie Schreiner, swear to keep it pure?"

Conrad and Anne-Marie answered in unison, "We do."

Frouja now introduced Heinrich Grabautschnik, who stepped forward and welcomed the couple in the name of the Party.

"The German State blesses your union," he said. "The German State stands by your union, especially, because it is the first real German marriage to be consecrated in the German Ostmark, birthplace of our Saviour, our Führer, Adolf Hitler."

A click of his heels, a wheel-about turn, and a sharp salute to the formidable man behind the fire. Fricka's guests, the bridal pair, the six little virgins and the six S.A. men followed suit. But the peasants did nothing. The heat of the fire, whose flames were lower now, permitting them to see more clearly, made them screw up their noses and wrinkle their eyes, which seemed to disappear into their faces. Some of them pushed their chins out or held an ear forward to hear better—that was all.

The speaker turned to face his silent audience again. "And it will not be the last such ceremony," he went on. "For we have set ourselves free from the alien and unworthy Christian marriage ceremony which was imposed on us by a scheming clergy in the thirteenth century. More than that—we have freed ourselves of the Christian faith, that Asiatic-Semitic religion, so alien and destructive to the German race. We have declared it for what it is —enervating and prejudicial to the development of strong, free, and independent men!

"The crucifix must go!

"It is a symbol of weakness. Christianity was nothing but an episode of a thousand years' duration, which is now terminating! For the German people there can be only one faith—faith in Germany!"

He gave the sign, and one of the little virgins danced forward holding a crucifix made roughly of two birch branches woven together, and cast it into the flames.

Suddenly there was a slight commotion among the peasantry as one woman in the front turned abruptly to part the crowd and leave the ring. It was Conrad's mother, Toni. She passed close by Dennis and Fehge, and they could distinctly hear her say in a strained, harsh voice, "God, strike him dead, God, strike him dead, God, strike him dead," until her words became mutterings and were finally gone with her.

Meanwhile another woman had pushed her way forward into the place left by Toni: Grabautschnik's wife, Clotilde. He had expressly forbidden her to attend the ceremony, and now, across the fire, he saw her. He gave her the look which all his married life had been instantaneously effectual. It did nothing to her now. She stayed to stare at the fire that had swallowed up the crucifix, her dirty, hard-worn hands clasped as in prayer, her pretty little face, that was always wan, coloured now by the fire. The tears rained down her expressionless features.

Grabautschnik could not take his eyes off her. He opened his mouth to continue his speech and had to close it again, his expression one of abject fury. He could think of nothing but the fact that at last, she, the moron, had gone completely off her head! He had always seen it coming. He turned and, without another word, strode back to his place.

The six little virgins were at a loss what to do. Heinrich Grabautschnik was to have given them their cue, and he had failed to do so. Their disturbed young eyes sought the authority of their leader, Frouja. With a harsh gesture the goddess indicated to them that they should proceed.

With a curiously lilting step, they thereupon danced forward and took Anne-Marie's wreath from her head. To the accompaniment of a quaint old song which they sang very sweetly in harmony, they cast it into the flames, the symbol of a virginity she had lost, theoretically, many weeks ago, a virginity which, in her lustful way, she had practically never possessed. It shrivelled and was gone like a dream. Then Fricka Reuther stepped forward and placed a wreath of myrtle on her daughter's head.

Anne-Marie's eyes were big as they rested on her mother, and she swayed slightly forward. Fricka's face was stern. Anne-Marie closed her eyes and stood stiff again, a little soldier in white batiste.

Now Kurt Schreiner came forward with the wedding rings on an old wooden platter of runic design, and the bridal couple were led by him to the altar, where followed the oath, their hands on the book, Hitler's *Mein Kampf*.

"I believe in the eternal new Reich. I believe in the new world outlook which was born in the soul of a man named Adolf Hitler. I believe that Adolf Hitler was sent to us as Saviour and leader of our German nation, our Reich, our People, who are united in their blood. I believe in this, his Almighty scriptural work, *Mein Kampf*, and swear to live according to its precepts to the best of my knowledge and ability. I pledge myself body and soul to my leader, Adolf Hitler, and to the German people, and I swear herewith loudly and publicly, 'Adolf Hitler—I will be true!'"

And those on the knoll chanted the oath like a credo.

Now it was Anne-Marie's turn. The girl's movements had become strangely wooden. The high-priestess took her by the hand and said to her and, in her huge voice, to all the others: "With Christianity a conception of the woman was brought to Germany which in no way coincided with the authentic German notion. She who had formerly stood on an equal footing with man became worthless and was classed below him. According to Paul, she was to be man's subject. This is the Jewish-Christian and German-alien conception of womanhood. We reject it! We have restored woman to her rightful and noble position—that of the great mother!

"Anne-Marie Schreiner, you are the noblest of wives, for you already bear in your womb the first of the many children which you will bear our state, our Führer, our glorious history. Do you swear that your child is pure?"

"I do," said Anne-Marie, in a very small voice.

"Do you swear that all your children will be pure in blood, and therefore in heart and mind?"

"I do," said the same distressed voice. And now it was time for Anne-Marie to say her little speech.

In a voice that faltered from the start, she began: "Oh, thou German God . . . from thy depths must I ever come, in dream and loyalty ripening to deed, with the power of will born of envy and need, when I reap, again will I be seed . . . If I fulfil . . . myself . . . in thee . . ."

Further she did not go, for a spasm went through her body which threw her up for a moment and then let her fall back, down the knoll, and into the fire had not Conrad caught her.

Fehge let herself drop astride the huge trunk which supported them and looked up at Dennis, her eyes wide with bewilderment. "Come on," he said. "Let's get out of here!" He took her roughly by the hand and pulled her after him. As the descent became steeper he let her go.

She took quick steps going downhill on the furrowed path slippery with fallen pine-needles, but he went down in the big, sure strides of his spiritual panic. Such nonsense! he kept saying to himself, such nonsense! But in his heart he could not dismiss it as nonsense.

"Stop!" Fehge cried suddenly, not because she was weary, but because she knew it was not good for him to tear down Schwarzenberg like that.

He stopped without turning round, and she could hear his laboured breathing. It was high time she brought him to a halt. Only now did she notice that they had reached the spot where stood the *Marterl* of the crucified Christ.

They both looked up into the path of sky which the tree-tops cut out for them. The moon was passing across it, the clouds hurrying over its white face, making it appear static in comparison with their wind-driven flight. "Let us rest," said Fehge, and sat down, simulating weariness.

He dropped on the road's soft, moss-covered bank beside her. The glare and the voices that had frightened her did not penetrate here. Slowly, unconsciously, she undid her braids and let the air loosen her hair. She ran her fingers across her scalp and wrinkled her brow. The loosening of hair and skin seemed to relieve the pressure on her mind as well. She sat, one knee hunched, her black hair like a shining silken cape round her shoulders and down her back; and with a small twig which she had snapped from its mother branch, she dug savage little holes into the hard earth. Her eyes stared unwaveringly straight ahead into an impenetrable thicket.

Dennis lay flat on his back, watching the high moon move as slowly as the hands of a clock. He spoke first. "I feel as though I'd come down from another planet."

She answered him out of her own thoughts, taking as little note of his as a character in a Tchekov play. "Did you see Conrad? I have never seen his face alight before. It made him look almost beautiful."

Dennis said he had not noticed Conrad particularly.

Fehge went on, and her savage digging with the futile little twig helped her to master the terror that still gripped her. "But you heard them. How they renounced the Saviour. You saw them burn His cross." Her cross, she couldn't help thinking, her little cross of birch-wood.

By her voice he realized how frightened she was. He rolled over on his stomach and looked up at her. "Yes," he said, "they have renounced Christianity. But our folk down there"—and he gestured toward the valley—"you wouldn't call them Christians, would you? You mustn't let it shock you too much," he went on, trying to soften for her, of whom he was so fond, what he could not take mildly himself, however hard and logically he tried.

She shook her head mournfully. "No. Our folk are not Christians. But they just have nothing. Those, up there"—her voice dropped to a clear, far-reaching whisper—"have something —something else!"

"Who are they?" she asked after a while.

"Those are Germans," he told her.

She turned to look into his face, and her great perplexity pained him, physically, in the region of his heart. "Why doesn't God stop them?" she asked.

There it was, the obvious question. He had to find the answer, and quickly. Now, least of all, could he let her down.

He groped in his mind till it hurt. Then it seemed as though the silence of the woods around them created the vacuum in which the answer was born. "Perhaps God thought we humans needed to see, with our own eyes, *what is sin*. Perhaps that is why He lets them grow so big."

The answer seemed to satisfy her.

He stretched out on his back as he had lain before, and the heavy scent of a patch of wild orchids near by made him feel a little sick.

He saw a shivering spasm pass through her body, and she said, "I hope He strikes them down *in time*."

The moonlight had almost covered the path of sky above them. Now it crept with silver fingers under the little wooden roof of the *Marterl* and over the body of the crucified Christ. Fehge's eyes rested on Him. "Perhaps He will have to come again," she said.

"The German poet Goethe said that if He were to come again, they would crucify Him again."

"Of course," she interrupted him. "That is what I mean. They must see Him die again. Only that will stop them."

He said, "I doubt whether that would make any impression on them . . . things being as they are." In the stillness of the night, under the fleeting light of the moon and the heavy scent of summer flowers, he could feel the frightfulness of the times in which they were living. "No," he repeated, "His suffering wouldn't impress them. If He performed a few miracles . . . walked on the water . . . raised a few dead . . . perhaps. But they would have to *see* it, all of them . . . we are living in a sceptical age."

His thoughts skipped suddenly to what had preoccupied him throughout the ceremony—not the people, but the glorification of the man. "What did you think of their new god?" he asked her. "That was his picture, you know, behind the fire."

She answered, "I didn't notice him."

Chapter Twenty-Eight

MUCH of the fear aroused in Fehge by the ceremony on Schwarzenberg was mitigated in the following weeks, during which she was allowed to join in the preparations for a Nativity play, the like of which had never been seen or heard of in the valley before. There had been a play every Christmas, at the school, with the school-children, but never one like this which was to be held at the inn, on a real stage that the Fichtenbach innkeeper, Aloys Reiss, had built in the inn's large dining-room, and which was to be acted, not only by the school-children, but by some of the girls and boys who had already graduated as well.

Stefanie, grown miraculously strong (the X-ray showed a complete standstill and partial recession of her illness), led the enterprise with such enthusiasm that all interests had to merge into it. Who could resist her? Sapponyi said one day to Thérèse, "This play is a remarkable thing. After thirty-five years of being separate kernels in one shell, Fichtenbach and Strubl have become one."

And he was right. There was not a person at the big house who was not in one way or another drawn into it; even the grouchy old bank director from Budapest had to cut out silver stars for halos. Dennis helped to build the stage, Andrea helped to paint the props, and Sapponyi put one of Strubl's empty cottages at the disposal of the players so that Stefanie would not have to go all the way to the inn every day for rehearsals.

At first the play was planned without the boys. That had been Melita's idea, because they were so unruly. Stefanie, who had often seen the young ruffians on the road, agreed. One of the big girls could be Joseph, and they could leave out the shepherds. But after rehearsals had been under way for a few days, a delegation of the boys came to the cottage and waited outside, dressed in their Sunday best and washed clean, while their spokesman, Brandstetter's Joseph, went in and scraped one foot back in a bow, took off his cap, and looked down to mumble his request that the boys would like to be in the play too, if they might. So they also became part of the enterprise, and the village of Fichtenbach became a closed corporation from the month of October onward.

Then came the casting of characters. Who . . . who would be the Holy Mother? She had only one line to say, but she was the star, no doubt about that!

"Let Julie be!" cried Fehge, and the others took up the cry, "Julie! Julie!"

Julie? With the crooked teeth and the watery, bulging eyes, and the vacant face? Stefanie looked at Melita in despair.

"Why, Julie?" Melita asked them.

"Because of her beautiful hair!"

What a dilemma! But poor Julie was taken sick in the nick of time, and that problem was settled without having to hurt her feelings.

"I think Fehge should be the Holy Mother," said Stefanie. It was really obvious. Where could she find a better Maria than this beautiful Jewish girl? But all the explanation she gave the children was, "Because she is the biggest," and that seemed plausible enough to them.

Wonderful shabby, glorious old things arrived in a big wicker basket from the Burgtheater in Vienna. Trattner had no time to visit Stefanie, but always the time to support a theatrical venture, even if it was nothing better than a Nativity play given by peasant louts. The cast-off costumes of Burgtheater actors and actresses, which meant the absolute aristocracy of European actors and actresses, were cut up and sewn into costumes for the children by Minna, a seamstress who lived in Pritnitz and had a sewing-machine. The children had to go to her for fittings of tarlatan, organdie, silk and satin, and bits of tarnished brocade.

The children of Fichtenbach went about like little gods and "became proud," as the Pritnitz children put it who were jealous. They were not allowed to watch the rehearsals; even the content of the play was kept a dark secret. All they could do was creep up to Minna's window and look in and gasp at what they beheld.

Dennis financed Minna and paid for the material needed for the stage and its props. He had offered to paint the scenery, but it turned out that the Herr Wirt could paint, and that he had always wanted to paint something big, and here, at last, in the back-drop for the scene in the stall of Bethlehem was his great opportunity! The Herr Wirt made up for years of artistic frustration and painted something gigantic in conception. When Dennis saw it he had to admit that it was better than anything he could have done. The Herr Wirt had not been hampered by any knowledge of technique. He had been free as a lark. In its crude way, his back-drop for the manger scene was a work of art.

They rehearsed for two hours every day. The children came with bundles of wood to build a fire in the iron stove, and Stefanie brought chestnuts to roast on it. Now they were almost ready.

Fehge let the bicycle coast down the hill with her. It went faster on the hard-packed snow than it had ever travelled on the dirt. The icy wind lashed at her face and made her struggle for breath. She was dressed for just this kind of weather, a Red Riding-hood cap of wool on her head, her lumber-jacket buttoned high in the neck, a red muffler tied in a knot, its ends breezing behind her. Her full, dark-blue skirt was of wool, her black stockings fitted high into her black woollen bloomers, her skirt clung, held in place by the pressure she created as she whizzed through the darkness of winter's late afternoon.

This evening was to be the dress rehearsal. Fehge was on her way to the inn. She would not have to pedal again except for the short, level distance past the fine new house that Anne-Marie and Conrad had moved into. Anne-Marie's much-acclaimed baby was growing inside her. It would come later than Stefanie's, which was due to arrive in February. Dennis still swore her to secrecy about that. It was the only time Dennis had ever asked anything unreasonable of her, so she felt that she must humour him.

Stefanie passed Fehge on the road, driving a little sleigh which the Baron had loaned to her for the winter, together with the roan which was moving now at a spanking trot. *Clop, clop, clop*, its hoofs beat on the hard-packed snow, and the bells on the harness jingled as the horse tossed its fine head and snorted into the cold air. Stefanie, wearing a Cossack hat of fur and a burly fur coat, was wrapped in a rug, and she cracked her whip at Fehge as she passed her, looking like a Snow Queen.

Fehge raised an arm in response and took her weight off the pedals, leaving the wheel free to go its fastest as the slope levelled off. The sled was putting an increasing distance between them. Fehge's eyes watered and the tears turned to ice on her lashes, fringing them with white. She moistened her lips that were parted in an unconscious smile, and the cold wind dried them.

Tomorrow, tomorrow was the day! When the music of the Ave Maria grew and swelled about her . . . that was one of the heavenly moments which came to one so rarely in life; that was the time when the inimical ceremony on Schwarzenberg was vanquished. She could feel it. Those others watching and listening tomorrow would feel it too. They wouldn't be able to help themselves!

It had been her idea to lift the Christ doll out of the manger and hold it in her arms and caress it like a real mother. The doll, strangely enough, had been given to her by Anne-Marie, of all people, when no one had been around to see. Fehge had dressed it, not with seed pearls and in satin, as Thérèse would have done, but in plain white cotton, though no less devoutly. Even its unruly hair had been made to lie smooth with a little oil and much brushing. That had been one of Dennis's ideas.

Fehge passed the Leitners' house and saw Annie coming from the stall. "*Hei-da!*" she cried. The play had made them all friends.

"*Hei-da!*" called Annie. "Going already?"

"It's time," cried Fehge, and whizzed by.

Annie ran into the house, untying her apron as she went, and soon she was on her bicycle too, whirring along in the direction Fehge had taken.

Moser's Creszentia was in the outhouse making soap. "Ready?" cried Fehge, and Creszentia dried the fat from her hands and tidied her hair as she ran into the house, and soon she was after them on her wheel. On bicycles, on foot, they all came streaming toward the little inn for the final rehearsal.

Tomorrow, tomorrow was the day! Dennis had done something truly spectacular. All the girls whose hair would be worn long were going to have it washed and waved at the hairdresser's in Pritnitz. The hairdresser hadn't been at all pleased at the influx of such a lowly clientèle. She was only in Pritnitz because her customers at Strubl made it worth while for her to stay in that backwater. "Snotnoses!" she had said in response to the idea. But what was being paid for couldn't be sneezed at!

Fehge would not be one of the chosen ones, for her hair would be hidden under her Madonna veil, but she was going to Pritnitz with all the others to watch the magical procedure.

Tomorrow, tomorrow was the day!

It dawned at last, December 23, 1933. The play was to start at six o'clock in the afternoon. It couldn't start any earlier because the cows had to be in and watered and milked, and the young folk had to get back from the factory. The peasantry from the entire countryside would be present, as many as the room would hold. But that was nothing compared to the fact that all who could make the trip from Strubl were coming, including most of the servants except for a skeleton staff which had to stay at the house. Even Trattner was coming—the great Trattner—and friends of his!

Three benches at the front were reserved for this nucleus of aristocracy. The rest of the room would not hold all the others, but what could the Herr Wirt do? He couldn't enlarge his inn!

All except the three benches at the front were filled by five-thirty. The stench in the large room which now looked tiny, so cramped was it by humans packed tight like sardines, was dreadful. Leather, wet from the snow outside, steamed in the heat, and as the waiting audience bought sandwiches and began to drink, the stench of beer and spiced sausage was added to the smell of leather, clothes, and cheap tobacco. How would the Strubl lungs stand it? Nobody cared.

First, Sapponyi came with Andrea. Head nurse and doctor away from Strubl at the same time—the play was making history! Trattner came next, with his party. They had come all the way from Vienna by sleigh and arrived at the inn with a jingling of their bells, undeniably the jolliest sound in the world. No one realized that the famous man was disturbed. He had had no time to see his daughter Stefanie for over six months. After Berlin, a motion-picture contract had taken him to Italy, and on his return, rehearsals had preoccupied him. This was to have been a happy Christmas reunion, and what had he found? Stefanie nearly seven months pregnant.

It was a disaster! To what extent, Stefanie could not yet know; he had not had a moment alone with her. But tonight he would have to tell her how things stood, that he hadn't a penny to spare, that what she lived on came from Hohenberge, her husband, and that Hohenberge would scarcely feel like keeping up his wife's expensive *apanage* if she were to be the mother of another man's child. It was, of course, too much to hope that the child was Hohenberge's. That would be much too simple.

Stefanie had laughed like the irresponsible child she had always been. Didn't she see what a mess she was in? Would she never grow up? Had she no feeling of responsibility whatsoever? No. The play, the play. . . . Damn the play! The entire village was in an uproar!

Well, let her enjoy it! She would have enough to grapple with later.

He looked about him, beginning to take an interest in his surroundings, able, as he always was, to put unpleasant things aside like a depressing role. He had looked forward to this evening. He believed in peasant art, and he knew Stefanie had a flair for the theatre—wasn't she his daughter? He thought that here she had undertaken something novel.

He was not disappointed. Half an hour later the lights in the room went out. Hushed silence followed. There were only two footlights. They burned blue and lighted the coarse sackcloth of the curtain which the children had garlanded with coloured paper flowers. Trattner could easily imagine what was going on behind it. The hearts of the children of Fichtenbach undoubtedly beat the same as the hearts of professional actors on a first night.

Stefanie was in the wings, ready to prompt. It had been left to Dennis to manage the intricacies of all the primitive contraptions. Lighting, for instance. The lights were blue now because they were shaded by blue tissue paper to which string was attached. Dennis held the other end of the string in his hand. When his cue came, he would flood the stage with light by no more complicated means than pulling the paper gently away from the bulbs, which could then blaze forth with all the voltage they possessed. A gramophone played "Oh Tannenbaum . . ." It was his job, too, to change the records and to create all the other noises required by the script. A little silver bell and a larger copper one stood on rungs of a ladder at his side within easy reach of his hands. Dennis was ready too.

But the children were not. They stood in the large dressing-room with its dividing curtain for girls and boys, their faces painted beautifully by an expert Stefanie, looking for all the world like the figures on a medieval animated set of chimes, and were involved in a political discussion.

"If Joseph is a Jew," Walter Reischer, who was to play Joseph, was saying, "then I don't play."

The whole unfortunate incident had been touched off by the Brandstetter boy's saying to the others, "Look at Reischer. He looks like an old Jew." Whereupon Melita had said thoughtlessly, "Why shouldn't he? Joseph was an old Jew." The answer had come from Reischer, who threatened to strike if this were true, so that the play was in great danger of losing one of its leading characters on the opening night.

Fehge, in a white gown, her blue head-shawl and halo in her hands, stood in the background with a troubled face. They hated the Jews. They wouldn't even play at being a Jew. . . . Why? Why?

One of the angels turned her face up to Melita. "Please blow my nose," she begged.

"Never have I seen so many runny noses!" Stefanie had said, on closer acquaintanceship with these children. It was true. Their noses ran all through the winter. After having painted their little faces, she had given the following instructions: "Nobody may blow his nose. Go to Fräulein Bahr. She will fix you up." That had been an hour ago. Since then Melita had blown uncounted noses. She wiped this one now and dabbed it absent-mindedly with powder from a puff in the pocket of her apron. How was she to settle this pending Reischer disaster? "Joseph" was walking behind the screen, probably as a preliminary to taking off his costume.

Stefanie came in, and Melita told her what was up. Reischer turned and waited to hear the Frau Gräfin's ideas on the subject. He leant on his long staff, sullen behind his false beard. He didn't look in the least like an old Jew.

Stefanie reminded herself that she shouldn't smile, and discovered that she didn't want to smile. It was really very sad. "Reischer," she said, "I have worked very hard at this play. You are not going to spoil it for me, are you?" And her back ached suddenly, as it had done on and off during the entire afternoon. It was a pain that seemed to snatch at her and then go away.

Reischer looked at her. She was so beautiful in the flowing robe that hid her swollen body, a robe of deep purple chiffon velvet that made her seem like a queen of the night, with the Hohenberge pearls at her throat. Her hair with the clear-cut streaks of white in it shone. She looked so well and so strong. Reischer looked away and tried to make a last stand. "*Na*, was he a Jew or wasn't he?"

Stefanie was torn between honour and the play she loved. She compromised. "I'll explain it to you afterwards," she said.

Reischer was smart enough not to look at her again. He moved in the direction of the screen. "Joseph" was leaving the play ten minutes before the curtain. "Come back," Stefanie cried in a shrill voice. "He wasn't a Jew," and she looked at Melita and gave a short laugh. Tears were in her eyes.

Fehge's head sank. Stefanie had lied.

The play began. The announcing angel stepped in front of the curtain and began to tell, in a prologue, a little of what was in store for the audience. "My God, isn't she beautiful!" said an audible whisper in the back.

"*Who* is she?" asked Sapponyi.

A peasant woman behind him leaned forward and whispered, "*Die Leitner Annie*," because they had all become one.

Even Sapponyi shook his head and said, "Unbelievable!"

Stefanie had painted on the girl's round, bland face two lovely perfectly arched eyebrows. She had given her long black lashes and peachlike velvet cheeks that blended naturally into her white skin—for Leitner's Annie was tubercular, and her skin was very white—and her own rough lips were completely hidden under the full cupid bows that had been painted there. Leitner's Annie, the cow-girl, was gone! Sapponyi's head went on wobbling a little for some time.

Now the announcing angel was through, without a hitch, without even that atmosphere of an impending hitch which so often creates nervousness among an audience listening to children perform. She drew aside the curtain for the first scene, which took place in a peasant room like the rooms the Fichtenbachers lived in, so they at once felt at home. On a chair sat Pfeiffer's Serafine, asleep by an open window through which streamed the light of an electric bulb moon. Pfeiffer's Serafine woke up to the right strains of music just as she had been taught to do. And there was Dennis, ringing the bells. Their sound crept beyond the footlights.

> "There are the bells of Saint Mary . . .
> And the moon shines in my window.
> I must have been asleep.
> For if the moon were not outside,
> It would be dark in my little room . . ."

Pfeiffer's Serafine was speaking high German, a thing she'd never been known to do before, and she was as magnificently camouflaged as Leitner's Annie had been, so that her own parents could hardly recognize her. They looked at their Serafine, and their mouths dropped open. Ludmilla Pfeiffer's hands were clammy. This bordered on the miraculous!

Now the bells rang out at Dennis's hand.

> "Didn't Mother say she'd be back at five?
> How light, how lovely is what I hear!
> Oh, why can't it be ever so,
> That I, alone, poised between sadness and joy
> Deep in my heart need nothing know
> But that it's Christmas Eve!"

Pfeiffer's Serafine didn't know what she was talking about, but she was not nervous. She felt at home in this accustomed setting, in a part that was well rehearsed. And Sapponyi thought: Ah yes . . . if someone comes along and teaches them with infinite patience how to speak and how to behave . . . Was that the solution? Bah! Who was to teach it? There weren't enough people to go round. And his head started to shake again in vexation . . .

Then Serafine rose and walked to the middle of the room as she

had been taught to do and began to take things from a drawer to
set the table as she had been taught to do.

> *"I wish there was something I could do,*
> *So that Mother would find it more friendly here.*
> *It is so empty, so sad in our room,*
> *Empty like my two useless hands.*
> *Oh, were they but full like my heart and soul!*
> *How lightly I'd hold them outstretched to my mother!"*

At these unheard-of and totally alien sentiments issuing from her
daughter's mouth, Ludmilla's eyes filled with tears which overflowed
and ran down her cheeks. But then, she was an emotional Slav!

Then came Serafine's play-mother, who was, in real life, none
other than Moser's Creszentia. With what awkward gestures she
caressed her "child"! How difficult it had been to teach these
children to caress and kiss as naturally as this mother now did. How
silly they had thought it, unaccustomed as they were to any outward sign of affection! Stage a fight with them—that they could
have appreciated! But a scene of tender greeting? It had been
very difficult for all concerned. Not only had Stefanie had to
cope with the children's uncouthness; the children had had to cope
with Stefanie's gentleness.

But Moser's Creszentia hastened over that hurdle and kissed
Pfeiffer's Serafine, whom she especially hated, on the cheek, as she
had been taught to do, and stood the way Stefanie had shown her
how to stand as she did it, and Serafine accepted the caress as she
had been directed. It made a show of real "upper class" affection
such as the peasants had never seen before. Many teeth showed in
grins.

> *"There you are, Karin, my child.*
> *How I would like to stay with you!*
> *But you know how the Herrschaften are—*
> *Festivities, visits, running about,*
> *What all has to be seen to till everything's ready!*
> *The ballroom, the kitchen, the children, the guests . . ."*

> *"Do you have to go out again on Christmas Eve,*
> *For other children, other people?"*

Alas, Moser's Creszentia did, but she had brought her little daughter a fairy-tale book to beguile the time and, after a few more studied gestures of affection and some more fine verses, she left her child, who returned to read her book in the moonlight. This was the moment when Dennis had to pull the string and flood the little stage with light as the first fairy entered upon the scene—Stückler's Erna as the Sleeping Beauty.

Stückler's Erna was so glamorous that every peasant in the room was transported. Stefanie had been clever enough not to dissociate the children completely from the garb they wore in real life. Instead, she had made their everyday clothes into something so magnificent that everybody could feel that even a dirndl had its place in heaven.

Erna wore a glorified dirndl with an apron covered with gleaming silver figures pasted on (the grouchy old bank director from Budapest recognized his stars) and a wreath of roses on her head and beads round her neck and roses in her hair, worn loose, as though she had been rained upon by blossoms. She cried:

> "Open your spirit and be not afraid,
> My little heart, in our Reich
> There shines a warm and lovely light.
> Each person, be he great or small,
> Is welcome to its blessings."

The Reich she was speaking of was the Kingdom of God. All the pious heads sitting down below understood very well what she meant, but very few of the heads sitting down below were pious. . . .

After several more and just as miraculous figures out of Grimm's *Fairy Tales* had assembled round the peasant child and had promised to take her to Bethlehem, the curtain was drawn on the first act by the announcing angel. Trattner whispered in Sapponyi's ear, "Miraculous!" All his worldly cares were forgotten, as always in the theatre. Clever Stefanie! This was better than Oberammergau!

Dennis sounded the little silver bell, the gramophone began to play "Silent Night," and the curtain rose on the scene that the Herr Wirt had painted. Now that they were warmed up down there in the audience, their admiration burst forth from them in an audible "Ah!".

On his back-drop Herr Wirt had painted an open central door through which you looked out into the black sky on to a firmament of stars. The Star of Bethlehem gleamed in large, crude exactness and sent forth a band of yellow light streaming across the sky, growing ever wider. Inside the stall were painted two symmetrical heads of cows on the one side and the head of an ass on the other. These animals glared woodenly into space as though turned to stone by the sanctity of their surroundings.

"*Who* is the Maria?" said one of the visitors from Vienna in a whisper that could be heard.

"Fehge," answered Sapponyi, as though everyone must know her, and Trattner added, "Stefanie's servant," and they both sounded as pleased as fathers.

Fehge's face had needed hardly any painting at all, which had nearly broken her heart. She sat before the manger in which lay the doll she had dressed. Beside her stood Joseph, and the three wore golden halos, round flat cardboard discs covered with gilt paper which stood up straight behind their heads. They caught the light and glowed softly. Fehge wore a royal-blue veil over her head and a white gown as in a Raphael painting; and Joseph, reassured now as to his Aryanism, wore his brown cassock and false beard. Shepherds and angels knelt and stood in adoration around the manger. The angels wore white gowns sprinkled with silver stars and starry halos such as the baroque Madonnas throughout Austria wore. And then the fairy figures brought in the little peasant girl.

When the village priest looked at the scene, he was astounded. This play was breathing forth an atmosphere he had tried in vain to get in his church.

When the gramophone began to play the Ave Maria, Fehge lifted the child from its bed of straw and took it in her arms, and kissed it and finally held it outstretched so that the peasant girl could see it. With a mother's pride, she spoke the only line she had to say in the whole play in answer to the peasant girl's question, "Oh, tell me, is this the beginning of the eternal Reich?" the words,

> "*All I can say is that I am a mother.*"

The Ave Maria played louder; and suddenly, down in the audience, Olga Retschnichek, star of the Vienna Opera, raised her heavenly voice and sang it, sang with the tears in her eyes and, sentimental as she was, felt that she had been born for just this moment, to sing the Ave Maria in these humble surroundings.

None of the children were surprised to hear the unexpected aria. It was just God's fitting blessing on the whole event. Then the play brought them all down to earth again, to the little peasant room where the child awoke from her dream to see her mother enter with the lighted Christmas tree. Serafine's big moment came when she would take her mother by the hand and lead her to the front of the little stage and tell her and those who had seen it with her:

> "*For now I know where Bethlehem is*
> *And where the Saviour lives,*
> *That He is there, in every love,*
> *And that no heart is lost*
> *That can feel love, that beats in love . . .*
> *Oh, if only all had seen it thus,*
> *How on this night love came to us!*"

But, of course, she didn't know what she was talking about. . . .

Then everyone sang "Silent Night." The curtain fell, and the visitors from Vienna began to applaud so that the peasants knew it was the thing to do, and they followed suit. The priest pushed his way through to Melita and asked her if she would give the play again on Christmas Day in Pritnitz, and Andrea, whose heart always expanded at Christmas-time (there was a time and place for everything), went back-stage to give Fehge a kiss. Even the innkeeper from Waldeck asked Melita whether she would give the play at his inn. It was not alone the desire to bring this little replica of God's

Kingdom to his village that led him to make the offer—the amount of sandwiches and beer consumed before and after the play was not lost on him.

Melita laughed and said she would see what could be done. Then, from behind, a big, husky man tapped her on the shoulder. She looked into his bleary eyes. She knew him, of course, the son of the postmaster in Pritnitz, not a bad boy, just a little drunk tonight. Why shouldn't he be? Beer drunk. It always made them belligerent later on, but now he was in the jolly stage, his face sweating and beaming. She turned round to say something to him. He clicked his heels, put his left hand on his stomach, raised his right hand and said, "I thank you in the name of our Führer, Adolf Hitler!"

Melita's face set rigid in the smile that had begun to lighten her face. The man laughed, and somebody slapped him on the back and led him off to the bar where the Madonna whom Fehge loved smiled her simpering approval. A little angel, with her nose running unhindered now and her make-up smeared, ran up to Melita and said, "The Frau Gräfin says we can keep our halos."

Melita pushed the child aside and walked to the entrance. The cold out there sent her back again to the dressing-room. Mechanically she found her coat and put it on, then went outside again. The door closed and shut out the light.

The people who had been huddled at the windows throughout the play to see what they could of the spectacle were dispersing. Melita walked across the hard-packed snow of the road. The moon was up and the unsullied snow glistened like diamonds. Across a wide expanse of field some wild animal had made little tracks with its hoofs. Melita looked back at the inn whose lights gleamed as prettily as in an illuminated picture-postcard. "Oh, if only all had seen it thus, how on this night love came to us!" Love? Melita's face grimaced in an unhappy smile. Love? They would drink and brawl at the inn until the strongest man had thrown everyone else out of the window, and knives would flash, for private jealousy, for political differences—just because some way had to be found to relieve the natural, latent belligerency of these people.

These people? These people were horrible!

Melita drew herself up tight and narrow with a long shuddering breath. What had the boy said? In the name of our Führer, Adolf Hitler. Christmas 1933. For him there was only one Reich, the Reich of Adolf Hitler's dreams. Tonight he had mistaken God's Reich for it. She wondered how many others had made the same mistake. And then she laughed bitterly, and the salt tears ran into her mouth. It was such an immeasurable let-down.

Chapter Twenty-Nine

STEFANIE walked restlessly up and down in front of her father, who was seated in the most comfortable chair in her room. Her cheeks were still flushed with excitement. She did not want to sit down. Not yet. Soon she would go to bed. She was tired, and the little straining pain in her back, which had grown steadier, now made her restless.

She was still heart and soul in the play, which had gone off so well. "But really, Papa," she was saying, "the rehearsals were even more fun than the play! If Bonsels could have heard his precious words on their rough tongues! His hair would have stood on end! Oh, it has been such fun! And, do you know, the priest wants us to give it in Pritnitz on Christmas Day, and the innkeeper from Waldeck wants it for his inn, and I shouldn't wonder if all the inn-keepers didn't come round asking for it! Oh, Papa, we shall have a wandering theatre! Somebody will give us a cart, and we will pack everything into it and travel from village to village with our play!" She paused. "Papa, you are not listening. Something is on your mind."

He told her. He had expected it to be a blow, but not to the extent evidenced by the deathly pallor of her face and the way she began to sway. Trattner rose and advanced toward her. "I'll call the nurse," he said. "Are you going to faint?"

She shook her head, and the piteous expression on her face cut into his heart. He pulled forward a chair for her, and she sat down heavily. The pain in her back had suddenly become excruciating. She would not faint. She must not faint. She must try to think. The sound as of a rushing train was in her ears; she felt sick; and she was in great pain. It was inconceivable that now, just at this moment, when she had planned . . . that she . . . that *they* should both belong to *him*! Louise, she thought. I must tell Louise. She will help us. We were always so close. Peter. Louise. And I.

She fainted. All that night she was unconscious, and in the morning labour began. The famous Professor Seifert was sent for from Vienna and remained with her all day, and still she did not recover consciousness. Toward evening her heart began to fail. She died shortly after midnight, and the child was taken from her after death. It was a boy, who weighed exactly four and a half pounds.

Andrea brought the child into Stefanie's room where Fehge was waiting, and the first thing she did was to put him into Fehge's arms. Then she slumped down in a chair, utterly exhausted. She passed a hand over her weary eyes that had seen very little sleep for two nights and was motionless for a moment. It was not alone the ordeal of birth and death and the vigil of two waking nights that had exhausted her. She had been through such trials before. It was the whole fantastic unconventionality of Stefanie and people like her, the careless way they lived their lawless lives. They seemed to be quite decent, fundamentally, so that you could not put your finger on the wrong. But it *was* wrong. This crass individualism. This disregard of every moral standard.

How could they be so carefree? How could they shake off responsibility and law and order so easily, as though it were not there? Where would this end—this reckless development of personality regardless of convention? Sodom and Gomorrha, thought Andrea.

Meanwhile Fehge held the boy in her arms. His little mouth twitched in a red face. His eyes were closed and bulged a little like two tiny soft pink cushions. He moved his head from side to side restlessly as though he were about to cry. She began to rock him, and the line she had studied carefully with Stefanie came to her mind . . . "All I can say is that I am a mother."

Andrea spoke without opening her eyes. "I doubt whether the little thing will live," she said, thankful that Trattner was not a Catholic and there had been no mad scramble to get the priest for an emergency baptism. That would have been the last straw. "If we could get him to Vienna to an incubator . . . perhaps . . ." But nobody seemed to care very much whether the child lived or not; and she thought, too, that it would be better off dead. She had done her best to bring it this far; now let God decide. "We must get him out of here," she went on, not able, after all, to leave the field, even to God. "Out of this room, out of this house. . . ."

"We can take him down to Dennis's cottage," said Fehge.

"Herr Seymour will thank us for that!" said Andrea.

"He won't mind! I know he won't mind! He . . . he . . . he won't mind."

Andrea took the child from Fehge's arms, which seemed to cling instinctively to the warm little body. "Go down and ask him if it would be all right, and you'll have to stay down there with the child until they've decided what to do with him."

Fehge ran all the way to Dennis's cottage.

Dennis took them both. Fehge put her hair up in a crown of black braids, in keeping with the dignity of her new position. She was housekeeper and nurse, a fine status to have achieved. The urge to become a nursing sister was, for the time being, submerged by this undeniably special assignment from God to care for this child, to wash it and feed it and keep it warm, to be its mother. But why had Dennis been so vehement, almost angry, about keeping that stupid secret? Now more than ever.

Seven days later the child was still alive and even gaining weight, which was entirely due to Fehge's ceaseless care. Both Sapponyi and Andrea admitted that. Fehge obeyed all instructions to the letter with a deftness and reliability that was astounding, but, more than that, she seemed to breathe life into the child by the intense way she watched over it. She would not let it die.

She knew nothing of the arguments that were going on about the child. Trattner had gone back to Vienna to see Hohenberge. Meanwhile Fehge cared for the baby in Dennis's cottage. The large room on the other side of the studio was theirs. It never occurred to her that this mode of living might be temporary. Dennis, who saw the end coming, groped in his mind for an explanation.

One evening she said to him, "I have thought of a name for the child."

"You have?" said Dennis. "What?"

"He was born on Christmas Day, so we should call him Jesus."

Dennis shook his head. "No," he said. "You can't do that. You can't imagine what an awful handicap a name like Jesus can be. In Spain, now, boys are often called Jesus, and I'll tell you a story to show you what a nuisance that can be. A friend of mine gave up his house in Spain and brought his entire staff to England with him. His chauffeur was called Jesus. One day when he was on his way home from London—he lived in the country in a province called Kent—he sent a telegram to his wife. 'Arriving on the four o'clock. Send Jesus to meet me.' And the man at the telegraph office handed the telegram back to him and said, 'You can't send that, sir. It's blasphemy!'" Dennis smiled at her. "You see. You can't do that to the little man. It wouldn't be fair."

Fehge's face clouded over, and she said nothing for a while. Then she went out of the room and came back with her Bible. "Listen," she said, and read to him, out of the Gospel of St. Matthew. "And she shall bring forth a son and thou shalt call his name Jesus; for he shall save his people from their sins. Now all this was done, that it might be fulfilled which was spoken of the Lord by the prophet, saying, Behold, a virgin shall be with child, and shall bring forth a son, and they shall call his name Emmanuel, which being interpreted is . . . God with us." She paused and looked up

from her slow reading. "We can call him Emmanuel, can't we?"
she said. "God with us."

"Yes," said Dennis. "We can do that."

"When will he be baptized?"

"You must wait. Just a little longer."

The plane was several minutes overdue. Oscar von Hohenberge
showed his impatience as he stepped out of it. To the three men
who were waiting with obvious obsequiousness to greet him he
said, "This damned plane! We are four minutes overdue, and I
thought it would be more!" He put his watch back in his vest
pocket. "Good afternoon, gentlemen."

Yes. He would be at the Embassy at nine o'clock precisely.
Yes. Ten o'clock next morning suited him excellently for Herr
Generaldirektor Schüler to put in an appearance. The Hotel
Imperial was where he was staying. Of course. But first of all,
gentlemen, he had to go to Strubl in the Wienerwald, where he
had a small matter to attend to. Where could he get a car to take
him? "Thank you. Very good of you, Herr Generaldirektor."
And he got into that gentleman's car and was off, leaving the
impression of a whirlwind, although he had moved quietly and
spoken in a low voice.

A little over an hour later, he was sitting in Sapponyi's office
opposite the Herr Medizinalrat.

"At first we thought the child would not live," Sapponyi was
saying, "and we really have this girl Fehge to thank for the fact
that the boy is alive today. Her care has pulled him through."

"Would she come with the child?"

"You can ask her. She seems deeply attached to him. If she
cares to, there is no one to stop her."

Hohenberge rose, as much as to say that he was ready to see the
child. Sapponyi said, "Wait. I will have him brought here."

It was Fehge who brought the baby, in his long dress, wrapped in
a soft white shawl. Fehge was wearing one of Stefanie's winter
dirndls which had been given to her. It was made of a flowered
material with a rich, wine-coloured background, cut high in the

neck with a tiny ruff of lace and buttoned down the front with round gold-coin buttons. She had dark rings under her eyes from lack of sleep, which gave her face an ethereal quality it ordinarily lacked. She looked so beautiful that even Hohenberge noticed it. There was something very soothing about her.

She came and stood in the middle of the room with the child in her arms and looked from Sapponyi to the tall, broad-shouldered man with the monocle and the peculiar square, shaven head. Hohenberge in no way showed his age. His lips were very thick, and his features heavy, especially the dissipated pouches under his eyes.

Hohenberge walked over to the child and looked down at it. "A boy," he said, with satisfaction in his voice, as though this fact could not be repeated often enough. Then he snapped to attention, and glared at Sapponyi. "And you really believe that the child will be healthy?"

"If you can pull him through this first year, he will have a good chance."

That reminded Hohenberge of what Sapponyi had said of the young girl here, who had done such a splendid job of looking after the boy. "And this is the girl, Fehge?" he said.

Sapponyi said, "It is."

Hohenberge's voice became honeyed, which, from him, sounded very unnatural. "And will she come along with us?" he said, and smiled at her, a smile she found utterly terrifying. It was his way of being friendly and jocose. He thought it was the right way to address a pretty young peasant girl. "I will pay her as good a salary as she can dream of. Well? What about it, my girl?"

Fehge looked from the man to Sapponyi and back at the man again, and she paled. "I don't understand," she said, and had to clear her throat two or three times before she could get out the words, "what the gentleman wants of me."

Sapponyi said, "This is the Count Oscar von Hohenberge. He was the husband of Stefanie von Hohenberge, whom we all loved. He has come to take the child with him."

Fehge could not find her voice for a moment. That was what

came of playing this absurd game of secrecy, of keeping that silly promise! Dennis had taught her the sacred meaning of a promise. But there were moments like these when it was a question of life and death! She must tell them! It was her duty to tell them. Dennis might not. Dennis had been so queer about this whole thing, all along. He might not tell, even now, but it had to be told!

"Fehge," said Sapponyi sharply, "what ails you?" She had behaved very oddly about this child. If he had not see it born, he would have believed it was hers.

She drew a deep breath and in a loud, strident voice that was totally unlike her own she said, "That is impossible. The Herr Graf cannot take the child with him because he is not its father."

Hohenberge drew himself back and up and looked at her disagreeably. Sapponyi became very nervous.

"Who, then, is the father?" he asked, after clearing his throat.

"Dennis," said Fehge. "Dennis is the father."

Sapponyi said nothing. He looked at Hohenberge, who was turning purple. He had been assured by Trattner that nobody had the slightest idea who the father might be. Stefanie's correspondence had shown nothing. Hohenberge now glared at Sapponyi. Trust the Jew to play him a trick like this!

Sapponyi opened his mouth to say something, but when he saw Hohenberge's rage he closed his lips tightly as though he had decided to keep to himself what he had been about to say. He sent for Dennis.

Meanwhile the three said nothing. Hohenberge walked softly up and down in a great rage. Fehge stood still, trembling a little. Sapponyi turned his pencil over and over between his fingers and stared at it. Suddenly, without looking at her, he said, "Fehge, you don't seem to realize that, according to the law, this child belongs to this man," and he designated Hohenberge with a hand that was limp at the wrist, "regardless of whom you believe to be the father."

Fehge stopped trembling and swayed a little. She was quite cold. "But," she said in a whisper, "that isn't just."

Sapponyi shrugged his shoulders. "If it were not so, anyone could come along and say, 'This child is mine,' even if it was the legal father's." She said nothing. "Couldn't he?"

Fehge's lips parted to speak. At first no sound came. "Not," she finally brought forth, "not if he speaks the truth. . . ."

Sapponyi's harsh laugh interrupted her. "Laws aren't built on the presumption that man speaks the truth. Besides," and he gave her a piercing look, "sometimes those who think they are speaking the truth are wrong. *It is often very hard to tell.*"

When they came for Dennis, he knew that Fehge had told. All the way back to the house, he fought his conflicting thoughts. The theory of complete individual freedom. What a mess had been made of it for him now.

When he entered the room, all eyes were turned toward him. Sapponyi did not stop for introductions. He plunged right into the matter. "Fehge has just told us that you are the father of this child."

In silence Dennis looked at the man standing where the light fell on him. He knew him at once. Stefanie had often spoken of him. He looked away. Freedom ended with parenthood as finally as with marriage. He took a deep breath. Then he turned again to Hohenberge with a look that seemed to measure the man inwardly and outwardly. After that there was no longer any doubt in his mind. He turned to Sapponyi and said, "That is true, Herr Medizinalrat. I am the father."

"You wish to take the child?"

"Have I not already done so?"

Sapponyi's face broke into the smile that he had tried several times during the last few minutes to control. He smiled, *because he knew who the father was.*

He turned to Hohenberge. "The matter now rests with you, Count."

Hohenberge hadn't taken his eyes off Dennis since the latter had come in, in his boots on which the mud had caked hard in the cracks, in his old English tweed breeches, his thick woollen lumber-jacket, a muffler loose at his neck, his pipe, out, still in his hands—

he had knocked it clear of tobacco before entering Strubl—his tousled hair, his kind, aesthetic, seeking, unaggressive and, to Hohenberge's way of thinking, unmanly face. Hohenberge couldn't take his eyes off Dennis.

The mother had been decadent enough. But this! This weakling. This Englishman. The father!

Hohenberge shook himself free of distaste. He turned to Sapponyi. "*Ich verzichte!*" he snapped out at him, meaning that he waived his claim, clicked his heels, turned his back on them, and strode out of the room.

Chapter Thirty

MELITA had consented to give the play in Pritnitz on the sixth of January, the feast day of the Three Holy Kings or Wise Men. It always amused Dennis how these world-over celebrations became disarranged as they travelled from land to land. Here, for instance, Santa Claus, or St. Nicolas, didn't come on December 25th, but on the sixth, and the children hung up their stockings for him the night before that date. And Christmas Day was just a day of relaxation following the all-important Eve when Christ was born and presents were handed out round the tree that the Christ-child had given. Now, on the sixth of January, came the Three Kings who drew the curtain on the whole festive season for another year. The children would dress up as kings and sing carols. They would go to Strubl, where they would be given cocoa and *Streuselkuchen*. Tomorrow the trees would be dismantled and burnt, and the smoke would smell of pine-wood.

The priest had agreed to give the children a hot meal if they came to play in Pritnitz, for they would have to remain there all day. About this the children were surprisingly sceptical. Pfeiffer's Serafine said to Melita, "If I were you, Miss Teacher, I wouldn't let myself in for it." But Melita shook her head at the girl. After all, the priest had promised.

She wasn't giving the play in Pritnitz to do the church a favour, but because she loved it and wanted everyone throughout the countryside to see it. Though Stefanie, who had created it, was dead, the play should live as long as possible.

They set out together for Pritnitz on the morning of the sixth, on a clear, cold day with sunshine that gave no warmth and the dry, cold air biting their skins. Fehge had not wanted to leave the baby, but Dennis had insisted that she should. He promised he would attend to him as faithfully as she did. "After all," he said, "I am the father," and Fehge had smiled, delighted that, at last, it was out.

As she walked beside Melita she could feel the cold air away down in her lungs. The glare of the sunlight on the soft snow of a recent blizzard made her eyes blink just as she used to long ago when her braids had pulled at her skin. Her feet sank deep into the fresh snow, which was not yet hardened by sled traffic. It was not easy going. The little troupe reached the assembly hall at eleven; Franz had already arrived with the props.

The hall was unheated and the children went through their parts with their coats on, feeling the cold even more than on the road outside. Erna made a grimace as she spoke about the warm and lovely light in her Reich, with her breath coming out of her mouth like smoke and her little red nose like a block of ice in her pinched, pale face. If he doesn't give us a hot meal, Melita thought to herself . . . but the priest had given his word.

She reminded him of it as the clock passed noon. He looked sheepish and said, of course, and went away, presumably to eat his own lunch, because he did not come back for an hour. At one-thirty the children were hopping from one foot to the other and slapping each other to keep warm. The props and dresses were in their places. Food, food, food was what the children wanted! Melita took them to the Lamb.

She seated them at two big round tables, where the same set of peasants played *taroque* on the same nights every week. She looked at her large group and sighed. Their lunch would cost her her next week-end in Vienna. What was the cheapest thing she could offer them?

Heinrich Grabautschnik came over and stood, his legs spread, his arms crossed, taking them all in at a glance. Melita started a hurried conversation with the waiter. But the children didn't share her inhibitions; they liked Heinrich Grabautschnik, he was a popular man, and well rid of his stupid wife, Clotilde, who had never come back to him after the ceremony on Schwarzenberg. She had died alone in the rain-drenched woods of a thing called "exposure," and a good thing too. Serafine said to Grabautschnik, "The parson promised us a meal, now the Teacher has to shell out!"

Melita tried to silence her with a glance, but Serafine was as proud of the generosity of her teacher as she was incensed at the meanness of her priest, and she intended to tell the world about it.

Grabautschnik looked at Melita and said jovially, "The party's on me."

He called over the waiter and told him what to bring—knack-wurst, sauerkraut, and home-fried potatoes. The children's eyes sparkled. They began to spin the beer counters on the table amidst shrieks of laughter. Only Fehge's eyes were big as they rested on Grabautschnik. She hadn't heard a word of the miraculous order; she only heard the words, "The crucifix must go."

Grabautschnik gave her stare for stare, and he thought, dis-passionately, that it wouldn't be much longer that she'd be sitting down at table with the others.

Then he crossed over to Melita and said, "You're crowded here. Won't you come over and join me?" And his head indicated where—a small table in a niche opposite. "You can keep an eye on them from there."

Her first natural instinct was to refuse. Then she could sense that he had something important to say to her, and she wanted to hear it, to fight it if necessary, and win. She had just suffered one miserable defeat. So she went with him.

After a long silence, filled only by the babel of the children's voices, Grabautschnik said, "There's going to be shooting soon."

Was that all he had to say—that the Nazis were going to try another *Putsch*? But she gave a start as he went on slowly to say, "You people are going to have to shoot it out before the summer."

She waited till she could feel that the skin on her face had cooled, then she said, "What are you trying to do? Provoke me into telling you something?"

He laughed and said, "No. You have nothing to tell me I don't know already. I'm much better informed than you are."

Melita's heart became leaden. She knew that he was right.

"You'll have to shoot it out, and you haven't a chance. You've waited too long. That's fatal. Nothing weakens an army like hanging around."

"We're not an army in that sense," she said bitterly.

"I know," he said. "That's why you haven't a chance. Letting the others choose their time!" His tone was contemptuous.

She clasped and unclasped her right hand, which lay on the table. How could she best extricate herself and get back to the children? Then out of a blue sky he said to her, "Fräulein Bahr, will you marry me?"

She turned white. "How dare you?" she said softly, her words caught in her throat.

He reddened at the insult of her obvious disgust. "Waiting for an academic man?" he said, and could not hide the sneer in his tone.

Pat in her mind was an answer, as a parting shot, "I want nothing to do with a man of your convictions." What she found herself saying, to her utter surprise, was, "It has nothing to do with that, Grabautschnik. I don't love you."

What a stupid answer for a girl of her political standing to give to a man of his! She could have screamed with mortification!

Grabautschnik was looking at her with undisguised contempt. "I don't love you, either, Fräulein Bahr," he said, and thought: Love? Does she think she can stand up beside women like Rosl and Hilda? "I am trying to win you for the Movement," he went on. "We need women like you, and you will soon be without a political home."

It was then that she noticed that Fehge was trying to catch her eye. Fehge rose when she saw she had attracted her teacher's attention, and Melita called, "What is it, Fehge?"

The waiter was bringing the first load of steaming plates. The spicy aroma of sausage penetrated into even the most stopped-up noses. "Ah!" cried the children in unison.

Above their clamour, Fehge said, very distinctly, "Will the Fräulein Lehrerin please excuse me? I am not hungry." And she left the room.

She went back to the hall and straight up to the priest, who was helping some men to arrange the seats for the audience.

"Why didn't you give us a hot meal as you promised?"

Her unwavering eyes made his falter. "Did I promise?" he asked her.

"Of course you promised."

"Well," he told her, "then I shall have to see what I can do about it, won't I?" And he was vexed with himself that he couldn't make the jocularity in his voice ring true.

She began to cry. She couldn't help herself, and the tears rained down her cheeks. "Oh, don't you see? It's too late! It's too late! Herr Grabautschnik's treated them all to a meal down at the Lamb!"

The priest stared at her as though she had taken leave of her senses. What was there to cry about then? Thanks to a kind God, Herr Grabautschnik had saved him at least fifteen *Schillinge*!

The children gave the play in Pritnitz with even greater success than in Fichtenbach. Here, in the large hall, there was more room; the audience was less crowded, with better air and a better view. The applause was deafening.

When it was over, the priest gave each child an orange.

The hall had held well over two hundred people. The price of the tickets had been twenty-five *Groschen* for adults and ten for children. The priest had made a tidy sum of money. The children tucked their oranges away and gave the priest a look out of eyes that were slits. *Ja, die Schwarzen*, the Black Ones, they knew how to bleed you and make the money to feed their own fat bellies! And that was why they did not join the new church army, the Catholic Action, but the Nazis, where a glorious future was being promised them by a new God. "Hitler breaks need! Hitler makes bread!"

It was Brandstetter's Theresa who started the chant. Her brother was a Nazi and she had learnt it from him. Now she led the children out of the hall to its rhythm. Yes. Adolf Hitler would set them free and pave their streets with gold!

On Monday, February 11, 1934, the storm that Grabautschnik had prophesied broke. The enemy had, indeed, chosen his time. The day before, Minister Fey of the Dollfuss Government, addressing a gathering of *Heimwehr* men, now incorporated in the Fatherland Front, said, "I can assure you, yesterday's conversations have brought us the certainty that Dr. Dollfuss is on our side. I can tell you more, if only in a few words. WE'LL GO TO IT TO-MORROW, AND WE'LL MAKE A THOROUGH JOB OF IT!"

They did.

Anton Bahr went to work as usual on that fateful Monday morning and worked until the news reached him and those working with him that shots had been fired in Linz. Then orders came from party headquarters to lay down their work and proceed to their places, unarmed. These orders were carried out in a spirit of grim determination. The fight to defend their rights, that Otto Bauer had promised them in Linz, had come at last.

At noon Dollfuss declared a state of martial law, and *only then* did the workers take to their secret arsenals. They were as meticulous as gentlemen. The first shots were fired in Vienna shortly after noon.

Anton, in his group, went to his home to find it already surrounded by the Dollfuss militia, which had set up cannon and was bombarding holes into a structure which still housed women and children. Thereupon he joined his "regiment." The fight was on.

He could not enter the Reumanhof, where he lived. It was one of those sprawling model apartment houses built by the Commune for its workers before the Dollfuss Government, set on killing its red heart, Vienna, had imposed such taxation upon that city that all further building was made impossible. A twentieth-century monument, Melita had used to call the Reumanhof.

They left it to its fate and fought their way to the Philadelphia Bridge, where they were able to hold their own that afternoon and night and on into the next day until they felt strong enough to take the offensive and advance on to the Margarethengürtel, which encircles ten of Vienna's boroughs.

This advance battalion, which included Anton, reached the Margarethengürtel but was forced to retreat because it met superior forces armed with machine-guns. The workers had only their rifles, and some had more primitive weapons such as spades and stout sticks. On this vain expedition, Anton managed to wrest a machine-gun from a *Heimwehr* man whom he had to kill. He closed his eyes for a moment to shut out the dead man's face, only to see again, in his mind's eye, the gaping holes of the Reumanhof that had been his home. With revulsion he thought that this was not what man had been cut out for. It was the weapon that made him think like this. He would not have minded killing the man with his bare hands.

But the machine-gun was a real prize. They retreated with it and with another, captured by someone else, and were fighting their way back to the bridge they had left that morning, the railway tracks in their rear, when, suddenly, fire was opened on them. An armoured car stood on the tracks, firing its bullets into their flank.

Anton was one of the first to fall. Bleeding from the mouth, he lay in the dust, fully conscious, and his first thought was: The railway workers didn't strike! There is no general strike! What am I doing here?

Suddenly and clearly he saw the entire country of Austria as Melita had always seen it, and he saw that it could not possibly have been on their side. He could see the people as she had seen them before he had clouded her vision with his theories. He remembered himself and Melly, starving children picking berries in the woods, and the people who had tried to stone them. Now he would like to have told her that she had been right. We are fighting for a lost cause, he thought. Melita was right all along. She never did love the people. They are not worth it.

Delirium was closing in on him, and he saw many things more lucidly now than ever before. The future, he thought, belongs to the extremes. The Right and the Left will fight it out. We—the sober ones—have no following.

Finally he saw "Bertha," his love, the precision machine which only he and his friend, Sylvester, knew how to handle—Sylvester, who had fallen already at the Gürtel . . . Bertha, that intricate tower of metal that chugged when she moved jerkily across a steel table. He could see her now, standing still in a deserted factory. He felt very lonely as he died, this man who had given his life for a lost cause.

The news of the fighting reached Pritnitz on the night of the thirteenth. No train ran so late. Melita took the car from Strubl, and when it was stopped on the outskirts of Vienna she got out and walked.

She arrived at her home the next morning. There were more gaping holes now than Anton had seen. Neighbours had brought him home and laid him on the bed, cleared of debris that now lay piled high in the corner. Frau Funke said, "I did the best I could. You can't go on living here anyway. They let him lie all day. They only just let us go and get him."

Melita nodded her head. The stench of gunpowder and burnt wood was dreadful. Anton lay, unrecognizably altered, a heap of mangled flesh. Shot. Run over by something. Christian soldiers had done this. Of course, there were no Christians, not in the whole wide world. Even Frau Funke, who had brought Anton home, might be a Nazi before the year was out. As soon as people started to think, there was no knowing where it would end. Melita sat down with her back to Anton on a chair that was whole and standing curiously alone in the centre of the smashed room. She was sitting thus, motionless, when the police came an hour later to arrest her.

Chapter Thirty-One

FEHGE lingered upstairs over putting Mani to bed. He was kicking his little legs happily into the air, placid, as all healthy, well-fed babies are, making little cooing noises. His bright black eyes watched Fehge, very much aware.

Whenever she was with the child, she could put aside the fear that was growing in her because God had not yet avenged His enemies. This fear had grown so tangible that it disturbed her sleep and appetite so that she was no longer as robust as she had been before. The sack of potatoes on her back would have been more than she could bear these days; but here, with Mani and Dennis, she had very little hard work to do.

Downstairs, the art dealer Fröhlich, who had been a patient at Strubl, was saying good-bye. He came often. He wanted to exhibit some of Dennis's pictures in his galleries in Vienna. He wanted to "discover" Dennis. And this was just what Dennis had managed to avoid until now. He did not want his art tempered by having to cater to public tastes and demands. It was his own, his very own, not created for any effect it might have on his fellow-men. And thus it was to remain. He had managed to explain this to Fröhlich without offending him.

Fehge watched the wizened old man leave the house. Really, he looked so much like a corpse, it was queer to see him walking about. Then, after a last smile for Mani, who would fall asleep quietly because he was an angelic baby, she went downstairs.

Dennis was already seated at his typewriter, about to continue an article he was working on. His articles he sold. They were a different matter. He wrote to be read, and he wrote only about what he knew. In writing you could do that. In painting, however much you reproduced, you created, and creations were something you had to be very careful with. You couldn't expose them carelessly to the world at large. Who could tell what effect they might have? Fröhlich had laughed and patted him well-meaningly on the shoulder. Now Dennis was thumping out words with one finger. The machine made a metallic *tick-tack* sound. He was writing an article on the Dollfuss assassination.

He looked up as Fehge passed through the room. Ute rose from the corner where she was lying and walked over to her mistress. She knew the routine of this house that ran like clockwork. Fehge would sit on the bench outside for a while, idling, until the late summer sun set. This was Ute's happiest hour.

Because Dennis looked up, Fehge felt free to interrupt him. She said, "Mani has the brightest little eyes. Like ripe, black cherries. I think he is going to be very clever."

Dennis removed his pipe, from which smoke rose transparently blue in spirals. "I'm sure he is," he said.

Fehge frowned. "There is something wrong with the eyes of Anne-Marie's child," she went on. "Today she was out in front of the house with it, alone, and she showed it to me. Its eyes do not focus. There is something wrong with the child."

Thus Fehge was the first to notice, and, through her, Dennis, what was soon to become the common gossip of the village—that Anne-Marie and Conrad's child was an idiot.

Fehge went and sat outside, and Ute lay down beside her, her nose on her outstretched paws, the brown of her hide reddened by the glow of the setting sun. Another hot day had passed. Fehge was glad of the window they had built into the other wall of Mani's room, thereby creating a cross draught. It was altogether delightful, the way Dennis had anything made that was needed. The cottage, now his own, had everything necessary in architecture and furnishings to make life thoroughly comfortable. Keppler had put in the window, and he had been friendly all during the day he worked on it. Dennis had said yesterday that when Mani began to walk he would build a fence round the house, and a gate. How far from the house? Fehge's eyes narrowed as she tried to gauge a suitable distance.

The sun set; the light turned blue, and the hills began to recede. It was time to prepare supper. Fehge rose and was about to turn when a figure stepped out of the woods, a woman in a dirndl, who carried a stick and wore a large knapsack on her back. She stood for a moment at the edge of the clearing, then advanced toward the house. Ute rose and growled, and Fehge held on to the dog's collar. But the dog was the first to recognize Melita. "Good evening, Fehge," she said.

Fehge ran forward, delight in her face. "Fräulein Lehrerin! So it wasn't true! You are not in prison!"

"No," Melita said, but she couldn't smile in response. "I am not in prison any more."

They clasped hands, and Melita bent to pat the dog. She could not seem to take her eyes off Fehge's face. Worry had given it a sensitiveness it had before worn only rarely.

"How happy you look!" Melita said, and couldn't free herself of the thought that had struck her as she had come upon Fehge sitting in front of the house, so much in possession: How content she looks. Like a young wife.

Dennis heard them and came to the door, and Melita's face lit up as though a sudden happy thought had filled her mind to the exclusion of everything else.

"Dennis!" she said, "dear Dennis! I have come to say good-bye."

The three stood together for a short while, talking softly, like conspirators.

"Someone helped me to escape," Melita told them, "not from prison . . . that would have been impossible. I was in a prison camp, so near you all," and her eyes wandered across the hills in the direction of Waldeck. "May I rest with you until nightfall? I dare not go on until it is quite dark."

They took her in. "Let us have supper now," said Dennis.

"You have not yet eaten?"

"Dennis doesn't like to eat supper until it is dark," said Fehge, and again Melita thought: She caters to his habits like a wife. But Fehge hesitated.

"What is it, Fehge?" asked Dennis.

"I want to show Mani to the Fräulein Lehrerin."

Dennis laughed and said, "Fehge is the proudest mother in the world."

He took Melita's knapsack from her, and she followed Fehge upstairs. Mani turned a sleepy head toward their softly approaching steps. His lids were sensuously laden with sleep. He smiled at Fehge and grasped her outstretched forefinger firmly. Then his eyes closed, and he fell asleep. His lips parted and he breathed through his mouth. Fehge leaned forward and straightened his little head, which was thrown slightly back, and his lips fell shut. His breathing could no longer be heard.

Melita watched Fehge. She thought how complete the picture was now.

They went downstairs again, Melita mechanically pouring out admiring phrases about the wonderful baby. Fehge hurried into the kitchen, and Melita walked slowly into the wood-panelled room that was living- and dining-room. Dennis was setting the table. Melita watched him silently for a few minutes. Then her eyes widened.

"Only two places?" she asked.

Dennis smiled. "Fehge won't eat with us."

He looked up at her, the silver poised in his big, manly hands, the fine old silver that had been his mother's dowry, that never tarnished here from one year's end to the other, and he went on, "I think that you once tried to improve Fehge's position by suggesting that she take a secretarial course in Waldeck. You didn't have much success with that idea, did you?"

Melita shook her head and felt absurd relief flood her heart. One's heart would not respond to reason, not even when one was as good as dead.

"When I saw her first this evening," she said, "I thought she had become your wife."

Dennis took up his little task again, and he chuckled as he set knife and fork and spoon as they should be, English fashion, the spoon atop the plate. "I can't even get her to take her meals with me," he said, and the answer made Melita grieve all over again. It was not a satisfactory denial.

Fehge waited on them. Melita ate stolidly, not with appetite, but because she knew that she would need all the strength the food could give her. Her eyes were those of a woman who has forgotten everything.

"Who teaches the children now?" she asked.

From a hill-top she had looked down at schoolhouse and garden in full bloom. Through the quiet air had been wafted up to her the tinkling sound of the brook where they built the dam together. For her the moment had been as bitter as gall.

Dennis was saying, "A young Catholic who, I think, missed the priesthood. The children frighten him, and he often comes up here to ask Fehge to help him." His amused glance rested on the girl. "Some day that young man is going to propose to Fehge."

Fehge flushed. Melita said, "I wonder if Fehge considers marriage something to get deep down into," and the girl laughed.

"How the Fräulein Lehrerin remembers . . . and understands," she said. "Now I will go and make sandwiches for you to take with you." And she left them alone.

The light of day was gone. Dennis turned on a lamp which flooded the table with light.

"I can't seem to grasp what has happened to you," he said. "It is so obviously unjust. And there is nothing a decent person can do about it."

"You had better get used to it," she said. "Justice is fast disappearing from our part of the world, and we didn't have to wait for the Nazis to come to us for that, did we?"

He said nothing. Melita went on, "What a long way we have travelled since that day when I explained the different factions in Austria to you in the form of a German lesson."

Dennis said, "Yes, and I have nothing fundamentally new to add to what I said then—that the most important thing is to learn to develop our own personal independence. Not to need another person; not to need anything material beyond what is necessary to keep body and soul alive. You ask to what end? I'll tell you. To *your* end. For the welfare of our fellow-men."

"Yes," said Melita. "You said something like that then, but I don't think you elaborated on it quite so much. And at that time you had no conclusion. The end you have just described you have learnt from Fehge." Suddenly her voice became vehement. "And what have I done except what you have just described? Lived for my fellow-men?"

He shook his head. "Not in the way I mean. Passively. Just by setting an example."

"Like Fehge?"

"Like Fehge."

She thought: If you could have loved me, I could have let my fellow-men alone, I could have been a good example. But you didn't take me. How could I concentrate on my lonely self, from whom I have constantly been trying to escape?

The one relieving tear of deep sadness rolled down her cheek, and the lump in her throat became bearable again. But the light of the lamp was not on their faces, so that he could not see that she was crying. Had he been able to read her thoughts, he might have come to the conclusion that all the trouble in the world was made by unhappy people.

The simple meal was quickly over, and by then it was dark outside. Fehge said, "I have put the sandwiches in the Fräulein Lehrerin's knapsack," and looked troubled. "I wish there were something more I could do."

"Thank you," said Melita. Dennis rose as she got up to go.

The two women shook hands and said good-bye without any pathos, as though they would meet again, and Fehge took the dishes away into the kitchen.

Dennis walked with Melita down to the edge of the road, where she shouldered her knapsack which he had been carrying for her by its leather straps. "Where will you go from here?" he asked her, and the question seemed to make the world very large.

She said, "I shall go as Fehge's parents would have done if they had lived," she pointed, "across these hills into Hungary; and from there we shall see. The face of the world is changing. You can tell that by its outcasts. You see, I have no passport, which makes me practically non-existent."

She gave him her hand, but he put his arm round her like a brother embracing his sister, hugging her close, and looked down at her face so near his. "Aren't you frightened?"

"No," she said, "not any more. I really don't feel anything any more. I am just going on the way I've learnt to go because I can't seem to think of anything else. I am sure I have become a very good soldier. Do you understand?"

"I think so."

"We are living in such a horrible world," she said, and he could feel a shudder course through her body.

Then he let her go, and she was soon lost in the dark.

Chapter Thirty-Two

ANDREA'S illness and Fehge's role in it played perhaps the most important part in creating among the peasantry the illusion that Fehge was possessed of supernatural powers. That she was a witch, that she could heal by the placing of her hands on the sick, had been bandied around, scoffed at and believed. But the part she played in Andrea's illness was not so easily put aside. First of all, the rumour came from Vienna. That made it very credible. And then, the people who were mixed up in it! Not peasants and country folk, but the most famous doctors in Vienna. This time Fehge's powers were not to be lightly scoffed at. Greater brains than those in Fichtenbach and Pritnitz had extolled them. All of this was true in a sense; but the playful irony that had accompanied the praise of the Vienna doctors had got lost on its way to the village, as so many things do when they start to travel by newspaper or word of mouth. But Hilda said that Fehge had prophesied the disaster years ago. She had heard her with her own ears! It came about like this:

On one early spring day after lunch in the year 1937, Andrea went down to Dennis's cottage to spend the rest hour with Fehge and the child, which she did whenever she could because they were the only creatures in the world whom she loved and liked to call her own. On this particular day her step, usually so light, lagged; and Fehge noticed at once, as she entered the house, that the nurse was not herself. Her lids drooped; she moved sluggishly. She felt sick and feverish, she said, and had taken her temperature—a sign that she was feeling very ill—and the thermometer showed 100°. Not much, but enough to make her feel the way she did.

She stretched out full length on the couch, her starched uniform lying in smooth folds, her cap spreading as she lay on it, regardless of creases. She put her hand to her forehead and said it was hot in the room, which really was pleasantly cool. She had not even looked round to see if the house was tidy, but had collapsed on the couch and closed her eyes. Fehge knew that Andrea must be ill. She had never seen her give way like this before.

How often had Andrea come to her, to her room at Strubl, then to the house she kept here, to scold that it was not tidy, that it was not clean, when it was both according to average standards! Today she had come not to scold but to rest.

Fehge immediately felt her heart warm toward Andrea. If the nurse would only give one the chance, one could be fond of her. But she had never given Fehge the chance. Ever since she could remember, Andrea had driven her, and Fehge had suffered and learnt. Now, with Andrea prostrate on the couch, a memory came back to her of a day long ago when she had still been under the deaconess's jurisdiction, when so many vexing things had accumulated, that, in the evening, when Andrea had found fault again, Fehge had burst out crying. Shaking with sobs, making no attempt to hide the tears that rained down her face, Fehge had lifted a warning little finger and pointed it at the irate nurse whose cheeks were blazing with temper. "You'll see," she had cried, like a Cassandra. "You'll see! Some day, something terrible will happen to you!"

Why did she think of it now when such scenes had long since passed away, when she had stepped out of the domineering woman's sway into a richer and fuller life than she had ever dared to hope for? But she did recall it. And Hilda, who had walked in on her vehement words, had echoed them. "The child is right, Sister Andrea. You'll get what's coming to you before you die."

Now Andrea seemed totally lacking in aggression, and Fehge felt sorry for her. "You should go to bed," she said gently.

Andrea opened her eyes and glared at her. "How can I take time off to lie in bed, with all I have to do?"

Fehge said nothing. Andrea fell asleep. This was the most astounding thing of all, to see Andrea asleep in the daytime. Fehge woke her when she knew it was time for her to go back to Strubl.

At first Andrea did not seem to know her. Her cheeks were flushed, and she had to collect her senses as though they had been scattered very far. "Yes, yes," she mumbled, and there was something very pathetic in the way she groped for her lost austerity. But a few minutes later she was her old, brisk self again—by sheer will power, because the fever did not leave her. It remained low and steady, and several days later Andrea could not move her neck. It had become rigid, and she was suffering from acute pains in her head. She could not get up and dress and do the rounds. Sapponyi, when told, did not believe it at first. Andrea could not come down? Andrea could not accompany him on his rounds? Why, then, she must be very ill!

It took only one glance for him to see that this was so. He called for his car and decided to take her to Vienna himself, and when he saw her step out of the lift, so aged by the paralysis that had fastened its hold upon her, supported by Fehge on the one side and one of the maids on the other, he thought: We shall not have her with us again. It can be only one thing.

Fehge drove to Vienna with them. Andrea had requested it.

Fully clad in cape and cap, she sat up straight all the way to the city, her face purple with the effort, the pain in her head almost driving her mad. But she never for a moment lost control of herself. She was polite to the chauffeur, to the doctor, and to Fehge—polite as she had never been in her life before. Fehge thought of it all the way to Vienna, how polite Andrea was in her stricken condition.

Sapponyi had telephoned to the Oberin, and she had told him to which hospital she wanted Nurse Andrea confined. The doctor there stretched Andrea out on a table and took off her cap, and she helped him with the intricate little button which had pestered her all her grown-up life. Well, it wouldn't annoy her any more.

For the first time Fehge saw Andrea without her cap. Even when she had come to see to the child in the night, sometimes, when Fehge had still been small, she had had on her cap, bulging at the back because she had not stopped to button it in her haste. Fehge admired her black hair, braided and coiled to form a thick, round nest at the top of her head where it supported the cap. She must look lovely with it down, thought Fehge. But it was scraped off her ears and pulled at her skin the way Fehge's hair had pulled in the days when Andrea had braided it.

The new doctor seemed to confirm what Sapponyi had feared and what Andrea now expressed in a loud, clear, slightly strained voice. "*Gell? Herr Doktor,*" she said, using the Silesian dialect of her childhood. "It is so, isn't it, *Herr Doktor*? Meningitis."

The doctor smiled down at her and stroked her hand. "You nurses know too much," he said.

With a smile that trembled, Andrea closed her eyes. Now she was ready to succumb. She had arrived at her destination like a lady, seated, not vomiting once as she had felt like doing; she had been polite to Fritz the chauffeur, to Sapponyi who had been very kind and always done the right thing by her—he was a gentleman, not like these new people . . . upstarts . . . small fry . . . she knew only vaguely whom she meant . . . she had said the right thing to Fehge. . . .

She opened her eyes. The pain would soon kill her. "Fehge," she said, "take my watch."

Fehge unhooked it from its brooch. "Keep it," Andrea said. It was hers to give. It was a fine old watch and had belonged to her mother. Then, "Thank you for everything," she said, quite clearly, and fainted.

Meningitis. Fehge did not know what it meant. Sapponyi said to the doctor, "Will she regain consciousness?" The doctor said, "I doubt it." Then Sapponyi left with Fehge and thought as he went that he would have to come back to Vienna for the funeral —yes, of course, he would. After all, eighteen years of faithful service. . . . Poor Sister Andrea. Still, she would have no more suffering. For her the worst was over. And for him? Oh, *Du lieber Gott!* What there was still ahead of him if he lived much longer!

But Andrea did not die. She did not have meningitis either. The next time Fehge came to see her, which was a week later, she could read the long name of the illness on the chart—*encephalitis meningo myelitis*, and before a month had gone by, twenty-three Vienna doctors had examined Andrea and treated her. None of them had been able to make her well. This care was not given her because the Bethesda Organization could afford twenty-three doctors, among them some of the greatest medical men in Europe, but because Bethesda nurses were very popular—every good doctor in Vienna called upon them—and because Andrea herself was known and liked for her keenness and reliability. Finally, and this was perhaps the most important reason, they came because the course of her illness was so unorthodox. One doctor brought his colleague, and he brought his, and so on. They ran to her bedside like passionate hunters after a famous stag. Where would they ever get a chance again to observe such a violent illness for such a long time? For the patient should, by rights, have been dead long ago.

The germ ran riot in her body. First she was paralysed on the right side, then on the left, then her vision forsook her, then she saw double. One day her heart-beats were irregular, the next day it was her breathing. The disease did what it wanted to do with her; its will was capricious. By God, medicinally she was a find!

Meanwhile she suffered the tortures of the damned like a heroine. The pains in her head never ceased. She could take no nourishment. She lay with an ice-bag on her head, looking as yellow as a chicken, with a mad expression on her gaunt face, yet perfectly patient with it all, with so much humorous understanding of those who came to—as she put it—"try out something new."

"It's all for the cat," she would say. "You doctors don't know what you're doing. You can't fool me. I'm in the same business. I'm just a guinea-pig for you. But do you think I mind? Not a bit of it! You can't kill me. The old heart won't give in. You'll see."

Of course she didn't mean it. She was sure that she was going to die, and she did not mind her suffering. Fehge's childish outburst had come back to her too. She had never quite forgotten it. She knew that she had caused others to suffer and had often been uncharitable in thought if not in deed. Now, this was retribution, and she accepted it gladly. She felt sure of heaven. The Saviour was very near.

But six weeks later, even Andrea began to believe that she would not die, for she lapsed into a state of chronic invalidism. She could not sit up. She could lift herself about six inches from the pillow when she pulled herself up by a stick that hung suspended horizontally from the ceiling like the swing she had swung on as a child when she had been a great tomboy. She could eat now and keep her food down. The pain in her head was dull and bearable. Only her back remained useless. Was this how she was going to end her days? That, dear God, would be a bitter pill indeed to swallow.

Andrea asked constantly for Fehge, who knew that she must arrange her life so that she would be free to go and see Andrea frequently. She took Julie into the house. She had taught the idiot girl to speak; now she showed her how to do the simple jobs about the house. In no time a little room had been added to the cottage for Julie.

Dennis was by now as accustomed to the girl, the first sight of whom had caused him to shudder, as were the peasants. Besides, there was no denying that Fehge with her infinite patience had done wonders by Julie. He would listen to them talking in the kitchen, to Fehge's bright chatter and Julie's sluggish tongue responding. He didn't know that outside the house, among strangers, the idiot girl still could not utter a word.

Fehge would leave Julie in charge, the food for the day prepared and standing cool in the cellar. There was nothing to do which was beyond the simple girl's capacity to carry out. Fehge would tie her big straw hat under her chin with a ribbon, fasten a shawl over her shoulders with a fine old Carinthian brooch which had been Stefanie's, and with a final wave of her hand be off. Without being conscious of it, Fehge dressed picturesquely. Round her throat, fitting tightly, she wore a piece of rare peasant jewellery, given her by Trattner because she was such a good girl. Tiny gold chains met in a big clasp at the front of her throat. The clasp had been moulded from an old Maria Theresa *Taler* and showed a robust baroque Virgin crowned like a queen with a chubby Christ-child seated on her ample lap. The jagged rays of a large sun shone behind them both. This piece of jewellery, of a type usually worn by older women, gave Fehge a quaint Old-World look and enhanced the aristocracy of her appearance. She looked like the daughter of a rich farmer, Dennis thought as he watched her go. At the bend in the road she turned to wave again. He lifted Mani to wave back, but the child was watching a bullfinch fly, and Dennis waved his pudgy little arm for him, the hand flopping. Julie, standing behind Dennis, waved too. Dennis turned to see a brief light of intelligence in her eyes. Truly, he thought, Fehge brings out the best in all of us!

Fehge would stay with Andrea all the day. Andrea's mind was unfortunately clear. She asked about the nurse who was taking her place, about those who had gone home, to heaven or to their families, about new arrivals, of which there were very few now; and from Fehge's telling she could sense the pall that hung over Strubl, a dying institution, like Austria, like herself. She said, "*Na, Kleines*, what will you say if I have to spend the rest of my life on my back like this?" and she laughed bitterly.

Fehge shook her head. "The Saviour won't let it happen," she said.

Before she went away she held devotional exercises as Andrea had taught her to do. "Come again," Andrea would say. "Come again."

Fehge did, regularly as the clock, every week, until one day the telephone message came to Strubl that Andrea was dying and wanted to see Fehge. Sapponyi sent her in his car.

Tilde, the nurse attending Andrea, had not had a night's sleep for over a week. She was a Swabian, with white hair like an Albino's, white eyebrows, and slightly pink-rimmed blue eyes, but pretty despite her lack of colour. So devoted was she to the headstrong Andrea that she refused to be relieved. Night and day she had watched this fluctuating illness, and now a great weariness overwhelmed her, for she had failed in her fight against death.

The disease had started its mad course through Andrea's body again and had at last found its way to the region of her heart and lungs. Her pulse was quick, then slow, her breathing like that of a person immediately confronted with death. It came in deep, shattering scoops and left in a short gasp, and it came less and less frequently.

"There's Fehge," she could still gasp as the girl came in, and she stretched out her arms. Fehge grasped her hands.

Then Andrea asked after everybody, just to show that she was clear-headed. As long as she was conscious, they were not going to whisper in front of her as she had so often whispered in front of the dying. She would have none of that!

"How long have you been like this?" asked Fehge.

"Since last night," said Andrea. "But I won't be like this much longer, eh, *Herr Doktor*?" and she said the last words in a loud voice.

The young house doctor who had received her was sitting at the foot of the bed. Now he shook himself out of a doze. He had been at her bedside all night, expecting that she would die in the morning, which she had not done. It was his free day, but he would not leave her to die with the assistant doctor. She had put up too good a fight.

The specialist from Pötzl had come in the morning as usual; he, too, had been surprised to find Andrea still alive. He had shaken his head. "*Gell*, Doctor?" Andrea had said, "you're surprised to find me still alive. It's the old heart that won't let me die. And I'm spoiling this young man's free day just by staying alive. I wish I could do him the favour of dying before noon, but I can't. I'd like some beer. I'm thirsty."

"Give it to her," said the specialist. "Give her anything she likes. There's nothing we can spoil here."

They gave her beer. "My, that tastes good," she said, and gave it right back again. Since early morning she had been vomiting almost incessantly.

Fehge said, "I won't let you go."

That made Andrea laugh. It came from her like a gasp. "*Bist ja grössenwahnsinnig,*" she said, and meant that Fehge was a megalomaniac.

Sister Tilde began to feel unsteady on her feet. "How much longer can this go on?" she said to the doctor.

He looked up wearily. "I give her till seven this evening. Not a minute longer. I have never seen anyone suffer so."

Tilde swayed. "That a human being can stand so much!"

Without looking up again, the doctor said in a dull voice, "Every illness exhausts itself in time. If the body can hold out."

Fehge whispered, "You think she may recover?"

The doctor shook his head. "The body usually gives in before the disease, as this body will."

Fehge tapped Tilde on the shoulder. "Why don't you get some sleep?" she said. "I'll watch her."

As though she had never refused similar offers, the pale young nurse tottered over to the couch and fell on it. She went to sleep at once and slept and slept, not waking even when the most frightful thing happened. Andrea began to hiccough. The hiccoughs threw her several inches high into the air, and she fell down on to the bed again and ceased to breathe. The doctor said, "Singultus!" and then, to Fehge, "Can you give an injection? Intravenous?"

She nodded. He on one side of the bed, she on the other, they gave Andrea two injections a. the same time. Then they stood above the motionless woman and waited. The doctor shook his head. Dead.

But she was not dead. She breathed again, easier now than before. She seemed to be asleep.

The doctor looked up at Fehge. "Where did you learn to give an intravenous injection?" he asked.

She nodded her head at the now evenly breathing Andrea. "She taught me," she said. "She taught me everything I know how to do."

The young house doctor went to bed in his room. Fehge said she would call him if there was any change. Tilde slept on and on.

Fehge sat down at Andrea's bedside and dozed. In the middle of the night Andrea woke up, and her body was very quiet, her breathing and pulse weak but steady. Nothing racked her body any more. In this state she could forget it, and her mind became very lucid. It was good of God to grant her a few such peaceful hours before she died! She could hear Tilde's even breathing and could see, by Fehge's attitude, that she too was asleep.

Her mind travelled out of the sick-room, away from Vienna, from Austria, where she had always been homesick, home to the little town of Hirschberg in Silesia where she had been born, and to the Giant Mountains, which surrounded it on three sides. Whenever anyone scoffed at the Riesengebirge because the mountain chain was low and flatly undulating, not jaggedly peaked like the high Swiss Alps and Italian Dolomites, she had always answered wisely that that was because they were so very old. Only young mountains had spikes. And did the Alps or Dolomites have a Rübezahl? Such a beloved old man of the hills. Even now she could remember the way the wind blew on the *Kamm*, the long, flat summit line. On the German side of the mountains were the tidy huts where one spent the nights on hikes or ski-ing tours; on the Czech side, the huts were sloppy and none too clean. The decency on the German side, the promiscuousness on the Czech side—she had found the same thing here, in the Vienna woods. But it had been a German man who had tumbled her when she was sixteen and changed her whole life. She mustn't think of it.

She had been dressed like a baker's boy, in white trousers, white shirt, white apron, and funny high white cap. She had borrowed the outfit from a real baker's boy for a fancy-dress party. Her father and mother had been there too. And she had cut funny capers in her tight-fitting little suit, and everybody had laughed. "*Ach, Du lieber Augustin*," they had sung, and one of the grown-up guests, a thick-set little post-office clerk, had said he'd take her home when it got late. Her mother and father had wanted to stay on a while with the grown-up folks and had been grateful for the young man's offer. And of course they had never known what had happened on the way home. One didn't talk about things like that to anyone, not about that, not about the terrible pains one had when one was menstruating . . . all these things were unmentionable. And he had been a German, this squat little clerk with the bullet head, a native of Hildesheim. He had told her about the famous old houses in that town, like dolls' houses, so quaint, so pretty, so excellently preserved that people came from all over the world to sightsee there. "Ah, our Germany," he had breathed heavily, "our beautiful Germany! And have you ever travelled up the Rhine, Fräulein?" he had asked. She was fifteen, and he was the first person to say "*Sie*" to her, "you," instead of the child's "thou," and to address her as Fräulein. "*Ein Rheinisches Mädchen beim Rheinischen Win*," he had sung in a pleasant baritone, and she had been not a little embarrassed to hear him sing on the street. She had been very sedately brought up. Then they'd taken the short cut through the park. When she had reached home the little white baker's suit was soiled with dirt from her struggle, and she could remember the nervous haste with which she had washed it and ironed it wet so that there should be no trace left of what had happened when her parents came home. How the iron had *tsished* and the steam risen from the wet linen! It was a sound and smell that had made her nauseous ever since. That was why she could never, never work in the laundry. Now that fear was gone too. She was going to die.

Fehge stirred and opened her eyes, astonished to find Andrea awake. She sensed the peaceful atmosphere of the room that, a few hours ago, had been so tortured.

Andrea said softly, "Now it won't be difficult any more."

The lack of struggle in the sick-room woke Tilde. Andrea smiled at her. "Fehge is looking after me," she said. "You can go on sleeping."

Tilde rubbed the sleep out of her eyes. "*Ach*," she sighed, "that was good." And tears of relief were on her lashes. She looked at Andrea. And then, after her first wonderment was over at finding her patient so much relieved, Tilde began to tell in whispers about a miraculous Dr. Sesenheimer. Her tone was conspiratorial. It seemed he was a homeopath, who had worked miracles. He had cured people whom the greatest specialists had given up as lost.

A homeopath! Andrea's lips curled. She had all the contempt of the medical man for these quacks.

But Tilde went on talking about him, and Fehge drank in her words, wide-eyed. Fehge, whatever Andrea might think, was as gullible as any peasant when it came to miracles.

In the morning, with Andrea still alive, and everyone more baffled than ever, Fehge cornered the specialist from Pötzl as he was about to leave and said, in a rush, because she was shy before him, "Please, may I go and get Dr. Sesenheimer?"

The specialist frowned down at her and drew in his chin. He was in a foul temper, so he only turned half an ear to Fehge. "Who? What?" She was probably some relative. "Bring anyone you like," he told her.

Fehge tied her shawl round her head and ran out of the hospital. Tilde had given her the address, and now she did what she had never done in her life before—she took a taxi.

It was not far, and she asked the driver to wait. She told the doctor's secretary that it was a matter of life and death, and the homeopath received her in a little private waiting-room where exotic fishes swam in illuminated glass tanks.

The man who stood before her was short and stockily built. He moved quickly and quietly like a projectile. His large brown eyes had a definitely hypnotic quality.

"I have heard of the case," he said, when she had done.

"Do you think you can save her?"

He shrugged his shoulders. "It is probably too late. They have sent for me when they thought no more harm could be done, haven't they?" and there was the trace of a smile on his lips. But he went with her at once.

The Oberin was angry that she had not been consulted. She had to pay the bills and answer for them to the Board. What would *they* say to the homeopath? She knew that many of her nurses went to him on the sly, and she had been curious to see the miracle man for herself. Now she could, without any responsibility on her part. She scolded Fehge, thereby clearing herself of all blame, and hurried into the sick-room.

When Tilde saw Sesenheimer, she rushed to him and kissed his hand. This extraordinary behaviour on the part of a sober deaconess could only be explained by her high-strung condition, due to exhaustion. But the Oberin could not consider that as an excuse when she was so sorely tried. This prolonged agony was wearing her out too. It was inconsiderate of Andrea to take such a long time to die. The Oberin gave Tilde a scolding and sent her out of the room.

Sesenheimer turned to Fehge. "Can you help me?"

She nodded her head. Sesenheimer was glad. He had taken a liking to the girl at first sight.

The young house doctor came in and greeted Sesenheimer breezily. He, like the Oberin, was glad to have this opportunity to see the man in action.

He explained the case briefly to Sesenheimer and told him what they had planned to do that day. "Embrocation . . . silver . . ." Fehge heard him say.

Sesenheimer shook his head. "I'm afraid it's too late for that," he said. "I would like to give it to her with injections." And with that the young doctor knew that Sesenheimer was no quack.

"Go right ahead," he said.

"Shouldn't I get in touch with her doctor?"

"I don't think you need do that," replied the young man. "He knew you were coming. He said you should go right ahead."

Sesenheimer gave Andrea two injections, the silver intravenously and another injection of elixir of hawthorn between the shoulder-blades. This, thought the young house doctor, is where the voodoo begins! He also prescribed some powders.

Andrea didn't wake up until five hours later, and when she did, the pains in her head were gone.

Fehge was sitting at her bedside, reading the little Catholic news-paper, *Rosegarden*, which so many of Austria's servant girls read. The late afternoon sunlight streamed into the room. It was feeling its way up the couch on which Tilde lay, asleep again.

Andrea lifted her head and it didn't hurt. She tried to lift it a bit farther. She could. Then it came to her that, once she had the strength, she would be able to sit up. She wiggled her toes. She could even move her legs freely. It was a great effort to move them, but she knew that the disease had left her body.

She put out her hand and touched Fehge. Fehge looked at Andrea, whose eyes were now free of pain. "He did it, didn't he?" she said.

Andrea nodded her head, but her words were not a clear affirm-ative. "You did it," she said, and smiled, and the tears rained down her cheeks. She was so weak.

Later Tilde confirmed her words. Fehge had done it.

Sesenheimer came and confirmed their belief. He took Fehge's arm and said jocosely, "This little girl did it." And the two women took his word for it solemnly.

There were many doctors, including Sapponyi, who, after hear-ing the case described in detail, said that it had been a coincidence. Andrea had undeniably stopped vomiting before the miracle man had been called in. When asked if the pains in her head had also ceased at that time, she said she couldn't remember. She didn't think so.

Be that as it may, Sesenheimer was now accepted by everyone.

The Oberin became his patient, and so did half of Vienna. People came to him from all parts of Europe, and he often repeated his jocose words, "Fehge did it."

The peasantry in and around Fichtenbach, when the story finally reached them, received a mystic version of it. The reports went that Andrea had been dead at least twice and brought back to life again. The homeopath remained a nebulous figure; they never got to see him. But they knew Fehge; she became the central figure of this miracle. They put aside everything they had ever known about the girl except what it now pleased them to accept —that she had supernatural powers. This began to take shape in their minds very clearly when Andrea's miraculous recovery became a fact they could see with their own eyes. For, a week after the homeopath's first visit, Andrea was sitting up in bed; three weeks later she was able to get up and walk; three months later she was back at Strubl.

Chapter Thirty-Three

IN the month of February, with the winter of 1937-1938 drawing to a close, the peasantry of Lower Austria was disturbed by a display of the Northern Lights. It came one evening at about seven o'clock. In a pitch-black sky, fingers of cerise light pointed from the horizon outward like the rays of a midnight sun. This light deepened into purple, then paled from cerise to blue, and it remained in the sky for several hours.

Toni, the dull-witted second-floor maid, was sure that the Communists had set fire to Vienna. That was what the light was. The other servants remained at the windows too, unwilling to go outside for fear the light might strike them down. Never had the Northern Lights been seen in that vicinity before, as far as anybody could remember.

Sapponyi and Thérèse put on their coats and walked out into the park. Word spread from mouth to mouth that the Northern Lights could be seen. The bedridden sat up to see through their windows, and those who could, walked out on to their balconies. One by one the lights in the rooms were put out, and Strubl lay in darkness. The light in the sky reigned supreme.

For weeks after, the peasantry continued to talk about the Northern Lights and wondered what it could portend. They were all agreed that it was a bad omen.

Sapponyi and his patients soon forgot it. They had other things to worry about. Another light was gleaming on their horizon, a political light, and its red glare lit up their sky as garishly as any Northern Lights.

Schuschnigg went to Berchtesgaden. When this happened, Dennis was not in the valley. He went away, once or twice a year, to France, to England, to Spain, to Italy—wherever it pleased him to go. He always left ample funds at Strubl to take care of his house and its inmates, and the impersonal forwarding address of some bank in the capital city of the country he was visiting. He did not correspond with anybody while he was away except for colourful picture-postcards sent to Mani and Fehge from the most out-of-the-way places. He never stayed away very long.

Sapponyi heard the news of the Chancellor's visit to the Führer before the rest of his countrymen were informed of it on the radio, through Trattner, who came on one of his occasional visits to see his grandson ; not that he was especially interested in the child, but he found that he could relax, unmolested, better at the cottage of the "mad young Englishman" than anywhere else. However old he grew, Dennis would never lose that title. The fact that Fehge had never asked for Trattner's autograph was almost a delicious relief, and she and Mani were a treat to tell stories to. Trattner's visits usually ended up with a stroll in the park with Sapponyi, and it was on one of these customary walks that Trattner said, "Just think ! As I was leaving Olga called me up and told me that Schuschnigg has gone to Berchtesgaden." He spoke the words lightly, since he could not feel their weight.

Then Sapponyi knew it was coming. That evening he said to his wife, "Let us go to Vienna tomorrow. I would like to take a house there for you. You would enjoy fixing it up, wouldn't you, my dear?"

She raised her eyebrows in amazement. "Why?"

He sighed. He wished he did not have to discuss it with her. Somehow he felt that she was not going to be with him in this, that she was going to hurt him, that from now on there would be nothing but pain.

He said, "I don't want to alarm you, but you may need the house one of these days. Things may turn out so that we may have to give up Strubl."

Thérèse was silent for a moment, then she said in a firm voice, "I can guess what is on your mind, Manfred, but I want to tell you"—she paused, not with emotion, but in order to weigh her words carefully—"should anything happen to you, I won't need a house in Vienna."

He knew exactly how she meant it. He had no illusions that what she said might mean that she was going to share death with him as she had shared his life. He knew she meant that she would enter a convent when the blow fell, as though freed. He could feel the pain that he had been anticipating. Suddenly he craved warmth. But it was much too late to build any fires.

It was too late in many other respects.

Chancellor Schuschnigg, heir of Dollfuss to the tight-rope of Austrian government, came back from his interview with the ridiculous little man who, it seemed, to the chagrin of many, was going to make history after all, and made his fiery speech of defiance in the Führer's face. He said, "They didn't leave us much . . . this Austria . . . but what they left us, that we're going to keep!"

It was a great speech, but it came too late. Then the Chancellor made his peace with the Social Democrats. Too late again! He began to gain a clear majority in the little country that could at last see the whites of their enemies' eyes. He began to loosen the reins of dictatorship, indeed he even promised elections, but it was much too late.

One by one Strubl's patients began to leave the valley. Those who were domiciled in Austria fled to their homes to be in familiar surroundings for the kill. Those from farther south or east went home to wait for it to come to them.

Fehge, who was often called upon during these days to help some such departing patient to pack, knew, too, that it was coming. Her little world was heaving as though an earthquake had struck it.

For the first time in her life, Fehge found herself in a condition that could be called sickly. Ever since that twenty-fourth of February, when the Chancellor had spoken—a speech she had heard, for they had all been assembled in the kitchen—she had not been able to eat or sleep. It had been like a fanfare for battle. She could tell that by the sudden gleam in eyes that had never sparkled before. It takes two to make a fight, she realized, and now there were two sides, definitely but much too late. They hadn't a chance, she knew that now. They were not filled with accumulated passion like the others. She could have wrung her hands with the futility of this tardily inspired war.

Yes, the sands were running exceeding low. God was certainly keeping her on tenterhooks. But He would strike, He would undoubtedly strike in time. For His people could not save themselves alone. If only she could have had certainty! But that nothing on earth could give her.

In the last fortnight she had lost over ten pounds in weight. Her eyes were big and woeful in her peaked face, and when she laughed, which she still often did—for she was anxious that no one should find out that she was so doubtful of God's timely deliverance—her beautiful white teeth were disproportionately large.

Sapponyi, who saw her only superficially these days, knew nothing of her condition, and it would never have occurred to her, nor to any of the peasantry to advise her, to see the doctor, not when she had no pain, not when she could still work. One went to the doctor only when one was ready to drop. Fehge had not reached that point yet. She had great reserves in her strong body which she drew on as worry tightened her throat so that she could not swallow.

Andrea, who saw the girl every day, and on whom her wasting condition was not lost, had diagnosed Fehge's condition as hysteria and treated her with doses of sharp anger. But so far she had not been able to get the girl's stomach to hold down her food. It never occurred to her to ask Fehge if she had anything on her mind. What could this simple girl, who had always been content with her daily life, which had not changed and which was not likely to—for Andrea could sense nothing coming—have on her mind?

Third-floor Hilda knew that it was coming too, but she was ready for it. Otto von Hapsburg no longer stood on her dresser. Instead, she had put there the picture of a man who also wore a little moustache, but whose face revealed, instead of Otto's pretty features, a low forehead, a formless nose, unhealthy sunken cheeks, and a thin, hard mouth. She had put the picture on her dresser in spite of the fact that, with her natural sense of beauty, she found this man, Hitler, who looked like a provincial waiter, hard to stomach as an idol. She also wore a swastika brooch on the inside of her dress lapel, ready for the day when she could wear it on the outside.

Heinrich Grabautschnik had asked her to marry him, and she had accepted him. He had promised her a position in the new world that was being formed, that of *Frau Gauleiter*, as big, he assured her, as that of the *Frau Baronin* had always been in Austria. That was what had struck home. As long as he didn't ask her to renounce the air she loved to breathe, the countryside she loved to see, the food she was accustomed to eating, and the people she was used to . . .

And Conrad knew that it was coming. He was in a position to meet it. He had money. That was all that mattered, for he had always been on the right side of the fence. There was only one cloud on his horizon—the child.

He was thinking of the child now, as he sat in the little morning-room of Fricka's house in Vienna, twiddling his cap, waiting for her to "receive" him, as she "received" everybody, even her own daughter, whose continued lack of respect in the face of the obvious position Fricka had acquired in the brave new world about to be born, riled her every time she had to see the girl.

Fricka had kept the house just as it always had been, not because she liked its memories that pricked her like thorns, but because she knew how it impressed people. And it was very important that she should impress people. She was organizing the Nazi Women's Organization in Austria and the movement for young girls, the B.D.M.—*Bund Deutscher Mädchen*. She was ready now. She was set to go. And the signal would come very soon.

She always kept Conrad waiting, as she kept everyone waiting, even when she was ready. Finally Conrad was ushered into the room that had been Maurice's library. It was still lined on its free wall-space by costly books. Its floor was covered by a thick Persian carpet with a rich design in reds and blues. In a corner a bright blue-tiled stove gave forth too much heat. The windows were wide open.

Fricka was taking leave of three well-dressed women. She stood like a ramrod behind Maurice's desk, nodding her head briskly at a final word one of the women was saying. The women did not shake hands in saying good-bye. Their right arms shot out in the Nazi salute, and they cried, almost in unison, "*Heil Hitler!*" Conrad would have liked to burst into laughter, but he controlled himself. Only the shiny little old, dark-red Chinese god on the desk didn't have to control himself. He held on to his fat belly and laughed and laughed.

The women had gone. Fricka said, "*Grüss dich*, Conrad. *Heil Hitler*."

He said, "*Heil Hitler*. How are you?" That was all a matter of form.

Then she said briskly, "Sit down and listen to me."

He sat. She stood and leaned forward over the desk, her two hands planted firmly on it. She said, "The child must go."

Conrad swallowed.

Fricka began to walk up and down, her feet making no sound on the carpet. Like a splendid cat, he thought.

"I saw Dr. Hauschnig yesterday," she went on. "The case is hopeless. The child will never be normal. It must go."

She paused. He said nothing. He had a lump in his throat from fear. It surprised him, but, he apologized to himself, this was different from any order he had received before. To do away with his own child . . .

His face showed his thoughts. Fricka said, "You have nothing to worry about. There is no reason why Anne-Marie and you shouldn't have healthy children yet. She was very young." And, he thought, there was that night I threw the loaf of bread at her, and it hit her in the stomach. He had to laugh, because he'd almost killed the child that night. What was he afraid of now when he was just being asked to finish the job?

But he was afraid. In the past years—in fact, ever since he had married—he had felt an urge for decency rising in him. It was the hopelessness of ever achieving that status in the way to which he had set his feet that had made him throw the loaf of bread at Anne-Marie. Conrad inexplicably felt trapped.

Fricka was saying, "It may interest you to know that I am working right now with a friend of ours on a law to make this sort of thing legal. There is no room in our glorious future for the insane."

Just then Conrad caught sight of a robin outside the window. It was building a nest. "Look," he said, and pointed.

Fricka saw the little red-feathered thing and smiled. "Yes," she said. "Spring is here."

The news that the German Army had entered Austria reached Strubl at two o'clock in the afternoon on March 11, 1938, a good three hours before the people of Austria were told of the resignation of their Government by their Chancellor, Schuschnigg. An Austrian general stationed at Salzburg, whose wife was a patient at Strubl, called her up and told her that the Germans at that very moment were pouring through the city's gates, that he had orders to offer no resistance. "I wanted to speak to you once more," he had stammered in a low voice, and hung up. Frantic efforts on her part to get the connection again had proved unavailing. Sapponyi was finally able to reach headquarters and ascertain that the General had actually shot himself upon hanging up the receiver. His wife now lay in a state of coma in her room.

The news spread like wildfire. Hilda could gather what had happened from the woman's delirious words before she became unconscious. Solicitously she asked if she could bring the Frau General anything? When the Frau General didn't answer, she straightened the covers, drew down the blinds, and tiptoed out of the room. Then, feeling delightfully heady, she ran downstairs to tell the rest of the staff, and on the way down she unbuttoned her hidden swastika brooch and fastened it on her apron where everybody could see it.

How brilliant was the sunshine under which the tragedy of Austria was being enacted. Never had there been such a dry spring! Day after day of cloudless blue followed a clear night sky carpeted with stars. The flowers were out weeks ahead of time, blooming profusely, but smaller because of the drought. The sun was hot at ten o'clock and brought the sweat out on your brow at noon. The purple pasque-flower was withering in its grey velvet chalice; last year, at this time, it had been just budding. Everything was ahead of schedule.

Sapponyi met the Baron in the park. The Baron was back at Strubl wrestling with a decision he had to make—whether to live a few years longer and die more or less on his feet, gay as he had lived until now, or whether to submit to a thoraco-plastic operation which would remove his good ribs to ease the pressure on his game lung and make more or less of a cripple of him for the rest of his life. That morning the Baron had told Sapponyi that he had decided against the operation. He had quoted the Chancellor in parody, "I haven't much lung left, but the little I have, I intend to keep!" and they had both laughed very heartily because they were both so worried.

Now the Baron grimaced as he saw Sapponyi walking toward him, expecting a reprimand because he was walking when he should be resting, between two and four. But as the doctor drew near and the Baron could see his face, he knew that an everyday reprimand was farthest from the man's mind. Sapponyi told him the news from Salzburg.

The big man's shoulders received the blow without sagging, but his head seemed to shrivel as his face grew grey, as his cheeks sank in and his eyes continued to glow in his dying face. He said nothing. What was there to say? Sapponyi spoke. "Let's have a walk," and the Baron turned and walked with him, away from the house, into the park, where everything grew wild, always tended carefully in its wildness, its luxuriant shrubbery guided to grow where it was best suited.

The Baron dug his cane into the earth and picked up scraps of gravel which he scattered on ahead. Once he started to speak, but his voice was thick. He cleared it and said, "This is, of course, a far worse day for Austria than 1918." Sapponyi's head was shaking a little, as it often did now, because he was old. "Assuredly," he said. "Assuredly."

"Well," said the Baron, a few minutes later, "now comes the German era."

"Ja. Ja," said Sapponyi, his head wobbling.

They reached a point from which you could see the Schneeberg, Lower Austria's highest mountain, with the snow still capping its peak. "Perfect weather," said Sapponyi. "Perfect weather." It seemed he had to say everything twice.

They stood for a while and looked at the view, then they moved on. "You and I," said the Baron, "belong to an era that died today."

Sapponyi's head nodded. He turned about-face when they reached an arbour, and they began to retrace their steps. He did this from force of habit. This was the place where, for over thirty years, he had turned back with Thérèse, every day between two and four, weather permitting. An era that had died today.

"Our fault, of course, is obvious," said the Baron. "We had nothing to offer our young people. The youth of a nation has no party discoloration. It is just young. Harness it, and your nation belongs to you. But if you fail to garner in the youth of a nation, they will fall prey to . . . to anything. Like this." Sapponyi's head nodded. "Besides," the Baron went on, "we had no leaders."

Sapponyi seemed to wake up. "Nonsense," he said. "We had no followers. He"—the Baron knew who was meant—"he has followers. He has"—he looked straight into the Baron's eyes, stopping to do so—"appeal. Does that astonish you? You only have to look at the people to understand it."

As they turned in at the drive, a car drove up. The Baron recognized his Steyr tourer. "My wife," he said, and hurried forward.

"Take it easy," said Sapponyi. "You've had a long walk."

The Baroness got out of the car. By the anxious expression on her face, both men could see that she knew. The Baron asked her, "How did you find out?"

"Rüdiger called me," she said. "Oh, Wolfgang, he is wild with joy!"

Her eyes were dry as she looked up at him, this plain woman with so much charm. The Baron's lips tightened. Sapponyi came up and kissed the hand of the Baroness. "Have you decided?" she asked, the sight of Sapponyi suddenly recalling to her mind why her husband was here and the great decision that had to be made.

Sapponyi let the Baron answer. "Yes," he said. "We have come to a decision. We are going to operate."

"Oh, thank God," said the Baroness, and her face lit up as though life had been returned to her. "I was so afraid . . ."

The Baron put an arm round her shoulder, and the three entered the house together. "I had almost decided to have a last fling," he said, "and make merry till I died. But then I decided not to. I'd like to have a little more time, time to get hold of Rüdiger, for instance, and beat the stuffing out of him."

The Baroness stopped, turned him about to face her, and put both her hands on the flat of his shoulders where his sick lungs breathed. "I'm so glad you decided to do the right thing, Wolfgang," she said. "But don't think you can beat this thing out of

Rüdiger. It's not as simple as all that. You see, we have nothing to offer him instead."

Sapponyi tiptoed away and left them alone.

Andrea was in the office—not that she had anything to do there. She was fiddling with an already perfectly tidy desk because she wanted to be reassured by Sapponyi that the unorthodox things she had heard were not happening. He came in, and she said at once, "It isn't true, is it, Herr Medizinalrat? All this nonsense about the Germans marching into Austria?"

She had been saying to herself that it couldn't be true because it wasn't right. Moreover, it couldn't be true, because these Catholics never spoke the truth, and besides, she hadn't seen it happen.

Sapponyi looked at her, and the flicker of a smile played about his lips. "You are funny, Sister," he said. "You never believe a thing until you've seen it, do you? It reminds me of the time when that young girl threw herself out of a third-floor window. Hilda saw her sailing past the second floor—do you remember? She rushed out into the passage and met you and said, 'The lady in 61 has jumped out of the window,' and you said, 'But not a trace of it!' and went right on doing the rounds. Because you hadn't seen it." He chuckled. "And there she was, lying on the ground, dead all the time."

Andrea blushed crimson. "The Herr Medizinalrat shouldn't joke if it is true. Is it?"

"Yes, yes," said Sapponyi, his head shaking again. Then he took down his white coat from its hook because it was time for them to do the rounds. "It is true."

Andrea struggled hard with the fact. It was true. It was wrong. It was true. Aha! This was one of those matters which were beyond her powers of comprehension. She became humble. She had faith in those in command. "Well," she said finally, "I suppose they have their reasons for doing it." She was a true German.

Sapponyi had heard her words. "Ready?" he said, and his voice was quite cheerful and strong. "Na, Sister," he went on as they walked slowly down the corridor, he buttoning his coat, she with her keys jingling and her starched skirts swishing, "now you're going to experience a blue miracle . . . when you see what comes rolling in here!" It was funny how his German Andrea had no idea, absolutely no idea whatsoever, what the Germans were really like!

Pritnitz was "taken over" that same night. Fichtenbach was overlooked as not important enough, and Strubl's day had not yet come.

But they, in Pritnitz, decided on a torchlight parade through Fichtenbach, up Schwarzenberg, where, on the summit, they would light a big swastika, the biggest swastika ever, and be free, at last, to do so!

They started off, flags flying aloft, torches flaring, party members first, then those who had been vacillating, then those who didn't care but thought it would be fun, until Pritnitz was depleted of its inhabitants. In the end there was no one to stay behind.

They passed the cottage, and Fehge heard them coming, their voices ringing out through the countryside as harshly as Conrad's drunken cries had once resounded, and she saw their lights glowing like another magic conflagration on the horizon.

She went to the door of the cottage, Julie like a shadow beside her, and moved sluggishly, step by step, across the garden path to the gate, and through it, to the side of the road.

They passed her by, oblivious of her. Her eyes widened, unblinking, her lips parted, and a little drop of saliva trickled out of the corner of her mouth down her chin. She wiped it away unconsciously.

"*Die Fahne weht . . . die Reihen sind geschlossen . . . S.A. marschiert . . .*"

The Horst Wessel song. Fehge heard its rhythm for the first time. Once Communists had marched to it with words of their own; then the Nazis stole it and now sang it to glorify a pimp.

It had come. The dam was down. The brown flood was pouring in—brown caps, brown faces, brown shirts, brown breeches, boots . . . *tramp, tramp, tramp* . . . feet marching with vigour, feet marching in time, in a way Andrea could have found no fault with. It had reached them at last.

Fear conquered Fehge's heart. There it was before her, what she had always sensed lay latent in the people. There it was—at large. *And God was doing nothing to stop it.*

The song passed her by and merged again into a rhythm of marching feet and voices chanting, "*Sieg Heil! Sieg Heil! Sieg Heil!*" Louder, louder, louder, passing her, then softer, softer, gone . . .

Gone? No.

Have you ever lived near a rushing brook and gone away for a few hours, a few days, perhaps far away, and still heard the water rushing in your ears? Thus the rhythmic intonation of the Nazi cry of "*Sieg Heil!*" lived on in Fehge's ears long after it had passed. It was in her ears until she fell fitfully asleep in her bed. She heard it when she awoke, and from then off and on, until it was silenced by an extraordinary event.

Chapter Thirty-Four

FEHGE woke up the next morning feeling queer. There was a lump in her throat, and to get rid of it she would have liked to scream. She began to be so afraid that she might cry out that this almost blotted out the fundamental fear of the flood that had broken in and made their old world disappear. What if she threw herself on the floor and screamed, as she wanted so badly to do? What a terrible thing that would be! She must not do it. She must get rid of this queer feeling.

She did not get up. Julie came to see if she was sick. "No," said Fehge, "only tired."

At last the solution came to her. She must go to church. Church had been the beginning of the end of fear when she had been a child. Church would help her now.

She dressed as quickly as she could, but she was overcome every now and then by fits of trembling, so violent that her teeth chattered in her head. These fits passed, leaving her more tired than ever. But she got through dressing somehow. Then she went and told Julie that she was going to church and would be back before noon. She smiled at Mani without really seeing him.

Julie looked at her so strangely that Fehge stamped her foot and yelled at her, "Don't look at me like that!" The tears began to come, and the lump in her throat threatened to choke her, but Julie kept on looking at her. Fehge ran out of the house.

After a few moments she stopped running. When she reached the inn opposite the schoolhouse, she thought she would go in and visit the little Madonna she loved. It would be a good stopping-place and would make her feel better.

The Frau Wirtin was at the bar, and she had her hand already raised in the new greeting. When she saw who it was, she dropped it and said pallidly, "*Grüss Gott.*"

Fehge walked over to the little Madonna. But she was not there. The frame was there, and the wooden shelf beneath it with the wild flowers in their glasses, her own small bunch of gillyflowers among them, their petals like little drops of blood. But in the frame was the picture of a man and the lighted candles were flickering on his little moustache and his cruel little eyes. That face! That face again!

Fehge wanted to say something, but, O God, not a word would come! The lump was thick in her throat. So she stretched out an arm, and with one sweep of her hand she threw glasses and flowers to the floor. Then, suddenly, she could speak, thickly, quite unlike herself. "What is the meaning of this?" she bellowed.

The Frau Wirtin came from behind the counter in a rage. When she saw the expression on the girl's face she backed away. A sane Fehge was already much stronger than she was, and, by God, this Fehge didn't look in any mood to be tampered with!

"What's the meaning of this?" Fehge shrieked again, and stamped her foot with impatience. "What's this buffoon's face doing on the altar!"

Holy Mother of Jesus! The Frau Wirtin had been an ardent Nazi for years and was going to be one again a few seconds hence, but in this moment she ceased to be anything at all! That was why she answered Fehge meekly, "But don't you know what's happened? The Führer . . ." What exactly had happened? She didn't know herself. But one of the phrases she had been taught to chant came to her mind. "The Führer has made us free . . ."

Fehge began to shrivel, and as she grew smaller, the Frau Wirtin grew in stature. "You idiot! Be glad there's nobody else here or they'd arrest you! You'd better get used to the new order of things. And fast!" But still she didn't dare tell the girl to pick up the mess of broken glass and bedraggled flowers on the floor.

Fehge didn't look at the altar again. In a humbled voice she said, "Please give me the Madonna that was . . . that was in the frame."

The Frau Wirtin went behind the bar and handed the little painting across to the girl. "Here," she said, "and now see that you get out of here!" Her voice, too, rose to a scream. These were nerve-racking times, even if you were on the right side of the fence. The whole scene had upset her dreadfully. How dared the girl! Oh, she would come to a sorry end, and that very soon too!

Fehge walked on down the road in the direction of Pritnitz. She felt much better; the lump in her throat was gone. The hot sun streamed down on her. Every now and then she wiped perspiration from her upper lip and the back of her neck. She held the wooden picture pressed against her breast. She would take it to church, where it belonged. She wasn't very clear about what had happened at the inn, nor did she want to think about it.

At the crossroads where her father had died, Fehge met Julie's mother. Sofie Gfrerrer said, "I was on my way to you. I want Julie home." Her voice was sullen.

Fehge said, "Is anything wrong?"

"Not yet," said the woman, and she looked nervously from side to side. "But I'm scared. You can't tell what's going to happen next. Last night they were all drunk, and Reischer's Walter went up to the big crucifix and said, 'Now we're going to give the Saviour a punch in the jaw,' and he did! And nothing happened to him. When things like that can go on, the end of the world's coming. I want Julie home." She didn't tell Fehge how her name had been bandied round as much as Sapponyi's last night—they were the only Jews Pritnitz had to vent its triumph on—nor how she had realized then that it couldn't improve their already precarious position if Julie went on working for the Jewess.

Fehge nodded her head. "I'll send her home immediately I get back."

The woman went on talking in a low voice. "We won't be here much longer. You'll see. Pepi"—she meant her husband—"never was a party member. They'll close us down. Rosl's been waiting long enough, and she'll see to it, and now she can too. D'ye know we've got a new mayor? Heinrich Grabautschnik. And a new postmaster. Overnight. I wouldn't believe it if I hadn't seen it with my own eyes. They were all ready to jump into the other men's shoes. Every man at his post. Hop-la! Just like that." And her tone could not conceal her admiration.

Fehge was in a hurry to get away. She wanted to put the Madonna in the church and get home. The fear had gone, but she was more tired than ever. And she didn't care who was mayor or postmaster. She hadn't known who had been before.

The woman saw that she wasn't listening. "*Na*," she said, "it's not going to be so easy for you either." But even this thrust didn't seem to strike home. They parted.

In the village square where the church stood, Fehge came to a stop. There was a crowd separating her from the church. In it she recognized Conrad, the centre of a group of young men in brown with bright swastika arm-bands. They had knives in their belts.

When Conrad saw her, his face lit up with triumph and he grinned. One of the boys standing next to him whispered something in his ear, and Conrad nodded his head.

Above their heads she could see the crucifix the Gfrerrer woman had mentioned, knocked askew by Walter Reischer's blow.

Fehge's eyes dilated, and the lump came back in her throat. "The crucifix must go," Grabautschnik had said, and there it was, toppling. He was getting his way, the devil was getting his way. *Where was God?*

She didn't see how gay the square was with its many swastika flags flying, especially the Lamb, which was swathed in them, and the many Hitler pictures wreathed with flowers and fir twigs . . . like the wreaths at Advent. She saw only the lopsided crucifix. That was enough. If God had done nothing when that had happened, He was going to do nothing at all.

Still clutching the painting, Fehge turned and walked back the way she had come. She took a roundabout way home, climbing up to the *Marterl* she loved on the Schwarzenberg. There He hung, the Saviour, seemingly eternal, looking down at her. His skin was porcelain pink, and the blood that flowed from His wounds was so red suddenly, that one would never guess how wind and rain had beaten down upon them.

She knelt and prayed. It was still and breathless about her. Wood and earth baked in the noonday sun. She finished her prayer and waited, as though for a message. None came.

"No," she said aloud, in a positive tone of voice, "He doesn't know what to do either."

When she got back to the cottage she said to Julie, "Your mother wants you home."

Julie stared at her for a moment in amazement, then decided not to ask any questions and went to her room to pack her few belongings. Fehge laid the little wooden Madonna on a table and left the cottage again. She walked straight up to Strubl and did what she had never done in her life before—asked to speak to the Herr Medizinalrat.

Hannes, the porter, raised his eyebrows at the unusual request, but after one look at the girl's face decided, like Julie, to say nothing. He rang the house-bell four times, which was the Herr Medizinalrat's signal. The sound, which echoed in the corridor, thereby accentuating the emptiness of the big house, provoked no sign of disturbance in Fehge's set features. On the contrary, when an answer was not immediately forthcoming, she said tersely, "Ring again."

This time the Herr Medizinalrat, on some floor or other, took off the receiver. Hannes spoke at his end. "In the lobby, Herr Medizinalrat," and, in a tone of slight contempt, "Fehge says she has to speak to you."

Sapponyi turned to Andrea, who was standing beside him. "It's for me," he said, nodding his head, and left her to finish the rounds without him.

Fehge was standing quite still, waiting for him. "What is it?" he asked, and wished that, of all people, she might be saved. What a hopeless wish, like all his bitter heart had ever formulated!

She began, "Herr Medizinalrat . . ."

"Yes?"

"I was down in the village."

"Yes?"

"Is there nothing that can stop them . . ."—she corrected herself, "get rid of them?"

He took her arm and led her to a window as though he wished to show her something there, but he only looked out on to the hills. He was thinking: She has lost her faith in God, or she would not come to me. And there is nothing I can do.

Aloud he said, "Nothing but a miracle can save us now."

When he didn't say anything more, she curtsied and said, "Thank you, Herr Medizinalrat," and went away.

Us, she thought, all the way down to the cottage! The Herr Medizinalrat had said us. Then he, too, was in danger. And God was doing nothing about it!

Fehge thought the day would never end. But the time finally came when Mani's lids were drooping, opening a little, drooping, Mani fell asleep.

Fehge went to her room and started to undress. She folded her clothes away neatly and got into her coarse cotton nightgown with the long sleeves and the high neck. It was one she had outgrown, so that it left her legs bare for several inches above her ankles. But it was not yet sufficiently worn out to warrant buying a new one.

She let down her hair, brushed and rebraided it. Then she washed her hands and face, growing more and more tired with every move she made. She thought she might sleep well tonight. She could not remember ever having been so tired.

Ute was ready for sleep too, her nose on her paws, her eyes opening every now and then reluctantly to watch Fehge. Fehge knelt by the open window to say her prayers. Then she got into bed. She had never been so tired! In the distance she could hear a song: "*Schlof mei Fehgele, mach zu dei Egele* . . ."

"Yes, Mother, I'll sleep."

"Fehge . . . Fehge . . ."

"Mother, leave me be. I'll sleep."

"Fehge . . . Fehge . . ."

It wasn't her mother calling. Fehge opened her eyes.

"Fehge . . . Fehge . . ."

Fehge sprang out of bed and ran to the window and looked down. It was Julie. "What are you doing here at this time of night?"

Julie was so agitated that speech had forsaken her. A flow of gibberish was all the answer Fehge got. But she realized that the girl was in distress.

She left the window and went down to the front door and let Julie in. "Now," she said, "what is it?" She was exasperated. If the girl was off in one of her ecstasies again . . .

Julie tried to speak but could not. Fehge stepped back a pace wearily. "Julie," she said sternly, "calm yourself."

The girl made signs to her that she should touch her. Fehge put one hand on each of the girl's upper arms just below the shoulder and squeezed them tight. "Now," she said again, "calm yourself."

Julie began to breathe evenly and, not taking her eyes from Fehge's face, said quite clearly, "They're coming to get you."

So it had come to her.

"Who is coming to get me?"

"Conrad," said Julie.

Of course. Who else? Conrad—the wave that had been sent

to engulf her. Everybody had their own particular wave that would inundate them.

"He says . . . he says . . ." Julie stumbled over the hard phrase which she had been saying over and over again in her mind ever since she had left the Lamb, where her parents had taken her in a pitiful effort to show that she was no longer working for the Jewess . . . "He says that you must be made an example of."

An example? Fehge couldn't follow. But the lump was in her throat again, and the shivering fits came back, making her teeth chatter in her head.

"Go upstairs," she said, and went up behind Julie.

On the way to her room she looked into Mani's. He was fast asleep. He had uncovered his legs and lay sprawled. She covered him. Then she looked down at the old dog, at her heels as usual. "Ute," she called softly. They would kill her. She went downstairs again and locked the dog in the cellar, where she whined for a while, then was still.

The two girls waited in Fehge's room. Fehge thought: I can't think of a thing to do. There isn't a thing I can do. There should be something, but I am too stupid to think of it. How can anyone be so stupid! And what disturbed her most was that she could not pray.

The shivering fits gave her no pause now. She trembled from top to toe unceasingly. Her eyes were enormous as she looked out of the window as far as the moonlight would let her, trying to penetrate the dark from out of which they would come. The road was clear, the sky light from a moon which was about to rise, like velvet. You could barely see the stars.

"There they come," said Julie.

Around the bend came the little flickering lights of bicycles being pushed up the hill. A dark mass moved around them.

"How many are there?" The lump would hardly let Fehge say the words. She was so cold, as though her blood had congealed hours ago. Yet she was bathed in sweat. She rubbed her moist hands against her nightgown and could feel the hardness of her thighs. She ached all over, and her legs felt as though water were running softly down inside them. I'm turning to stone, she thought.

Julie's eyes were on her. "Don't look at me, stupid," she said, and her voice was like a little child's. Suddenly she spoke in the jargon of her fathers. "Look down the road. How many are there?"

What a silly question! Julie couldn't count.

The group walked into the moonlight.

"Four, five, six, seven . . . three of them are girls . . ." Fehge said, and her voice was husky. "What do they want from me? I have turned to stone."

The group came up the hill to the door of the cottage and stood in front of it for a while, whispering. Then one of the men knocked, and Ute barked. "She's got the dog in the cellar," someone said. "Good," said the boy who was knocking. "But keep your revolver drawn just the same. The bitch may not be locked up."

He looked up, as though trying to guess which room was Fehge's, and she saw that it was Conrad. He saw her white figure move away from the window and yelled, "There she is . . . the witch!"

Julie drew away from the window with Fehge. "What are you going to do?" she said.

Fehge didn't answer.

The group had meanwhile discovered that the door was not locked. This easy entry shocked them for a brief moment, then the noise of their tumbling into the quiet house could be heard above, their voices preceding their steps as they mounted the stairs.

"Open the door," said Fehge, "or they may go into Mani's room and frighten him."

Her voice sounded as though she were in a trance. The last thing Julie heard her say in that strange voice was, "Dear Saviour, help me."

Julie went to the door and opened it. The group, Conrad in the lead, had reached the top of the stairs. They were looking at the doors, wondering which could be Fehge's bedroom. One boy already had his hand on the knob of the door that led to Mani's room. "Here," cried Conrad. "Here's Julie," and he stepped forward, pushed the idiot girl back into the room and swung the door so hard that it banged sharply against the inner wall. Conrad in the lead, the group entered the bedroom.

"Put on the light," said Conrad. Somebody did—click—and the room was flooded. Eyes blinked.

The boys were in S.A. uniforms and wore the swastika arm-band on their sleeves, the girls wore their dirndls. They were all three girls who had gone to school with Fehge. They stood on tiptoe in the rear, trying to see what was going on. Fehge turned slowly and faced them, as though on a pivot.

A scream rang out, a long-drawn wail from Julie's throat, and she fell on her knees and cried "Maria! Maria!"

The boys stopped dead. The girls stood higher so that they could see between the boys' heads, and then they too saw, and, like Julie, screamed and, one by one, fell on their knees. The boys around Conrad began to back, slowly, until they stumbled into the girls. Two knelt down as the girls had already done, the others turned and fled.

Conrad stood alone, facing Fehge. But Fehge could not see him. Her eyes were closed, and the blood trickled slowly from her forehead over her lids, its fall broken only by her lashes. It trickled on from there, down her cheeks, in broken, uncertain channels. She held her hands stretched straight down at her sides, and from two open wounds in her palms the blood dripped to the floor. The wounds of Christ were in her feet, above the instep, and the red blood trickled out of them, down her foot, between her toes where she stood on the wooden boards of the floor which sucked it up.

Suddenly there was a stir. Ute. Ute had stood up on her ageing hind legs and had managed to slip open the latch that locked her in. Up the stairs she had bounded and now threaded her way like a streak of lightning between the kneeling people to her mistress, who put out no hand to greet her, to tell her what a clever dog she was, who said nothing at all.

The dog stopped dead in her tracks. She backed a step and

growled, her short hair bristling, then, with a loud, sharp howl, she turned and fled into the night.

Still Fehge stood motionless, not seeing, not hearing—and Conrad, as still, facing her. His cheeks were hollow as from long fasting, his eyes bulged, and he held his teeth gritted so tightly together that his jaw seemed locked. All the signs of youth had left his face. He was an old man.

He raised a shaking right arm and his three longest fingers touched the blood on Fehge's cheeks. "*Ahhh*," he bellowed, "*ahh . . . ahh . . . ahh . . .*" and turned and ran out into the night.

They found him next morning where he had hanged himself from a tree behind the summer-house. Ute was never seen or heard of again.

Chapter Thirty-Five

THE Führer had been expected in Vienna on Saturday, March 12th. On Sunday, the 13th, he still hadn't arrived. He was in Linz, but he did not put in an appearance in Vienna. Why? Nobody knew except those who kept quiet about it. But there were some who realized that there were not enough National Socialists in Vienna to make his reception as spectacular as it had to be, and this fact soon became self-evident when all the faithful Nazis from a radius of more than a hundred miles around Vienna were rounded up and brought to that city to chant a mechanical welcome to the new god.

Pritnitz was sucked into this net which spread over the countryside around Vienna in all directions. They came to Pritnitz and they came to Strubl, where they took Fritz, the chauffeur, Franz, the coachman, Hannes, the porter, and Otto, the boy who cleaned the shoes—all of whom had been party members; and they commandeered Sapponyi's car.

These hooked fishes rode to Vienna like all the other fishes, packed into trucks, as tight as sardines. They had to stand all the way in their leather coats and brown breeches, their heads bare, shivering a little when the cold draught of the speeding car hit them, squirming in their shoes as their feet ached from standing still and cramped. A swastika flag grew out of the front of each truck and flapped inconsiderately into the faces of the rear ranks of men. Some had been singing when they had started on their way, but the wind soon took the breath out of their open mouths, and they became silent. They swayed in unison, and they thought in unison, that the great new era, which they had laboured, suffered and fought for, had dawned, at last. . . . But as they grew tired, their brains, unaccustomed to thinking, lapsed into coma. They would arrive in Vienna in just the desired state of mind.

As they approached the city, the highways merged and traffic became more congested. The trucks slowed their pace and rolled along in single file.

This congestion was not helped at all by the fact that there was another stream of traffic coming the other way. This pilgrimage was not mechanized, it had not been organized, it was spontaneous. The people walked on foot or rode on bicycles or drove in carts. The trains leaving the station were filled with them. Their throng, too, was augmented at merging highways so that the line doubled and trebled, becoming such an obstruction that the trucks had to slow down almost to a standstill. The pilgrims finally were forced off the road, walking in the ditches but not halting their advance.

These pilgrims were not going to Vienna. On the contrary, they had their backs turned to it, and they were not facing north either, where the Führer was waiting for his herd to be assembled where a new sun was rising. They were satisfied with the old, because suddenly it shone with a new light that warmed them.

The story of the stigmata of the girl Fehge had travelled fast. Such stories do. Now, two days later, there was not a parish in Lower Austria of any size which was ignorant of the fact that a Catholic girl but of undeniably Jewish origin, living in a hamlet near the village of Pritnitz, had been blessed with the stigmata of

Christ. There was scepticism, but not among the peasantry. It was they who carried the story, from relative to relative, from friend to friend, from village to village. The story grew, as such stories will. The girl had made the dumb speak, had brought the dead to life, had healed the sick. A sinner had hanged himself. The stains of her blood were still wet on his fingers when they took him down.

Slowly, like a monster rearing itself from sleep, the pilgrimage started. The faithful, the curious, the eager—they gathered together in groups, found a leader, and decided to set forth at once, for who could tell when their journey would be forbidden, as visits to the stigmatized girl in Bavaria had been forbidden by a cautious clergy?

Small preparations. All that was needed, really, was a faithful heart. Forgotten were politics and the fact that the little country was without a Government. Without a Government? No, indeed. God had spoken. God still reigned supreme.

As the vanguard of this strange army reached Pritnitz, Sapponyi was informed of the matter. He was seated at Fehge's bedside in one of Strubl's rooms into which she had been moved as soon as news of the "Strubl miracle" had reached the main house. By the window sat His Excellency Bishop Riehl, his mauve cap providing a soft spot of colour in the otherwise sombre room.

His visit to the stigmatized girl was by no means official. The *Bischöfliche Ordinariat* would stand aloof from her for some time to come, until all danger of fraud had been eliminated and the people, in their ardour, forced an issue. But the Bishop had had a visit to make at Strubl, and that had given him the welcome excuse to see the girl. He was therefore now at her bedside incognito.

Fehge lay on the bed with her eyes closed. Where the wounds were, she was lightly covered with soft linen cloths. At first they had tried to treat and bandage the wounds, but, in her semiconscious condition, she had cried bitterly and had been in such evident agony that they had to let her be. Now, without medication or the prescribed form of bandage, they seemed not to trouble her so much.

There she lay, as white now as her covers, her face gaunt and strained, as it had never been in real life. She was asleep, but her sleep seemed to bring her no peace. Every now and then she moved her head restlessly from side to side.

Sapponyi had just looked under the light bandage on her hands and had been able to ascertain that a thin, pink healing skin had formed over the open red gashes. The wounds were disappearing.

He had just told this to the Bishop, who nodded his head and seemed relieved. "It would be a blessing for her," he whispered, "if this did not recur." And for us all, he thought.

Andrea came in with the news that pilgrims were arriving in Pritnitz in droves. Sapponyi looked at the Bishop, who said tersely, "I was expecting this."

Sapponyi, in whose eyes the light had been snuffed out two days ago, seemed suddenly to come to life. He had been told about the creatures who had been herded in trucks to Vienna and the purpose of this herding, and he could visualize the scenes now being enacted on the road. He who had thought he would never laugh again, laughed now. "Isn't it strange, *Hochwürden*," he said, "this . . . shall we call it 'contra-pilgrimage' to the Jewess Fehge?"

The Bishop winced as the doctor didn't spare him and reminded him of the embarrassing fact that the stigmatized girl was of Jewish origin. "I'm afraid we are all going to find it very embarrassing before it is over," he said.

"Not I," said Sapponyi. "In the position in which I find myself, nothing on earth can embarrass me any more. That this should happen under my roof, I consider a sort of personal recompense from God, if I may be so presumptuous as to say so. It has heightened my self-esteem. I shall die a self-respecting man." And he followed the amazed Bishop out of the room.

Andrea remained standing at the foot of the bed and looked down at the sleeping girl whom she had brought up to woman-hood. She felt like the proverbial hen who has hatched the duckling's egg. In her eyes was a pathetic expression of horror as she looked at Fehge. She had seen the bleeding stigmata with her own eyes; there was therefore no possibility of dismissing it with her favourite phrase, "But not a trace of it." And Sapponyi had probed the life out of her after it had happened, questioning her mercilessly about every detail in Fehge's physical life, everything she knew, even the embarrassing fact of Fehge's menstruation periods, which had ceased half a year ago, so the girl had confessed to her—no, not confessed, spoken of it easily, unencumbered by false shame as was Andrea. Yes. Sapponyi had made Andrea repeat everything. What was he trying to do? Take away from the thing its quality of the miraculous and find a rational explanation in science?

Andrea couldn't see it that way. How she would have liked to, but she could not! It was a miracle, and Andrea was learning to accept it as such, very grudgingly because the stigmata of the girl went against the grain. Andrea had believed so firmly in God. It was almost unfair of Him, if she might say so, to impress Himself upon her in such a bizarre manner. Or had she not believed firmly enough.

Andrea was hurt and bewildered. Incomprehensible things were going on, and she was not thinking of the hordes that had overrun Austria. Of them she had had no time to think, and she had not yet seen them. She would soon have ample opportunity to do both.

Chapter Thirty-Six

TEN days later, an elderly man whose thin grey hair looked as though it never had been combed, stood in front of Sapponyi's desk in extreme agitation.

"I am sorry," Sapponyi was saying, "but I cannot let you see her. I have strict orders . . ."

"From whom do you take orders?" Moritz Behrendt shouted.

"From whom I please. And when I can't do that any more, I shall abdicate."

"Herr Medizinalrat," Behrendt began again, now almost in a whisper, "this is no time for witticisms. I must see the girl Fehge."

"I am sorry," Sapponyi repeated. "In order to avoid complications I have promised not to let anybody see Fehge until the Bishop's *Ordinariat* has come to a decision about her status."

"To whom have you made this promise?"

"To Hochwürden Bishop Riehl."

Behrendt beat with his fist on the desk that stood between them. "So!" he yelled. "So! Hochwürden, Bishop! And the Cardinal was received yesterday by Adolf Hitler! What do we owe the Church now, Herr Medizinalrat?"

Sapponyi paused to let the other man's ire die down. He had never conducted conversation in a vehement tone in his life, and he was not going to start now. He was not going to do anything as long as he lived that he had not been accustomed to doing. Finally he said, "And what do I owe you and your party? You made a mess of it just as much as the Black Ones did."

Behrendt ignored the thrust. He knew the man in front of him too well. He leaned forward and said, "Look. Let me tell you why I want to see this girl."

When he had finished, Sapponyi was silent for a while, then he smiled, then he threw back his head and let out a laugh that was no less hearty because it was so soft. Ever since he had laughed in front of the Bishop ten days ago, this thing, this strange event, had brought him face to face with a hundred different situations, all of them entertaining in their way. This, now—what Moritz Behrendt was proposing—was the most fantastic of them all. A climax. Preposterous. And absurd. Still . . . you could never tell. Incredible, utterly incredible, was what had happened to the ridiculous little housepainter, the flesh-and-blood puppet of a twentieth-century Germany, with his hollow name of "leader"! Leader? Was there ever a man so led, more than that—driven—by his people's basest instincts and desires? No. Sapponyi would never again say "impossible" to any proposal.

And what had they to lose?

There was Moritz Behrendt, who had spent the last four years, ever since the ill-fated February civil war, in prison and concentration camp. Three weeks ago he had been set free as a part of Schuschnigg's too-late peace with the Social Democrats. It could only be a matter of days now, perhaps hours, until the Gestapo took him back into custody and then—no, by God, Behrendt had nothing to lose!

Behrendt's party? Sapponyi couldn't help admiring the man for not having escaped to pretend, as so many others like him were doing, that a great party which had died under Dollfuss's cannons away back in 1934 still had life in some hospitable capital city or other. If anything at all could still be done for Austria's defunct Social Democratic Party, it could only be here on Austria's native soil. With Behrendt's fantastic idea? Sapponyi was not sure, but, as he had decided a moment ago, nothing was impossible nowadays.

And he, Sapponyi? He had nothing more to miss on this earth except, perhaps, if he were lucky, the final reality of the loss of Strubl. And Fehge? He could not worry about Fehge; he could not presume to. She could look after herself.

He rose and said, "All right. Come with me. I will take you to her."

Fehge was sitting at the open window of her room, her hands folded in her lap. She wore white mittens to hide the pale marks still visible on them, and she wore a white kerchief such as the older women in that vicinity wore round their heads. It hid the marks on her forehead.

She could feel her strength returning to her like new warm blood in her veins. But a dazed feeling prevailed. She still suffered from pains in her head and nausea in the face of anything but the plainest food. Her legs felt weak, and she dragged them a little when she walked. But Sapponyi had assured her that there was nothing wrong with her; these were all still symptoms of tiredness; she should rest and not over-exert herself until she felt she could lead a normal life again. She hoped this would be soon. She did not like this state of not being herself.

She turned her head as the door opened, and when she saw

Sapponyi with a stranger she rose. The sight of the stranger did not disturb her. Whoever the Herr Medizinalrat brought to see her was welcome.

"Fehge," said Sapponyi, "this gentleman would like to speak to you."

"I will fetch chairs from the other room," said Fehge.

Behrendt made a quick, nervous gesture. "Please let me."

Fehge stepped back and reddened with embarrassment, and Sapponyi put a hand on Behrendt's arm. "I think Fehge would like to get them," he said, and Fehge walked past them, flattening herself a little. "Only bring one," said Sapponyi. "I can't stay."

Fehge brought the strange gentleman a chair, and Sapponyi went away and left them alone. "Won't you sit down?" said Behrendt.

"If the gentleman wishes," said Fehge, and sat.

Behrendt seated himself opposite her. He had motioned her into the chair she had been sitting on before, where the light fell on her face. It had not changed much since that day, twelve years ago, when he had looked down at it in a kitchen in Linz. Her clear-cut features were perhaps less oriental now with her full-grown body and face making her eyes less dominant. He knew types like her from Bavaria, from Silesia, from the Balkans. The oriental dress of her fathers would have suited her less today than when he had seen her last. How well she had assimilated!

He smiled to her, and she smiled back to him. Then she looked down at her fingers and began to play with them. She stroked the place where the pink spot was under the mitten and felt the healing prickle of her skin. Behrendt looked at her hands, worn by hard work, the knuckles a little swollen, the clean, slightly reddened hands of a hard-working girl. How simple she is, he thought, and suddenly his heart sank. For the first time he had the feeling that his mission might not succeed. He had been so sure. Why, else, had it happened? God—for now he, too, suddenly believed— God could not let such a thing happen without a purpose. And the purpose could only be the one that had inspired him and raised all his fiery hopes of victory in defeat, that had carried him like some volcanic eruption from the coffee-house in Vienna, where he had read about her stigmata in an obscure little provincial paper, here to Strubl within three hours. But now, face to face with the girl who had revived his dead hopes, his spirit flagged. He felt before he began that he had made a mistake.

"Fräulein Fehge." The sound of his own voice surprised him. Whatever I say, he thought, is going to sound dreadful.

She helped him by bursting out laughing. "Nobody's ever called me that," she said in the village dialect.

"What?" said Behrendt.

"Fräulein . . . Miss Fehge," and she was still laughing. "My," she said then soberly, "it's good to laugh again."

He began once more. "Fehge," and still his voice was pompous, "we do not meet today for the first time. Twelve years ago you spent a day in Linz, and I saw you there, just as you were finishing your work in the kitchen. Don't you remember me?"

She shook her head slowly. "Excuse me, sir," she said, "I don't."

He smiled. "You had a big problem then—what to do with your earned *Schilling*."

She laughed softly. "I never know what to buy, even now."

She paused; he sat silent. "Fehge," he began again, "you are a Jewess, are you not?"

She answered him, "My father was a Jewish pedlar. He died down where this road runs into the Pritnitz highway. And then my mother died. Because she wouldn't eat *Trefe*. She kept her laws. And I keep mine."

She spoke with great dignity.

So she was conscious of her origin. That was important. "You know," Behrendt went on, "how terribly this man who has taken over our country has persecuted your people and what he will do to those of your race over here."

Fehge shook her head. "I don't know anything about that, *gnädiger Herr*," she said. "I never go anywhere."

"Do you read the papers?"

"Well. Not the papers the *Herrschaften* read," and she mentioned the little Catholic paper which she read.

"Very well, then," said Behrendt, sitting back. "these Nazis—you know them. You have seen them. They will destroy your race."

"They will destroy everything," said Fehge, and her eyes grew big. "*Ach, gnädiger Herr*, they are like the locusts in the Bible. They will leave nothing as it was."

Behrendt stared at her, then he got up, walked up and down once, sat down again and pulled his chair closer to hers. "Tell me," he said, weighing his words, "*tell me exactly what you think about it all.*"

"About what?"

"About what has happened here."

"*Nun*," she said. "He went and freed them like he always promised he would."

Behrendt was disappointed, but he didn't show it. "That was only silly talk," he told her. "That is how he deceives the people, telling them he will make them free."

"But he did make them free," Fehge interrupted him, and with sudden animation she lifted both hands and he could see the pink marks on the palms where the mitten gaped a little. It gave him a turn.

"He did," she repeated vehemently. "They are free now, at last, to do as they please."

Behrendt opened his mouth to say something, then he closed it again. He passed his hand over his brow and down the side of his face. He was confused. "You don't understand," he said. "He didn't free them; he let them loose. Freedom . . . freedom is quite another thing."

"It is?" said Fehge. "What is it, then, if it isn't to be free to do as you please, like the animals we would be if we didn't have God in us?"

Behrendt would have liked her to go on, but she didn't. She paused, definitely. It was his turn.

"There is a freedom," he said, "to worship as you please, to say what you please, to write what you please . . . to . . . to be yourself!"

She looked at him for a moment. Then she said, "What good is that freedom when you have people who don't want to worship? Who want to speak and write and do evil?"

Behrendt nodded his head with a stupefied expression on his face. "I think," he said, so low that she could scarcely hear him, "you've got something there."

"You and I," said Fehge, politely including the *gnädiger Herr* in her recommendation, "we are not free. We are tied by a thousand chains. God's chains. And are they not beautiful?"

Then, with a sort of simple grandeur and in an altered tone of voice, she said, "But the *gnädiger Herr* wants me to do something for him or he wouldn't be here. What is it?"

Yes. What was it? She drew him back from far away. He took a deep breath. "Fehge," he said, "I want you to save us."

Fehge put the tips of the fingers of both hands against her breasts in a gesture that told, at once, her bewilderment, and seemed to ask, "Me?" But she only said slowly, with the fear growing in her eyes, "What does the *gnädiger Herr* mean?"

Now he would have to start building this thing up from the bottom. "Fehge," he began, "in this village and in Pritnitz and for miles around, there are people waiting to catch a glimpse of you."

Fehge's heart began to beat wildly with the old fear. What did he mean?

Behrendt went on relentlessly. "They have come from all over Austria to see you, hundreds of them. They would come from Bavaria if they had not been refused entry into the Ostmark!" He spat out the new word contemptuously. "The Nazis are allowed to stream in like a brown flood, but the pilgrims of faith are turned back at the border."

"The pilgrims of faith?" she said. "Where are they going?"

"To see you."

She rose from her chair and stood behind it, gripping its back.

It took her farther away from him and put something between them. Then she asked, "Why?"

"Fehge," and now Behrendt spoke fast, "yours is a great mission. On the day when they were herding men together from all over the country to greet the Führer in Vienna—they had to do that, Fehge, because that city did not want him and if its people alone had been left to greet him, he would have seen nothing but sullen faces, so they collected their ruffians from far and wide. And as those hundreds were being herded toward the city, other hundreds were moving on foot, spontaneously, Fehge, of their own free will, to the girl who had been blessed with the stigmata, who had made the dumb girl speak and the dead woman come to life and the villain hang himself. . . ."

"But I didn't do that!" she interrupted him and backed against the wall as though she would like to have disappeared through it. "I didn't do any of that! Not I! Not I!"

"No," said Behrendt, "not you. But their faith in you. Fehge, I represent the people of Vienna, and those hundreds out there who would rather worship God than Hitler. Not their Cardinal, who turned his back on Christ this morning and went to see the anti-Christ. No. I mean those out there who in spite of everything will never lose sight of the cross because they carry it in their hearts. Lead them, Fehge! Lead them! As Joan of Arc once led an army. Go out to them and tell them you will lead them! Go out to them, walk among them, talk to them. Tell them to drive out the invader. They will rally around you—an invincible army. An army the Nazis will not be able to break. They don't dare touch you. They would like to, but they don't dare. They will fall back abashed before your followers. Go out to them, Fehge. Gather them round you. Tell them to fight and drive out the enemy!"

Behrendt was sitting forward on his chair, gripping the ends of its arms, looking up into her face with such intensity that she could not take her eyes off him. He thought: If I can get her to do it, we could make history. She had evidenced a power that is beyond the comprehension of man. She is more powerful than they, with all their apparatus of war. For her, they would fight with their bare hands, and the armed enemy would become vulnerable with fear, the fear of the unattainable. . . .

At last she spoke. She said, "You have no right to tell me these things. Such a message must come from God. What you say that I should do is overweening."

Silence. Then Behrendt's low words, coming from him drop by drop, "Overweening? Are you not being overweening when you believe that this miracle was lavished on you by God for no greater purpose than to save your life?"

She answered him as slowly, "Why not? It may seem wasteful to you that such a miracle should be lavished on someone as insignificant as I am. But not to Him, Who can do nothing too lavish because everything is in His power. Besides," she added softly, "I am afraid you think too well of those pilgrims of faith. If they are really here to see me, as you say, then I am sure it is not because their faith is so much greater than the Cardinal's, but because they hope to gain something for themselves." She leaned forward and said with deep feeling, "Why do you think they go to church, sir? Because they love God? No. Because they covet heaven." Her tense body relaxed again, and her voice sounded tired. "No," she repeated, now seemingly negating everything in general, "you and I know very well that they can gain nothing from me except what I can do for them with my two hands."

It was over. What had Sapponyi said at the door of her room like a parting shot? "I want to draw your attention to one thing . . . I am sure this is not your miracle."

Their silence was broken by the shrill whooping of a siren and the roar of a motor. A car was speeding up the hill, round the curve and up the drive to Strubl's front entrance. It was full of brownshirts. Its long motor was mounted with a swastika flag. "Storm troopers," said Behrendt, and then, feeling quite sure, because it was so timely, "They have come for me."

The S.S. men were in a foul temper, not because they didn't enjoy a hunt—that was as good as the cops and robbers of their boyhood days; but the quiet, contented crowd waiting in Pritnitz had disgruntled them, and the monument of flowers on the graves of the Jewish pedlar and his wife—that had been the last straw! Heinrich Grabautschnik had tactlessly pointed it out to them, a fragrant pyramid built by faithful hands on the hitherto neglected graves of Moishe and Dworje. Remove it? Grabautschnik, a staunch Nazi, had advised against it, and they had sheepishly pretended to forget all about it. However, it still rankled.

They had picked up two S.A. men in Pritnitz to show them the rest of the way. Walter Reischer was one of them. He had not wanted to go along, but he had had his first taste of Prussian discipline and had come along, after all, like a lamb. "Please God," he had prayed to himself all the way up to Strubl, "please God I don't have to see *her*!"

As they tumbled out of the car, Reischer the only reluctant one, it was very evident that this was what they had been cut out for —hunting and killing. At last they were free!

Sapponyi came to the door to meet them. Whom had they come for? Behrendt? Himself? Or both.

"Guard the front and back. He may try to escape by the balconies or cellars," one of the S.S. men said, and saw Sapponyi. "Behrendt!" he said. "Where is he?"

"If the gentlemen will come this way," said Sapponyi, and waved with his hand in the direction of upstairs.

The S.S. men drew their guns. The third man said, "I'll stay down here. This may be a ruse."

"I am sure he is not armed," said Sapponyi.

"Don't give us advice, Jew," said the S.S. man, and poked Sapponyi in the ribs with the gun. "Show us the way."

Sapponyi moved on ahead. Andrea, standing at the back of the large entrance lobby, watched the whole procedure, the high spots of colour in her cheeks which always were there when someone was dying. As the little group turned their backs on her, two big tears rolled out of her wide-open eyes. She was trembling from head to foot. "*Na sowas,*" she whispered to herself. "Well, of all things!" The world was standing on its ear.

At the door of Fehge's room they halted. "He is with the girl Fehge," said Sapponyi very solemnly, "here."

But he made no move to open the door. Neither did the others. They looked from their guns, then to the closed door from behind which there came no sound, then at one another.

The S.S. man who seemed to be the leader said to one of his comrades, "Go on in and bring him out. I'll stand guard here."

"*Nee*," said the other, with a sheepish chuckle, "I don't want to see the girl. You know . . ." His voice trailed off.

Sapponyi looked at Reischer and saw that the boy looked green. Sapponyi was enjoying this little interlude. "Why don't *you* go in, Reischer?" he said. "You and Conrad Schreiner knew her well. You can't be afraid of her."

The S.S. men were so relieved at this solution that they missed the implication regarding their fear. They all looked at Reischer, who began to tremble. "Go on," said the S.S. man. "You don't need a gun. Go in and get him."

"Yes," said Sapponyi, merciless, "go in and get him!"

Reischer looked from one to the other, then he opened his mouth wide and began to blubber like a stuck pig. "I can't," he wailed. "I won't. I'm afraid."

Sapponyi took over as the others stood transfixed. "What are you afraid of, Reischer? You tore down all the *Marterln* between here and Pritnitz. You made a swastika fire of them, and you got drunk watching it. God didn't strike you dead as you desecrated them. What are you afraid of now? The devil will protect you now, as he did then!"

Reischer bellowed. Sapponyi turned and knocked hard on the door. "Come out, Behrendt," he called. "They have come for you." If Behrendt didn't come out soon and put an end to this scene, he would lose his reason. For suddenly it was no longer amusing to see the ignorant beast in man—not to this extent, anyway. But from within the room there was still no sound.

Fehge and Behrendt stood and sat as they had been before. When she spoke it was in a whisper. "What are you going to do?"

"Go out to them!"

"Stay here," said Fehge, as she realized with a sudden sense of uplift that her room, like church, had become a sanctuary.

Behrendt shook his head. "No," he said. "I didn't come to save myself." He rose. "It has been a great privilege to see you again," he said, and shook hands with her gently, sensing the hurt under her little white mittens.

But she laid a hand on his sleeve and pointed to the open window. It was then that Sapponyi rapped at the door and called out to Behrendt to surrender. "Why don't you try to escape?" she said. "It is not a high jump."

He shook his head. "I am really not interested in saving myself." He spoke calmly, as though nothing untoward were going on outside, although Reischer was roaring at the top of his lungs. "I came to you, I suppose, in a moment of mental aberration, to save . . ." He raised his hands in a helpless gesture and let them fall again. "I suppose to save the thing itself. The idea. Now I know it is no use." He spoke very gravely but with a tranquillity that lighted his face.

"Sapponyi was right. This was not our miracle. I think, perhaps, we put the stress on the wrong thing. On freedom." His whole being was moved by sudden understanding. "It should be on servitude! The right kind of servitude. As you put it, the right 'chains.'"

He stopped speaking, still staring at her. "I mean," he added in a more even voice, "that's just something to start out from. If they don't kill me and I preserve my reason, I'll work it out. You'll see." And he walked out of the room without further adieu, as though he would really be back a few years later with a solution.

She heard a sharp slap outside the door and the bellowing stopped. Their footsteps disappeared down the passage. Then she felt a dreadful pain in her head and everything went black. Andrea found her an hour later, lying on the floor, and put her to bed.

Chapter Thirty-Seven

THEN Dennis came back. He did not go to Fehge at once. First he was closeted with Sapponyi in his office for two hours. He went there seeking reassurance. It couldn't be true, this wild story he had picked up on the train between Vienna and Pritnitz! It was one of those fantastic peasant distortions. Fehge had hurt herself, cut herself, bled—and this was what had been made of it. It could not be true!

"It is true."

In those three words, Sapponyi denied him reassurance.

"Such things don't happen," Dennis said vehemently.

"Of course they happen!" the doctor replied.

Then he had proceeded to explain Fehge to Dennis in a perspective from which Dennis had never chosen to observe her—psychologically. There could be no denying that Sapponyi's diagnosis was sound and sane. Dennis could recognize all the symptoms as Sapponyi stood them up before him, and, medicinally arranged like that, they led up to the phenomenon of stigmata as to a logical goal. First—her intangible fear of people in general; then that fear becoming more real as she witnessed the growing terror of the outnumbered concentrated on a tangible enemy, and, finally, the physical results culminating from her rigid control . . . ah, had she not been so controlled, everything might have turned out quite differently; she might even have committed murder and by now been dead herself!

Sapponyi went on, "Now let us turn from the psychic aspect to the physical one. You are following me?"

Dennis nodded his head. He was, but with great difficulty, due to his emotional rejection of Sapponyi's approach to the thing. He was busy groping for his own now that it had become a fact.

Sapponyi spoke with the penetrating quality of a school-teacher in front of a particularly dull class, checking off the items one by one on his fingers as he mentioned them. "Here you have the symptoms of hysteria rising rapidly to a crescendo. First—the cessation of the period of menstruation a little over six months ago. Second—insomnia, resulting in an increased nervousness which it required an ever greater amount of self-control to hide. Third— the incapacity to retain food, with its inevitable loss of weight and a resultant thinning of the skin tissues, and finally, the conquest of mind over deteriorating matter—the effusion of the blood into those channels where the mind wants it to run—the stigmata.

There it was—the sound and scientific observation.

Dennis rose and strode over to the open window, from which everything looked as it had every other spring. He said, "I know you will think me unreasonable, but I reject all the fine proof you have just chalked up for me."

"You prefer to believe it was a miracle?"

"It was a miracle."

Sapponyi's face aged all of a sudden. "You are very lucky," he said. "We scientific men are handicapped in reaching such a comforting solution," and he threw the scissors with which he had been toying on to the desk, where they fell with a clatter.

"I wouldn't call my solution comforting," said Dennis. "I don't presume to think that any of us could be saved in such an easy manner."

Sapponyi said, "That reminds me of something else I must tell you," and he recounted Behrendt's visit.

When he had finished, Dennis said, "And what *is* to become of her?"

Here, too, Sapponyi was helpful. He could draw a picture of Fehge's future that figuratively made Dennis's hair stand on end. A life on earth under constant supervision, a life actually only beginning after death, after canonization—if it ever came to that, when the girl, now a saint in heaven, really began to function.

"Not Fehge!" Dennis said, as vehemently as he had ever said anything. "Not Fehge!" And then, more reasonably, "There are enough saints, don't you agree with me, Herr Medizinalrat?"

Sapponyi answered him obliquely. "Why don't you take her away with you?"

The words stood out as clearly in Dennis's mind as the words "Fehge has God" had done thirteen years ago. He could never let her go. He could not bear the thought of her leaving him, not even to anything as glorious as God and heaven—at any rate, not until she was dead. He was irrevocably tied to her. Not father and mother, not marriage, not parenthood, not religion, not politics were nets that caught you—only love. When you loved you were no longer free. He had never been free since he had set eyes on Fehge. It was as simple as that.

It was late afternoon when he finally walked into her room. He found her in an apparent state of coma. Actually she was conscious, had been for days. But she kept her eyes closed and did not respond to her surroundings because, in her mind's eye, she saw those who were waiting for her as Behrendt had told her they were, and she could not face them. The last thing in the world she wanted to do was lead. To follow and to serve—ah, yes; but who and where and to what end? Now?

When Dennis walked into her room she did not open her eyes, and his step was too soft for her to recognize it. But when he spoke, her heart leaped. He would help. He had always helped.

He came over to her bedside. Still she did not open her eyes. But he had seen the colour rise faintly to her cheeks at his first greeting. He knew she was bluffing, like a child that pretends to be asleep. And that was what she looked like, her age lost under the bedclothes, her long hair in its braids winding snakelike down them, her face so much thinner, paler, smaller. Her forehead was still bandaged, and she wore the mittens. He was glad of that.

"Hello," he said again, and then spoke the redeeming words. "Come on, young lady, *jetzt mach' aber Schluss*," which is the equivalent of "Snap out of it."

The corners of her mouth curved to a smile. She opened her eyes and looked into his. Thank God, she could be herself again!

"Come on," he said. "Sit up. There's nothing the matter with you."

She sat up, raised her knees a little, supported her elbows on them, and laid her head on her hands. "I know," she said. "I'm only afraid. Of them. How shall I ever get away from here."

"It was high time I came," said Dennis. He sat down, crossed his legs, and looked at her.

"It was indeed."

Dennis tipped his chair. "And now," he said, "we must think of a plan of action to get you out of the mess you're in."

He groped for his pipe and pouch, but remembered that he could not smoke here. Meanwhile she eyed him sombrely. Then, quite suddenly, she spoke. "He said something which constantly troubles me."

"Who did?"

"The gentleman who came . . . who wanted me to . . ."

"I know whom you mean. What did he say that leaves you no peace?"

"That it was overweening of me to believe that God sent this miracle to save only my life."

"And what was your answer to that?"

"I said the first thing that came into my mind, that it might seem a great thing to him, but what a small thing it really was for God to do, Who can do anything."

"That was a very fine answer."

"No. It doesn't satisfy me. While I have been lying here, I have been thinking of all the others, who are in danger of the Herr Medizinalrat especially. He must be saved too."

"We can do nothing about that," said Dennis. "This is like a flood, and in it, I believe, man's help is going to count very little."

"Are you sure?" she asked him.

"Quite sure. To think otherwise would be overweening."

To whom else would he have dared voice this undoubtedly heinous thought? In his mind's eye he could see all those the world over who were so eager to help and save those who were floundering now in this sea of woe, and they seemed to scream at him, "Wrong! Wrong! Wrong!" "I don't care," he threw back at them in his mind. "*Look to yourselves!* You cannot conquer

361

this thing, you have no right even to fight it, unless you are pure in your own hearts. Your fight must begin within yourself." But he could not drown out their voices crying against him.

Fehge, however, seemed reassured. "I have come to one conclusion lying here, and I am determined about that," she said.

"What is it?"

"My life belongs to God because He gave it to me a second time. I must spend it serving Him."

Dennis smiled. "And what, pray, have you been doing until now?"

She brushed aside the remark and spread her hands apart in an eloquent gesture. "And now tell me—how am I to do it here?"

Dennis answered what had been on his mind all the time. "I intend to take you and Mani to England with me."

She opened her eyes wide and echoed in a whisper, "To England?"

"Yes."

She screwed up her eyes and reconstructed, in her mind, the map of Europe which she had studied with him. "That is much too near," she said. "The brown flood will come there too, and we shall be just where we are now."

Dennis said, "It's not very far, I'll admit. But I promise you they won't get there." He rose and looked down at her from the foot of the bed. "I think there will be war, and we in England will fight them." He saw her pupils dilate. "But we shall win," he went on. "It will be the great battle of the powers of good against the forces of evil. And you can help. God!" he cried out suddenly, as the idea in its magnitude struck him. "What a perfect creature you are for the times facing us!"

"Why?" she asked.

"Because you are out of yourself. You don't stand, as we do, in the centre of our own petty little private lives as in a ring, hemmed in, hampered. You are completely free." He stared at her as though he had just found her. "Because you are unburdened by yourself." And that, he thought, was why Fehge had never attached herself to anyone; even love required, to begin with, an awareness of oneself which she completely lacked. This, however, he kept to himself.

She couldn't have followed him had she been trying to; but she was very busy with her own thoughts concerning this strange new future that he was offering her. "Mani is growing big," she said. "He won't need me much longer. I can become a nursing sister in England, can't I?"

"No!" Dennis's voice was harsh. "First you will learn my country's language. There's more to it than 'Dearly Beloved.'" His voice softened. "Although that is one of its most important phrases. Then you will train to be a nurse. As Andrea would say, 'What's worth doing at all is worth doing well.' And then, when the time comes, you, at least, will be ready."

Twilight had fallen before they spoke again, and then it was Dennis who said, "It may be difficult to get a passport for you. Perhaps the simplest way to accomplish our purpose will be for you and me to get married."

Fehge's mouth fell open.

"Don't let that worry you," he went on calmly. "It will be just a formality. I think that otherwise we shall have great difficulty in getting a passport for you."

She found her voice. "Marriage is never a formality," she said. "It is a sacrament. And it would be most unfitting for a gentleman like you to marry a girl like me." The flush of indignation gave her cheeks the first colour they had had in days. "If that is the only way out, then I shall stay here," and her lips drooped as though she were going to cry.

Dennis wanted to smile. She looked like a little ikon Madonna with her kerchief about her head, and the melancholy set of her features.

"Why can't you take me as what I am—your maid?" she suggested. "Can't a maid go so far away?"

Dennis said, "Oh yes. That's been done often. Only now, circumstances being what they are, it may not be so easy. But we'll try it and see how far we get," and her face became radiant again.

In the end it was all perfectly simple, thanks to the agitated state of mind into which the stigmata of the girl Fehge had thrown Heinrich Grabautschnik, the new mayor of Pritnitz, who could not prevent this Jewish girl from stealing the show.

His position was altogether not a happy one. They had not made him *Gauleiter* as he had been led to expect. He had a feeling that if he had been married to the school-teacher Bahr—who, he had meanwhile heard, had died a ridiculously futile death fighting on the wrong side of the barricades in Madrid—he might have acquired the hoped-for position. But his marriage with Hilda had evidently spoiled that. Was the New Order not going to be as social as it had promised to be?

Meanwhile he was mayor of a community that was not showing at all the right amount of *esprit de corps*. There had been the death of Anne-Marie's baby. From colic. What reaction could one expect but one of relief toward the timely death of such an unfortunate child? But Kurt Schreiner, who had been called in on the case, had behaved, after it was over, like a madman. Grabautschnik, who had been depending on the district doctor's help in organizing the jollifications in Pritnitz and surroundings, had found a singularly morose and useless man on his hands. And why? The child was better off dead. But Anne-Marie hadn't seemed to think so either. Her crazed behaviour after its death had struck another dismal note. The stigmata of the girl Fehge had been the last straw, followed, as it had been, by Conrad's ghastly exitus and his mother, Toni's, death-defying—and what was far worse, Führer-defying—words spoken as she had stood under the tree from which his feet had dangled at just about the height of the breasts which had fed him, words that had been clearly heard and eagerly passed on by the men who had come to take him down, "Thank you, dear God, that you have saved him from Adolf Hitler, the devil." Dreadful. And demoralizing in its effect on the village. The girl had to be got rid of. But how?

Nobody could advise him, not even the Gestapo. They didn't want to be responsible for the disappearance of an object of such an overwhelming display of sincere, unpropagandized devotion.

Not during these first weeks that were to be given over to "re-joicing," until the plebiscite on April 1, when the people of Austria would give Adolf Hitler their "*Ja*." So what was he to do? Let this thing go on? Let it grow? Into what? The implications of Behrendt's visit to the girl had not been lost on Grabautschnik. No! It was impossible! It had to be stopped!

But the calm, patient life continued to pulsate around the stig-matized girl in Fichtenbach. The inns were filled to capacity for miles around, the houses to the last bed, with pilgrims sleeping on the floors and in the barns, and hundreds of others encamped in the near-by fields, all waiting to see her. The continuously fine, pre-summer weather stood Fehge in as good stead as it did the Führer.

One morning Heinrich Grabautschnik came to a conclusion. Why should he rack his brains and, in the end, perhaps ruin his career by doing the wrong thing, when the Church would surely know a way out? The girl could be put in a convent. He sent for the Bishop.

When the famous man arrived and was ushered into Heinrich's office, Heinrich did not rise nor did he ask the Bishop to be seated. He pretended to be very occupied because he had made up his mind to begin by snubbing the Bishop, since, as Mayor of Pritnitz, he had lost the assurance he had possessed as innkeeper of the Lamb. The Bishop, however, was a man who never lost his assurance. He therefore sat down without being asked and arranged his robes. Then he leaned back, folded his arms, and waited with the most complacent expression in the world on his face.

It was his background that gave him this steadfastness. Even now, when his Church was face to face with one of the most serious crises in its history, he was not afraid. They would weather this storm, as they had weathered all the others. Nothing had inspired him with so much confidence as the contra-pilgrimage to the girl Fehge.

"Good morning," said Heinrich, looking up, childishly deter-mined not to give the Bishop any title. "I want to know what you are going to do about the girl Fehge."

"The *Ordinariat* has not yet been able to come to a decision," said the Bishop. "We need time to observe the case."

"We can't give you time," said Heinrich.

The Bishop shrugged his shoulders. "If you remove the girl from our jurisdiction . . ."

That was not at all what Heinrich meant. The Bishop was being very exasperating, especially in his disregard of the power that stood behind Heinrich.

Grabautschnik looked at the elderly man with his smooth, round, purple cap and his black robes, and remembered old paintings in which men attired like him were portrayed. How far back it all went! Heinrich scratched his head, drew his hand over his face, screwing up his nose with it, and sniffed.

"The girl has to go," he said. "Disappear."

"Making people disappear comes under your jurisdiction," said the Bishop.

"This is no joking matter," said Heinrich, raising his voice.

"I was not joking," said the Bishop evenly.

Like Sapponyi, he was a man of science too. He did not believe that the stigmata of the girl Fehge had been a miracle. He did not believe in the miraculous quality of most of the stigmata evidenced by various women in recent history. It was proved that no woman had bled from the wounds of Christ before the stigmata of the Holy St. Francis of Assisi in the thirteenth century. Since then, innumerable women had aped this holy man's sufferings out of sheer hysteria, and he did not believe in accrediting them for that reason alone with the same exalted position the great saint enjoyed. They were not worthy of that. But he could not succeed in classifying the girl Fehge with these morbid psychopaths. After all that Sapponyi had told him about her, especially their final conversation that had taken place before the event itself, which he remembered word for word, there seemed to the Bishop to be an impetus of valour underlying the paroxysm that had later overwhelmed her which filled him with admiration.

"She must go," Heinrich repeated. "The people are still there, waiting to see her. She is taking their minds off what they should be thinking of now."

"Of giving the Führer their 'Ja.'"

CHAPTER THIRTY-SEVEN

"Exactly."

The Bishop nodded his head. "Yes. I do see. The situation is very embarrassing for you."

"And for you too," said Heinrich, leaning forward and pointing his finger at the Bishop. "For you too, Bishop. What if Fehge takes it into her head to lead these people? To form a movement of her own? A Church of her own? What then? Why did she have the stigmata? Only because she identifies herself with Christ!"

This little bit of analysis was by no means the result of astute thinking on Heinrich's part. His unschooled brain was not equipped for such perspicacity. It had come from a higher presence to whom he had been commandeered a few days ago for a discussion of the girl.

"If she can do it once, she can do it again," he went on. "And then, Bishop, you would find yourself out of business! Not that I think she has it in her. . . ." How Hilda had laughed when she had heard about it. . . . "Well, of all things," she'd shrieked, and laughed and laughed. . . . "*Die Fehge!* Did she win out after all?" And her voice had sounded pleased.

Heinrich wasn't at all sure that Fehge didn't have it in her. Nothing breeds success like success, and there were others, like Hilda, for instance, ready to follow anything new.

"Not that I think she has it in her," he repeated, "but neither had Christ. He just had a good propaganda ministry working for him. Your Church!"

This *bon mot*, too, Heinrich had gleaned from higher up.

"Somebody else might get the idea this time and pick out the girl Fehge and build a Church round her. Why not? What words can't be put into the mouth of such a stupid peasant lout? What deeds can't be attributed to her? Already she has made a dumb girl talk, a dead woman live, a sinner hang himself! I don't know how many blind and lame have learnt to see and walk just by going to sit in her seat in church! What's it going to be like when she starts going out again? When they really see her? Who knows how far things might eventually spread?"

He was thinking, too, of the flowers that had been heaped high on the graves of her parents. He had been present at the service in Leonding, where the graves of the Führer's parents had been honoured ... he could recall the metallic click of heels, the salutes and "heils" and the harsh commands. There was undeniably something more spontaneous about the tribute in Pritnitz, and the mound of flowers was undoubtedly higher. . . .

The Bishop said, "I think you have less to fear from the girl Fehge than from any other of our children who have been blessed with stigmata."

"Why?" asked Heinrich.

"Because," said the Bishop, and leaned forward, "she is of Jewish origin. She least of all will lend herself to any aggressive movement, and that is what you fear, isn't it? Aggression."

Heinrich stared, started to speak, shook his head. He must remember that one. He must tell that one to them higher up. He had stumbled over enough of *their* traps.

"We are not afraid," he mumbled, and added, with a shout, "of anything!" and he thumped on the desk with his fist.

The Bishop got up. "Have you any suggestions as to what I should do? Your leaders have closed the borders so that no one of Fehge's race may leave."

"The girl may leave the country. Any time. Let her go anywhere she likes as long as she gets out of our territory. Come to me for the necessary formalities. But one thing is understood: nobody must believe that the Party has anything to do with it. Is that clear?"

And that was why, when Dennis cautiously began to take steps toward procuring a passport and exit visa for Fehge, he found all doors opened wide to him; and before he knew where he was, with profound salaams and nothing but the most polite treatment at the town-hall in Pritnitz and at Police and Gestapo headquarters in Wiener-Neustadt, he was in possession of the precious document.

He immediately telephoned his triumphant news to Sapponyi and asked him to see that Fehge was packed and ready, for they were leaving by the night train from Vienna.

When he came into her room late that afternoon, he laid the little pink-brown booklet ceremoniously on the table in front of her and said, "This is your passport."

She picked up the important document and looked carefully and methodically through it. It was issued by a Republic that had ceased to exist, but it was valid enough. It said, among other things, that Augusta Siemohr's profession was that of maid, that she was born when and where unknown, that her domicile was Strubl, her face oval, her eyes brown, her hair black, and that she had no other marks of identification. . . . On one page was the snapshot Dennis had taken of her a few days ago, a good likeness, and a place for her to sign her name; on another page it said that this passport was good for all European countries, and directly opposite that was the exit visa with the Gestapo stamp, the swastika on its wheel with the eagle flying overhead.

She put it down and said, "Do I have to travel under this sign of the devil?"

"Not for long," he told her. "You'll be a British subject soon. In five years."

She picked up the document again and read aloud, "Valid for all European countries," and looked up at him. "For England too?"

"Of course."

"Why do they accept a thing like this with the devil's sign on it if they are going to fight it?"

He put his hand over hers. "Your mind runs along such simple channels, Fehge, and the world is a very complicated place."

She held the passport in uncertain hands. Her faith in the fine new world was a trifle shaken. Dennis's faith on this score had never been as firm as he had led her to believe. Pray God, he thought now, that she won't be disappointed. That when it comes it will really be a fight with a clear-cut issue, with the powers of evil and good clearly divided. Pray God, that on our side the powers of evil are not permitted to creep in!

Fehge was thinking of Melita, who had said that the lack of this document made her practically non-existent. Her hands grasped it firmly again. Uncertain of its real value as she might be, it did make her a citizen of this world. She looked down at the fine woollen travelling suit that Dennis had bought for her, in a colour of green like the moss in the woods, which, she had noted only a few moments ago in the long mirror, undeniably made a lady of her. Then she looked up at Dennis and smiled at him frankly with a carefree expression on her face that he had not seen before. Until now, even as a little girl, she had always worn a slightly troubled expression. He wondered if, at that moment, she was not putting her trust completely in him. The thought made him catch his breath sharply. Then he said to her, very solemnly, "This is our last evening here, and we are going to dine together," and she answered him without a change of expression. "All right. I'll be down in a minute."

When he had gone, she went over to the open window and looked out on to the valley. She could see the roof of their cottage where Julie had helped Dennis to pack all their belongings and cared for Mani while she had been here in the big house. She would not see the cottage again. She was saying good-bye for the hundredth time, to it and to the big mountain with its rocky hollow tooth, and to the small hills that were green and softly hillocked, to the road, to every rut and curve in it, and to the brook that overflowed in spring, with the long reed grass lying flat in its rushing waters, with the little waterfall in the bend of the road (which was out of sight) that had a lacy coverlet of ice in the winter and whose banks were yellow with primroses in the spring. She had said farewell again and again to the field flowers and birches, to the deer and the birds, to the berries and mushrooms, to the evergreens and leaf trees. Now, suddenly, a formation of airplanes came roaring across the hills. Above Strubl they separated. Twelve—she counted them—flew east and twelve flew west. She watched the noisy grey birds, and her lips parted, and she tilted her head a little to one side.

Tomorrow it would be over, this hard life, this dear life, and a new life would begin.

Chapter Thirty-Eight

THE end of Strubl came like the final unravelling of a knot. In those last days, Sapponyi's almost constant prayer had been, "When they come, dear God, let it be the Germans, not the Austrians!" It was the prayer on the lips of every man who knew he could expect the Gestapo and arrest.

When they came for him, had he been there, he could have seen at once that his prayers had been granted. The group that drove up with the usual aplomb consisted of six German Gestapo men. But Sapponyi was nowhere to be found.

Andrea received them. She looked like a whipped dog. She had looked like that ever since her first contact with her new brown countrymen. Sapponyi, watching her change, had often thought of the Nietzschean sentence, "It is an incomparable distinction to enter this noble and subtle world. To do so one must certainly not be a German."

Now, when they told her that they were going to arrest this Jew-doctor because he had permitted abortions to take place in the Sanatorium, she flew into a rage, to her great relief.

"Nonsense!" she said. "Not a trace of it! I've been here over eighteen years, and there's never been an abortion unless it was to save the mother's life!"

She had better be careful what she said, they taunted her, she, a Bethesda sister, before she disgraced her entire organization! They were in it anyway up to their necks, since so many of their nurses had worked for Jewish doctors. And hadn't she just admitted that she had served a Jewish doctor for over eighteen years?

Andrea's lips tightened. She wouldn't deign to answer. To tell the truth, she didn't know what to say. Rabble, was all she could think of! Rabble! And her own people too!

Then Schreiner appeared on the scene. He and Fricka Reuther would bear witness for the prosecution. Andrea felt momentarily relieved. Of course, the nasty little Austrian doctor was at the bottom of it all!

But where was Sapponyi?

The few patients left were assembled in the living-room and told that they must go. Before they went to their rooms to pack, they had to sign a paper to the effect that they had left of their own free will because they no longer wished to remain under the care of a Jewish doctor. This document was then preserved, with thousands of others like it, to form the factual basis for a future book of German history.

Meanwhile a thorough search was going on for Sapponyi. A guard was stationed outside the house to prevent his escape, and his immaculate flat was turned upside down. Thérèse spent the entire day putting things to rights again, all by herself, for she had no servant left. And at the end of the day no one would have known that the devil had been housed there that afternoon. But Thérèse had a crick in her back, and a feeling of weariness overwhelmed her so that she almost wept.

Still there was no trace of Sapponyi. Down in the cellar several skylights had been found open. Perhaps Sapponyi had, after all, escaped to the woods before the guard had been stationed. They sent men out with bloodhounds, but they did not find him. Late that night, the chief Gestapo officials returned to Vienna, leaving a guard at Strubl.

It was on the next day at about three o'clock in the afternoon when Andrea, who had gone up to the attic to get down her belongings there—for she was leaving that evening—heard groans from one of the mansard rooms which had been used by the servants in the days when Strubl had been full to overflowing but had now, long since, been in disuse, where, as far as she knew, only trunks and boxes were kept with the inventory of the floors that were closed. She had shown the Gestapo men up here the day before. Who was in that room? She tried the door. It was locked.

She fetched old Seppl the groom, the only manservant now left them, and he broke in the door. On the dusty mattress of the cot lay Sapponyi. He was groaning and in a stupor. Andrea felt his pulse. It was very weak. He had evidently taken something.

She picked up a bottle of pills from the floor and looked at it, then she shook her head. Sapponyi opened his eyes. Incredulous they were, as reason came back to him, and Andrea sent Seppl out of the room. Would he tell? Right away?

"Are they still here?" said Sapponyi out of dry lips that parted with difficulty.

Andrea nodded her head.

"I am terribly thirsty."

Andrea did not stir.

"I know what you're thinking," he said in his parched voice, and the trace of a smile curled his lips. "That a doctor should make such a mess of suicide!"

Andrea succeeded in answering his smile, but her heart bled. She could feel it. Like red-hot drops inside her.

Sapponyi got up shakily. She moved to help him. "Leave me be," he said.

He walked over to the window. Then he was sick. He wiped his lips with a handkerchief, for which he fumbled in his pocket, his back turned to her.

She let him alone. She stood watching him, and then she heard a dripping sound. She looked down. Blood was dripping on to the floor at his feet.

She ran to him and turned him round. He had slashed his wrists with a small penknife, and as she struggled with him he cut himself again and again.

Six deep wounds he inflicted upon himself until he ceased to struggle and she could help him back on to the worn mattress where his servants had lain. Then she dressed his wounds.

The guard came. Seppl had not told, but such things spread, as though of their own accord. An ambulance was sent for, and while they waited for it, Andrea went to tell Thérèse. Thérèse said she would go to him. Andrea told her, "Follow me. I will show you the way."

Thérèse had to let Andrea show her the way, for she did not

know the house she had been part of for so long. She had been through it only once, and that thirty-five years ago, when it had been consecrated.

With bowed head, holding up her skirts, which were unusually long and old-fashioned, she moved softly in Andrea's wake, the picture of mildness, avoiding the eyes of the few servants who were left, who came from wherever they were to stare at her. "Look . . . the Frau Medizinalrat . . . in the house . . ."

The lift no longer ran. Andrea gave Thérèse no pause for breath, and she didn't ask for any. Quietly, without a word, the two women ascended flight after flight of what had once been the beads of Fehge's daily rosary. At the door of the little mansard room stood an S.A. man on guard. Another was posted inside the doorway. "Here," Andrea said as she flung open the door, and Thérèse moved ahead of her, but not into the room.

Sapponyi turned his head and saw her. "Come," he said. "Come here, Thérèse. Come closer."

She shook her head from side to side, and her eyes were filled with horror. "Manfred," she whispered. "Manfred . . ." and her small pitiless whisper carried strangely across the musty room. "Do you realize that you have committed a mortal sin?"

He stared at her for a moment, then his mouth twisted into a smiling grimace and he laughed and laughed until he coughed.

Like a flash, Andrea stepped past Thérèse and to his side. She leaned over him, like a Pietà mother, and took one of his hands in both hers. "Do you hear that, Sister Andrea?" he said in short breaths, "I . . . I have sinned!" And he began to laugh again.

"*Sh . . . sh . . .*" said Andrea. She was trembling from top to toe. To Thérèse she said, "If that's all you have to say, you'd better go away."

Gone were superior and inferior, swept away. The levelling process had set in.

Andrea stayed with Sapponyi. He spoke only once more, to say, "I'm glad that Fehge got away. She . . . she was something rare."

God had given Sapponyi one chance; he did not get another.

With the ambulance came a group of Austrian S.A. men, rowdies from the suburbs of Vienna. Their pay-off for the spade-work they had done for the Party was live Jewish booty—in this case, Sapponyi.

They made him get up and undress. Because he was so old, his body looked very pitiful, and its transparent skin gleamed white. His white bandages were all he had on.

The men formed a circle round him, sitting tailor-fashion on the floor, and they made him kneel in the centre and do a series of unmentionable things before he died.

Seppl told Andrea about it, sparing her no detail, his eyes wild in his head. She listened to every word without once interrupting him; not even when he was through did she say, "But not a trace of it!"

When he had gone away, she went into Rosl's room. It was Rosl's day off. Andrea went to the waitress's closet, chose a simple, dark-blue dress, took it with her to her room, took off her habit, and put on the dress. It did not fit badly. She did not look at herself in the mirror.

She buttoned the dress down the back with fingers that were perfectly steady. Then she rebraided her hair from the back to the side and did it up again Dutch style, in round nests over her ears, which was the way she had done it as a girl. It softened her features, but nothing could have softened her expression.

Then she made a bundle of her habit, crumpling her hood without hesitation, tucking her brooch safely away. Her other things were already packed. She took her purse, which held a substantial sum of money that belonged, of course, to her organization, and went back into Rosl's room. She left several *Schillinge* notes on the table, much more than the dress was worth. Then she went downstairs to telephone to Pritnitz for a car to carry her and her belongings to the station.

As she reached the lobby a car drove up. Mechanically she paused to see who was coming. Out of it stepped her Oberin, the golden cross swinging from a cord at her waist.

The old lady took in Andrea at a glance. Her eyes flickered, but

375

she said nothing. She had heard of the doings at Strubl, and that was why she was here, to protect her girl, Andrea, from any harm. She had come almost too late.

Andrea took a few steps in the Oberin's direction, as though without volition, like a sleepwalker. She held the bundle outstretched in her arms. "Here," she said, "is my habit," and her voice had a whimper in it like a tired child's. "The rest of my things are in my bag ... here. The money ... I will get work and return the money ..." Her voice went dry in her throat.

What was she doing? Revolting? But how did one revolt? She swallowed. How did one revolt? The question grew big inside her. How did one revolt?

The Oberin spoke. In a very gentle voice she said, "Andrea, I have come to take you home." She could see how Andrea was trembling.

The Oberin went on, and now she spoke in the dialect of Andrea's homeland, Silesia, from which province of Germany she also came. "Don't protest, Andrea," she said. "It's no use. We are too small. But in God's eyes we count, as they do not. If you want to have a few days alone, to find yourself, you may have them."

Andrea bowed her head. The Oberin had her bird in its cage again. Her voice became sterner. "And after that you will take up your duties in the laundry. As long as we live, Andrea, it is our duty to obey. Remember that."

Remember that? How could she ever forget it? She had heard the Führer's first Reichstag speech, to which every good German had listened, and now she could remember his final words distinctly, "All that I ask of you is obedience ... obedience ... OBEDIENCE!"

His voice had risen to a hoarse shriek. Then had come the great silence of a dazzled audience, followed by the roar of a thousand people who had at last heard what they wanted to hear. Obedience ... to the laundry? Obedience ...

Andrea took a few more steps forward until she was standing close to the Oberin, who took the bundle from her trembling fingers and put her other arm round Andrea. Andrea's body began to shake with sobs.

The following Sunday when, from the pulpit of her church in Vienna, Andrea for the first time heard a prayer for the Führer's health, she bowed her head to hide the tears that rolled down her cheeks. Obedience, obedience, obedience. . . .

The tide of the brown flood sucked the faithful down from the hills about Strubl where they had been waiting. The girl Fehge was gone. No denying it. She had been spirited away. And on the day they learned that fact, the Bavarian "field kitchen" arrived in Pritnitz. The jolliest-looking men in the world came with it, Bavarians all, in spick-and-span uniforms. They served goulash and had their photographs taken with the children of Fichtenbach and Pritnitz; and on the following Sunday, there the pictures were in an illustrated paper! Well, of all things! And a band played on the square! This was a good, heart-warming thing that had come to them, enveloping them all in its goodwill. They couldn't help but have faith in it. Their hearts were full of hope and something akin to love welled in their hearts, and the old people's eyes were full of tears all the time. "My Lord, my God, isn't that beautiful!" The fine young men. The good warm soup . . . a little watery . . . but one didn't look a gift horse in the mouth. Ludmilla Pfeiffer slapped her daughter Serafine when that one refused the food with the words "I'm full." She had just eaten at home. But just then and there almost everybody wanted to feel that they had been very hungry and that this good thing had fed them.

They danced to the music till late in the night, and their new mayor stood drinks all round. Oh, they thanked their Führer, Adolf Hitler, again and again and again until the mountains re-echoed the sound. And the flowers withered on the graves of Moishe and Dworje.

The tide of the brown flood lapped at Strubl's foundations and inundated the big house. It was turned into a maternity home for the poor, with Schreiner in charge. When the first Fichtenbacher gave birth to her child in the house that to them had meant *Herr-schaften* since they could remember, an almost audible sigh of satisfaction rippled over the countryside. The Führer had indeed opened to them the gates to paradise. What these children were being born for, what world they were being born into, did not interest them in the slightest. They had no comprehension of that sort of thing, not when it was pending, not when it came. Their lot had always been hard, and it would continue to be hard; but at last someone had paid attention to them, and that gave them satisfaction.

In the end the valley remained more or less as it had always been. The Gfrerrers were gone, no one knew where to, but Rosl didn't take over their inn. She now owned a hotel in a Viennese suburb that had once belonged to a Jew, and she had bought it for a song. *Heil Hitler!*

Anne-Marie went to seed in her fine house. Her mother gave her only enough to keep body and soul alive, and she hadn't learnt how to be, nor had she any talent for being poor. Soon hers was the most slovenly house in Fichtenbach, more slovenly even than that of Slovak Ludmilla Pfeiffer, and the peasants began to say, "She spins," which, in their tongue, meant she was going crazy.

The new teacher was a Bavarian and he organized the children into Hitler youth for the boys and B.D.M. for the girls. Now when school was out their good-bye greeting of "*Sieg Heil*" rang out into the clear mountain air instead of the former *Grüss Gott*. And the brown of the Nazi uniforms blended in with the dirt colour of the road, not like the *loden* green that had stood out in the distance. For the rest, everything was the same—the sky, the mountains, the flowering fields, and the icy brook which never dried up, not even in the hot month of August.

Printed in Great Britain
by T. and A. Constable Ltd
at the University Press
Edinburgh